Her Last Hope

OTHER TITLES BY LOUISE GUY:

Everyday Lies

Rival Sisters

A Life Worth Living

A Winning Betrayal

Her Last Hope

LOUISE GUY

LAKE UNION
PUBLISHING

This is a work of fiction. Names, characters, organizations, places, events, and incidents are either products of the author's imagination or are used fictitiously. Any resemblance to actual persons, living or dead, or actual events is purely coincidental.

Published by Lake Union Publishing, Seattle

www.apub.com

ISBN-13: 9781542016032
ISBN-10: 1542016037

Cover design by Sarah Whittaker

Printed in the United States of America

For Robyn. You define friendship.

Chapter One

With her head bowed, Abi stole a glance from under her dark sunglasses at the handful of mourners surrounding the grave. She wasn't sure what shocked her more: that she was burying her husband or that so few people had turned up for his funeral. Had they got the wrong date? How was it possible that people could turn so quickly on the man who'd only recently celebrated his fortieth birthday attended by close to two hundred friends and family? Rumours were flying around but nothing had been confirmed. How could they doubt their friend's integrity, and regardless, why weren't they there to support her and Hayden?

A squeeze of her hand brought her out of her thoughts and she managed a weak smile. Thank God for Mel. Her sister had rushed to Melbourne from Geelong minutes after receiving the phone call from Abi. She'd been incredible at keeping sixteen-year-old Hayden fed, helping Abi with the funeral arrangements and making many of the phone calls to advise family and friends of the situation. Tony, Mel's husband, had arrived earlier that morning, in time to join them for the funeral. Abi hadn't had a chance to talk to him properly yet, but the coolness that radiated from him confirmed he was only there out of obligation. She wondered how many others were there for the same reason? Laila, her best friend, smiled as Abi caught her eye. Laila was genuine; she knew that. It was hard to believe, though, that out of Eric's family, only his brother, Gabe, had turned up. His parents hadn't even made the trip. Fresh tears spilled down Abi's cheeks as the reality of how life had changed in an instant stabbed at her. It hadn't just changed for her, there was also Hayden to consider.

From the moment Abi found Eric she'd been in denial, unable to comprehend that her husband could have taken his own life. He loved her and Hayden; adored them. Even his note didn't convince her. *I love you both so much. Use my life insurance. You're strong, and you'll be fine. Tell everyone I'm sorry.* She'd called the police, certain he'd been murdered. But their investigations had confirmed there had been no one else involved. And as the police investigated further and news of Eric's business dealings came to light, the note made more sense.

Feelings of uncertainty plagued Abi even now, while Pastor Phillip read a prayer as the casket was lowered into the ground. It was incomprehensible that Eric would do something that was not only illegal, but high-risk, and which he knew could destroy their family and friends. But he had, leaving her questioning whether she had really known her husband at all.

She placed a hand on her son's shoulder. His face contorted in a grimace as he folded his arms across his chest. He hadn't wanted to come. He believed what they were saying about his father. He was angry and upset, and as hard as she'd tried, Abi hadn't been able to get through to him. She had, however, insisted he attend the funeral. He'd regret it for the rest of his life if he didn't. Now she was beginning to question her decision. In fact, since discovering Eric's body, she'd been questioning every part of her existence.

Angry tears pricked the back of her eyes. She wasn't sure who she was mad with. Eric? Their friends who'd deserted them? Hayden for not only believing what was being said but seemingly blaming her too? Herself for being oblivious to her husband's business dealings?

The pastor, at Abi's request, read a short poem before indicating to Abi that the service was nearing completion. Nausea filled the pit of her stomach as his words blanketed her. Mary Elizabeth Frye's 'Do Not Stand at My Grave and Weep' had been completely the wrong choice. The faces surrounding them held anger and questions, not tears. Other than Laila, Mel and herself, she wasn't sure anyone required tissues.

She took Hayden's hand and moved closer to the graveside. She dropped the single white rose she'd been holding on to the casket, tears once again blurring her eyes and spilling down her cheeks. 'Goodbye, my love.' Her voice was a whisper. She looked across at her son, expecting him to drop his rose too. But his eyes were fixed firmly on the horizon. Abi glanced back to where they'd been standing and sucked in a breath. A single white rose lay trampled on the ground.

Chapter Two

Lucinda Manning had never been involved with a legal case before, and had certainly never imagined sitting in Queensland's Dorford District Court waiting to learn of her husband's fate. Would he be allowed to return home, or would he be taken away from her and their four-year-old, Max?

She clenched her fists as the court was called back in session for the judge's verdict and sentencing. The stress of the past few weeks had been enormous. Ryan had been arrested on suspicion of drug possession, assault, and breaking and entering. While the charges looked indisputable, Ryan's lawyer had assured them he'd do his best to minimise Ryan's involvement in the eyes of the court. The victim of the assault was still in a coma, and without any eyewitnesses, the prosecution's case was weak. Did that mean he would only be convicted for the drugs and the break-and-enter? Was there even the slimmest chance he might be let off with a fine or another punishment that didn't require jail time? Lucinda crossed her fingers. Hope was all she had to keep her going right now.

She felt Ryan's eyes on her many times throughout the hearing, and did her best to keep her expression neutral. Her stomach was a jangle of nerves and her hands were sweating, but she'd learnt over the last few years that showing no reaction was the safest path.

The judge read through the charges and asked the defendant and his lawyer to stand for the delivery of his verdict. Ryan locked eyes with Lucinda as he stood.

Lucinda felt a squeeze of her hand. She kept her eyes forward, not turning to look at her mother, but grateful for her support. She sucked in a breath and held it while the findings were read.

'In the matter of the state versus Ryan Manning . . .'

Lucinda found herself tuning out as the judge read through his findings and considerations. All she wanted to know was what sentence would be handed down and whether prison time would be served. Eventually, the judge reached that part of his summation.

'. . . on count one, of possession of MDMA, you are sentenced to twelve months' imprisonment, to be suspended after six months. On count two of assault and breaking and entering, I sentence you to five years' imprisonment, to be suspended after two years.'

A second squeeze of her hand reminded Lucinda to breathe. Ryan didn't flinch as the judge spoke. His eyes remained locked with Lucinda's as he mouthed, *I'll be out soon.* He continued to watch her as he was led out of the courtroom.

Lucinda exhaled. It was finally over. Thirty months, the minimum he would serve, was not *soon*. She and Max had two and a half years before there was any likelihood of Ryan reappearing. Thank God.

Rachael, Lucinda's best friend, was waiting outside the courtroom when Lucinda and her mother, Tess, appeared. Lucinda continued to keep the neutral look on her face; you just never knew who was watching. Rachael hurried over to them.

'Six years in total, partially suspended,' Lucinda said before Rachael even asked. 'He'll be in prison for two and a half.'

Rachael let out a long breath. 'Hallelujah.' Her voice was barely audible as her eyes scanned the people milling about outside the courthouse.

Lucinda's mother put an arm around each of their shoulders and lowered her voice. 'Come on, lovely ladies. We're going back to my house. I've organised a special lunch, and we can talk freely there.' She squeezed the two women closer. 'The champagne's already on ice and we still have three hours before Max needs to be collected from kindergarten.'

Lucinda allowed herself to be led to her mother's car. She wasn't going to argue. It was as if the lid had been taken off the pressure cooker she'd been forced to live in since discovering she was pregnant five years earlier.

Half an hour later, the three women lifted their champagne flutes.

'To freedom,' Tess said.

'And to making better choices moving forward,' Rachael added.

Lucinda shivered. 'I can't imagine going near another man for the rest of my life. Not after this experience.'

Tess laughed. 'You might change your mind down the track. You've just been unlucky.'

That was an understatement.

'Have you given any more thought to my suggestion?' Rachael asked.

'What? Leaving Dorford? Disappearing?'

Rachael nodded. 'As much as I'd like to say you've now got freedom, you haven't. Ryan's going to have you watched the entire time he's inside. I guarantee it. He'll demand visits from both you and Max. He'll completely control you, Lu. I know. Mum lived that nightmare for ten years before she died.'

The room fell silent as the three women digested Rachael's words. Her mother, Joan, had lived a nightmare. Rachael's stepfather was sentenced to life imprisonment after murdering a police officer during a robbery. Joan had assumed she was finally free of the man who'd controlled her life for over twenty years, but she wasn't. He'd made demands from inside the prison, and when they were not met, he'd ordered his colleagues on the outside to deal with Joan. She'd been roughed up, threatened and forced to live in constant fear. She'd gone to the police for protection, but it hadn't been enough. Her husband had arranged to have her house burnt down with Joan in it. It had been devastating for Rachael and a massive shock for everyone in Dorford.

'As much as I'd hate you to go, Rachael might be right,' Tess said. 'Ryan's controlled you for the last five years. You need to break away from that. It's no way to live.'

'I am right, Lu; you know it. Ryan's dangerous. Ever since Max was born his threats have escalated, and they're not empty threats.'

Lucinda ran her fingers over the scar on her arm as Rachael's words settled over her. Ryan never made empty threats, but it was the threats against Max that worried her the most. Ryan would never physically hurt his son, but he'd not hesitate to carry out the biggest threat he had held over her on several occasions. Unless she did precisely what he told her, she would never see Max again. Six months earlier, when she'd refused to deliver drugs to one of his clients, he'd threatened her with this. She'd stood firm; she couldn't be part of something she was so against. But then Max and Ryan had disappeared for ten days and not made any contact with Lucinda. She was frantic by the time they returned. From Max, she learnt that they'd been on holiday at the beach and he wished she'd come, but that was all. Ryan had said nothing until Max was in bed later that night. Then he'd grabbed her, his hand holding her chin so she was forced to look him in the eyes.

'You ever say no to me again and he'll be gone for a lot longer than ten days. In fact, you might never see him again.'

Lucinda's legs had crumpled beneath her. Ryan hadn't let go of her, his grip tightening as she sank to her knees. 'Do you understand?'

Lucinda had nodded, tears running down her cheeks, a tight pressure settling on her chest as the enormity of her situation enveloped her. That pressure was still present now, six months later.

'I worry for you too, hon,' Tess said. 'I'd hate for you and Max to go, but it might be the safest option.'

'Where would we go?'

'Melbourne,' Rachael said. 'I know a guy who could set you up with a new identity. It's expensive, but it would give you a fresh start.' She pulled out her phone and wrote the details down on a piece of paper.

Lucinda took the paper from Rachael and stared at it. 'Melbourne? I've never been there, and I don't know anyone. Sydney would be better. I've got friends in Manly.'

Rachael shook her head. 'It has to be a fresh start. Your friends would be the first place Ryan would look for you. Melbourne would be perfect. You should probably consider a change of look too.'

Lucinda's hand automatically went to her head. 'What, my hair? Cut it?'

Rachael nodded.

'Oh no,' Tess said. 'Lucinda's hair is gorgeous. Clients of mine would kill to be natural blondes for a start, but to have such long, gorgeous hair too.'

Lucinda loved her honey-blonde locks, but perhaps Rachael was right. She swallowed, doing her best to hide her reaction, and smiled at her mother. 'It's only hair, Mum. It's not a big deal.'

Tess shook her head. 'I'm not cutting it for you. You'll have to get someone else to do it.'

'In Melbourne,' Rachael added. 'There's no point doing it here in case someone sees you and reports back to Ryan.'

Lucinda nodded. In the scheme of the decisions she needed to make, her hair was minor. The thing she couldn't imagine was moving away and starting again. She had her part-time dental nurse job, her friendship with Rachael – and, of course, there was her mum. If her mum came with her, then maybe, but she couldn't imagine Tess would ever move. She had her hairdressing salon and her friends. It would be too much to ask. But if Lucinda still went, she'd never be able to come back. How would that work? Max would never see his grandmother and she'd never see her mum. It was unimaginable.

Lucinda sat bolt upright in bed the next morning and took several deep breaths as she tried to calm herself. Then she jumped out of bed and ran down the hallway to Max's room. She knew it was only a dream, but she still had to check. Relief rushed through her as she watched him sleeping peacefully. Ryan hadn't taken him. She closed her eyes, thoughts of Ryan still haunting her. Since his arrest, he'd made nightly appearances in her dreams. Sometimes he was just there, watching her, but at other times, he threatened her and hurt her. Often the dreams were a re-enactment of things he'd done in real life, but last night was different. He'd placed Max in the passenger seat of his car, and as he drove towards a lake, he'd shouted out of the window: *You'll never see either of us again*. She'd been frozen to the spot, unable to scream or move as the car slipped under the water.

Now that she was awake, she reminded herself that Ryan was in prison. She needed her subconscious to understand this and allow her a decent night's sleep. Telling her subconscious this was one thing, getting it to listen was another.

A little before nine, she dropped Max at her mother's and then headed towards Aloha, a five-minute drive away. A ninety-minute yoga session would help sort her thoughts and, more importantly, quieten them. Bikram yoga had been a lifeline for Lucinda when she'd discovered it two years earlier. Initially, she'd struggled with the heated yoga room, but after a few sessions, she'd started to enjoy sweating and looked forward to the amazing feeling she had following the final relaxation at the end. Without yoga, she wasn't sure how she would have coped with her life with Ryan.

As she moved through the breathing exercises and into the poses, Lucinda tried to block out her thoughts. She didn't need to make a decision right this second on whether she could continue living in Dorford.

The ninety minutes disappeared, and as she lay down for the final relaxation pose, she wiped the sweat from her eyes. Wouldn't it be bliss if she could stay in this bubble permanently, and not have to deal with the stresses Ryan's lifestyle had brought? How she wished they'd never met. An image of Max entered her mind as she had this thought. As her grandmother used to say, *every cloud has a silver lining*, and in this case, she would be right. Ryan's dark, menacing cloud hung over every second of her days, only lightened by Max's presence. She could put up with pretty much anything, and had, for the sake of her son.

Chapter Three

Abi pulled the bed covers over her face, her head throbbing with a dull ache. She'd hardly slept in the weeks since Eric's death, and when she had, she'd woken to enjoy a split second of normality before the full force of her new reality crashed down on her again.

She ignored the gentle knock on her door, hoping Mel would assume she was asleep and go away. She was relying far too heavily on her sister, but the thought of dragging herself out of bed and dealing with anything was incomprehensible. She needed to be left alone. It was the only way she could block everything out, which right now was her only coping mechanism.

'Abs?' The door opened a fraction.

Abi remained still, wishing her away.

'Abs.' Mel's voice was louder this time. 'You need to get up. You've got the meeting with your lawyer at ten.'

Abi squeezed her eyes shut, her headache worsening. She'd met with Ross, their lawyer, two days after Eric's death, and was advised that a criminal investigation was underway and she could expect all of their assets to be frozen while she was investigated. The meeting would provide an update.

Mel pushed the door wide open and came into the room. She drew back the curtains before pulling the bed covers down.

Abi opened her eyes and stared at her. Mel had the look of someone who'd been up for hours. Showered, dressed and bright-eyed. Her caramel, shoulder-length hair perfectly straightened. Abi hated to imagine how she looked. She'd made an effort ten days earlier for the funeral, styling her long black hair into a braided bun and even doing her make-up, but since then it had been an effort even to shower, let alone do anything else.

She sighed. 'I'm not really up to it.'

Mel smiled, but Abi could see the concern in her eyes. 'You don't have much choice regarding the lawyer, and anyway, Hayden needs you. Something's happened.'

Abi sat up. Hayden should be at school. 'Is he okay?'

'He's downstairs, and yes, physically he's okay, but he's very upset. The school told him he was no longer enrolled.'

'What?' Abi threw the covers off and got to her feet. 'Why on earth would they say that?'

'The fees for this term are unpaid, and in light of what's happened, they're not letting him stay.'

Abi stared at Mel. 'Eric didn't pay them?'

Mel shook her head. 'No. Tony and I would offer to help you out, but that's not feasible at the moment. And anyway, from what Hayden said, I'm not sure he's welcome there anymore.'

Abi's heart began to pound. 'I can't believe they'd do that to him. We've been paying fees at that school for years. Why didn't they ring me rather than talking to him directly?'

'Apparently, they did. I assume your phone is switched off?'

Abi nodded mutely. She was doing her best to avoid the world, and switching it off was one of the few defences she had.

'Abs, Hayden needs you. I know how tough this is, but you need to pull it together for him.'

A lump rose in Abi's throat. Mel was right. Drowning in misery, she was letting the people who were most important to her down. She blinked back tears and nodded.

Mel immediately drew her in for a hug. 'You're going to be fine. You're the strongest person I know. You'll get through this, Abs, you will.'

Abi wasn't so sure she would *get through this* when she saw her son's pale face as he sat at the kitchen table scrolling through his phone. She pulled out the chair opposite him and sat down.

'Hayden?'

He looked at her, his blue eyes flashing with anger. 'They threw me out. Said they'd called you twice in the last few days and you hadn't bothered to call them back. Thanks for the extra dose of humiliation, Mum. As if what you and Dad did wasn't enough already.'

Abi took a deep breath, trying to decide how best to handle this. 'I'm sorry, Hayd. I am. I turned my phone off, and they couldn't reach me.'

'Well, turn it back on. Dad killing himself isn't all about you, you know. It affects both of us.'

'Hayden.' Mel approached them, a warning in her voice.

Abi held up a hand to stop her. 'No, he's right. The current situation affects all of us and plenty of other people too. And yes, I need to pull myself together and start trying to fix some of what's happened.'

Hayden snorted. 'Fix it? How do you intend to do that? You and Dad stole close to five million dollars from your friends and family and lost it all. I don't see a quick fix with that.'

Abi felt the sting of his words; he might as well have slapped her. If this was what her son thought, she could only imagine what the friends and family who'd been affected were saying. 'You need to understand that I had nothing to do with your dad's business dealings. There's no way I would have gone along with what he did. But I know your dad well enough to feel certain he didn't steal anyone's money.'

She hoped Hayden hadn't heard the waver in her voice. The evidence against Eric was damning. Did she believe what she'd just told her son? She took a deep breath. For her sanity, until there was concrete proof he'd deliberately deceived them, she needed to.

She continued, 'An opportunity came up and he invested it where he thought he was going to make everyone a substantial return. Much more than their original investment would have.'

This time Hayden laughed. 'You're still telling yourself that? Why would Dad put everything on the line by doing something illegal if it was for everyone else's benefit? He did it for him. You both did. You encouraged friends and family to put their money in a capital guaranteed investment and told them they couldn't lose anything, but instead Dad invested nearly five million dollars in a high-risk property development without their permission. God, you even helped some of them get loans to do it. I'm amazed you're not in jail.'

Abi rubbed her pounding forehead. 'I never encouraged anyone to invest in a property development, and if your father had mentioned it to me, I would have stopped him.'

Hayden pushed back his chair. 'I guess the police will confirm one way or another whether they believe you were involved. I hope you're aware of how many years in prison you could be facing.' He shook his head before turning and storming out of the kitchen.

Abi placed her head in her hands and groaned. He was sixteen, had just lost his father, his world was in turmoil, and she'd pretty much checked out. Of course he was angry.

'You okay?'

Mel pulled two cups from the kitchen cupboard and switched on the coffee machine as she waited for Abi to respond.

Abi looked up at her. 'You believe me when I say I didn't know Eric made that investment, don't you?'

Mel crossed the kitchen and sat down next to Abi. 'Of course I do. You do realise Hayden's anger is because he's scared of what might happen?'

Abi nodded. She'd done her best not to think about the possible consequences for her in all of this, but losing everything and going to jail were possibilities. She shivered at the thought. She'd spent more time trying to get her head around what Eric had done, and the fact that he'd driven himself to the point of taking his own life, than worrying about herself. She needed people to know that he wasn't the terrible person they all thought he was.

'I honestly believe he was trying to be the hero, Mel. Turn everyone's money into a fortune and surprise us all. He should never have done it, but if all had gone to plan, we'd be celebrating. He didn't *steal* the money. He was investing in something he thought would provide huge returns. No one's going to lose out anyway.'

'What do you mean?'

'His life insurance.' Abi blinked back tears. 'His note said to use it. It should cover nearly all of the debt. It cost Eric his life, but it will all be paid back. There will also be his superannuation payout.'

Mel reached across and squeezed Abi's hand, sympathy filling her eyes. 'You need to get ready. Your meeting's in an hour. And Abs, I need to go home today. I'm sorry, but I've got to get back to work, and Tony needs me. I have to try and work things out with him.'

'What do you mean *work things out*?'

'He's upset about how things have turned out. He's not convinced Eric's motivations were as pure as you suggest. But, if the money's going to be repaid, then he'll be fine. He definitely won't believe you had anything to do with it if you give up the life insurance money to cover the debt.'

Abi sighed. She'd known Tony was angry with her, but Mel had done her best to shield her from him by sending him home after the funeral, and that was the last time she'd seen him. She hadn't had an opportunity to convince him of her theory: that what Eric had done had been for the benefit of those around him. That he hadn't lied upfront to their friends about his real intentions for their investment funds, but the property development opportunity had come later. But had it? That was the one thing that still didn't sit well with her, and she'd done her best to push it from her mind. They'd always discussed everything. For him not to tell her was not just unusual, it was unheard of. But, for her mental health, right now she couldn't afford to dwell on it.

After a teary farewell with Mel, Abi pulled herself together and drove to St Kilda Road to the offices of Law One. She took a deep breath, pushed open the office door and stepped inside. Rosemary, the elderly receptionist, glanced up, her face hardening as Abi approached the front desk.

'Take a seat.' She indicated to the waiting area. 'Ross won't be long.'

Abi nodded, doing her best to ignore the frosty greeting, and sat by a window overlooking Queen Victoria Gardens. She'd give anything to be sitting under one of the Moreton Bay figs with Eric on a picnic rug, enjoying the autumn sunshine. Instead, she was about to meet with his lawyer to learn what her husband's business dealings and death meant for her and Hayden. *Death*. It wasn't a word she could associate with her husband. She gave herself a mental shake; she doubted she'd ever come to terms with it.

Ross appeared moments later. His face was grim, his usual friendliness absent. 'Abi, come through to my office.'

Abi stood and followed him along the corridor to his corner office. He motioned for her to enter and take a seat, and pulled the door shut behind him. He sat down at his desk and cleared his throat a few times.

'That's it?' Abi asked. 'You have nothing to say? He was your friend, Ross. You didn't even come to the funeral.'

Red splotches appeared on Ross's cheeks. 'No, I didn't. Under the circumstances, I didn't think it appropriate.'

Abi shook her head, unable to hold the sarcasm back. 'Thanks for your support.'

Ross stared at her for a moment. 'You are aware that I was one of Eric's clients, aren't you? I turn fifty next month, and thanks to your husband I've lost most of my savings. Savings Eric convinced me to contribute to what I understood was a capital guaranteed investment, not a high-risk property development.'

Abi bowed her head. She'd done her best to block out the reality of the impact Eric's actions had on those who'd invested. She looked up, her face flushed with heat. 'I'm so sorry, Ross. I hadn't realised. And I do appreciate everything you're doing for me.' A thought crossed her mind. 'Would you like me to use another lawyer?'

Ross sighed. 'No. I want to help you. Eric was my friend, and I thought I knew him pretty well. When we went through the details just after he died, I knew from your shocked expression you knew nothing about the investment. We both knew him well enough to hope he was trying to do something good for us.'

Tears filled Abi's eyes as relief washed over her. 'Thank you, Ross. It means a lot to know that someone else believed in him.'

Ross's eyes hardened. 'The word I used was *hope*, Abi. I *hoped* he was trying to do something good for us. I *hoped* that the initial investigations would be proven wrong. But they weren't. I think you need to get your head around the fact that Eric wasn't the person you thought he was. He was involved in fraudulent activity and if he was still alive would be prosecuted in a criminal trial. I've spoken with a number of our mutual friends, and it appears he had us all deceived. No one can believe it, to be honest.'

Abi swallowed. Ross's words were harsh, but even she had to admit that the idyllic picture of her husband was no longer so black and white. It had merged into a shade of grey. Perhaps when Ross realised how she intended to divide Eric's estate, he'd feel a little more forgiving. But there were a few other matters to discuss first. 'What happens now? Am I going to be charged?'

'It appears not. I heard from the securities department this morning, and they said they were satisfied with their investigations of you and would not be pursuing it any further.'

Abi's mouth dropped open. 'Really? But last week you said that, as the spouse, I would most likely be held responsible for his actions. And of course, there's the work situation.'

'While there are ethical arguments about what you did at work, there's nothing illegal in your dealings. The loans you initiated all went through the correct approval channels, and you didn't personally handle the ones for any family members, just friends. You weren't a director in Eric's company so aren't liable. He had no other staff, so the business will go into the hands of a liquidator to see what other monies are invested and how that will be managed with Eric's clients.'

'But the money Eric lost, there's no way to recoup it? No insurances against it?'

'No, it's gone.'

Abi swallowed. 'Do you know who's been affected?'

Ross pushed a document across the desk to her. 'Here's a list of the clients and what their starting balances were.'

Abi scanned down the list of fifteen clients – all friends of hers and Eric's, as well as Mel and Tony. A dull thud started in her forehead as she saw the amounts everyone had lost. She looked up at Ross. 'Eric would be gutted if he realised what he'd done.'

Ross raised an eyebrow. 'I assume that's why he decided not to stay and face the music. It leaves many questions unanswered and, unfortunately, a lot of people believe he's taken the coward's way out.'

Abi's eyes filled with tears. 'He didn't kill himself to escape or because he's a coward. He did it so everyone would be paid back.'

'What do you mean?'

'His life insurance. It's worth four million dollars. It was on the note he left. To use his life insurance and to tell everyone he was sorry.'

Ross pushed a hand through his thinning hair. 'Which is why you continue to defend him?'

Abi nodded.

'I'm sorry, Abi. I assumed you were aware that Eric changed your policies last year.'

'I am. He wanted us to have at least four million dollars each if something happened to the other one. He couldn't get one policy for that amount so took out two separate ones for each of us, both with two-million-dollar payouts in the event of death. It won't cover the entire debt, of course.'

Ross flicked through the papers in the file and pulled one out. 'Unfortunately, Eric didn't check the fine print before ending his life.' He passed the paper across the desk to Abi. 'There's a thirteen-month wait period for the suicide clause to be valid. According to this, the suicide clause becomes active in just over three months, on the thirteenth of July.'

Abi glanced at the policy date and closed her eyes. Eric had ended his life for nothing. Her stomach churned as the irony of the date occurred to her. July thirteenth was her birthday. Not a day she'd be celebrating this year.

Ross cleared his throat and she opened her eyes to look at him. 'What is there, then? There must be money somewhere else we can use to pay some of this back. His super?'

'His superannuation is worth around four hundred thousand. It will settle any outstanding personal debts his estate shows. I'm not sure, at this stage, when – or if – it will be released to his beneficiaries. We probably won't know until the criminal investigation is complete.'

'At least I can continue working and start trying to make all of this right.'

'How do you mean?'

'I need to pay everyone back. I can't let Eric's . . .' She hesitated. Eric's what? Bad decisions? Deliberate deception? No, she pushed the last thought from her mind. She had to believe there was another explanation. '. . . transactions impact our friends and family like this.'

'It's millions of dollars,' Ross said. 'I think you'll be doing well to cover off the expenses for your current lifestyle. You're down to one income, with a high mortgage, the upkeep of a large house, school fees and general living expenses. From what I understand, all of your savings were tied up in Eric's business and the property development. Paying back the debt will take you decades, if not more than your lifetime.'

'What about my life insurance? Can I use any of it?'

Ross sighed. 'No, you can't access it now. In fifty or sixty years, assuming you live a long life, your policy will eventually pay out to the families who've lost money if you rewrite your will to reflect that.'

'That's not going to be much help that far ahead. Half of them probably won't even be alive.'

'No, but their children will be, and it will all get passed down.'

'I can sell the house and anything of value that we own.' Selling the house would also give Abi a fresh start. While a forensic cleaning company had removed all traces of what had happened, Abi doubted she'd ever be able to step foot in Eric's home office again. 'There's also an investment my parents left me when they died. It's worth at least two hundred thousand. That will be a start, but there must be something I can do now to pay people back?'

'Honestly, I don't think there is. It's nice to see that's your priority, but I think it's your finances you need to be concerned about, not other people's.'

Abi rubbed her forehead. The dull thud of her headache intensified as she realised the irony of her situation. She was worth a fortune dead, but nothing while she was alive.

Abi sat in her car in the underground car park of Law One for a few minutes, letting the reality of the situation sink in. Then, remembering Ross's words about him contacting a number of their *mutual friends*, she pulled her phone from her bag and scrolled through the contacts. She'd avoided everyone since Eric's death, switching her phone off and not returning calls, but now she needed some answers. She took a deep breath as she stared at the name on her phone screen.

Dylan Sawyers.

Dylan and Eric had been friends since high school. They'd caught up most weeks for a game of squash and a beer, and Dylan was the instigator of many boys' trips. They'd been as close as brothers. If anyone knew about Eric's business dealings, Dylan would.

Dylan answered on the first ring. 'Abi?'

'Yes, it's me, Dylan. How are you?'

'I should be asking you that. I've called a few times, but your phone went straight to voicemail.'

'I switched it off,' Abi admitted. 'I don't want to talk to anyone at the moment.'

Dylan sighed. 'God, I miss him. Nothing's the same. I can't even bring myself to go to the squash courts. Sorry, I'm sure you're suffering a lot more than I am.'

If only he knew just how much. 'Did you know, Dylan? Did you know what he was up to?'

Dylan hesitated for just a second.

'You did, didn't you?'

'Not exactly. Abi, I'm a cop. He knew I'd never be able to turn a blind eye if I knew he was doing anything fraudulent. But . . .'

'But what?' Abi's heart rate quickened.

'But I've realised since Eric's death that there were a couple of occasions where he did allude to risky business opportunities that could provide huge returns. One was about eighteen months ago. He was excited at the time. He didn't go into any detail of what the opportunity was, but he insisted on supplying all of the alcohol for our weekend up on the Murray River to celebrate. Considering eight of us went, that was quite an outlay. He did that a few other times too, over the years. Just said things were going well and he wanted to share his good fortune. He paid for that fishing trip four of us took through the Kimberley, for instance.'

'Really?' That was the first Abi knew of that. Eric had been excited about the ten-day trip and had had a wonderful time, but she wasn't aware that he'd funded it.

'He was a very generous man, Abi. Very generous.'

'What happened with that opportunity he mentioned? Did he celebrate when it paid out?'

'That's the thing,' Dylan said. 'A few months back he turned up to squash quite upset. He said he'd had a bad day and proceeded to take it out on the squash court. Smashing the ball like he wanted to kill it. When we had drinks later, he said he'd got himself into a bit of strife with the investment he'd been so excited about. Again, he didn't tell me what it was but did say he'd been premature in buying the drinks on the fishing trip.'

'What sort of strife?'

'Financial, I assume. But he said another opportunity had presented itself that would fix his problem. He just didn't have the capital available to invest in it. Over a couple of beers he said he had an idea of how to raise the capital, but he wasn't sure if it was ethical.'

Abi sucked in a breath. 'Do you remember when that was?'

'Three or four months ago, I'm not sure exactly. I told him his ethics weren't something to compromise and to make sure he stayed true to himself, and more importantly operated within the law. Eric laughed it off. Said I was the wrong person to confide in and it wasn't that big a deal. That he'd stretched the boundaries of ethics before. We left it at that. I'm so sorry, Abi, I feel responsible.'

'What? You had nothing to do with it. You didn't even know what Eric was dealing with.'

'I know, but I've been a police sergeant now for over ten years, which is why I didn't pursue the conversation. Something niggled at me that it didn't feel quite right, but Eric was my friend. As soon as I started any kind of investigation, I'd be obligated to see it through. If only I had. I might have been able to stop Eric investing in the property development in the first place, and stopped him from taking his life.'

Abi blinked back tears. 'It's not your fault, Dylan. Eric got himself into trouble and he didn't see any way out. He didn't come to any of us for help. Do you think the investigation might show up any other fraudulent transactions?'

'I hope not. Eric did mention other opportunities in the past where he'd taken calculated risks. Some paid off, some didn't. Again, he never went into the detail, and most of the time I assumed it was his own money he was risking. I never thought he'd risk clients' funds unless he was authorised to do so.'

'Is there anyone else he might have worked with or discussed things with that you know of?'

'Just you. Until today I assumed you knew everything.'

'You knew more than me. I thought my husband was an honest businessman. I'm currently being proven very wrong.'

Dylan sighed again. 'If you need anything, anything at all, just let me know. Okay?'

It was on the tip of her tongue to say that, unless he had a few million dollars spare, he probably wasn't going to be much help, but she didn't. None of this was Dylan's fault. He'd lost a close friend too. Instead, she thanked him and ended the call. If Dylan didn't know the detail of Eric's dealings, then it was unlikely any of his other friends did.

She started the car and manoeuvred her way out of the car park and into the street. As she drove along St Kilda Road, away from the CBD and towards East Brighton, she wasn't sure what to think. What if the property development wasn't the only unauthorised investment? What if the investigation showed more debt? She shook her head. No, she needed to believe this was a one-off. She'd asked Ross for a copy of the sheet with all of the clients' names and outstanding debts. She'd have to work out a way to fairly divide up the funds she had. If she sold the house and cashed in the investment her parents had left her, she would have some money. Hopefully, Eric's superannuation would become available too. But splitting the money fifteen ways meant no one would receive much. She'd have to hold out hope that the investigation found some profits within the company that could pay back the debt.

Her phone rang as she turned off Nepean Highway into Hampton Street. The caller display showed it was Ivan, her boss.

'Is this a good time, Abi?' Ivan's deep voice exploded into the car.

Good time? Was that even a thing anymore? 'As good as any, Ivan. I'm sorry I haven't been in touch. Things have been a bit hectic with everything that's happened.'

Ivan cleared his throat a few times. 'No need to apologise. I hope Eric's funeral went well, and things are being sorted out.'

'They are, thank you. I appreciate the extra time off you've allowed me. I'll use this week to get myself ready for coming back next Monday, if that's alright?'

The phone line was silent for a few moments, then Ivan spoke. 'Look, normally I would have this conversation in person, but with you on leave, we'll have to do it this way. I hate to do this, but we're going to have to let you go.'

'Hold on.' Abi pulled the car over to the side of the road, her head thumping even harder than it had previously. 'What? Why? I was just with my lawyer. He said I was in the clear, that the investigation showed I didn't do anything legally wrong.'

'Legally no, ethically yes. Four equity loans in two days for family and friends? Come on, Abi. I'd be questioning that at the best of times, but then all four clients lose their money in an investment orchestrated by your husband.'

Abi drew in a breath. The loans for Mel and Tony and three close friends were to ensure they could take advantage of the capital guaranteed investment. If she'd had any idea that Eric would use the money for something else she'd never have helped push them through. 'I didn't do anything wrong, Ivan. All of the loans met the criteria they needed to for approval. And I didn't do the one for my sister. Briana did.'

'They were approved for a scheme your husband devised to use the money for his own purposes, and no, you didn't do your sister's, but you did put in requests for Briana to rush it through. I'm sorry, Abi. While I'd like to believe you had nothing to do with Eric's . . .' He cleared his throat. '. . . Eric's downfall, we can't have you working for us. We're not trying to be unfair, and I hope you can understand the position we're in.'

Abi brought her hand up to her throat. Was she being fired? 'But I've been with Bank East for twelve years. I've never done anything wrong.'

'Until now.'

'Ivan, my lawyer just confirmed I'm clear of any wrongdoing. Firing me isn't legal.'

Ivan cleared his throat again. 'I'm not firing you. The bank is restructuring and unfortunately several jobs have become redundant, yours included. You'll receive a letter and a redundancy package.'

Abi fell silent. Of course they didn't want her working in the bank. Was she that surprised? No one was going to want anything to do with her after this.

'Look, Abi, I'm sorry. I realise you're going through a tough time, but the situation is already damaging the bank's reputation. Have you seen any of the news stories?'

Abi had deliberately avoided all news channels since Eric's death. She'd heard from Hayden that *everyone* knew what had happened, that it was all over the papers and television, but she'd chosen to ignore everything.

'No.' Abi's voice was barely a whisper.

Ivan sighed. 'Probably a good move. Take care of yourself, okay. I'll have your belongings packed up tomorrow and your items shipped to you. You'll receive an official letter with the redundancy details. There's no need to come back.'

Abi's mouth dropped open as Ivan ended the call. He didn't even want her to come into the office? She gripped the steering wheel as her body started to shake. Her entire world was falling apart.

A pain settled in Abi's gut as she drove the rest of the way home. How was it possible life could have changed so dramatically and so quickly? Tears rolled down her cheeks. Eric had done this to her. Whatever his motivations were with the investment, he'd ruined her life. She reflected on Dylan's comment about Eric saying he'd *stretched the boundaries of ethics before.* What did that mean exactly? And if he'd spoken of needing capital three or four months back, then that tied in with when he'd suggested inviting a group of twenty friends, mostly couples, over for a Saturday-afternoon barbecue. When she'd asked what the occasion was, he'd replied, 'No real reason, it'd just be nice to see our friends.'

On the day, he'd talked to everyone about an investment opportunity. Even at the time, she'd thought it was unlike him to be pushing friends and family to invest in something during a social event. He usually kept business apart from their personal lives. In fact, up until the barbecue he'd always said he'd preferred keeping clients and friends separate. That if anything went wrong, or if he was to lose a lot of money, it was better that it wasn't within their social circles. But at the barbecue, he'd done what she now realised was quite a hard sell.

'You'd be mad not to invest,' he'd said, turning the beef skewers expertly as he addressed a small group of their friends. Abi had been refilling wine glasses but stopped, frowning when she realised he was talking shop and wondering if *this* was his real reason for inviting everyone over. He'd looked up and seen her staring, and his blue eyes crinkled at the edges as he smiled and waved her over.

'I was just telling these guys about the capital guaranteed investment I mentioned last night. Like I told you, this one's going to have higher returns than anything we've ever done.'

'And our investments are guaranteed?' Tony asked.

Eric nodded. 'Yes, that's the whole point. It's a protected investment. So if you invest ten thousand, for example, there's a hundred percent capital guarantee. That means that even if it performs badly, you'll still receive your investment amount back in full.'

Alexandria Goldberg looked thoughtful. 'And you're expecting high returns?'

'On the conservative side, we're predicting a twenty-five percent return in the first six months.'

Jerry, her husband, whistled. 'That's crazy.'

Eric nodded again. 'It is, and like I said that's a conservative estimate.' He started moving the cooked skewers on to a plate. 'It's likely to be much higher, so if you have any spare funds, consider coming in on it. I don't usually push my investments with family or friends.' He laughed. 'Can't imagine the barbecues and holidays would be as much fun if I lost anyone's money, but this is different. For a start, the worst-case scenario is you only get back what you put in. So the downside is your money's sat doing nothing for six months, which isn't ideal, but it's not dire either. The upside's enormous.'

'If we wanted to invest, how do we go about it?' Tony asked.

'Just let me know how much you want to put in and I'll organise the paperwork. The opportunity closes in two weeks. That's the only catch. So if you have funds you need to get released from elsewhere then it might be tight.'

Abi could see the interest in her friends' faces. It did sound like an excellent opportunity. She just wished Eric hadn't turned a barbecue at their home into a sales pitch.

Eric clapped the tongs together and called out to the larger group. 'Food's ready. If everyone wants to take a seat at the table, we can eat.'

Half an hour later, the talk turned back to Eric's investment opportunity. This time it was the Goldbergs who initiated the conversation. 'I'm interested,' Jerry said. 'There's plenty of equity in our house in South Yarra we could use.' He turned to Abi. 'We did our home loan through you and Bank East, Abs. Can we use the equity?'

'You could certainly apply for an equity access loan. People do them all the time.'

Eric laughed. 'With interest rates as low as they are, everyone should be taking their equity from their homes and investing it elsewhere. You'd be crazy not to.'

As the afternoon progressed, Abi found that many of the couples were discussing Eric's investment opportunity, and quite a few had asked her if she could help them access their equity. Of course, she could only help those who had loans with Bank East, which of the twelve interested couples was only four. She was, however, able to provide the others with information on who to speak to at their bank.

Now, as she pulled into her driveway, Abi was jolted from her thoughts. June Cherry was standing by her front door, and she didn't look happy.

Abi took a deep breath, pushed open her car door and stepped out on to the driveway. She forced a smile on to her lips. 'June, what a surprise.'

By the look on June's face, it wasn't a nice surprise. She had her hands on her hips, and her eyes flashed with anger. 'We need to talk.'

'Of course. Come in and have a drink. I'm sure we could both use one.'

June didn't move. 'I don't want a drink. I want an explanation.'

Abi swallowed. 'For what exactly?'

'For why you encouraged me to take equity from my home when you knew I couldn't afford to lose money?'

'Hold on, I never encouraged you. You came to me.'

June snorted. 'After Eric laid down a *you can't lose any money* investment plan. Yes, I asked you to do the loan for me. Yet not once did you tell me I should be careful. That what I was doing was high-risk.'

Nausea churned Abi's stomach. 'June, I had no idea that Eric was going to invest in the property development. Like you, I believed the money was going into a capital guaranteed investment. There was no reason at all to warn you about that. The capital was guaranteed. You couldn't lose.'

'But I did. I lost four hundred thousand dollars. And guess what, Richard knew nothing about it.'

Abi's arms tingled with discomfort. 'You didn't tell him?'

June shook her head. 'The house is in my name, I didn't need to. I was looking forward to surprising him with my little windfall in six months. Instead, I now have to tell him our mortgage has increased significantly, and I've lost what equity we did have.' June's face drained of anger and tears welled in her eyes. 'How do I tell him?'

'Oh, June. I'm so sorry. I don't know what to say.'

'How about, *I'll repay you, June. Don't worry at all. My husband's the prick, not me.*'

Abi swallowed. 'Let me assure you, that is my plan. I've just seen my lawyer, and every cent I can get my hands on will be distributed between those Eric's let down.'

'Let down?! Are you for real? *Stolen from*, you mean.'

Abi forced herself to ignore the accusation. 'The problem is my assets aren't going to cover the loss. I'm hoping there's money in the company to help, but until the investigations are complete, I have no idea how much.'

'Just make it clear, Abi. Am I getting my four hundred thousand back or not?'

Abi shook her head slowly. 'At this stage, it's doubtful. I'm doing everything I can to repay as much as possible, but it's close to five million dollars. It's not going to happen overnight.'

June shook her head. 'I'll never forgive you. You encouraged me to invest in his scheme. You made the appointment, and you pushed through my application. If I'd gone through normal channels, it wouldn't have been ready in time for Eric's cut-off date. But having you on my side meant I was able to invest. How you're not in prison, I have no idea.' She turned and walked to her car. She looked back at Abi as she opened the driver's door. 'I'm going home to tell Richard. I suggest you lock your doors tonight. I can't imagine he's going to be too happy.'

Abi didn't reply. June was angry, which she understood. She also understood in that moment that she was the enemy. None of their friends would believe she was innocent. She looked so guilty, it was no surprise Ivan had fired her. Anger welled inside her as she pushed open the front door and made her way inside. How could Eric leave her with this mess? It was bad enough that he'd done what he had, but to leave her to face the music on her own was unforgivable.

Chapter Four

As Lucinda weaved her way around the play equipment, she felt a sense of relief. It was ten days since the court case, and here she was with Max at the park. The black cloud that had been hanging over them for years finally felt like it had lifted, and in the last few days so had the pressure in her chest. Rachael's predictions of Ryan controlling her from prison hadn't materialised. She hadn't heard from him. Out of sight, out of mind was a real possibility. She could only hope that was the case. She reached the swing and helped Max up on to the seat, still deep in thought.

'Push me high, Mumma,' he squealed.

'Higher than high!' Lucinda pulled Max back towards her before letting him go, the rush bringing another excited squeal. How simple it would be to be four again. To rewind and start fresh and not make dangerous decisions as she had with Ryan. Although, when she thought back, she could see why he'd fooled her. He'd been charming. He'd whisked her off her feet, and by the time she'd become aware of the many secrets he'd been keeping from her, she was too far gone to walk away.

To walk away. She pushed Max higher. If only she had walked away. But then she wouldn't have Max, and he was the one good thing that had come from the last five years. Him and Rachael. Rachael was the only friend who'd stuck by her when they'd realised

Ryan's true nature. She didn't blame any of them. A drug dealer and criminal was hardly the person you wanted at your weekend barbecue. Her heart sank a little as she thought of her best friend. Rachael was still trying to talk Lucinda into moving to Melbourne, but she wasn't sure she could do it.

'You have to get out of here, Lu,' she'd said just two nights ago, when she'd dropped in to see Lucinda with a bottle of wine. 'I'm surprised you think you can still live here after what's happened.'

'But he's in jail,' Lucinda had argued. 'He hasn't made any contact, and I don't think he will. I'll be fine for at least the next two and a half years. That's when I need to think about moving.'

Rachael shook her head. 'You're naive if you believe that. He'll have someone watching you. I know you don't want to leave your mum and Dorford, but you need to be safe. Ryan might be in prison for drugs and assault, but we know he's capable of much worse. While he might not have physically killed anyone himself, he's organised others to do that for him. Steph can back me up on that.'

Lucinda shivered at the reminder.

Steph was a mutual acquaintance of Rachael and Lucinda. Her husband, Colten, worked with Ryan and was currently serving eight years for armed robbery. When Lucinda had first met Ryan, Steph had done her best to try to warn her off him. To hint at the type of work he and Colten did. But Lucinda was too infatuated to take notice. After she and Ryan had married, she'd spent more time with Steph, and as Ryan's moods changed from charming to arsehole more frequently, she'd started to listen. That he was dealing drugs, threatening people and had a criminal record had been a complete shock. He'd told her he was a pharmaceutical rep. When she'd finally questioned him, he'd just laughed at her.

'I am a pharmaceutical rep. I deal the highest-grade MDMA in Queensland. Ask anyone. They can rely on me for top-grade gear.'

Lucinda had decided at that exact moment that she had to end the relationship. She couldn't believe how naive she'd been. How many times Steph had tried to warn her and she'd ignored her. She'd also put up with unacceptable anger and violence from Ryan. She'd found herself making excuses for the bruises when he chose to leave his mark on her. Even as she reflected on it, she couldn't believe she'd allowed it to continue. That she'd stayed with a man who had no respect for her.

Steph had been concerned when she announced she was going to leave Ryan. 'You need to be careful. He's not going to be happy with you leaving. You'll need to be smart about it.'

Lucinda never had the chance. She found out a few days later she was pregnant and had stupidly put the packaging from the pregnancy test in the bin. Ryan had seen it and been ecstatic. He'd held her tight, told her she'd made him the happiest man in the world. Tears had filled her eyes as she'd struggled out of his grip. 'I can't do it, Ryan, not with your lifestyle.'

He'd taken her by the shoulders. 'Can't do what?'

'This.' She'd waved her hands around. 'Us. I was going to tell you it was over. The pregnancy doesn't change that.'

The grip on her shoulders had tightened. 'It changes everything. You and this baby are my family, my only family.' Both Ryan's parents were dead and he'd distanced himself from his extended family. When he'd first told Lucinda about them he'd been less than complimentary. *Bunch of bloody losers, the lot of them. As far as I'm concerned they're dead to me.*

Right at that moment, she had wished she could be dead to him too.

'You don't get to tell me when it's over,' he'd said. 'You're carrying my kid, and you'll stay. If you don't, you'll be very sorry.'

When he let go of her, Lucinda had rushed to the bathroom, emptying the contents of her stomach into the toilet bowl. Relief had washed over her when she heard the roar of Ryan's motorbike and the squeal of tyres as he drove away from the house. She could breathe again, but for how long? How could she live with a man who controlled everything she did? Who threatened or hurt her whenever she went against his wishes? She had to get away from him, but how?

She'd spent the majority of her pregnancy trying to work out how she could escape, but as each day passed and her stomach grew, Ryan became more and more possessive of her. Telling her what to eat, how they would raise their son. The only upside to being pregnant was he kept his threats and anger to verbal only. She had nine months where she didn't have to fear another split lip or try to explain away a black eye. Ryan had made it clear that he wanted a son and would not tolerate a daughter. It was a ridiculous thing to say but had at least given Lucinda a glimmer of hope, and she'd spent the pregnancy praying for a girl. If it was a girl maybe he'd let her go. But as soon as Max came into the world, Lucinda's hopes of a future without Ryan had slipped away.

Tears filled her eyes as she continued to obey Max's demands of being pushed higher. It was unthinkable that she'd brought Max into a world so dangerous and so far removed from the one in which she'd grown up. At least they had a reprieve for now.

When Max was finally too tired and hungry to play any more, Lucinda brought him over to the picnic rug and handed him his lunchbox. His eyes widened with delight as he saw his favourite cream cheese sandwiches. He grabbed one and stuffed it into his mouth.

Lucinda laughed. 'Slow down, buddy.' The laugh died on her lips as a shadow crossed the picnic rug. She turned, a tremor rushing through her body as a tall, solid man, dressed in black leather with a teardrop tattoo below his left eye, stood over her.

'I have a message from Ryan. He wants you to bring the boy to see him tomorrow at three.'

Lucinda stared at him. 'Why didn't he just ring me if he wanted to get a message to me?'

'Because he wasn't convinced you'd accept his call or take his request seriously.'

The guy reached inside his jacket, causing Lucinda to flinch. Was he going to pull out a gun in full daylight, in a playground in front of Max? She moved her body to block Max's view of what was going on.

The man pulled out a piece of paper and held it out to her, and she relaxed slightly, feeling stupid. 'He needs some money. This is the number for the processing officer at the prison. Speak to them before you go to see how you organise that.'

Lucinda took the piece of paper from him and nodded.

'Make sure you're not late tomorrow. If you are, I'll be coming back to visit you, even if I don't like what Ryan's told me I need to do. Don't put me in a position of making you find out what that is.'

Lucinda shivered as he walked away.

She slipped the paper into her pocket and turned to face Max. She'd managed to keep Max away from the prison up to this point, as Ryan had agreed that while he was being held before the court case it was best to shield him from it, but now things had changed. Rachael was right. Ryan would control her from prison just as effectively as he had done when he was at home. Her stomach roiled as she realised the messenger must have followed her to the park; that she was being watched. Rachael had said Ryan would do this, but Lucinda honestly hadn't wanted to believe her.

Max's grip on Lucinda's hand tightened the next afternoon, as he climbed out of the car and took in the high fences with the coiled barbed wire at the top. Lucinda hadn't been sure what to tell Max about the visit to the prison and why his dadda was in jail. She decided not to say anything and to use Max's questions to provide the information he asked for.

'I don't like it here.' Max's lip trembled as he stared wide-eyed at the fence. 'Want to go home.'

Lucinda knelt in front of him and pulled him to her. 'There's nothing to be scared of.' If only that were true. 'But Dadda wants to see us, and this is where he's living at the moment.'

'Why is the fence scary?'

Lucinda looked to where Max pointed. The fence was scary; the whole place was. 'It's to protect Dadda and his friends that are on the other side. Nothing can get in to harm them.'

'Like dinosaurs?'

Lucinda smiled. 'Dinosaurs definitely couldn't get through this fence.'

Max nodded, seeming to accept this, but his usual chatter wasn't present as they made their way to the security gate. Lucinda squeezed his hand as they went through, before being led into a building where a prison official met them. The woman smiled at Max.

'You're a very handsome-looking young man. Are you here to visit someone special? Your daddy perhaps?'

Max nodded, his eyes still wide as they darted all around the room. He was unsettled, and Lucinda didn't blame him.

The prison official winked at Lucinda before returning her attention to Max. 'Now, I have a very important job for you. Are you up for it?'

Max looked to Lucinda before nodding slowly.

'Great! Well, see this funny-looking machine' – she indicated a large metal detector, similar to the one at airports – 'I need you to walk through to the other side.' She leant close to Max, lowering her voice. 'If you have superpowers, the lights will turn green as you go through. If you don't, then they'll be red.'

Max didn't need any more encouragement. He dropped Lucinda's hand and hurried through the metal detector. His eyes widened as the lights turned green, and he flung his arms in the air, giving a celebratory whoop.

Lucinda walked through after him, surprised when the light turned red.

The guard frowned then pointed to her ears. 'No jewellery or belts.'

Lucinda had completely forgotten. She removed the offending items and walked back through the metal detector. This time the light turned green.

'You've got powers too, Mumma,' Max shouted.

'I'll just check Mummy's bag with my magic wand,' the guard said. 'Make sure there's no kryptonite in it, as that might affect your powers.' Lucinda placed her bag on a table and it was quickly searched. Next was biometric scanning. On her first visit to the prison, she'd been enrolled in the system, so on subsequent visits an iris scan confirmed her identity. Once that was complete, she stored her belongings in a locker, took Max's hand and waited for the guard's direction.

'Okay, young man,' the guard said. 'Head through this door and you'll find a room on the other side where your daddy is waiting for visitors.'

Lucinda and Max walked through the doorway to a large meeting room. Tables and chairs were set out in rows, and several men in khaki sat behind these desks. Some wore handcuffs, but most just sat there staring straight ahead, waiting for their visitors.

'There's Dadda.' Max clapped his hands together. He pulled at Lucinda's hand and dragged her to the back of the room where Ryan was sitting. His face broke into a genuine smile when he saw Max. He stood, looked over at a guard who gave a quick nod, and came around the table so he could hug Max. The little boy threw himself into his father's arms.

'It's fantastic to see you, buddy,' Ryan said. 'I've missed you so much.'

'Can you come home now, Dadda? Grandma gave me a new puzzle I want to show you.'

Ryan ruffled the little boy's hair. 'Not today, bud, but soon, I hope. Why don't you come and sit down so I can have a chat with you and your mum?'

Max followed his father's instructions and sat down at the table.

Ryan looked at Lucinda and opened his arms to her.

She took a deep breath and stepped into his embrace. Regardless of anything she felt about Ryan or the situation, she knew better than to antagonise him.

'Thanks for coming.' Ryan released her from the hug. 'It's so good to see Max. I can have two hours of visits a week. Let's see how we go today and then work out how many times a week you'll both come. I'm thinking twice a week for an hour, but if that's too long for Max, we might make it three visits at forty minutes each.'

A tight pressure returned to Lucinda's chest. *Three times a week?* 'That might be a bit tricky to organise with work and Max's kinder.'

Ryan frowned. 'No, it won't be. You work part-time. One visit can be on the weekend and the other one or two through the week.' His eyes were cold. 'You'll work it out. You owe me that, at least.'

Lucinda didn't respond. She didn't owe him anything.

'I've got good news. I'll be out of here a lot sooner than the courts say. I've got a plan.'

A shiver ran down Lucinda's spine. 'What sort of plan?'

Ryan nodded towards the guard. 'Nothing you need to worry about. Just know that I'll be home within a few months.'

Lucinda nodded, unable to formulate words. *A few months?* Her stomach churned at the thought. But then, visiting the prison three times a week was hardly ideal either.

'Now, come and sit down and tell me what you and Max have been up to.'

An agonisingly slow hour passed, with Ryan asking questions about what Lucinda had been doing and Max too. He seemed to want to know every minute detail of Lucinda's activities, and she was careful to be as accurate as possible. If he was having her followed, she couldn't afford to mess up. Who knew what the consequences would be?

'Mumma, I'm hungry.' Max interrupted Ryan as he began grilling her to find out if she'd done anything social since he'd been in prison. 'Is it dinner time yet?'

Ryan laughed. 'That sounds like it's time for you two to head off.' He ruffled Max's hair. 'Thanks for coming, Lu. This will all work out okay, you'll see. I'll be home before you know it, and in the meantime you'll be visiting so often that this place will feel like a second home.'

Lucinda nodded. Rachael's idea to leave, and leave now, was advice she needed to consider seriously. Ryan was going to run her life from prison, and if he got out in a few months, what was she going to do then? Be forced to sell drugs for him and any other criminal activity he decided she should participate in? If she was going to leave it would have to be now.

An image of her mother popped into her mind. If only Tess would come with her, it would be so much easier.

Tess's eyes widened as she realised what Lucinda was asking of her. They'd put Max in front of the television and were in the kitchen preparing dinner. 'Leave my home, my friends and my business?'

Lucinda nodded. 'I know it's a huge ask, but Max and I have to go. I can't stay here. Ryan's quite likely to get out of prison in a few months, and even if he doesn't, he's going to control me from inside. He's a dangerous man.'

'And you'd go to Melbourne, like Rachael suggested?'

Lucinda nodded. 'We'd need to cut off all contact with everyone. We can't risk someone knowing where we are.' Tess's face paled, causing Lucinda's bottom lip to tremble. 'I can't think of another solution, Mum. I need to keep us safe.'

'What if I didn't come. Then what? Would I ever see you again or hear from you? Are you cutting off contact with me too?'

Lucinda blinked back tears as she saw the fear on her mother's face. 'We'd have to be careful. Hopefully we could stay in touch. If we got you a prepaid phone untraceable to you, then we could call each other still. As for visits, probably down the track. If we can convince Ryan you had nothing to do with me leaving then eventually he'd leave you alone, but initially I imagine he'll have someone watching you.'

'I can't just pack up and leave my entire life behind. I've worked so hard to establish Trims and Tones, and the salon staff rely on me. What would I tell them?'

'I'm not asking you to, just putting it out there as an option.'

'Maybe in a few months I could give some thought to selling the business and coming and joining you. I'm just not ready to make that decision now. And he might not even be let out early. He has a non-parole period of over two years. I don't see how he could get out before that. If we're lucky he'll serve out his sentence and then he won't be out for years. Is there a need to rush away so quickly?'

'Whether he gets out in a few months or a few years he's not going to let me live my life the way I want to. Two or three times a week we're going to have to traipse into the prison, which just isn't good for Max or me. I need to be able to live, not have my life put on hold while he's in prison – and then turned into a nightmare once he gets out.'

Tess nodded. 'How I wish you'd never met him.'

'You and me both, Mum.' Lucinda turned her attention to the salad she was making to accompany her mother's chicken. It was awful that she was putting Tess in this situation. Awful for both of them. And Max would miss her dreadfully. But it was a choice she had to make for their future. Live in fear and misery forever, or have a chance at freedom and a new life.

Chapter Five

Without Mel to keep her on track, Abi had no motivation to drag herself out of bed the next day. Hayden was home from school and she hadn't had the energy to do anything about it. Her initial anger and threats to storm the school for answers had faded into oblivion. Of course they wouldn't want him there. A considerable number of Eric's clients were parents at the school. Quite a few had lost their money in the property development, and several others were now awaiting the outcome of the insolvency investigation to find out whether their investments were secure or whether there were any additional fraudulent deals. It wasn't something Abi had given any thought to until Ross mentioned it. She couldn't begin to imagine how she'd feel if she discovered he'd misused other funds as well.

It was close to five by the time she finally threw off the bed covers. Music was blaring from Hayden's room and she couldn't stand it any longer. She needed to pull herself together. She showered, dressed and pulled back the curtains. Her stomach rumbled; she hadn't eaten anything since the previous morning. But worse than that, she hadn't spoken to Hayden, let alone fed him or checked on his well-being. She was a shit mum. That had to change. Even making this decision, she felt stronger.

She ran a brush through her hair, checked her pale reflection in the mirror, then strode down the hallway to Hayden's bedroom.

The smell was the first thing to hit her as she opened the door. Her hand covered her mouth and nose as her eyes scanned the room. Dirty plates and glasses covered every surface. Hayden was lying on his bed, eyes closed, she assumed listening to the music. She moved into the room, her foot kicking a pizza box. She opened the lid, reeling from the smell of the half-eaten pizza.

She switched Hayden's stereo off and turned to face him.

His eyes flew open and he sat up. 'What are you doing?'

'Coming to check on you and apologise.'

Hayden opened his mouth and closed it again. She imagined he was expecting her to fly off the handle about the state of his room.

'Apologise?'

She nodded. 'For letting you down since Dad died. I'm not coping very well, to say the least, but I'm going to do my best to turn that around.' Her eyes flittered around the room. 'Let's start here. You take all the dirty clothes to the laundry, and I'll start on the plates and rubbish.'

Hayden hesitated for a moment before climbing off the bed and standing. He started to pick up the clothes without arguing. One small victory at least.

Abi was stacking the dishwasher when Hayden came into the kitchen. He sat down at the island counter.

'Want some dinner?'

He nodded.

Abi closed the dishwasher and opened the fridge. There was a note stuck to the shelf: *Lasagne in freezer. Already cooked so microwave is fine.* Her heart swelled with gratitude towards Mel.

Ten minutes later, they sat opposite each other at the kitchen table, both hoeing into the food.

'When did you last eat?' Hayden asked, his eyes widening as Abi shovelled in another forkful.

She put her fork down, realising she was being a pig. 'Breakfast yesterday, and I think that was a cup of coffee. I'd better slow down or I'll be sick.' She raised an eyebrow. 'This is quite a situation we're in.'

Hayden continued to eat, his expression blank.

'First thing we need to do is get you back into school.'

'The grammar?'

'No, we can't afford it. Sorry, but it's the secondary college.'

The colour drained from Hayden's cheeks. 'You're kidding?'

Abi shook her head. 'No, there are going to be some big changes around here. Dad's life insurance isn't valid, so I'm afraid that we don't have anything but a lot of debt. We're going to have to sell the house and a lot of our belongings.'

'Good, I definitely don't want to live here anymore. You'd think Dad could have at least killed himself somewhere else.'

Abi flinched. Hayden's words lacked any compassion, yet she understood what he meant. She hated even walking past the permanently closed door to Eric's home office.

'Where are we going to live?'

'I'm not sure. I'll start doing some research tomorrow. We'll probably be okay for a little while. Even if we sell the house quickly, there will be a settlement period. I'll try and find something close to the secondary college so that it's not a huge commute for you.'

Hayden pushed his plate away, stood and walked out of the kitchen.

'Hayden,' Abi called after him. 'Hold on. We need to discuss this.'

He stopped in the doorway and turned back to face her, his eyes flashing with anger. 'What's to discuss? You and Dad fucked us over, and now I have to pay for it with shitty schooling and a crappy house. Just let me know where you put the rest of Dad's guns. I might want to use one.'

Abi's mouth dropped open as Hayden stormed up the stairs to the second floor. A huge part of her wanted to go back to bed and curl up in the foetal position, but a stronger part of her said *no*. She had to be the adult here. She had to make their lives right again, whatever *right* might look like.

Her phone rang, breaking into her thoughts. She glanced at the screen: Mel. Tears immediately filled her eyes. It often seemed like Mel had ESP. A phone call would come at the exact moment she needed it. She picked up the phone and put it to her ear.

'Hey hon, how are you?'

Abi burst into tears at the love in her sister's voice. Thank God there was someone who knew her and treated her the same as always.

'Oh, Abs, don't cry. What's happened, other than the obvious?'

Abi dried her eyes on her sleeve and took a deep breath. 'Let's see. Hayden's being awful, I lost my job yesterday, and it looks like Eric's life insurance isn't going to pay out.'

'What, why not?'

'He changed policies and the suicide clause isn't valid. There's some superannuation but nowhere near enough to pay anyone back.'

'Oh, geez. That's awful. I'm so sorry.'

Abi gulped. 'You shouldn't be apologising; it's me that should be. I can't pay you back yet, Mel. I can't pay anyone much at all. A bit, of course, once I sell the house, but hardly anything in the scheme of things.'

'Abi, it's not your fault. You shouldn't feel guilty for something you had no control over or involvement in. I mean it. We've lost some money. So what? There are many more important things.'

Tears started to roll down Abi's cheeks again. She was so lucky to have a sister like Mel. 'Okay, then let's not talk about it. Cheer me up, tell me something about you.'

Silence greeted her.

'Mel?'

'I think I'll call you back another time. You've got enough going on without me adding to it.'

Abi sat up straighter in the chair. 'Don't be silly. What's going on?'

Mel sighed. 'It's Tony. He's moved out.'

'What?'

'He's not as forgiving about the money. Honestly, I think he knows deep down you weren't involved, but the fact you were able to hurry the equity loan through makes him suspicious.'

'He blames me?'

'He blames both of you.'

'Okay, but why would he move out? It's not your fault.'

'He's making me choose between you and him. Says you've screwed us over and shouldn't be part of our lives anymore. That if you are part of my life, then he's not.'

Abi sucked in a breath. She couldn't lose Mel as well. 'Do you want me to come and talk to him? Try and convince him I knew nothing?'

'Not at the moment. He's behaving awfully and I don't want anything to do with him. He knows you, Abs, and he should know you wouldn't be involved with something illegal.'

'If only the life insurance was there,' Abi said. 'Then at least he'd know I had nothing to do with it when I paid you back.'

'I can't believe Eric didn't realise,' Mel said. 'His death was pointless.'

Abi sniffed and wiped the tears from her face.

'Oh shit,' Mel said. 'Sorry, I shouldn't have said that.'

'No, it's true. At least you knew him well enough to know that taking his life was a selfless act, not a coward's act like everyone else is saying. It was purely for the life insurance, but yes, completely pointless. Now, enough about him. What are we going to do about you and Tony?'

'Nothing for now. I'm too angry with him. We're better leaving it for a while and cooling down. But you need to get out and do something. You can't sit at home dealing with this all alone. As soon as you hang up, you're to ring Laila, okay?'

'I'm fine, Mel.'

'No, you're not. You're to ring her and organise a catch-up with plenty of wine involved. I'll be texting her in an hour, so if you don't ring her, I imagine she'll ring you.'

Abi gave a little laugh. 'You've always been so bossy. Okay, I'll ring her. But you look after yourself and let me know if there's anything at all I can do to help.'

'Thanks, sis. Love you.'

Abi smiled as she ended the call. She opened up her contacts and selected Laila's number. Mel was right. She probably did need to debrief over a glass of wine.

The next evening, Abi hesitated before reluctantly climbing out of the car. When she'd told Laila what was happening, her friend had immediately gone into problem-solving mode.

'You're coming to me for dinner tomorrow night, no arguments. I'm inviting Carly, Jude and Mia, and you'll see that you do have friends and support around you.'

'Only Jude turned up to the funeral.'

'I know, but I've spoken to the others since and they know you weren't involved in what Eric did. Also, none of them were affected by the investment. We've all been friends for years and you need to be surrounded by kindness right now.'

Laila was right, of course, kindness was what Abi did need, but her gut churned as she made her way up the path to the front door. She wasn't convinced that kindness was what she was going to find tonight.

Soft jazz combined with laughter floated down the hallway from the living area when Laila opened the door. She immediately pulled Abi into a hug.

'Wow, something smells amazing.' Abi drew in a long deep breath. She hadn't eaten since Mel's lasagne the previous night, not having the stomach for anything much, but the fragrant aromas of lemongrass and ginger made her stomach rumble.

'Your favourite Panang curry,' Laila said. She linked arms with her friend. 'Now, come on through. The girls are all here, and the wine's open.'

The laughter died as Laila and Abi entered the open-plan living area. Jude was immediately up on her feet, her arms outstretched. Abi sank into her friend's embrace, pushing her reservations aside. It was a relief to know that Laila had been right. These were her friends, they knew her, and they knew she would never do anything to hurt anyone.

Jude gave her one last squeeze and then pulled away. 'Come on, let's get you a glass of wine and then you can tell us how you're going. I can already tell by how thin you are that you're not eating enough.'

Abi ignored the comment and smiled at Carly and Mia. Both avoided eye contact. Okay, maybe she'd been too quick to feel relief. She gratefully accepted the glass of Merlot that Laila held out to her and took a large sip. She was going to need Dutch courage by the looks of it. She sat down on the couch next to Jude.

'How are things?' Jude's enquiry instantly brought tears to Abi's eyes. It didn't take much these days.

'Not great,' she managed.

Jude handed her a tissue. 'Sorry, I didn't mean to upset you. I imagine it's difficult.'

Abi nodded. 'I'm trying to get my head around things, to be honest. I've lost so much in such a short space of time. My husband, my job, my friends.' She looked pointedly at Carly and Mia. 'I understand that people think I was involved, but I wasn't. Now I'm trying to work out how I'm going to pay back the money that was lost.'

Jude sucked in a breath. 'But it was millions. Is that even possible?'

Abi shrugged. 'Probably not. I have a little bit of money, and I figure I can sell a lot of our furniture and artwork.'

'What about the house?' Carly asked. 'That must be worth a mint.'

'To the bank, not to me,' Abi said. 'Even when it's sold I'll probably only end up with a few hundred thousand. That will be split between everyone who's owed money, but it hardly makes a dent in the overall debt.'

'Do you have to sell it?' The shock on Laila's face made Abi grimace. 'I thought you would at least be able to keep your house.'

'I'm going to sell everything I possibly can to show everyone I intend to pay back the debts. But even if I wasn't doing that, without a job I can't make the mortgage repayments.'

'God, why would you want to live there anyway?' Carly shook her head. 'Not exactly a home full of happy family memories.'

Jude shot a murderous look at Carly before turning back to Abi. 'What will you do? Where will you go?'

'I started looking online at some rentals today,' Abi said. 'It's the only option for the moment. We'll need to move away from Brighton, of course. It looks like we might be able to afford to rent something small in Gardenvale. We'll see.'

'There are always spare rooms here if you need them,' Laila said.

Abi smiled, knowing that, as much as she'd hate to have to take it up, the offer was genuine.

'How's Hayden coping?' Mia asked. 'It can't be easy on him.'

Pain stabbed at Abi's chest as she thought of her son. Last night had been a disaster, and he'd ignored her every time she'd tried to communicate with him today.

'He's pretty upset. Not only has he lost his dad, but major changes are happening for him too. He's starting at the secondary college tomorrow. We can't afford the school fees at the grammar, and they kicked him out anyway.' Although Abi wasn't convinced she'd get Hayden to the secondary college. After she'd got off the phone with them that morning, she'd tried to talk to Hayden about it, but he'd just turned his stereo up so he couldn't hear her. Eventually, she'd given up and left him alone.

'But he's been there since he was five,' Jude said. 'Surely the school would have some compassion? When Henry Garcia's mother died, they gave him a scholarship and paid his school fees so he could finish his schooling. Hayden must be entitled to something like that.'

Abi shook her head. 'The dean of admissions was a friend of Eric's. He lost quite a bit of money in Eric's investment so won't be doing us any favours.'

'That's fair enough,' Mia said. 'You can hardly expect any preferential treatment after what's happened.'

A breath caught in Abi's throat. Mia's feelings were written all over her face, her words laced with venom. Abi glanced at Laila. Why had she invited Mia if she knew she was going to be like this? She could tell immediately from Laila's face that she was as shocked as Abi.

'Come on,' Laila said. 'Abi's living a nightmare. She's not expecting preferential treatment, but she is expecting our support.'

Mia put her wine glass down and stood. 'I'm sorry. I had hoped I could be a bigger person and rise above what's happened. But I can't. I'm going to say goodnight before I say something awful.' She turned to Abi. 'I do feel sorry for the situation you're in, but unfortunately I find it very hard to believe you're completely innocent in what's happened. You and Eric were one of the closest couples I know. I applaud you for trying to do the right thing now in repaying people, but your actions are too late. You should never have helped your friends refinance their houses. If it weren't for your greed, no one would be suffering now.' She squeezed Laila's arm on the way past and mouthed *sorry* before making her way out of the room.

Carly stood as the front door closed behind Mia. 'I have to agree with Mia. I lied to my husband tonight about where I was going because I'm too embarrassed to admit I'm socialising with you, Abi. We're counting ourselves lucky that the bank was unable to push through our equity loan in time for Eric's investment.' She grimaced as she spoke. 'We'd be five hundred thousand dollars poorer right now if they had. If we'd banked with Bank East to start with you probably would have rushed the equity application through for us, and we'd be as devastated as half of your other friends right now. The fact you were asked to leave your job confirms that I'm not the only one who doesn't trust you. Now, I'll leave you ladies to your meal.' She turned to Laila. 'Happy to do this again one night, but not if Abi's invited.'

Laila shook her head. 'I can assure you there won't be another invitation until you've apologised to Abi. She's innocent, and both you and Mia should be ashamed of yourselves.'

Abi lowered her head. She didn't want to see Carly's reaction and instead listened to her footsteps, waiting to hear the closing of the front door. As much as she appreciated Laila's words, if she were standing in Carly's shoes she'd probably be feeling very similar. Abi had helped Mel and three of her and Eric's friends acquire loans to invest in Eric's business. As much as she wanted to believe she hadn't played a role in what had happened, inadvertently she had. Was it possible he'd set her up? It was only four clients, but collectively it was well over a million dollars of the investment. She gave herself a shake. No, Eric wouldn't have done that to her.

Laila was quick to bring the bottle of wine around to top up Abi's glass and refill Jude's.

'Just ignore them,' Jude said. 'They're arseholes.'

Tears spilled down Abi's cheeks as she shook her head. 'They're just saying what everyone's thinking.'

A few hours later, Abi pushed open the hand-carved front door Eric had insisted they add to their *dream home* and was hit with the deep thump of bass from Hayden's second-floor room. She sighed, locked the door behind her and walked down the long hallway to the kitchen. She wasn't in the mood for a repeat of her last conversation with him. She sank on to a stool at the kitchen counter and lay her head in her hands. After the scene with Mia and Carly, she'd been unable to eat more than a few mouthfuls of Laila's curry. She'd felt terrible pushing it around her plate but just couldn't stomach it. How was she ever going to move forward, with people blaming and hating her? It was bad enough that some of her friends had turned on her, but to think that her son had too was heart-breaking.

Abi lifted her head from her hands, pushed herself up off the stool and walked determinedly to the staircase. The way Hayden was behaving towards her wasn't acceptable, and she was going to make sure he realised this.

Hayden was lying on his unmade bed, his eyes closed, his foot tapping to the beat of the music that screamed from his speakers. Clothes littered his floor, and empty plates and glasses covered most of the surfaces again. How had he managed to achieve such a mess in the space of a day?

Abi studied her son. It was hard to believe he was nearing six foot. Physically he was a man; mentally and emotionally he still had a lot of growing to do.

She walked over to his sound system and turned down the dial for the volume. Hayden's eyes jolted open.

'What are you doing?'

'I need to talk to you. It's important.'

Hayden sat up, leant against the headboard and folded his arms across his chest. 'What?'

Abi stared at her son. Eric would be shocked if he were here to see the attitude Hayden had adopted. But of course, that was the problem. He wasn't. 'I wanted to talk to you about Dad and about what's happened.'

'Why? There's nothing we can do about it now.'

'No, we can't change the situation, but we can control how we react to it. You can't go on like this. Being so angry. He was your dad. It's okay to be sad that he's gone.'

Hayden's eyes flashed with anger. 'Sad? Are you kidding? He completely fucked up my life. He was a lying, cheating scumbag and I doubt this was the first time he did something like this.'

Abi sucked in a breath. 'We don't know that for sure.' And she certainly hoped the investigation would show it was an isolated event. 'At least wait until we have all of the facts before you make assumptions.'

'We have enough facts already. Dad was a criminal and his business dealings confirm that. What else are you waiting for?'

Abi sighed. 'Honestly, I don't know. It's all been such a shock and I never would have believed your dad could have done something like this. I guess I'm trying to come to terms with the situation.'

'Yeah, right.'

'What's that supposed to mean?'

'There's no way Dad would have done *something like this* without you knowing. He's killed himself so can't confirm what he has or hasn't told you, and you're letting him take the fall because he can't defend himself. You're as bad as each other. He set up the deal, you organised loans, and then he stole the money.'

Abi took a deep breath. Within seconds of finding Eric, her thoughts had immediately gone to Hayden: to how he would cope with the situation of his father's death; of how devastated he was going to be. At no time had she imagined he'd react with such immediate and intense anger. Surely it wasn't a normal reaction? 'I'd like to organise for you to speak to someone.'

'What, like a shrink?'

Abi nodded. 'You've experienced a huge shock and a huge loss. Everyone deals with grief differently, but all I've seen from you since Dad died is anger. Having someone help you work through the stages of grief could help.'

Hayden's expression hardened. 'I don't want to speak to you or a shrink about any of this. Dad's dead. We're broke. My life's fucked, and you and Dad are to blame.'

'I wish you'd believe me when I tell you I had nothing to do with Dad's business dealings.'

'As if. Even Gabe thinks you had to be involved.'

'Gabe?'

'He rang this afternoon. He wanted to talk to me.'

Abi stared at her son. Gabe had hardly had anything to do with Hayden since his birth. She couldn't see any reason why that would change now Eric was dead. He'd come to the funeral but had hardly spoken a word to Abi. Since then, like many others, he'd not contacted her at all.

'He said he's going to come and talk to you. That he has a proposition that could help us out.'

'He's coming down from Sydney?'

'Yep. Said he'd ring you and come down next week.'

Abi couldn't imagine what her brother-in-law would have to say. Based on prior communications, whatever it was it wouldn't be good. And if he'd led Hayden to believe she was to blame then it wasn't going to be an enjoyable conversation.

'Okay, but in the meantime, I need you to believe me. I had nothing to do with your father's financial dealings. My work is related but still had to go through proper checks and processes. Everything I do is above board.'

'*Your work?* You're unemployed, remember.'

The iciness in Hayden's words was impossible to miss.

'Is it money?' Abi asked. 'Is this why you're so angry? I get that it's upsetting to have to change schools, but money comes and goes. That's not the end of the world.'

Hayden shook his head. 'We're losing our home, most of our belongings and I have to change schools. Kelly dumped me, by the way, so I can thank Dad for that too. So, while this might not be the end of your world, it's certainly the end of mine.' He stood and walked over to the sound system. 'Now, based on your little announcement this morning, I have to psych myself up to go to a new school tomorrow. One where I won't know anyone, yet my gut feeling is they'll all know my father killed himself after financially ruining most of our friends and family. So, if you don't mind, I want to think about my options.' He turned the music up louder than before.

Options? What does he mean about options? The thought whirled in Abi's head as she backed out of his room. At least he'd agreed to go to the secondary college, that was a start. But the word *options* plagued her. He didn't mean he'd kill himself too, did he? She stopped, went back into his room and turned his music down again.

'What do you want now?' Hayden demanded.

'What do you mean by *options*? You aren't thinking about doing anything drastic, are you?'

Hayden stared at her for a minute, recognition dawning in his eyes. 'Like Dad did?'

Abi nodded.

Hayden's lips curled into a snarl. 'I'm not that gutless. I face my problems. Don't worry, I have no intention of killing myself. If there's an afterlife I'd see Dad, and right now he's the last person I want anything to do with. My *options* are whether I even bother finishing school. I'm old enough to leave, you know?'

'You are. You're old enough to do a range of things. All I ask is you think through all of your options carefully before you act on any of them. Something good will come out of this; you mark my words.'

Abi tensed as the words left her mouth. Could she have just suggested that something good would come out of Eric's suicide?

To her surprise, Hayden nodded. 'I believe you on that one. After speaking with Uncle Gabe, I realise there is the possibility for something amazing to come out of all of this. I just need to trust that you'll support what he has to say.'

A nervous chill ran up her spine. Hayden and Gabe had spoken and come up with a plan Hayden was pleased about. She couldn't begin to imagine what it would be, but the one thing she knew was that Eric would be turning in his grave if he thought his brother would be able to assert any influence over their son.

Abi's stomach clenched the next morning as she watched Hayden reluctantly walk towards the entrance of the secondary college, his head bowed despondently. She'd offered to accompany him, but he'd looked at her as if she were crazy.

'I'm not a little kid. I'll be fine.'

He looked anything but fine.

A wave of grief rushed over Abi. She closed her eyes, her throat tightening as she gripped the steering wheel. *Oh, Eric, why did you do this to us?* The tears started to flow freely down her cheeks. She'd already learnt she couldn't control them. When grief hit, it hit like a truck. Nothing prepared her for it. Since Eric's death, she'd been so busy trying to understand what had happened and get her head around her next steps that she hadn't had the chance to grieve properly for everything she'd lost. She'd lost her partner, her best friend. That was the hardest. That he was unable to talk to her; that they could no longer try to work out a solution together. But she'd also lost her reputation and most of her friends, and that was his fault. Her sadness morphed into anger each time she had this thought.

It wasn't like Eric to run away from a problem, or at least that's what Abi had always believed. He'd tried to fix problems, and his life insurance would have been the one solution he could think of. If only that had been the case and his actions hadn't been such a waste.

Her body reacted physically at the thought of his death. The image of him lying in a pool of blood, the side of his head missing, was not something she would ever be able to forget. Her stomach contracted and she pushed open the car door and retched. She sucked in deep breaths, trying to get herself under control. While she needed to deal with these feelings, the school car park on her son's first day wasn't the best place to be trying to cope.

Abi did her best to push the overwhelming thoughts from her mind and pulled the car door shut. She blinked back tears as she pulled out on to Marriage Road. You often heard stories about how life could change in an instant, and for her, it certainly had. She wished her parents were alive to be of support, but her mother had died only months after Mel was born and her father had died of a heart attack two years ago, aged sixty-five. It had been an enormous shock to all of them. Although, if he were alive now, what was happening would probably have brought on a heart attack anyway.

Eric's family were of no support. Eric had certainly lived up to their opinion of him: the black sheep of the family. Never fitting in. Going against the family's wishes by moving to Melbourne and marrying a woman of whom his mother didn't approve. *She cheated on Gabe, she'll cheat on you too* had been her ongoing mantra. Abi hadn't cheated on Gabe, but the way he'd reacted to their break-up implied she had and he would never forgive her.

As she had this thought, her phone rang. Her stomach roiled as Gabe's name flashed up on the screen. She took a deep breath and accepted the call.

Chapter Six

Lucinda ran her hand through her newly cropped, light brown hair as she gazed out of the hotel window, taking in the twinkling lights of Melbourne's CBD. It was hard to believe that she'd done it. Within twenty-four hours of the visit to the prison, she'd reached her decision and she and Max had fled Dorford. Now, two days later, they were in Melbourne. Her heart ached as she thought of how she'd fled without giving her mother or Rachael the chance to say a proper goodbye. She'd left Tess a note and a package with a prepaid mobile phone in it, deciding the less she knew about her plans, the better.

She wasn't surprised that Max was fast asleep. He hadn't slept well on the bus or trains, and their day since arriving in Melbourne that morning had been jam-packed. First, the trip to St Kilda to visit Rachael's contact and obtain their new identities, before finding accommodation for the night and a mobile hairdresser to deal with Lucinda's hair. Max's had been cut short, but he didn't look drastically different like she now did. Seth, Rachael's contact, had given her two choices of name for her new identity: Francesca or Hope. She hadn't needed to think about it. Of the two, there was one obvious choice – the very thing she needed right now. Hope.

She checked her watch. It was after seven and her mother should be home from work. Lucinda slipped her new phone from her pocket.

To her relief, Tess answered on the third ring.

'Oh, thank God, I've been hoping you'd call. I've been sitting here since lunchtime willing the phone to ring. I wish you'd waited and said goodbye, Lu.'

Lucinda kept her voice low so as not to wake Max. 'I couldn't, Mum. It could have put you in danger. I explained that in the note, and also why you can only use the prepaid to call me.'

'I know, hon. You've done the right thing, I just wish it wasn't like this. And I have some worrying news, I'm afraid.'

The tremor in Tess's voice caused the hairs on the back of Lucinda's neck to rise. 'What's happened?'

'Ryan's furious,' Tess said. 'He knows you've disappeared and he's making all sorts of threats.'

A heaviness settled in Lucinda's stomach. 'He knows already? We only left on Wednesday.'

'One of his mates turned up this morning demanding to know where you were. Ryan sent him to speak to you and he couldn't find you. I told him I was as shocked as Ryan is. He told me that Ryan wanted to see me, and I needed to make an appointment immediately to go in. He stood over me while I rang the prison and organised visitation. I'm going in tomorrow.'

'Oh God, what are you going to say to him?'

'That I'm sick with worry that you and Max seem to have disappeared. There's nothing else I can say.' She hesitated for a moment. 'Oh, Lu. I wish you'd said goodbye.'

Lucinda blinked back tears. 'I just couldn't, Mum. And it's not goodbye; we can speak on this phone all the time. Just make sure you hide it well when you're not using it. Can you ring me after you see him tomorrow and let me know how you go?'

'Of course. Just be careful, won't you? I'm worried about you and Max.'

'There's no need to be. We're safe. I won't tell you where we are, and then you're not lying to Ryan when you say you don't know.'

'Okay, I'd better go,' Tess said. 'The pantry floor's uncomfortable, but I'll ring you tomorrow after I see Ryan.'

'What? Hold on, why the pantry floor?'

'Because the phone's in here and I'm paranoid that guy's still hanging around. I've closed all the curtains in the house so he can't peer in. I'm just not taking any risks.'

Pain throbbed in the back of Lucinda's throat. She couldn't believe she'd brought these problems on both herself and her beautiful mum. All because she'd been infatuated with a man who'd turned out to be a monster.

'Call me tomorrow night, Mum.'

They said their goodbyes and hung up, nausea overwhelming every emotion Lucinda felt. Had she made a mistake trying to run from Ryan? No, she was certain they had to leave. But should she have insisted Tess come with her? She sighed. Even if she had, Tess would have stood her ground. Her life was in Dorford.

Lucinda's heart raced. She and Max were on the bus waiting to leave the bus station at Dorford when a black van screeched to a stop in front of the bus. She didn't have time to react. Ryan was out of the van and up the stairs of the bus in a matter of seconds. His eyes locked with hers as he strode down the aisle. He didn't speak, just grabbed her by the hair and dragged her out. She screamed for help, but no one did anything. Conversations and laughter continued around her. How could they not see what was happening? He pushed her down the stairs and as she slammed into the curb the bus door closed. She tasted blood as she screamed again.

'Stop screaming and wave to your son,' Ryan said.

She looked up as the bus pulled out into the road. Max's face appeared at all of the windows. There were at least twenty of him. His hands were against the glass and his anguished cry of 'Mumma' rang out.

Ryan laughed. 'You'll never see him again, you stupid bitch.'

Lucinda sat bolt upright in the hotel bed, her heart pounding. She swallowed. It was only a dream. She was in Melbourne. She and Max were safe. She got up and quickly checked on Max before going to the bathroom and splashing water on her face. The dream seemed so real. Even if the events hadn't taken place, there was no mistaking Ryan's anger. It was as it was in real life, often triggered by the smallest of things.

She glanced at the clock. It was only five, but there was no way she'd get back to sleep. She needed a cup of tea. Lucinda shuddered as she switched on the kettle. It was the same Smeg retro design that they'd had in the house in Dorford. She ran her fingers over the scar on her arm as the water boiled. It would be a year now since she'd earned that scar. All because she'd laughed when Mikey, a friend of Ryan's, asked him if he was dressing to look like the Godfather or if his appearance was just a coincidence. Ryan had laughed along at the time, but the moment Mikey left, Ryan had turned on Lucinda.

'Don't you ever embarrass me like that again.'

Fear had flooded Lucinda the moment she saw the flash of anger in his dark eyes. She was in the process of making them tea. She had no idea what he was talking about. Still, it didn't stop her from trying to avoid what she'd learnt was generally inevitable. She put the kettle down and immediately went into defence mode. 'I'm sorry, babe. It definitely wasn't intentional.'

He'd snorted. 'Yeah, right. Laughing along with that prick Mikey when he makes a stupid comment like that. I dress how I like to. I'm not copying anyone or trying to be anyone.'

'I know that, and you look damn hot.' Lucinda had done her best to plaster a seductive smile on her face and approached Ryan, hoping she could play to his ego.

Desire replaced the anger in his eyes for just a split second before he punched her in the chest, hard. She reeled back, and before she could catch her breath he grabbed her by the hair. 'You do not laugh at me, ever. Do you understand?'

She did her best to nod as tears came to her eyes. The pain was made worse by the shock. He let go, pushing her roughly into the wall, and she crumpled to the floor.

'I'm going to pick up Max from your mum's. I'm sick of him spending so much time with her. Get your shit together while I'm out.' A look of disgust crossed his face. 'If Max sees you like that, I'm going to be very angry.'

She'd closed her eyes, trying to catch her breath, when they jolted open as she screamed in pain. He was standing over her, the kettle in his hands, pouring boiling water on her arm. She rolled out of his way, and he'd dropped the kettle and walked out of the kitchen. It had taken months for the burn to heal and she would always wear the scar as a reminder.

Now she took a deep breath and, with a trembling hand, poured water for her tea.

It was just a dream. They were in Melbourne and they were free. Hopefully she would never suffer at Ryan's hands again.

Lucinda was sitting staring out at the city skyline two hours later when Max woke. She'd spent the time trying to work out their next steps. Their first priority was finding somewhere to live. Having never been to Melbourne, she wasn't sure where to start. They had the whole weekend ahead of them to orientate themselves before contacting real estate agents on Monday.

'Mumma!' Max jumped out of bed and flung himself into Lucinda's outstretched arms. 'Can we go on more trams today and to the zoo and on that wheel thing?' He pulled himself out of her arms and pointed out of the window to the Melbourne Star, which they could just see in the distance.

'I'd say we could definitely do more trams today,' Lucinda said. She'd already thought that a day exploring some of Melbourne's suburbs would give them a feel for suitable areas. 'And possibly the big wheel later. We'll leave the zoo for another day when we can go when it first opens and stay until it closes.'

'Okay.' Max rubbed his belly. 'I'm starving.'

Lucinda laughed. 'Let's get you dressed and then we can go downstairs to the restaurant. We have a buffet breakfast included.'

Max's eyes widened. 'Like the one in Fiji?'

Lucinda nodded. 'Just like that one, I hope.' The three of them had been to Fiji for a week the previous year, and the highlight for Max, other than the kids' club, had been the buffet breakfast every day.

Max rushed to get dressed, and five minutes later they exited the lift in the lobby area and followed the sounds and smells to the dining room.

'Can I have anything I want, Mumma?' Max asked once they were seated.

'Without making yourself sick, you can.'

'They have ice cream,' Max said, his eyes widening as he looked across at the large display of food.

Lucinda laughed. 'Okay, maybe you can't have anything you want. Let's stick to breakfast food. I don't imagine anyone actually eats that.'

'He does.' Max pointed to an elderly gentleman sitting at the table next to them. The man smiled and waved his spoon in the air.

'You haven't lived until you've had ice cream for breakfast, young man.'

Max grinned and turned to Lucinda. 'See, Mumma. I haven't lived. I think I should start.'

'Let's see if you have any room left after you eat some proper food, okay?'

Max nodded.

'You listen to your mum,' the man said. 'She knows what she's talking about. Look at all my plates. I've had at least nine courses before the ice cream.'

'William!' An elderly lady – his wife, Lucinda assumed – sat down opposite the man. 'You're not annoying these lovely people, are you?'

'It's fine,' Lucinda said. 'Just hearing about the merits of having ice cream for breakfast.'

The old lady clasped her hands together and appeared to take a deep breath before smiling at Lucinda and Max. 'Ignore my ridiculous husband. Who on earth eats ice cream for breakfast? A growing boy needs eggs and fruit and all sorts of good things. As we all do,' she said, looking pointedly at her husband.

Max nodded but kept sneaking glances at William, who was licking his spoon and waggling his eyebrows at Max.

Lucinda stood. 'Don't let us interrupt your meal.' She smiled and led Max to the buffet, where they filled their plates before returning to their table. The elderly couple were now enjoying coffee.

'So,' William said, winking at Max, 'are you on holiday? There's lots to see in Melbourne.'

Max shook his head. 'No, we live here now. Don't we, Mumma.'

Lucinda nodded. 'Just moved.'

William's eyes widened. 'Well, aren't you lucky. Moving to a hotel like this with a buffet breakfast every morning.' He lowered his voice and whispered conspiratorially to Max. 'Imagine how many bowls of ice cream you'll be able to eat.'

Lucinda laughed; the twinkle in the old man's eye was infectious. 'We're not planning to live at the hotel. Just until we find a permanent place.'

'Melbourne's a beautiful city.' The woman smiled. 'I'm Dot, and this big oaf' – she nodded at her husband – 'is William.'

'I'm Max,' Max immediately said. 'And this is—'

Lucinda cut him off before he could say her name. 'I'm Hope. Are you on holiday?'

Max had already shovelled in a spoonful of scrambled eggs, and thankfully didn't say anything about Lucinda's name change.

She shook her head. 'No, we're having a special weekend for our wedding anniversary. We've been married fifty years today.'

'Congratulations!' Lucinda said.

'Fifty *wonderful* years,' William added. He reached across the table and squeezed Dot's hand. 'Couldn't ask for a better wife.'

Lucinda blinked back tears at the obvious love the two held for each other. It was a million miles from anything she'd ever shared with Ryan.

'You okay, love?' Dot asked.

Lucinda nodded. 'It's just lovely to see two people still in love after fifty years. I haven't been fortunate in relationships.'

Dot tutted. 'More fool the silly men is all I can say. Now, love, William and I have lived in Melbourne all of our lives, so if there's anything you need to know just ask away. We can certainly try and supply the right answer.'

'We need a house,' Max said. 'A big one with a fort and a lake.'

William gave a hearty laugh. 'Is that right?'

Max nodded. 'My favourite park at home had both of those so it would be good to have them in my garden. I could go there every day then.'

Lucinda picked up her teacup and took a sip. If Dot and William were any indication of how lovely people in Melbourne were, she'd made the right choice to come to this city.

'Do you know what area you plan to look in?' Dot asked.

Lucinda shook her head. 'I don't know Melbourne. I need to be close enough to the city to catch public transport once I start working, but somewhere cheap. I can't afford much, to be honest.'

Dot nodded, the lines on her forehead deepening as she gave thought to Lucinda's problem. 'You know, the area we live in has some older apartment blocks. You might find something in Elsternwick or around that area. There's a train station that brings you straight into the city, and lots of buses.'

'And,' William added, 'lots of parks.'

Max's eyes lit up. 'Really?'

He nodded. 'We have one right near our apartment, with a lake and a big playground. There's no fort, but it's still lovely.'

'Can we go there, Mumma?'

Lucinda smiled at Max's enthusiasm. 'We can certainly add Elsternwick to the list of suburbs we're going to look in. Maybe we'll even take a trip out there today and look around. Familiarise ourselves.'

'Yay,' Max said. 'And we can go to William and Dot's park?'

'If we can find it.'

Dot pulled out a pen from her bag and started writing on a napkin. 'Let me give you some directions and information, so you know exactly where to go.'

'And why don't I help this young man get another helping of food while you two women chat about that,' William said.

Max jumped to his feet. 'Is that okay, Mumma?'

Lucinda hesitated for only a second before nodding. 'Of course.' She smiled at William. 'Thank you, that's very kind of you.'

William mock-saluted her. 'My pleasure. It's lovely to meet such nice people. Dot and I have moved around a bit recently, and we lack company, don't we, love?'

Dot looked up from what she was writing and nodded. 'Not this morning though.'

Lucinda continued to sip her tea as she watched William take Max on a tour of all of the buffet areas. Max returned a few minutes later with a bowl of fruit salad. Lucinda couldn't help but notice William wink at him as they sat down.

'Look, Mumma,' Max said. 'This is very healthy.'

'It's a great choice, Max. Well done.'

His eyes narrowed. 'Once I eat all of this, could I please have some ice cream?'

Lucinda almost laughed as she saw William's face looking nearly as hopeful as Max's. 'Of course you can.'

Max grinned and began eating the fruit.

'Here you go.' Dot pushed two napkins across to Lucinda. 'There are some directions here to a few parks in the area, and also which train to catch from Southern Cross Station. I've put our contact details on a separate napkin in case you do move to the area. Make sure you look us up if you do.'

Lucinda took the information gratefully. 'We will, thank you.'

William rubbed his hands together. 'Okay, Dottie. Time we left these two young ones to their day.' He waggled his eyebrows suggestively. 'I've got plans for us this morning.'

Dot flushed and swatted his arm playfully. 'Too much information, William. Hope doesn't want her breakfast spoilt.'

Lucinda laughed at William's look of indignation.

Dot pushed her chair back and stood. 'Good luck with the house-hunting, dear. And do look us up if you're in the area, won't you?'

Lucinda nodded and smiled as Max said his goodbyes.

'I like them,' he said, finishing his fruit salad. 'We should live where they do. Can I get ice cream now?'

'You can.' Lucinda stood to help him get a bowl. She'd have a look at rental prices in Elsternwick when they returned to their room, and see if the area was feasible. Dot and William had certainly made it sound attractive. If nothing else, it gave them a place to start their search.

Chapter Seven

While Abi had done her best to push thoughts of Gabe from her mind, his phone call replayed in her mind over the weekend.

'I'm flying down to Melbourne next week, Abi, and want to talk to you. Would you be free for me to take you out for lunch or dinner?'

The last thing Abi wanted to do was sit across from Gabe over a meal. She told him she had plans but would be available at one thirty on Wednesday if he'd like to come to the house. She'd then gone on to ask him what he wanted to discuss.

'It's something we need to go over in person,' he'd said.

'Yet you've already spoken to Hayden over the phone about whatever this is?'

Gabe hesitated. 'I needed to gauge his interest before I spoke to you. I'll see you next week.' Ending the call, he hadn't allowed her to ask any further questions. Hayden had given her no more insight, clamming up as soon as she asked. 'Speak to Gabe; he'll explain when he's here.'

Now, Monday morning, she'd decided to forget about Gabe until he arrived on Wednesday. She felt positive. It was the start of a new week, and she was going to get herself a job and begin the process of re-establishing herself. But with every phone call she made, Abi's face grew hotter. The shame she was being made to feel was devastating. By lunchtime, she'd exhausted her pool of contacts. Every single conversation had brought one of two results: *I'm sorry, Abi, we just can't take the risk.* Or, *I can't believe you'd have the gall to even ask after what you and Eric have done.*

No one was going to employ her. It wasn't just banking contacts she'd rung. She'd rung people who'd always told her they'd love to use her administration skills if she was ever looking for a change. She was willing to do anything. However, the reality was no one was willing to hire her. It was still hard to get her head around the fact she was now a widow and that her husband had made the choice to make her one. Would he even have done it if he wasn't a member of the gun club, which had given him such easy access to a weapon? She bet none of her other friends' husbands had a Smith and Wesson they lovingly cleaned and admired after each club meeting.

She did her best to push the thought from her mind. Something she realised she was becoming an expert at when it came to thinking about Eric and trying to make sense of the situation.

Right now, she needed to work out how she was going to survive. Her payout from the bank would last a couple of months. She'd been through all of their expenses and cancelled a lot of the automatic payments. She'd cancelled the cleaner, the gardener and all of what she considered luxuries. It had reduced their monthly outgoings significantly, but they still had to eat and pay utilities – now, and when they moved into something smaller. She'd cashed in the one investment that had been in her name and planned to distribute the money evenly between the fifteen families that had been affected by Eric's losses. The investment had been left to her by her father, and at a little over two hundred thousand dollars it only gave each of the investors thirteen thousand. As the smallest investors in Eric's scheme had invested seventy-five thousand and the largest close to a million, it was nothing more than a token. She would send each payment with a letter explaining how deeply sorry she was, that she intended to pay back every cent, and there would be more coming once the house and contents were sold.

The one item she had managed to sell so far was a painting by Tom Roberts. Dylan had always joked with Eric that if he ever wanted to sell it, Dylan would buy it immediately, and he had. Abi was pretty sure it was worth less than the twenty-five thousand Dylan insisted she take. It was a lovely gesture, and she was happy to see it go to someone who loved the artist's work. She'd earmarked the money to give to Alexandria Goldberg. The Goldbergs had lost more than anyone else in Eric's scheme, and while twenty-five thousand wasn't much, she wanted to offer it as a goodwill gesture.

Her phone rang, causing her to jump. Had one of her contacts changed their mind? She pulled the phone towards her, seeing Laila's name on the screen. Her heart sank momentarily. It definitely wouldn't be about a job.

'Hey, you.' She managed to inflect some enthusiasm into her voice. 'What's happening?'

'I've got the afternoon off, so I'm inviting you over for drinks. I imagine you could use one by about now?'

Abi laughed. 'You couldn't be more correct. What time do you want me?'

'Anytime from two. I should warn you, though, Alex is dropping something in to me. She said she'll be doing that at about three. So if you aren't in the mood for bumping into her, perhaps come a bit later.'

Abi thought of the money she'd planned to give to Alex. 'Actually, I want to see her, so that will work well.'

'She's a bit mad at you, Abs. It might be a repeat of the way Carly and Mia behaved.'

'That's okay; my skin is being toughened every day. I can drown myself in your wine once she leaves.'

Laila laughed. 'Definitely. I'll put another bottle in the fridge now in case it gets ugly and we need more.'

Abi hung up, promising to be at Laila's at two. She took her chequebook from a pile of papers and wrote out a cheque for Alex before slipping it into an envelope, which she put in her bag. She wondered whether Alex would be able to see past her anger to realise Abi was trying to make amends.

Abi sank into Laila's plush couch, grateful that she had at least one friend's support. They'd only been talking for a few minutes when the doorbell rang.

'Brace yourself.' Laila stood to open the door. 'She's early.'

Abi gulped her wine as Laila left the room. She heard the two women chatting as they made their way back to the open-plan living area.

Alex hesitated the moment she saw Abi before turning to face Laila. 'You could have warned me.'

Laila shrugged. 'Why? We're all friends. Aren't we?'

Alex pursed her lips and turned back to look at Abi. She raised her eyes at Abi's half-empty wine glass. 'Bit early, isn't it? Or is this how you cope these days?'

'Don't be a bitch, Alex,' Laila said. 'Abi's having an awful time and we're trying to drown some of her sorrows. It's the Bay of Fires Pinot Gris you're always raving about.' She raised an eyebrow. 'I was going to offer you one, but it's obviously too early for you.'

Alex shuffled from foot to foot for a moment before relenting. 'Oh fine, there's no point me standing watching you two drink. I might as well join you. It's not as if life's exactly rosy for me right now either.' She glared at Abi as the words left her mouth, before choosing to sit in a chair as far from her as possible.

Laila went to fetch another glass.

Abi's hand shook as she reached into her bag and pulled out the envelope. Previously she would have described Alex as one of the kindest and loveliest women she knew. She and her husband owned Fleming's, a hatted restaurant in Elwood, and they were about to open another one in South Yarra. Alex was always organising charity events at the restaurant and was regarded as one of Melbourne's women of influence. She laughed at this title anytime it was mentioned, but it was true. She had a fantastic network that she called on to support her charities and contribute to the community.

'How's the opening coming?' Abi asked, clutching the envelope to her.

Alex narrowed her eyes. 'You are kidding, aren't you?'

'What do you mean?'

'The bank foreclosed on South Yarra three days after Eric destroyed us.'

Abi closed her eyes. *Oh God.* She knew that the Goldbergs had lost close to a million dollars, but she'd assumed, and hoped, they had several investments. They appeared to be doing so well, and Fleming's must turn over a good profit. She opened her eyes and looked at Alex. 'I'm so sorry. I had no idea.'

'Yes, well, that's the reality. We trusted Eric to look after us, and he let us down. We've still got Fleming's, thank God, and the apartments in Elsternwick, but it will be a long time before we can look at opening a second restaurant. Keeping the house and the kids at their schools are our priorities right now. Thanks to Eric, and of course your efficiency in hurrying our equity loan through, we have a huge mortgage to service.'

'Alex, I knew nothing about the property development when I helped you with your equity loan. I need you to believe me. If I'd had any idea of Eric's plans, I would have stopped him. There's no way I would have allowed him to do something outside of the law.'

'If that's really the case, Abi, you obviously didn't know your husband very well.'

Abi almost laughed. Alexandria's words couldn't be more accurate. She was beginning to think she hadn't known him at all. She held the envelope out to Alex. 'I know this isn't much, but it's a start. I am planning to pay back every cent you're owed. Unfortunately, it might take some time, but I will do my best. As soon as the house is sold, I'll be dividing the proceeds between everyone who lost money.'

Alex looked at the cheque. 'You're right; it's not much.' She tucked it in her bag. 'Look, Abi, I appreciate what you're trying to do, but I don't see how you'll ever make things right. What are you going to do for work? No one will employ you in banking and, to be fair, I don't blame them. I certainly wouldn't trust my money with you after what's happened.'

'It wasn't Abi's fault,' Laila said, returning with a glass of wine for Alex. 'She's as much a victim in this as anyone who lost money. Except she's lost more. She's lost her husband, her assets and her career. Eric set her up, Alex.' She smiled apologetically at Abi. 'Sorry, hon, but I'm beginning to think that he did. That barbecue where he was so persuasive about the investment, encouraging everyone to get equity from their homes and then pushing you to look after the clients that could apply through your bank. You have to admit it was a bit over the top for a safe capital guaranteed investment.'

Abi stared at her friend as Alex accepted the glass of wine. The hardest thing about hearing Laila's words was the possibility that they were true.

Alex sipped her wine, remaining silent for a moment before her face softened. 'Abi, if Eric has screwed you over I'm sorry. We all thought he was a good guy.'

'I did too,' Abi murmured.

'Do you have a backup plan for work?'

'I honestly don't know. All of my knowledge is in banking and administration. I thought I'd have more chance in administration, but after the series of disastrous phone calls I made earlier today, I'm not so sure.'

'What about Fleming's?' Laila said. 'You were telling me the other day that you need more staff. This way you'd have someone hardworking who you know, and you'd be helping Abi out. You said you needed a bookkeeper, didn't you? It would be a start.'

Alex laughed. 'You have to be kidding. Jerry's a generous man, and he's already expressed to me that he thinks you've been put in an awful position, Abi, but I can't see him letting you anywhere near our finances.'

Abi nodded. 'That's okay. I'm not expecting help from anyone. I'll find something. Even if I have to work at the supermarket and pack shelves, it will provide an income.'

Alex tapped her manicured nails against her wine glass. 'Where are you going to live once the house is sold?'

'I've been looking in Gardenvale, but I'm not completely sure yet. I have to work out what we can afford, which won't be much. We might have to move further out, but I'm hoping we can stay in that area as Hayden's moved to the secondary college.'

Alex nodded, frown lines appearing in her forehead.

'What's that look for?' Laila asked. 'You look like you're in scheming mode.'

Alex managed a wry smile. 'You know me too well.' She turned to Abi. 'Look, I can't employ you at the restaurant. For a start, a lot of our friends eat there and probably wouldn't be too happy seeing you. But I do need an on-site manager at the Elsternwick apartments. The job comes with a two-bedroom apartment and a small salary. Would that help?'

Tears filled Abi's eyes. 'Really? You'd do that for me?'

'It's a job, so you'd be doing it for me. It's an old apartment block and attracts some less-desirable elements, which is why I like to have someone living in and managing it. You'd be responsible for leasing the apartments, doing regular inspections and coordinating any maintenance that needs doing. There are twelve apartments in total. One would be yours, and currently ten of the other eleven are rented. Number one priority is getting the other apartment rented. What do you say?'

Abi wiped her cheeks, nodding. 'Thank you so much.'

Alex sipped her wine before smiling. 'Don't thank me yet. You haven't seen the place. You don't have to move in straightaway, but you would need to handle everything else immediately as there are some urgent maintenance issues.' She laughed. 'Take a look at it tomorrow before you commit. Compared to what you're used to, it's a shithole.'

Abi wasn't sure she'd describe the older-style, two-storey brick apartment building as a *shithole*, but it was definitely less desirable than she'd hoped. Alex had dropped her a set of keys earlier that morning with a list of instructions. Scanning the list now as she sat in her car in the street outside the building, Abi realised she had a lot to do. Four of the apartments had maintenance issues, and a prospective tenant was arriving in an hour to look at the vacant apartment. She needed to familiarise herself with everything before the woman arrived. According to Alex, it was the worst apartment in the block and she was to *rent it as long as she's not a druggy or a criminal.* She hadn't elaborated on why it was so bad, but Abi assumed she was about to find out.

She pushed open her car door and walked up a small path to the front entrance. The garden was overgrown with an abundance of weeds. Looking at the list of job requirements, it appeared the garden was also Abi's responsibility. Luckily the apartment block itself took up most of the land area, so it wouldn't be a huge task to bring the garden under control.

Abi entered the foyer and climbed the stairs to the second floor, where she walked down a light-coloured corridor to apartments eight and nine. The vacant apartment was right next to the one available for her and Hayden. She decided she'd look at their apartment first. She took a deep breath as she unlocked the door and moved inside. This was going to be their new home. Her heart sank as she looked around. It was fully furnished, with mismatched seventies-style furniture. The dull, shabby browns could hardly be considered retro. The apartment housed a small kitchen with space for a table and chairs, and an even smaller living room with one couch, a television and a coffee table. The two bedrooms were both about the same size with single beds, and there was one communal bathroom. Abi stared into the bathroom. It was smaller than her pantry and in desperate need of updating. She sighed, wondering how on earth she'd sell this to Hayden. Even bringing some of their furniture and belongings with them would make it a hard sell. She let herself back out of the apartment and moved to the vacant one next door, to view it before the prospective tenant arrived.

She pushed open the door and stepped inside. A musty smell greeted her. She wrinkled her nose and walked into the small living area and opened the windows. Then she moved into the bedrooms and did the same. The layout was identical to the apartment next door, but the paint was peeling, the carpeting worn and the sparse furniture in even worse condition. She was amazed you could even call this apartment furnished. The smell was worse closer to the windows, and Abi put her nose to one of the curtains, reeling as she did. They stank. A combination of smoke and something else she couldn't identify. She checked the curtains in the bedrooms, and they were all the same.

She took out a pen and a notepad and started making notes. The curtains needed washing; there was only one chair for the kitchen table; the yellowing walls needed a coat of paint. Her phone rang as she added more maintenance to her list. It was Alex.

'Are you still interested now you've seen what a dump it is?'

Part of Abi wished she could say no, but this was a lifeline and she needed to take it. 'Of course I am. I'm just making a list of what needs to be done on apartment nine. I doubt anyone will want to rent it in this condition.'

Alex laughed. 'You'll be surprised, and we can only do essential repairs at the moment. Nothing cosmetic.'

'But it needs some paint and chairs and a few other things.'

'Not essential. Sorry, Abi, but that's the reality right now. We can't afford to do anything that isn't considered essential. If you look at the maintenance issues I gave you for the other apartments, you'll see the type of things I mean.'

Abi had already scanned the list. An oven needed repairs in one apartment, there was a broken window in another, and the hot water had stopped working in two others. She had the name of a handyman to call who, according to Alex, could fix nearly anything.

'I have to go,' Alex said. 'Let me know how you go renting out apartment nine. Like I said, as long as they're not a criminal or druggie then rent it. Once you've gone through their application, of course, and rung their references.'

After agreeing she would, Abi hung up and took another look around the apartment. The mattresses on the beds were lumpy, and if she was honest, it had no appeal at all. She couldn't begin to imagine the sort of person who would willingly rent it.

Abi found herself apologising as she showed the woman, who'd introduced herself as Hope, and her little boy around. 'I'm sure we can do a few things to make it more comfortable. Washing the curtains should make a difference to the smell.'

Hope laughed. 'It's cheap and it's in a good location.' She'd given Abi a very brief rundown when they'd met, telling her that they'd recently moved from interstate for a fresh start. 'We met an elderly couple on Saturday morning who raved about Elsternwick, and exploring the area over the weekend made me realise why. It's perfect for our needs, as is this apartment.'

Her four-year-old, who'd introduced himself as Max, didn't look convinced. 'It's tiny, Mumma,' he whispered. 'Where would I sleep? The beds are yuk. I'd have to sleep on the floor.'

'I'm sure they won't be that bad,' Hope said. She turned to Abi. 'I'll fill out an application, if you have one. We'd like to move in as soon as possible if you accept us. The hotel we're staying in is rather stretching our finances.'

Abi stared at Hope for a moment. She was well dressed, as was Max, and seemed educated. Her short, brown hair was nicely styled, and her green eyes were bright and engaging. She definitely wasn't on drugs and Abi's gut feeling said not a criminal. She'd be a perfect candidate for tenancy, but Abi couldn't help but wonder what circumstances had driven her interstate to start again in something so cheap and rundown. That wasn't normal, was it? But then Abi's situation was hardly normal, so she wasn't one to judge.

She leafed through the file Alex had given her and handed Hope an application form. 'Fill this out, and I'll process it immediately. Assuming all is in order, you can move straight in.'

Hope sat down on the one kitchen chair and began filling in the form.

Abi glanced over it quickly when she'd finished.

'Are you working now?' she asked.

Hope shook her head. 'We only got here a few days ago, but I have plenty of leads for work. I can pay the first two months' rent in advance, if that makes a difference?'

Abi smiled. 'I'll let you know.' She glanced at the form again. 'I've got your number. Now, I'll get on and go through your application and give you a ring this afternoon. Hopefully I can get on to your references, and we can finalise everything quickly.'

It was surprisingly quick to run through Hope's application. She'd supplied mobile numbers for her references and Abi got on to her previous employer straightaway. She quickly learnt that Hope was a competent and reliable administrator and had a glowing recommendation from her former landlord. She stared at the form once more before deciding to ring Alex.

'How did you go?'

'Good. I've checked her references, and they're glowing, although . . .' Abi hesitated.

'Although what?'

'I don't know. I'm just not sure they're genuine. There was something I couldn't put my finger on. Maybe she'd spoken to them beforehand to make sure they said all the right things.'

'Most people do when they supply references, or give fake ones. A lot of landlords never bother checking them. What was your gut feeling? I'm more interested in that and whether she can pay the rent.'

'She's lovely and can pay the first two months upfront, on top of the bond.'

'Perfect, tell her it's hers as soon as she can move in. There's a lease in the information pack I gave you this morning. Get her to sign that and get the bond and rent from her. And what about the apartment for you and Hayden? I told you it was pretty horrible.'

'It'll be fine. And Alex, I appreciate your help. I know this is a complicated situation.'

Silence greeted her at the other end of the phone line.

'Alex?'

'I'm here. I'm sorry too, that you're going through all of this. It's hard to separate you and Eric, which is why so many of us are upset, but I can see you're trying to put things right.' Alex gave a little laugh. 'Your new living situation is going to be a testament to that. It's not what many people would choose.'

'Unfortunately, I'm no longer in a position to choose. But again, I appreciate what you've done for me. I'd better go and organise things with the new tenant and get these other maintenance issues fixed up.'

Abi rang off with mixed feelings. She was grateful to have a job and somewhere to live, but she'd be lying if she didn't admit that it was going to be a huge adjustment.

The next morning passed in a flash for Abi. She dropped Hayden at school before going on to the apartments to give her new home a thorough clean. She arrived back at her house a little after one, giving her enough time to have a quick shower and prepare for Gabe's arrival.

Now, showered and dressed, she glanced at the clock. Gabe would be here any minute. She wrapped her arms around herself as she thought of her brother-in-law. From the day she met Eric, she'd done her best to distance herself from Gabe. She hadn't cheated on him as he'd led his parents to believe. They'd been out twice, both times in a group of friends, and seeing too many signs of his arrogance she'd come to the conclusion that friends was all they would ever be. Towards the end of their second date, at a party where he'd ignored her in favour of smoking dope out the back with his friends, she'd met Eric. Her heart had skipped a beat when he'd smiled at her. The attraction was instant.

She'd done her best to let Gabe down gently, but it hadn't gone well. She'd learnt that he was fiercely competitive, and losing a girl to his younger brother was not something he was going to do happily. As the relationship between Abi and Eric intensified, so did Gabe's hatred towards both of them. Eric tried talking to him many times, but in the end, gave up. It was the Christmas they announced their engagement that Gabe threatened her. They'd just finished clearing the lunch table at Gabe and Eric's parents' house when he turned to her. Eric was outside with the rest of the family, and it was just the two of them. 'I can't believe you turned me down and are marrying him. You must have a screw loose.'

Abi had done her best to be nice. 'I can't help who I fell in love with, Gabe. And I'm sorry. I've told you that before. I hope you'll be happy for us.'

'Happy? You'll pay for this. One day, when you least expect it, I'll take something you love away from you. Then you'll see how it feels.'

Abi had stared open-mouthed at Gabe. They'd been out twice. To suggest he loved her was ridiculous. 'You don't love me. You just don't like the idea of Eric having something you now seem to think you want.'

'Whatever,' Gabe said. 'Just remember what I said. One day you'll regret humiliating me.'

Other than Eric, the only person who'd believed Abi's story was Eric's elderly aunt, Rhea. She'd overheard part of the exchange between Abi and Gabe, and assured her she'd speak to her sister. Eric's mother, however, had accused Rhea of being a troublemaker and refused to discuss the matter further.

As a blue rental car pulled into the driveway at precisely one thirty, Abi did her best to shake off the feeling of foreboding.

Hayden's excitement as she'd dropped him at school that morning worried her more than if he'd stayed in his miserable funk of a mood. Whatever Gabe was offering was hugely attractive to Hayden; she just couldn't imagine it would be anything she'd want to agree to.

Gabe climbed out of the car, a large bouquet of lilies in one hand, his briefcase in the other. He looked up, and Abi's heart caught in her throat. For a split second, the crooked smile, the closely cropped jet-black hair and cobalt eyes could have been Eric. There was no question that they were brothers. Gabe was two years older but, like Eric when he was alive, Gabe kept in shape and had a full head of hair, so it would have been difficult to tell who was the eldest.

He strode up the driveway to the front door and held out the flowers. 'For you.' He leant in and kissed her on the cheek. 'Imogen remembered that lilies were your favourite, and as she can't be here she wanted you to know she's been thinking of you.'

Abi took a step back, surprised. Gabe hadn't brought flowers to the funeral and Imogen hadn't attended. In fact, she hadn't heard from her sister-in-law at all since Eric's death. She'd assumed that, like the rest of the family, she was humiliated by her brother-in-law's actions. Still, Abi wasn't going to question an act of kindness.

'Thank you. Please tell her they're beautiful and she's right about lilies being my favourite.' She motioned for him to come inside. 'I was about to make some coffee. Would you like one?'

'I'd love one.' Gabe followed her into the kitchen, sitting down at the island counter and watching as she filled a vase with water and added the flowers. 'I imagine things have been very difficult.'

Abi nodded, turning her attention to the coffee machine. 'They have. They still are.'

'Hayden mentioned you lost your job and he's had to move schools. I assume the house will be sold?'

'It's already on the market. The agent hasn't put a sign up yet as she thinks it will sell quickly, so they probably won't need to. Two groups are coming through tomorrow morning.'

Gabe nodded. 'And what about you? Where will you go?'

'A friend's given me a job as an apartment manager in Elsternwick. The salary isn't much, but it comes with a two-bedroom apartment. I'm getting it ready at the moment and we'll move as soon as the house is sold.' She looked at Gabe. 'I haven't told Hayden yet, so if you don't mind keeping that to yourself. He's not going to be very happy about it.'

Gabe nodded. 'Of course. That's very generous of your friend. You're lucky to be surrounded by people who care about you.'

Abi snorted. 'Most of my friends aren't speaking to me. Hopefully that will change over time as I pay people back.'

Gabe raised an eyebrow. 'I thought he lost millions?'

Abi nodded. 'He did. But even if it takes me the rest of my life, I intend to pay every cent back. Eric thought his life insurance would cover everything.'

'You're not the type to run away from your problems, Abi. Not like Eric. As much as I'd like to believe he thought his insurance would cover his mistakes, I wouldn't count on it. I think he'd kick himself that he didn't get away with whatever he was trying to orchestrate. He definitely wasn't the brother I thought I knew.'

Abi fell silent. Gabe didn't know Eric; he'd had nothing to do with him for years, and right now, his speculating was more painful than she was able to deal with. She passed a cup of coffee across to him and remained standing on the other side of the counter. 'What was it you wanted to discuss?'

Gabe put the coffee cup down and opened his briefcase. He took out a folder and rested his hands on it. 'Imogen and I want to do something for you and Hayden. We realise you're in an awful situation and we're in a position to help.'

Abi's legs began to tremble. Was he going to offer to pay back their debt? Would he even have that kind of money? Even if he did, he'd be the last person she'd imagine would help her. She made her way around the counter and pulled out the stool next to Gabe. Her voice was barely audible. 'You're going to help us? You'd be that kind?'

Gabe's smile didn't reach his eyes. 'We're family, Abi. Of course we intend to help, and this is how.' He pushed the folder in front of her.

She looked at the cover and then back at Gabe. 'Sydney Grammar School?'

Gabe nodded as he sipped his coffee. 'Both Eric and I went there, and Imogen and I would like to offer to send Hayden to finish his schooling. He's year twelve next year, and finishing off at a school like that would open so many doors for him. Doors that Eric's legacy may otherwise have closed.'

'But it's in Sydney?'

'It is. We'd like Hayden to live with us while he's there. We have plenty of space, so he'd have a large room and an entertainment area to himself.'

Abi stared at him, trying to get her head around what he was offering. 'You and Imogen want to pay the fees? This is what you mean by helping us?'

'We do. Eric and I rarely saw eye to eye, but the one thing we agreed on was the importance of a good education.'

They weren't offering to help pay back the debts, or even keep Abi and Hayden together, but they were offering to help her son. Abi wasn't sure what to think. 'You could have offered to do this for him here. Kept him at his old school.'

Gabe shook his head. 'In Sydney he'll get a fresh start. He won't have Eric's reputation hanging over his head. He would have been made an outcast here. Too many families have been affected by Eric's downfall.'

He was right; it was the one thing Abi had considered a positive about moving him to the secondary college. No one there had been personally affected.

'Imogen and I will extend our help to sending him to university too. If he gets the marks he needs, of course.'

Abi stared at Gabe. It was an incredibly generous offer, but it was Gabe. Gabe, who Eric had despised. Gabe, who thought he was superior to everyone. Sure, he was incredibly lovely and generous right at this moment, but that was because he wanted something. What she couldn't work out was how this was going to advantage him. Gabe didn't do anything to be nice or to be generous unless he would benefit. 'Gabe, you hardly know Hayden. You might be related, but you're basically strangers. I can't imagine why you'd want to do this.'

'I don't know him because Eric chose to keep away from the family. He made it very clear we weren't good enough for him. We now have a chance to reconnect with Hayden, and I'd like to take it. He's my blood, Abi. What do you say? I can hang around the rest of the week while he packs his things and we can fly back together on Saturday. Imogen has organised a fitting with the uniform department on Monday morning and then an interview with the head of the year where he can select his subjects. They've said he can start as early as Tuesday.'

This was all rolling far too quickly for Abi. She'd just lost Eric. She didn't want to lose Hayden too. 'They have a place available at such short notice? I thought the waiting list was years long?'

Gabe's smile was more of a smirk. 'The principal and I go back a long way. He was able to pull some strings.'

Abi took a sip of her coffee. 'It's a very generous offer, Gabe . . .'

'But? It sounds like you were about to add a *but*.'

Abi nodded. 'But I don't understand why you'd want to do this. You and Eric weren't close, and you hardly know Hayden. You don't have any kids, and suddenly you want a teenager living with you. Why?'

Gabe shifted on his stool. 'Hayden's my only nephew and I'd like to do this for him. There's no hidden agenda or ulterior motive. Sure, Eric and I were very different from each other, but that's not something I hold against him. He had different beliefs, and that's fine, it's what makes the world go around.'

'You know he'd say no if he was alive, don't you? He wouldn't want Hayden being influenced by you.'

'He's not alive, so it's not relevant. It's what you want for Hayden that counts. From what I understand, you can't offer him anything right now other than a roof over his head and a public education.'

'And me,' Abi said. 'He's always had me and always will.'

'From what Hayden told me, he's angry at you right now. He doesn't believe that you weren't involved in Eric's business decisions. In his eyes, he's lost both of you, and every other part of his life is imploding. Let me turn it into a positive for him. We'll get him to start seeing a psychologist so he can work through some of this. He needs an outlet for his anger, and if he stays here, it's probably going to be you. Also, he's about to turn seventeen. It's his second-last year of school and he should be able to make this decision himself. If he wants to stay here then fine, but if he wants to come, that's what we're offering.'

Abi nodded. It would make a massive difference to Hayden's future, but every fibre in her body screamed *no*.

'Hayden needs family around him at a time like this,' Gabe added. 'He'll get that in Sydney. Mum and Dad want to see more of him and so do the extended family. Eric kept you all away from us, and we want to rectify that.'

'They want to see me too?'

Gabe blushed. 'Well, of course, if you come up to visit, but I was referring to Hayden. What do you think?'

Abi sighed. 'Honestly, I don't know what to think. I've just lost Eric, and now you want to take Hayden from me. It doesn't leave me much, if he was to go.'

'You can visit, and I'm sure he'll want to come home on the holidays. It's only a quick plane flight.'

'After living the lifestyle of the rich and famous with you and Imogen he's hardly going to rush back here to the apartment I'm moving to.'

'Maybe not, but you're welcome to stay with us anytime.'

Abi nodded. 'Hayden will be home soon. I guess we chat to him and see how he feels about the idea.' As much as Abi wanted to say no, she couldn't come up with any good reason that wasn't her being totally selfish. If only she could go with Hayden, but that would mean putting up with Gabe daily, and that definitely wasn't a scenario she wanted.

Gabe stood. 'Why don't I come back at five? You and Hayden discuss the opportunity, and if he wants to come, I'll take you both out for dinner to celebrate. It'll give you a chance to express any concerns you have, without me being there.'

Abi slid off the stool and followed him to the front door. 'Thank you, that's incredibly thoughtful. We'll see you at five.'

She held the door open and watched as he climbed into his rental car. From an objective perspective, Gabe's visit had been one filled with generosity and kindness. But Abi found that hard to swallow. It just wasn't Gabe. The question was, what was his real motivation?

Hayden slammed through the front door a little before three thirty. He dropped his school bag in the hallway and called out to Abi.

'Mum, are you home?'

'In the kitchen.' She was sitting at the kitchen table waiting for him to arrive. For the last hour her mind had been a whir. If he went, what would she do? She wasn't ready for her baby to leave the nest. Not that he was a baby, but he was only sixteen. She sighed – her needs weren't a reason to prevent Hayden from taking advantage of this opportunity.

Hayden appeared in the kitchen doorway seconds later. 'Where's Gabe? Did he come?'

Abi patted the chair next to her. 'Come and sit down. Yes, he came earlier, and he's left so you and I can have a chat.'

Hayden hurried over to the table, excitement in his eyes. It was the first time since Eric's death she'd seen any animation in him.

'Did he tell you about the school? It's one of the best in Australia.'

Abi nodded. 'He did, and it's a very generous offer from both him and Imogen.'

Hayden's smile fell. 'But? I can already tell you're about to say *but* and then give me some bullshit reason why I can't go with him.' Abi stared at her son. He was so full of anger, and when had his language deteriorated so badly? 'You can't stop me going. I'll go whether you say I can or not. Gabe's got plans for me. I'll finish at the school and then go on and do law like he did, at the University of Sydney. I can intern at his firm and work there once I graduate. He's going to groom me to take over one day. This is an opportunity bigger than anything Dad would ever have been able to give me.'

So that was the ulterior motive: he was looking for someone to take over the firm. It wasn't really an ulterior motive. It made sense that he'd want to keep it in the family, and it provided Hayden with another opportunity if he was interested in law.

'I thought you wanted to work in finance,' Abi said. 'It's all you've ever talked about.'

Hayden rolled his eyes. 'You think after what Dad did that I'd be able to be successful in finance?'

'Hayden, your father would hate to see you make this decision. He and Gabe have never been close. He's always believed Gabe only operates for self-gain. That he's arrogant and egotistical and only out to get things for himself.'

Hayden let out a loud laugh. 'Well, that's a joke, isn't it? I think, looking at how Dad's chosen to exit this world, his opinion of Gabe means nothing. Maybe if he'd spent more time with his brother he'd have developed better work ethics and done things within the law. You can't point the finger at Gabe for being anything but generous. He's throwing me a lifeline when I'm drowning.'

A heavy feeling settled in Abi's stomach. Hayden had idolised Eric up until this point. She'd never heard him say a bad word about him. Now, pure hatred coated every word. 'But Hayd, you hardly know Gabe. It'll be like moving in with total strangers.'

'I don't care. I can move away from all of this shit Dad left behind and start again. I hardly know Dad's family, which is crazy. They're blood, and I'd like to get to know them. Gabe's looking out for me. It's more than Dad did.'

Abi closed her eyes. She couldn't imagine how she was going to get the message through to Hayden that Eric had loved him. That, regardless of what he'd done, Hayden had been so important to him. She opened her eyes and took her son's hand. 'If I agree to you going to Sydney, there's going to be a condition.'

Hayden withdrew his hand from hers and folded his arms across his chest. 'What?'

'Gabe's offered to organise some counselling for you. After all that's happened, it's important you talk to someone. Hopefully you'll come to realise through that process that Dad loved you enormously. There are a lot of things I don't understand about him right now, but that is one thing I'm absolutely certain of. I also need you to believe that I wasn't involved in what he did. I had no knowledge at all of it. I honestly have no idea how I can prove this to you, but it's the truth.'

'I can go to Sydney then?' Hayden didn't comment on anything Abi had said, but she could see the hatred in his face when he looked at her. He didn't believe her.

'Gabe's coming back at five to take us out for dinner and discuss it further. If you think you'll be happy living with him and Imogen, then, as much as I'm going to miss you, you have my blessing to go.'

A wide grin spread across Hayden's face.

'But, Hayden, I'll expect you to stay in touch, okay? And I'll expect you home for the school holidays.'

Hayden nodded, although Abi could tell he wasn't listening. 'When do I move?'

'Gabe said you could fly back with him on Saturday. He's organised meetings and uniform fittings at the school on Monday, and you can start Tuesday.'

Hayden leapt to his feet. 'I'll start packing now. Call me when Gabe arrives. I can't wait to thank him. You've no idea what this means to me.'

Abi lowered her head to the table as Hayden bounded out of the room – and, from the sounds of it, up the stairs two at a time. Tears pooled in her eyes. She understood that it gave him something to look forward to and the opportunity to get away from everything that was happening around them, but it hurt how easily he'd turned his back on her.

Chapter Eight

Lucinda paced up and down the small living room area, willing her phone to ring. Her mother hadn't called on Saturday as promised; instead, she'd sent a text saying the visit to the prison had been cancelled at the last minute and rescheduled for Wednesday afternoon. She hadn't given any more information, just said she would call then. Lucinda checked her watch for the millionth time then pulled her cardigan tightly around her. She wasn't used to the temperatures plummeting into single figures overnight.

She stopped in front of the apartment window and looked out to the darkened street below. Moonlight cast shadows from the leafy trees on to the road, and a couple walked past hand in hand. As they passed under the street light, the man reached across and twirled the woman's hair around his finger before pulling her to him and kissing her. It was a simple, intimate gesture, but Lucinda shuddered and quickly closed the curtains. How she wished she could close off the memories too. Her wedding day was the last time Ryan had playfully twirled her hair around his finger, as he'd told her how lucky he was and how happy he was. Two days later they'd been ordering drinks at the hotel where they were honeymooning, and he'd taken her hand and told the waiter that his wife's favourite drink was a Bacardi, lime and soda. She'd laughed and said that must be his other wife, but she'd love a vodka, lime and soda. She'd thought nothing of it until they returned to their room and Ryan approached her. She'd shivered with anticipation, expecting they'd spend the afternoon in bed. Instead, when he reached for her hair, he grabbed a handful, demanding an apology as he reduced her simultaneously to her knees and to tears.

She pushed the memory from her mind, instead focusing her thoughts on the small apartment. Dot and William's suggestion of Elsternwick had been perfect and she could hardly believe how lucky she'd been to find accommodation so quickly. And the fact that Abi had been happy to check her references immediately, and allow them to move in the same day, meant there'd been no reason to look at any others. It had been such a relief to realise that her fake references of her mother and Rachael had worked. She didn't mind the fact that the apartment needed improvements; she and Max could get organised over the next few days while also getting out and exploring the area further.

She did wonder why Abi would be moving into these apartments. She'd seen her drive off in a very new-looking Audi. She dressed beautifully, had perfectly manicured nails, and with her shiny, long black hair looked like she'd recently walked out of the salon. Everything about her suggested she had money. While the apartments were basic and functional, they were a massive step down from what Lucinda was used to, and she imagined an even more significant step down for Abi. Maybe Abi was running from something too? How ironic would that be?

Lucinda's thoughts were interrupted as her phone rang. She grabbed it from the coffee table and answered it.

'Mum?'

'Hi, love.' Her mother sounded exhausted.

'Are you okay?'

'Yes, just a stressful few days. It would have been better to get this meeting over on Saturday rather than have to wait four days.'

'Why was it postponed?'

'Ryan did something at the prison. I'm not sure what, but they revoked his visitation rights for a few days. He had a bruised cheek, so I expect someone looked worse off than he did.'

'Did he threaten you?'

'No,' Tess said. 'Surprisingly, he seems to believe me. I turned it on a bit. Said I couldn't believe you'd go without telling me. He did make me promise to contact him if you were in touch. He also said I might get random visits from his *colleagues* to check up on whether I've seen you or not, and save him using his prison calls to ring me.'

'What exactly does that mean?'

'He *said* they'd just ask me. The reality, I suspect, will be a bit different. Rachael had one of his colleagues visit her today.'

Lucinda sucked in a breath. 'Is she okay?'

'Yes. Apparently the guy was quite polite. He asked if she'd heard from you and then asked to see her phone. She handed it over, and he scrolled through it. I assume he was looking for messages or phone calls to you. The last calls from you to Rachael were from before you left, and her calls and texts to you once you left went unanswered. It all matches up to us having no idea that you were going to leave. Thank goodness for the prepaid, Lu. That was such a smart idea.'

'Did he say anything when you met him? Did he suspect I might be somewhere?'

'He didn't let on a whole lot. Just wanted me to know that he'd be watching me, I guess. That's okay, I've got nothing to hide, other than this phone, which lives in the bottom of a cereal box when I'm not crouched on the floor in the pantry using it.'

Lucinda wasn't sure whether to laugh or cry at her mother's description. It was ridiculous on the one hand and totally necessary on the other.

'Rachael said to tell you she misses you.'

Tears welled in Lucinda's eyes. It was hard to imagine not seeing her best friend again. 'Tell her I feel the same.'

They spoke for another ten minutes before ending the call, with Tess promising to call Lucinda if anything else happened with Ryan. She hung up, mild relief settling over her. As hard as this had been so far, it looked like she'd managed the first part of the journey: escaping unseen.

The next morning, once Lucinda and Max had finished their breakfast, she crouched down next to her son and said, 'I need to talk to you, Maxy. It's important.'

Max sat up straight, a serious expression on his face. 'I have my important ears on.'

Lucinda smiled. 'We're going to go for our walk soon, and if we bump into anyone, I need you to play along with something for me. Do you know what my middle name is?'

Max frowned. 'Is it Hairy Maclary?'

Lucinda laughed and tickled his stomach, causing him to scream with laughter. 'No, it's not, you silly billy. It's Hope.'

Max stopped laughing, and his serious expression reappeared. 'No, I don't think so. It's something else.'

Lucinda shook her head. 'No, it is Hope. I have two middle names, Hope and Emma.'

'Emma.' Max rolled the name around on his tongue. 'Yep, it's Emma.'

'Well, as I said, I have two middle names. Emma's one, but the one I love best is Hope. And I've decided I like it better than my real name, so as we are having a fresh start here in Melbourne, I'm going to tell people that's my name.'

'What about Lucinda?'

'I'll be Lucinda when we go back to Queensland, but in Melbourne I'm Hope. Do you think you can remember that?'

Max nodded. 'Can I still call you Mumma?'

Lucinda pulled him to her and cuddled him. 'Of course; I'm just letting you know in case Abi or someone else calls me Hope, so you don't get confused. And I don't want you to mention that I've changed my name. It's our secret, okay?'

Max nodded. 'I love secrets.'

'I know you do, and you're the best at keeping them.'

'Can I tell Grandma when I speak to her next?'

Lucinda nodded. 'She's the only one you can tell. And there's a reward for you every week that you go without telling anyone my secret.'

Max's eyes widened. 'Really?'

Lucinda nodded. 'A new Matchbox car every Saturday morning. But if you tell anyone my name used to be Lucinda, then there's no car. Deal?'

Max nodded, excitement flooding his cheeks.

Lucinda checked her watch. 'Let's put our coats on and go and find the beach. I could use some nice sea air in my lungs.'

Max jumped off the bed. 'Okay, Mumma Hope. Let's go.'

They locked up and walked down the stairs.

'Hello, Mrs Abi,' Max called as they walked down the narrow pathway to the footpath in front of the building, where Abi was talking to a well-dressed woman. 'I'm going to the beach.'

Lucinda smiled and waved. 'Sorry to interrupt, Max is a little excited about our outing.'

'Are these our new tenants?' the woman with Abi asked.

'Yes, let me introduce you. Hope, Max, this is Alexandria. She owns the apartment building.'

Alexandria smiled at Hope before turning her attention to Max. 'And will you be going swimming, Max? That coat of yours looks like it might be waterproof.'

Max laughed. 'No, silly. It's far too cold. Where we come from it's warm, and you can swim all the time.'

'Really?' Abi frowned. 'I didn't realise the weather was warm enough all year round in Perth.'

Lucinda's cheeks flushed. 'Only if you're crazy like Max. But no, definitely not swimming today. We'll wait until summer, I think.' She smiled at Alexandria. 'It's lovely to meet you. We're very pleased to have been accepted as tenants, and I'm sure we'll love living here.'

Alexandria laughed before stopping herself. 'Sorry, I just don't expect anyone to love living here. We'd like to do more with the building, make it nicer, but we're not in a financial position to at the moment.'

'Would you be happy for Max and I to paint the walls in our apartment?' Lucinda asked. 'We'll supply the paint and do the work. It would give it a nice lift.'

'Of course you can,' Alexandria said. 'We might even have some paint left over at Fleming's. My family own a restaurant in Elwood. We renovated last year and have a lot of tins in storage. Would you like to use that, or would you prefer to buy your own? There are probably some brushes and rollers too.'

'If you have spare that would be wonderful. Thank you.'

'You're very welcome.' Alexandria hesitated then spoke again. 'I recall Abi saying you weren't working when you applied for the apartment.'

Lucinda's gut contracted. 'No, but I'm looking and have plenty of savings if it takes me longer than anticipated. We'll be fine to pay our rent.'

Alexandria nodded. 'I wasn't prying, but I have some waitressing shifts available at the restaurant. I'm not sure if you have any experience or would be interested, but I like to employ more mature staff. We are a fine-dining restaurant, so I don't want teenagers serving. It means we also pay above minimum wage.'

Lucinda couldn't believe it; it couldn't be that easy to get a job, surely? 'I'd love the opportunity. Thank you, Alexandria.'

'Call me Alex. If you're free tomorrow, come in, and we can fit you for a uniform and give you a few hours to learn the ropes. I could use an extra pair of hands on the lunch shift. Ten for a uniform fitting and then a shift that runs through until two.'

Lucinda hesitated, her eyes falling on Max. 'I appreciate the offer, but I haven't had a chance to find day care for Max yet. If I can get that sorted out this afternoon, then I could come in tomorrow. If not, would it be possible to make it next week? I'm sure I can be organised by then.'

'I'll look after Max for you,' Abi said. 'I was planning to be here for a few hours in the garden tomorrow. He can help me for a little while and then we can play some games or go for a walk. Whatever you're comfortable with.'

Alex clicked her fingers. 'Great, it's all sorted. Now, I'd better get moving. I'm glad everything's working out here, Abi. Under the circumstances, I wasn't sure.'

Lucinda watched with interest as Abi's cheeks flamed red. She looked embarrassed rather than flattered by what appeared to be praise.

'I'll see you tomorrow, Hope. Abi can give you the restaurant's address. Black shoes and minimal make-up, please. We'll supply a white shirt and black skirt, and we have lockers for you to store your clothes and belongings. If you can bring your tax file number and some identification, we can get you all set up.' She began walking down the path towards her Range Rover, stopping when she reached Max, who was busy watching a snail cross the path. 'Have a good swim, Max, and watch out for the twelve-legged jellyfish, won't you.'

Max's eyes widened as Alex laughed and continued on to her vehicle.

'Wow, I wasn't expecting that,' Lucinda said to Abi. 'Thank you for offering to babysit. I'll see if I can get him into day care but would love to use you as a backup.'

'Find a day care for next week, but not tomorrow,' Abi said. 'I'd love to look after Max.' She frowned. 'I'm not having the best week, and I think a four-year-old would be the perfect distraction for me.'

'Is everything okay?' Abi's eyes filled with tears, and Lucinda immediately felt awful. 'I'm so sorry, I didn't mean to upset you.'

Abi shook her head. 'You didn't. I'm just a bit emotional at the moment.'

'Would you like to talk about it?' Abi hesitated. Lucinda could see her weighing up whether or not she wanted to divulge her personal issues to a stranger. 'I understand if you don't. Believe me, I'm the last person who talks about her problems.'

'It's been a tough couple of months,' Abi said. 'My husband, Eric, passed away and my son's moving to Sydney on Saturday to live with his aunt and uncle.'

'Oh, you poor thing. I'm so sorry to hear about your husband. That must be very difficult.'

Abi gave a wry smile. 'That's an understatement. I'm beginning to get myself sorted out but Hayden leaving is a real curveball. He's only sixteen, and I wasn't expecting to lose him so early.'

'Why Sydney?'

'Eric's death has left us in a difficult financial position. His brother is very wealthy and has offered to put Hayden through Sydney Grammar for his last two years of school. I had to pull him out of private school here, so Hayden sees it as an amazing opportunity.'

'But you don't?' It was written all over Abi's face that it wasn't what she wanted.

Abi shook her head. 'No. I don't trust my brother-in-law, and I'll miss Hayden. He isn't coping with Eric's death very well, and I'm not sure running to Sydney's going to help.'

Lucinda stared at Abi. Here she was thinking she had it tough, and look what this woman was going through. She'd been right when she'd wondered whether something had happened to force someone of Abi's status to move into the apartments. Still, she would never have guessed this scenario.

'Now,' Abi said, 'looks like Max is ready for the beach. Alex said she wanted you at Fleming's at ten tomorrow. How about I arrive at nine, and that will give you plenty of time to get to Elwood. There's a bus that leaves across the road from the apartment block that'll take you there. It couldn't be easier.'

The next afternoon, Lucinda was relieved to be the only passenger to exit the bus at the stop closest to the apartment building after the completion of her first shift at Fleming's. She'd been sure that morning when she caught the bus to Elwood that she was being followed. Four others had got off at the stop Abi had told her to get off at. While three had gone in the opposite direction, a man with a menacing scorpion tattoo running down his forearm had walked closely behind Lucinda as she made her way along Barkly Street. She'd heard a television blaring from one of the houses, so she'd decided to pretend she was going to visit and stopped outside it, her heart pounding. If he wanted something from her, then she'd rather know now, and in a place she could see people were home if she needed to call for help. The man had reached her, smiled and continued on his way. She'd remained rooted to the spot until he was out of sight. When her heart rate eventually calmed, she'd told herself off for being so paranoid and then continued on to the address she'd been given for Fleming's.

Now, as she stepped off the bus, she felt a combination of exhilaration and exhaustion. Her first shift had gone well. She'd been given a short training session and then allocated a small section of the restaurant to look after to get used to the processes. Alex had been incredibly friendly and welcoming, as had the other staff. She'd filled in her paperwork and had been pleasantly surprised to find that, not only was the hourly rate above the minimum, but the tips were shared among the staff at the end of each shift. She'd pocketed more in cash for the four hours she'd worked than she would usually take home in a day.

She hurried from the bus stop to the apartment block, keen to see Max. She was incredibly grateful to Abi for offering to look after him, and thankful she'd met someone she felt she could trust. She was going to need to get used to relying on day care and strangers to look after Max, which was going to be a huge mental adjustment. She'd done it in Dorford, of course, but here, having taken on a new identity and hiding from her past, it felt completely different.

She could hear Max singing 'I'm a Little Teapot' as she scaled the stairs to the second floor, and, as she pushed the door open, Abi called out that she needed another cup of tea. Lucinda grinned as Max rushed to her and threw himself against her legs.

She bent down to hug him. 'Sounds like someone's having fun,' she said, smiling over the top of Max's head at Abi, who'd stood when she came in. 'Thank you so much.'

Abi smiled. 'We've had a lovely time, haven't we, Max?'

Max nodded. 'The best. Can Mrs Abi look after me again?'

'Of course she can, if Mummy lets her,' Abi said. 'How was your first day?'

'Great,' Lucinda said. 'Alex is lovely, and the restaurant is beautiful. That's quite a business to own. I assume they're doing very well.'

Abi's cheeks flushed. 'Fleming's has done well for years. I'm glad you had a good day. I'd better get my things together and get back home. It's Hayden's last night tonight and I plan to cook him something special.'

Lucinda couldn't help but notice how quickly Abi changed the subject about Fleming's. It was as if she wasn't comfortable discussing it. She'd also acted strangely the previous day when Alex had made a comment about things working out *under the circumstances*. Lucinda was intrigued, but certainly not going to pry. She slipped her hand inside her pocket and removed the tips she'd earned. 'I'm hoping you'll share this with me, Abi. It's my tips. You've been looking after Max while I've been there, so it's only fair.'

'Don't be silly!' Abi said. 'There's no way I'm taking your money. If anything, I probably need to pay Max. He helped me do some weeding in the garden while you were out and I'm being paid for that. Don't forget I'm earning an income looking after the apartment block.'

Lucinda continued to hold the money out. 'I know, but I'd be paying day care if he was there. I hate to ask you to do something for nothing.'

Abi patted her arm. 'It wasn't for nothing. You gave me something too. Being with Max took my mind off what's happening tomorrow. I got much more than you'll ever realise from today. Put your money away and go and enjoy the muffins that are on the counter.' She winked. 'Max made them for your afternoon tea.'

'They're Grandma's recipe,' Max said, walking over to the counter to inspect them. 'You know, the ones she says you need the Queensland sun to make them grow.'

Lucinda froze. How much had Max told Abi about them?

'Max wasn't completely sure of the exact ingredients,' Abi added, 'so we googled blueberry muffins on my phone to check.'

'Lucky too,' Max said. 'Did you know blueberry muffins don't have mayonnaise in them?'

'Mayonnaise? Why on earth would you think they had mayonnaise?'

'Grandma uses something white. Abi thought it might be yoghurt.'

'Sounds like your mum's a great cook,' Abi said. 'Did you see much of her before you moved to Melbourne?'

'All the time,' Max said. 'I even had sleepovers sometimes. She lived just around the corner, didn't she, Mumma?'

Abi frowned. 'Sorry, I thought she lived in Queensland. I must have misunderstood.'

'She does. In Dorford,' Max said. 'That's where—' He stopped, the excitement in his face dissolving as he looked at Lucinda's face. 'Is everything okay, Mumma?' His lip quivered. 'Did I say something wrong? I didn't say anything about the secret.'

Lucinda forced a smile. 'No, Maxy, you haven't said anything wrong. But how about you thank Abi and then go to the bathroom and wash your hands, ready for a muffin. Abi needs to get back to her house now.'

Max threw his arms around Abi's legs. 'Thank you, Mrs Abi, I love you.'

Abi laughed and leant down to hug him. 'You're very welcome, Mr Max, and I think I can honestly say I love you too.'

Max giggled, pulled away and ran to the bathroom.

Abi turned to Lucinda, her face full of kindness and compassion. 'I'm a very private person, Hope, and respect the privacy of others. Max suggested you have some secrets that he's keeping about your life before you came to Melbourne. It's absolutely none of my business, although if you ever need someone to talk to, I'm here. I don't judge and I don't offer unsolicited advice, but I am a good listener.'

Tears filled Lucinda's eyes, but she blinked them away. 'Thank you.' She wasn't ready to say any more.

Abi nodded and picked up her bag from the counter. 'Okay. Let me know how you go with day care. If you can't find one for next week, I'll definitely be able to help out.'

Lucinda nodded. A lump had formed in her throat as a result of Abi's kindness, and she didn't trust herself to speak without breaking down. Abi had enough to deal with at the moment, without adding Lucinda's issues to her load. But the fact she'd offered was a true testament to the type of person Abi was.

Lucinda walked the other woman to the door and took a deep breath. 'I hope all goes well with Hayden.'

Abi's smile didn't hide the sadness in her eyes. She reached out and squeezed Lucinda's arm. 'Thank you. Me too.'

Chapter Nine

Saturday morning came around far too quickly, and Abi found it hard to believe that her son could appear so excited while all she felt was dread. His bags were packed, and he'd been hovering around the living room windows for the last ten minutes waiting for Gabe to pull into the driveway to take him to the airport.

Hayden turned to Abi as the car arrived. 'He's here. I'd better get my bags outside.'

Abi followed her son to the front door and picked up one of his three bags, ready to help him with it to the car. Gabe strode up the driveway.

'We're so excited this is happening, Hayden. I see big things – huge things – ahead for you.'

Hayden returned his grin and went to open the boot of the car.

Gabe turned to Abi. 'I know this is difficult, but it's for the best, you'll see. He's going to do so well in Sydney. I've already got some of my business contacts lined up to meet him. It'll be good for him to meet some of their sons and be socialising with the families that make this country run the way it does.'

Abi didn't comment. Eric would be turning in his grave if he knew Hayden was going off to live with Gabe, where he would be influenced by him and witness his elitist opinions and lifestyle. Anger welled inside her. If it weren't for Eric, none of this would be happening. She opened her mouth, about to say something, then shut it again as Hayden came towards her. It wasn't his fault that Eric had taken away every opportunity they could possibly give him. As much as she'd love to say, *You can't go, I've changed my mind*, she knew that she couldn't. Instead, she hugged Hayden to her, not caring whether he was embarrassed or not by her display of affection. He was only sixteen and he was moving away from her; she would get her hug in.

'Mum!' Hayden removed her arms from around him. 'It's only Sydney, not the other side of the world.'

It might as well be the other side of the world as far as Abi was concerned. Everything was happening too quickly. She was a creature of habit, and change didn't sit well with her. 'It's a big deal to me. You're all I have. I'm going to miss you terribly.'

Hayden's face softened. 'You can call me, and I'll be home for the school holidays.'

Abi nodded. 'I know.' She blinked back tears, doing her best to smile. 'Ring me when you land in Sydney so that I know you're safe.'

Hayden rolled his eyes. 'I'll text you.'

Gabe jangled his car keys. 'We'd better go if we're going to make this flight. I'll keep in touch, Abi, let you know how he's going – and you can ring me any time.'

Abi nodded, wrapping her arms around herself as Hayden and Gabe climbed into the car. Five weeks ago she'd lost her husband, and most of her friends in the process, and now she was losing her son. Was there anything else to lose?

Close to five, a car honking from the driveway had Abi pull herself up off the couch. After Hayden and Gabe had left, she'd had no motivation to do anything but mope around. She opened the front door and smiled. Mel. She could always count on her sister to pick the right time to turn up.

Mel bounded out of the car, a bottle of champagne in one hand and a small overnight bag in the other. Abi laughed at her sister's mood.

'What are you doing here?'

'Come to cheer you up.' Mel threw her arms around Abi and pulled her into a tight hug. 'I figured Hayden left this morning, so you've probably been curled up in the foetal position ever since.'

'That's a pretty accurate description.'

'I decided I'd come and visit and stay the night. Tomorrow morning we'll go for a nice long walk along the beach and have some breakfast. Breathe some fresh air into your incredibly pale face. After that, you can show me the new apartment before I go home. But for now' – she waved the bottle of bubbles at Abi – 'we'll drink this and hopefully get rid of any sorrows.'

Abi followed her sister into the house, her mood lifting immediately. 'Thanks, Mel,' she said when they reached the kitchen. 'You have no idea how much I needed this today.'

Mel's eyes were filled with sympathy as she met Abi's gaze. 'I think I do know. You're going through a rough time, Abs, losing both of them so close together. I know Hayden's only in Sydney, but it's still a massive adjustment. Especially when he's with Eric's pig of a brother. You're looking too pale and too thin. Are you eating?'

Abi sat down at the kitchen counter and pointed to the cupboard that housed the champagne flutes. 'I'm eating enough, and you're right, the adjustment is massive. I can't even begin to imagine what the future looks like for us now. Hayden's talking about doing uni in Sydney too. He's still got this year and next of school left, so if you then add four years of uni, possibly more if he specialises, then that's at least six years of being away.'

'You could always move to Sydney.'

'I know, and I guess I might do just that. I'd miss you and Laila though. Also, I can't see how I could afford it. I doubt Gabe would want me living with them, and to be honest, I wouldn't want to anyway. Sydney's prices aren't affordable at the moment.'

Mel poured the champagne and passed a glass across to Abi. 'Here's to a new start. Hopefully one with a happy ending.'

Abi clinked glasses with her and sipped the golden bubbles.

'As much as I love that you're here, I assume you and Tony are still apart?'

Mel nodded, put the bottle in the fridge and came and sat down next to Abi. 'Yes, his ultimatum is still in place. You or him.' She sighed. 'I can't imagine what's going through his mind. He knows how close we are and that, other than Hayden, we're the only family we've both got. Why he'd want to split us up, I don't think I'll ever understand.'

'He blames me. It's as simple as that. He doesn't believe that I didn't know about the investments, and thinks Eric and I have manipulated you both into investing and then losing the money. The problem is, on the surface, that's exactly what it looks like.'

'I know, but he should trust me,' Mel said. 'If I say you're not to blame, then he should agree with me.' She placed her champagne on the counter, untouched.

Abi raised an eye. 'What's going on? Normally I have to fight you for the bottle you drink it so quickly.'

Mel gave a small smile. 'There is another reason I wanted to see you today. I've got some news.' She rubbed her stomach, her smile widening.

'Oh, Mel!' Abi put her drink down and pulled her sister to her. 'This is amazing news. How long have you known?'

Mel pulled back from Abi, tears of joy in her eyes. 'I suspected a couple of weeks ago but waited until this morning to do the test. I'm about eight weeks.'

'That's amazing news. What about Tony? Please tell me you've told him?'

Mel's smile slipped. 'No, and until he apologises, I have no intention of telling him anything.'

'But after everything you two have been through, surely you want him to know. He'll want to be at the ultrasounds with you. You know how much he wants this. You can't leave him out of it now.' Abi was shocked that Mel could even contemplate not telling her husband. They'd been trying for a baby for over ten years. Five years ago they'd been through three rounds of IVF, but none were successful. Two miscarriages and immeasurable heartache had led them to the decision to let nature take its course. Two years ago Mel had told Abi that they'd made peace with the fact that they weren't destined to be parents.

Mel's jaw set in a hard line. 'He's behaving in a way that makes me not even recognise him. I don't want him to miss out either, but if that's what ends up happening, then it's just too bad.'

'You realise that he'll blame Eric and me if you don't tell him, don't you?'

'How do you figure that?'

'Because you'd be together if it wasn't for us, so anything he misses out on he'll use as ammunition against me. I get why you don't want to tell him, but I still think you should. And if you want me to guilt you into telling him, I will. This adds a whole new layer of stress for me and what happened. You need to tell him, and you need to get back together. You don't want to be having a baby and raising it on your own – or, worse still, having to split custody. I can't even imagine what that would be like when the baby's a newborn. You'll be so attached and then have to give him or her up on the days Tony has custody.' Abi shivered. 'It would be awful.'

Mel remained deep in thought for a few minutes while Abi sipped her champagne. Eventually she spoke. 'You're probably right. I hadn't thought beyond right now, to be honest. I'll think about it. No guarantees, but I will think about it. He has to accept you as part of my life, though, if he wants me in his.'

'You could always try and negotiate with Tony over me,' Abi said. 'I understand if he wants me out of *his* life, but that doesn't mean I have to be out of yours too.'

Mel nodded. 'I could give it a try. Perhaps I'll see his reaction to that suggestion first, and that will help me gauge whether I tell him about the pregnancy.'

Abi smiled. 'Pregnant. I can't believe it. I'm going to be an aunt. Finally, a piece of good news.'

The next afternoon, Abi waved Mel off as she pulled away from the curb and headed in the direction of Geelong. It had been so lovely to see her, even if the visit was quick. They'd enjoyed a walk and breakfast in St Kilda before having the *not so* grand tour of the Elsternwick apartment. Mel's shock at the size and state of the place hadn't gone unnoticed, but her suggestion that fresh paint would give it a lift and some of the furniture from Abi's guest house would fit into the small space perfectly was appreciated.

Now, as Abi walked through each room of the dream house she and Eric had lovingly planned and built thirteen years earlier, she was overcome with an overwhelming sense of sadness. She'd thought after Hayden had left that she'd lost everything, but she realised there was definitely more to lose. And having just signed the sales contract, her house was yet another thing that was officially lost.

The real estate agent had contacted her that morning with the *good news* that the first couple who'd been shown through had put in an offer above her asking price. 'And they want a thirty-day settlement,' the agent had excitedly told her. 'They really want the house, Abi, which is why the offer is above your asking price. They aren't willing to risk losing it. The wife described it as her dream home. She can't believe how perfect it is.'

It was perfect, or at least it had been. It was perfect when they'd been a happy family; when she'd dreamt of their future together, of retirement, of Hayden getting married and providing them with grandchildren. But now she honestly wasn't sure what was keeping her going. Repaying her friends and trying to make up for what had happened was her only real motivation to carry on. She could only hope that when the insolvency investigation was complete, Eric's business would have some profit to distribute to those who'd lost so much.

She ran her fingers over the oak dresser. Handed down from her grandmother, it held so much sentimental value. But it would have to go. In fact, almost everything would have to be sold. Abi had organised for Clarkson's Fine Art Auctions to host a home contents auction. She would keep a few essential pieces of furniture for her new apartment, but the rest would be sold, and the money would go towards repaying Eric's debts.

She stopped in the living room in front of a wall of photos, and took the middle frame off its hook. It had always been her favourite photo. Eric and her on their honeymoon, standing hand in hand, the white buildings of Santorini behind them, their roofs perfectly matching the intense blue of the surrounding Mediterranean. It had been pure bliss.

A single tear rolled down Abi's cheek, and she brushed it impatiently aside with her sleeve. To this point she'd kept her fury at bay, her concerns being more about Eric and why he did what he did. But now her grief and anger was burying any compassion she had for her husband. Whether he'd thought through the implications of his actions or not, she'd never know, but to leave her widowed with her life turned upside down was unforgivable. She glanced at the photo one more time before raising it above her head and slamming it down on the dresser. Glass went in every direction and Abi dropped the frame. It was tempting to take more photos from the wall and give them the same treatment, but the sensible part of her brain kicked in. She was the one who was going to have to clean this up, and also, she didn't want to damage any of the furniture that could be sold.

She sighed. At thirty-nine, less than three months before her fortieth birthday, this was her life. Her new life. A life she'd never imagined and definitely didn't want.

Chapter Ten

With Max still sleeping, Lucinda sipped her coffee, enjoying the stillness of the early morning. She looked out of the second-storey window on to the leafy street below. The area was beginning to grow on her, although she wasn't sure it would ever feel like home. It was hard to believe that she and Max had been in Melbourne for nearly two months. She still found herself looking over her shoulder as she walked down the street, convinced someone would be watching or following her. She hardly recognised herself. She'd had her hair cut again and now sported a short pixie cut. She ran her fingers through it. She had to admit she quite liked it, and it definitely gave her a sense of comfort that it would make it harder for anyone Ryan might have sent to find her.

The name Hope, however, was still taking some time to get used to. She had to listen carefully and respond when people used her name. It was mainly at work, and then of course with Abi. She smiled, thinking of her neighbour and new friend. She missed Rachael and their regular catch-ups but was finding that the more time she spent with Abi, the more she enjoyed her company.

A gentle knock on the front door jolted Lucinda from her thoughts.

She opened the door to find Abi, coffee cup in hand, grinning at her. 'Ready?'

'For what?' Lucinda had no recollection of making plans with Abi.

'Yoga. The way you were talking about it the other night made me realise how much you must be missing it. You said there was a class at eight this morning.' She glanced at her watch. 'It's only just past seven. I'm here to look after Max.'

'I'm not sure . . .'

'No arguments. You've got plenty of time to get dressed, grab your mat and go.'

At Abi's insistence, Lucinda walked the few blocks to Yoga Life. She'd been unable to explain to Abi why she was hesitant to go to the studio. Initially, she'd been delighted to discover a yoga studio within walking distance of their apartment, but on the day she'd been in to enquire about classes she'd got a weird vibe. She was sure it was her paranoia, but it had been hard to shake. She was convinced the yoga instructor who talked her through the various payment options was staring strangely at her. It was the feeling she got from random strangers in the supermarket, at the park and pretty much anywhere she went. She knew it was her concerns about being found by Ryan, but there was something about the instructor that didn't sit well. Luckily, this morning's instructor was Luke, not Mary, so hopefully she would be able to relax and enjoy the class.

After storing her belongings in a locker, Lucinda pushed open the door to the studio, the heat immediately embracing her. She found a place at the back of the room and unrolled her mat. There were five minutes before the class started, so she lay down, closed her eyes and allowed her body to adjust to the heated room.

She opened her eyes and stood when Luke entered and welcomed everyone to the class. There were at least thirty people now standing on their mats, waiting for him to start the first breathing exercise. Lucinda did her best to keep her eyes on herself in the large mirror that covered the front wall of the studio, but no matter how much she convinced herself it was just yoga, the same uncomfortable feeling she often got when she was out settled over her. Her eyes did a quick scan in the mirror, her heart catching in her throat as she saw Mary in the second row, to her left. Mary's eyes connected with hers before refocusing her gaze on her own reflection. What was it about the woman that unnerved her so much? She'd definitely never met Mary before, but was it possible the other woman knew of her? That they had some kind of connection that went back to Queensland?

Lucinda finished the class completely distracted. She was positive Mary had looked at her several times, but each time the woman's gaze would revert back to her own in the mirror. When they reached the final Savasana, Lucinda's mind was whirling. So much for having some time out to calm her mind. If anything, the yoga session had unsettled her. She wasn't sure whether to hurry out of the studio and never return, or to confront Mary and find out why she was staring at her.

The decision was made for her when she finally rolled up her mat and quietly left the studio. Mary was hovering around the water cooler, ostensibly refilling her bottle, but Lucinda knew she was waiting for her. She collected her belongings and walked over to her.

'Did you want to speak to me?'

Mary blushed. 'Was I that obvious?'

Lucinda nodded. 'Do I know you from somewhere?'

'I'm not sure,' Mary said. 'I'm sorry, you probably think I'm creepy. I was trying to place you the other week when you came in to check out the studio. It's driven me nuts ever since.'

Lucinda didn't comment, just waited for Mary to continue.

'It's just you look so much like someone I used to know a few years back that I can't stop looking to see if you could be her. Her name wasn't Hope, though. You haven't changed your name by any chance, have you?'

A slight chill ran down Lucinda's body. Was it possible Mary *did* know her?

'Sorry,' Mary said before Lucinda could answer. 'As I said, I know I sound crazy. You're new to this area, aren't you, or at least new to the studio?'

Lucinda nodded. 'Yes, I moved from Perth recently.'

Mary frowned. 'Perth? Definitely not who I'm thinking of then. Perth's a great city. Do you know many people here?'

Lucinda shook her head. 'No, just settling in still. I'm working, so most of my spare time's taken up with my four-year-old.'

'I have a four-year-old, too,' Mary said. 'They might like to have a play together one day.'

Lucinda hesitated. There was still something about Mary that didn't sit quite right. 'I'm sure Max would enjoy that,' she said finally, wiping the sweat from her face.

'Perfect.' Mary's voice sounded excited, but her eyes and face said something else altogether. She looked puzzled or confused.

Lucinda gave herself a shake; she was reading far too much into this woman's expression. She'd mistaken her for someone and then put out an offer of a play date.

Mary walked over to the reception counter and picked up a card. She held it out to Lucinda. 'My mobile's on this. Just give me a ring anytime you think Max would like to catch up. We could meet at the park and the kids could play. Zeb's always looking for new friends.'

Lucinda smiled and took the card from her. 'I'll give you a call to organise something.'

'Fabulous. Now, I'd better have a shower. I'm teaching a class in about twenty minutes. Namaste.'

Lucinda watched as the yoga instructor made her way to the change rooms. She wondered if she'd ever get over being suspicious of people. They'd moved here for a fresh start but if she worried that every person who crossed their path had links back to Ryan, how would she ever move on?

She took a deep breath, pushed open the door of the studio and walked out on to the street. She should be happy that she'd just met someone who could possibly be a friend for both her and Max, rather than being suspicious and concerned. She tucked Mary's card into her purse, making the decision to call her and set up a play date. Max would love it, and it might help her adjust to the idea of being less suspicious and making new friends in Melbourne.

The next morning, Lucinda and Max rugged up and headed out to the park. Max marvelled at the fiery oranges and reds of the liquid amber trees that lined the roadsides, as they made their way through the streets to Trendall Park. It was every four-year-old's dream. Not only did it have Max's favourite – swings – but it had a cannon at the entrance, a bandstand and a small lake. The established trees gave it a restful feeling, which helped Lucinda relax more than usual and be less inclined to check over her shoulder every two seconds.

Her thoughts went to Mary as she pushed Max on the swing. This would be the perfect place to meet up with her. She had thought about ringing her that morning, but she didn't want to look too eager. She had flipped from being suspicious of Mary to suddenly being afraid she might scare her off if she contacted her too quickly. Lucinda raised her eyes to the sky as she had these thoughts. Was she losing her mind? She would usually have considered herself level-headed and rational. Now, however, as her thoughts raced from paranoid one minute to self-doubting the next, she was questioning herself.

After ten minutes on the swing, Max said he wanted to run around and explore on his own. Lucinda sank down on to one of the park benches that gave her full visibility of the playground. There were only a handful of kids playing on the equipment, and she imagined the chilly autumn air had kept many people indoors for the morning. She smiled as an elderly couple wound their way, arm in arm, along a path surrounding the park. They reminded her of the couple she and Max had met at their first buffet breakfast when they'd arrived in Melbourne. She squinted as they neared, her smile broadening as she stood and waved. It *was* Dot and William!

The elderly couple's smiles reflected Lucinda's as they reached her.

'Hope, dear, how wonderful,' Dot said, squeezing her arm. 'We'd hoped you might contact us.'

'Let's sit,' William said. 'I'm exhausted.'

They sat down on the bench Lucinda had been occupying.

'I planned to get in touch,' Lucinda said, 'but I lost your details. I'm so sorry. Max was very disappointed when I realised.'

An excited *whoop* travelled from the playground, and Max came hurtling in their direction. He threw himself into William's arms.

Lucinda reached for him immediately. 'I'm so sorry. Max!'

William beamed. 'Don't be sorry. That's the best greeting I've ever had. How are you, young Max?'

'We live here now,' Max said. 'Just around the corner.'

William's face flushed with pleasure. He turned Max around and pointed to an apartment block. 'See that building? Dot and I live on the third floor. See, the balcony with the large pot plant and the telescope. That's us.'

'Ooh, a telescope. What do you use it for?'

'During the day I look at birds in the park, and at night I often watch the stars.'

'Yay.' Max pulled away from William. 'Watch me.' He dashed back to the play equipment and waved to them.

A look passed between Dot and William, and Dot's lip trembled.

'Is everything alright?' Lucinda asked.

Dot nodded, and William took his wife's hand. 'You'll have to forgive Dot, but Max has similar features to both our son and grandson when they were this age. We noticed it the morning we met you in Melbourne. Unfortunately, we lost our son ten years ago. He was a grown man, of course, not Max's age, but burying a child is not something any parent wants to do, no matter what their age is. And our grandson has been far too busy for us for many years. We hardly know him.'

'I'm so sorry to hear that.'

Dot sniffed. 'Don't mind me. I'm just a silly old lady.' She wiped her eyes. 'Max is a gorgeous little boy.'

'Do you visit the park often?' Lucinda asked.

'Most mornings you'll see us here around this time,' Dot said, 'and often we do a shorter walk in the afternoon and feed the ducks. We bring pellets for them now that you're not supposed to feed them bread.'

'Perhaps you and young Max would like to meet us later this afternoon?' William said. 'We'll bring the pellets and Max can do the feeding.'

'He'd love that,' Lucinda replied. 'Thank you.'

Dot patted her hand. 'No need to thank us, it's lovely to see you again. We've no family to enjoy so it would be our pleasure to spend some time with both of you. If you'd like to, of course.'

Lucinda nodded. She was already missing her mother and knew Max would be too. Temporary grandparents would be a welcome change.

On their second visit to the park for the day, Lucinda watched as Max ran up and down the lake edge excitedly throwing pellets to the ducks. She was standing with Dot, who suddenly announced she needed to sit down.

'Just watching him is exhausting.' The older lady gave a little laugh.

Lucinda took her arm and led her to one of the park benches, while William remained with Max as he fed handfuls of pellets to the ducks.

'William's loving this,' Dot said. 'It's such a treat for him to spend time with a young person. Me too, in fact.'

'It must have been very hard, losing your son.'

Dot's eyes filled with tears. 'It was. He was involved in a car accident. We were able to donate his organs, at least. Some consolation, I guess.'

Lucinda sucked in a breath. 'How awful.'

Dot nodded. 'We haven't ended up where we thought we would. I always imagined a house full of kids and grandchildren. But we were only blessed with Billy. His son, our grandson, moved away with Billy's ex when he was little, so we never got to know him. It feels very sad to reach old age and not be surrounded by the love of family.'

Lucinda didn't know what to say to this, so fell silent as Dot struggled with her memories. Dot was the first to speak.

'We come to the park a lot to watch the kids, and we imagine what could have been, but today is special. Thank you, Hope.'

'You don't need to thank me,' Lucinda said. 'Max is having a lovely time and so am I.'

'No, I do need to thank you. You've given us a real lift right when we need it. William's had a few health issues of late, and with no family around it's difficult.' She gave a small laugh. 'An afternoon of someone else's company makes a world of difference.'

Lucinda's heart ached for the older lady. She had to admit, the afternoon had given her a lift too.

'You and Max are welcome to join us for dinner tonight,' Dot said. 'William bought some extra chicken just in case you felt like a night off cooking.'

'Oh, no. Thank you, but we can't tonight.' Lucinda's response was automatic. It was one thing to meet the couple at the park but another altogether to go to their home.

Dot patted her hand. 'No worries, love. It's a treat in itself to spend an hour or two with you.'

Seeing the disappointment in the older woman's face, Lucinda immediately felt awful. 'Perhaps we could meet at the park for a picnic next weekend instead. I'm working Thursday and Friday but will be free on Saturday.' The park remained neutral ground and gave them a chance to get to know each other better. While the older couple appeared lovely, Lucinda still needed to be careful. 'That way we can both bring some food and Max can run around and leave us to chat.'

Dot's face lit up immediately. 'That sounds wonderful.' She took a piece of paper and a pen from her bag. 'I'll give you my phone number and if you need to cancel, just call. We'll understand.'

Lucinda didn't reply, just waited for Dot to finish writing out the details. Dot was giving her an out if she needed it, which she appreciated but hoped she wouldn't feel the need to use. She needed to make life 'normal' in Melbourne for her and Max, and this was a good start. They were both missing Tess, and while William and

Dot were older than Lucinda's mum, they provided a comforting presence for which she was grateful.

As she had this thought, Max ran over to them with William doing his best to keep up.

'This young fellow's going to wear me out.' William laughed, wiping his brow. He winked at Lucinda. 'And he tells me you have a secret, one that's worth a Matchbox car.'

Lucinda's smile faded and her head whipped around to look at Max. 'Max, you're not to discuss our private matters with anyone.'

'But I didn't tell him the secret, just said I had one that I'd never reveal.' He closed his mouth firmly and pretended to turn a key and throw it away. 'It's safe with me, Mumma.'

William laughed. 'Don't worry, we all have secrets, and we aren't planning to interrogate Max for yours.' He sank down on to the bench. 'One I'll let you in on, though, is I'm not as young as I thought. Keeping up with this young man might bring me to an early grave.'

Dot laughed and patted his knee. 'Hope's suggested we meet her and Max here on Saturday for a picnic.'

William's eyes lit up. 'That sounds lovely.'

'I'll make a pavlova,' Max said.

Lucinda laughed. 'That might be a bit fancy for a picnic, Max.'

'It's my favourite, and we can put it in a big box and bring it.' He turned to William. 'Could I please have some more pellets for the ducks?'

William held out the bag to him. 'Just one more handful or they'll explode. They've had a bit more than usual this afternoon.'

The three adults watched as Max ran off to feed the ducks.

'He's a credit to you, Hope,' William said. 'An absolute credit.'

Lucinda smiled. 'Thank you. That's a lovely thing to say.'

'Just stating a fact,' William said. He narrowed his eyes, a smile playing on his lips. 'Now that I've stated my fact, I'd like to suggest we stick to Max's plan of a pavlova? It's my favourite too, and Dotty never makes it.' He patted his almost flat stomach. 'Says I don't need the sugar.'

Lucinda laughed. 'Okay, a picnic with pavlova. It sounds perfect.'

By the time Saturday morning rolled around, Lucinda was tired, her feet aching. She'd worked two long shifts at Fleming's on Thursday and Friday, and standing on her feet all day and into the evening was taking its toll. She'd been lucky to get a place at the local child-care centre for Max, but it wasn't permanent. At the moment she had to ring each day to see if they had space, and luckily she had Abi as a backup.

She stared out of the window as the rain bucketed down. She'd been up early with Max to make the pavlova to take for the picnic with William and Dot. With this weather, though, they'd have to postpone. It was a shame about the pavlova, although she was sure Max would be happy to eat it over the next few days. He was in the bedroom watching *Peppa Pig* on Lucinda's iPad while she sat on the couch in the living room massaging lotion into her feet, hoping it would help. She glanced at the coffee table as her phone pinged with a text message.

Please contact Dr Mizue at your earliest convenience.

Lucinda stared at her phone. This was her mother's code for *call me*.

Tess answered on the first ring. 'Oh, Lu, thank goodness I got you. It's Ryan, he's had me revisit him. Apparently, his lawyer's found grounds for him to appeal his sentence. He'll be back in court next week.'

Lucinda's stomach roiled. 'What grounds?'

'Something to do with the man he was accused of assaulting that was in a coma. He's woken up and come forward and said that Ryan didn't hurt him; and, in fact, tried to help him during the attack. That someone else was involved. Ryan's lawyer thinks it's enough to get the original sentence overturned.'

Lucinda was silent, trying to digest this information. 'Why did he call you?'

'He wanted to reassure me that as soon as he's out, he'll do everything he can to find you and Max and ensure custody of Max reverts to him. He even asked me whether I'll be involved and support him when he's a single father. I'm worried it was a warning, Lu.'

'You think he knows that you're in contact with me?'

'I don't know for sure, but it seemed a bizarre thing to suggest. That I'd want to help Ryan take Max from you.'

'Does he have any clue where I am?'

'I don't think so. He told me he's had a private investigator look into your disappearance, but so far it's all been dead ends. That's one good thing at least.'

'And he still doesn't know we're in touch?'

'Of course not. I just wanted to keep you up to date. Ryan's asked me to go to court to be supportive of him. I will, of course, so I can let you know what happens. I'll be devastated if he gets out.'

'Me too.' Lucinda would be more than devastated – *terrified* was more accurate. 'I'm so sorry to have involved you in all of this.'

'Don't be silly. I'll play along as if I'm on Ryan's side at the moment, but make it clear that it's more because I want to see you and Max rather than because I'm siding with him. I think that's more believable than me appearing to be in favour of his plans.'

'You're right, it does sound more realistic.'

'Okay, well I'd better go. I've had one of the others open up the shop for me this morning, but I have a client at ten, so I need to get there. I'll let you know what happens.'

'Okay. Thank you, and I love you, Mum.'

'You too, hon. Look after yourself, okay?'

Lucinda ended the call, a sense of foreboding settling over her. This was not what she needed today or any day. She'd been dreading the moment when Ryan's sentence ended, but that was supposed to be more than two years away. It was breathing space, if nothing else. But if he got out sooner, she wasn't sure what she would do. Suddenly Melbourne's population of close to five million seemed very small.

It won't happen, she tried to convince herself. *He's guilty, and he'll have to serve his time.* As much as she wanted to believe that, she also knew he'd done it before. Paid off victims, usually before the court case, so he didn't end up in prison.

'When are we going to the park, Mumma?'

Lucinda's head snapped up as Max came into the living room. She pointed to the window. 'I'm not sure we'll be able to, Max. I was about to come and chat to you and suggest we give Dot and William a call and postpone.'

Tears filled Max's eyes.

Lucinda held out her arms to him. 'We can do it another day, Maxy. There's no need to get upset. I'm sure you and I can play some games today, and maybe even watch a movie on TV later.'

'But we made the pavlova. It's William's favourite. He'll be so disappointed, and I wanted to see them today. I miss Grandma and Daddy and my kinder friends and Rachael.' The tears started to spill down his face. 'I miss everyone.'

Lucinda hugged him tighter and rubbed his back as he cried harder. She knew how he felt. She didn't miss Ryan, but she certainly missed her mother and Rachael. 'How about I call them and see if we can drop some of the pavlova over to them?'

Max pulled back from her and wiped his face. 'Really? To their house?'

Lucinda nodded. 'We won't stay long, just drop off the dessert and say a quick hello. We'll make plans for the park for another day.'

'Yay,' Max cried and started dancing around the room. 'Ring them now, Mumma, ring them now.'

Lucinda smiled and reached for her phone. She'd put Dot's number in it after they'd returned from the park on Sunday. Dot answered on the third ring.

'Dot, it's Hope.'

'Oh, hello, love. I thought you might call to cancel. How very disappointing this weather is today.' She gave a little laugh. 'William was up early making a roast dinner to bring for the picnic.'

'Really?' Lucinda couldn't help but laugh. 'That's an unusual choice for a picnic.'

'That's what I said, but he insisted it would go well with the pavlova. Anyway, let's try again next weekend, shall we? If you're free, that is?'

'We are, but we also thought we could drop some pavlova over to you and William. We'll wait for the rain to ease a bit and then walk over. You live near the park, so that's not far from us.'

'That would be lovely.' Lucinda could hear the smile in Dot's voice. 'Hold on a minute, love.'

Lucinda waited, hearing Dot relay the conversation to William. She couldn't make out what he said, but Dot's voice was full of excitement when she spoke again.

'Why don't you come for lunch, after all? It's all cooking, and it was supposed to be for the four of us. Seems silly for you to deliver dessert but not stay. What do you say?'

Lucinda hesitated. She'd wanted to keep things casual with the older couple until she got to know them better, but was she being overly cautious? She'd already offered to go to their house to drop off the dessert, so did it make any difference if they stayed? It would take her mind off her mum and Ryan and everything that was going on in Dorford.

'Hope?'

'Sorry. Yes, that sounds lovely. What else can we bring?'

Lucinda did her best to push thoughts of Ryan and his potential release away as she and Max huddled under a large umbrella and made their way to Dot and William's. They lived in a new apartment building not far from the park, near Glen Huntly Road. Max pressed the button on the lift for the third floor, and did a little dance when the doors opened. Apartment 303 was almost opposite the lift – and Max hammered his fist on the door, beaming when William flung it open.

'Hey, Max,' William said, ruffling the little boy's hair. 'Have you got that pavlova you promised me?'

'Mumma's carrying it,' Max said. 'She didn't even drop it, and she had to carry the umbrella too!'

William laughed and wiped his brow. 'Phew! We'd uninvite her if she did. Now, come on in. Dot's in the kitchen. She's making her world-famous roast potatoes to go with my special lamb.'

Max's eyes bulged. Two of his favourite foods.

William smiled and leant forward to kiss Lucinda on the cheek as she left the wet umbrella by the door and entered the apartment. Its high ceilings were a surprise, making it feel spacious and inviting. 'Lovely to see you, Hope.' He held out his hands. 'Let me take the dessert, and I'll show you through to where Dot's slaving away.' He winked. 'I promise not to eat it before dessert time.'

Lucinda laughed and handed over the plastic container.

'You're here,' Dot exclaimed, as William brought Lucinda and Max through to the open-plan kitchen with its adjoining living area overlooking Trendall Park. He placed the container on the bench and took off the lid for a sneak peek.

'That looks delicious.'

Lucinda had to agree, it did. 'Max did a great job with the decorations,' she said.

'And the pavlova,' Max added. 'I made all of it.'

'Really?' William said. 'Well, that deserves a reward. Follow me while Dot finishes getting lunch ready. I've got a little treat for you.'

Max looked to Lucinda for permission. She nodded. 'Go and see what William has for you and then come and tell me. It sounds rather exciting.'

Max followed William out of the room, and seconds later, Lucinda heard him shriek with delight. 'Play dough, my favourite! And a proper table and everything.'

'Go and have a look, love,' Dot said, as she opened the oven door to check on the potatoes. 'William's rather proud of the set-up in the spare room.'

Lucinda saw why straightaway. A large bedroom, devoid of a bed or any bedroom furniture, greeted her. In one corner a small table and chairs had been set up, and three mounds of coloured play dough sat on the table with a rolling pin and cookie cutters. On the floor in the middle of the room was a large box with the words *Train Set* on the side. Next to that sat what looked like a brand-new blackboard with chalk pieces. 'Wow.' She couldn't help the word escaping her lips. 'You didn't buy any of this just for Max, did you?'

William blushed. 'Yes and no. Dot made the play dough fresh this morning after you agreed to come to lunch, and the train set is an old one from when my Billy was a young lad. The blackboard, however, is new. Dot has been wanting one for ages to write notes on in the kitchen, so she finally twisted my arm to get one yesterday. She can use it for her own purposes after he's gone.'

Lucinda's face flushed with pleasure. How incredibly generous this couple was. 'You shouldn't have done that, but I'm very grateful. I'm sure Max will have a ball.'

He already was. He'd selected the blue play dough and was pummelling his fists into it.

'Why don't you go and keep Dot company,' William suggested. 'Max and I have important creations to make.'

Max grinned up at him and held out the orange play dough. 'You make orange cookies, and I'll make blue.'

'Deal.' William pulled out the chair opposite Max and sat down. He winked at Lucinda. 'We have secret men's business to get on with, if you don't mind.'

Lucinda smiled and retreated to the kitchen. 'How can I help?' she asked Dot as she entered the room.

'You can take a seat at the counter and pour us a glass of bubbles.' Dot took a bottle from the fridge. 'They're my favourite but I rarely get a chance to drink them. William and I aren't very social.'

'Really? That's a surprise. You're both so outgoing.'

Dot took two champagne flutes from the cupboard above the stove. 'Everything changed when our Billy died. Friends just stopped calling. It was very odd. We assumed they just didn't know what to say. We've moved three times since he died, each time to see if we can have a fresh start. We've only been in this apartment a short time.'

'You've had a rough time,' Lucinda said.

Dot nodded and smiled as Lucinda handed her a glass. 'Here's to you and your beautiful son, and for helping liven up an old couple's week.' She raised her glass to Lucinda. 'Tell me, what's been happening with you?'

Lucinda told Dot about her job and laughed about her aching feet.

'What do you do with Max while you're at work?'

'I've been using the local day care but haven't been able to get a permanent place as yet. On the days they can't have him I have a neighbour who's usually able to look after him.'

'Usually?'

'Yes, Abi's been wonderful. This Monday's the first day she can't have him, but I'm hoping a place will become available last-minute at the centre. I'm second on the cancellation list so it should.'

'Drop him to us.' Dot's eyes widened in delight. 'We'd love to have him. There's no need to waste money on day care or feel indebted to your friend when he could just come here.'

'Oh, no,' Lucinda said. 'I couldn't ask you to do that.'

'You're not asking, I'm telling you. Assuming you trust us, of course. We can take him to the park, and we can bake and do all sorts of things. We'll keep him very busy, I promise you that.'

Lucinda blinked back tears. Why was this woman being so kind? She hardly knew her yet she was offering to look after Max.

'Really,' Dot said, 'he can come to us as many days as you need. It would breathe some life back into us. If I'm honest, you already have.'

Lucinda thought for a moment. She'd hesitated in coming to their house for lunch, would she actually now agree to have them look after Max? She might not need to, as it was likely a place would come up at the centre, but having a backup would mean she wouldn't be letting Alex and Fleming's down.

'He can be a bit of a handful at times,' she said finally. 'I'd be worried he might exhaust you.'

Dot laughed. 'If he does, we'll turn on the television and use it as a break for half an hour or so. I'm sure a little bit of entertainment won't hurt him. William' – she raised her voice – 'I've got a massive surprise.'

William came into the kitchen. 'What's going on?'

Dot beamed at her husband. 'We're going to be Hope's backup on Monday to look after Max. If she can't get a place at the day care centre, he's coming to us.'

William's cheeks flushed and his eyes lit up in delight. 'Really? Can we pay the day care to make sure there isn't a place?'

Lucinda smiled at his enthusiasm, realising she could hardly say no now. The couple were so genuinely excited it was touching. 'Just a backup, William, but only if you think he won't be any trouble. I'd hate for you to think I'm taking advantage of you.'

'Trouble?' William snorted. 'You wouldn't even know the meaning of the word. Max will be no trouble at all, you mark my words.' He rubbed his hands together. 'I think I'd better join you with the bubbles.' He moved into the kitchen and started opening cupboards. Lucinda watched with interest, as an enormous weight lifted from her shoulders. She knew she needed a more permanent solution with the day care centre, but with limited availability and her shifts continually changing it wasn't easy. Now she would have Abi, and Dot and William as backups. As much as she hated relying on others, she realised she was very lucky.

'What are you doing?' Dot finally asked William after he'd opened and shut every cupboard in the kitchen.

'Looking for a champagne flute.'

Dot opened the cupboard above the stove and took one down, frowning as she did. 'You should know where everything is by now.'

William's face coloured for a moment before he brushed the comment aside with a laugh. 'It's new to me every day, darling. That's the benefit of dementia.' He winked at Lucinda.

'Ignore him,' Dot said, filling his glass. 'He's got no sense of direction and would forget where his head was if it wasn't screwed on.'

They raised their glasses in a toast before William returned to what was now being called the playroom.

'Men are useless,' Dot said, rolling her eyes. 'I could leave the glasses next to the bottle, and he still wouldn't find them.'

Lucinda laughed, enjoying both the teasing and the sounds of laughter coming from the playroom. 'He might not be able to find a glass, but he's wonderful with Max.'

Dot nodded. 'He is, and that's what counts. Now, let me get this meal on to some plates, and we can eat.'

As they sat down at the beautifully decorated kitchen table for lunch, the phone rang. William jumped up. 'Start without me; I'm sure I won't be long.'

'Who's he talking to?' Max asked as Dot started to carve the meat, and William's voice rose.

Dot strained to listen. 'I have a feeling it might be a friend we haven't seen for a long time. He rang earlier and left a message on our machine.' She smiled at Max. 'He's your mum's age and is called Jonesy. Billy, our son, was his godfather. We think of him as a grandson even though we're not related. He and William are very close.'

Lucinda watched Dot with interest as she explained who William was speaking to. While Dot's words suggested she was pleased to hear from this man, her body language said something else altogether. Her whole body appeared to have tensed, and she'd paused partway through serving the lamb.

'Are you close with Jonesy too?'

Dot nodded, her eyes returning to the meat which she suddenly seemed to remember she was carving. She carried on, passing plates to Max and Lucinda.

Whoever this Jonesy was, the phone call had certainly rattled Dot.

The older woman held out the bowl of roast potatoes to Max, who looked to Lucinda for guidance.

'You can choose a potato,' Lucinda said.

William returned to the room just as their plates were full of lamb, potatoes and broccolini. He raised an eyebrow at Dot, took a deep breath and sat down. 'Jonesy's back in town. He's been away for close to three years,' he explained. 'Like a grandson, he is. I've invited him to lunch on Monday, Dot. I hope that's okay?'

Frown lines creased Dot's forehead. 'Let's confirm Monday morning. If young Max ends up coming to us, we'll make an arrangement for another day.'

William ran a hand through his thick grey hair. 'He was fairly keen to come on Monday.' He reached for the bowl of potatoes and ladled some on to his plate before turning to Lucinda. 'If Max comes to us and you'd prefer him not to meet him, then just say the word and we'll change the arrangement. He's a good bloke and I think you'd approve of him.'

Heat crept up the back of Lucinda's neck. While she didn't want them changing their plans for her benefit, she definitely didn't want Max being introduced to a man she hadn't met. It was a big enough thing to leave Max in Dot and William's care; after all, she hardly knew them. She cleared her throat. 'It's most likely there will be a place at the day care for Max, but if there's not, I'll change my shift. It's no big deal. That way, you can catch up with Jonesy, and everyone's happy.'

Dot tutted. 'Don't be silly. If he comes to us on Monday, we'll change Jonesy to the evening after Max has gone. That way *everyone's* happy.' She patted Lucinda's hand. 'Don't worry, we'll be looking after Max as if he was our own. We'd never let anyone hurt him. Once you get to know us more, you'll know you can trust us.'

Lucinda flushed an even darker shade of red. She wanted to object and say it wasn't a case of not trusting them – but that wasn't true, and Dot was perceptive enough to realise this. At this stage, Lucinda was wary of everyone. It wasn't personal, just a fact. She'd fled Dorford, taken on a new identity and was hiding from her husband. And while she believed Dot and William were good people, trusting anyone to keep her secrets, or to keep her safe, was going to be a hard task at any stage.

Chapter Eleven

Abi sank into the plush cushions of her bright-white chaise lounge, relieved she'd decided to furnish the small apartment with her own furniture and belongings. She'd opted to bring the chaise and two armchairs rather than a couch, as the living-area space was tiny. She'd also repainted the walls, which gave the apartment a lift. The dark door frames, skirting boards and kitchen cupboards were a constant reminder of how old and dated the apartment was, but the fresh paint on the walls and stylish furniture improved it. Right now, however, with the rain crashing down outside, the bleakness of the day reflected both the apartment and her mood.

She'd felt sick to her stomach three weeks earlier, watching the home and contents auction that Clarkson's auction house had conducted; items that had cost thousands of dollars sold for hundreds. She'd also sold her Audi A4 and bought a second-hand Toyota for a fraction of the cost.

The one upside to moving had been keeping busy. When she was physically active, it was much easier to focus on the task at hand and block out all Eric-related matters. There were times, though, particularly when she lay down at night to sleep, where she'd find herself trawling through conversations and incidents from the past. She wanted to believe he'd never done something like this before. But then she remembered the late-night visit from a distraught client a year ago. Eric had taken him through to his home office, but Abi had still got the gist of their conversation. The man's money was invested in a fund he hadn't been aware of. Eric had explained to her later that the client was confused. The money he'd invested had been authorised for any investment Eric's company chose to use it for. Abi had had no reason to question this. It was a perfectly plausible explanation. But it had happened a few times over the last few years, and now she was beginning to dread the implications.

Abi sighed, forcing her mind back to the present, and she picked up her phone from the wide armrest. She'd left six messages for Hayden in the last two weeks and he'd not responded. She had no idea if he was even alive. She pressed the button for his number, and it immediately went to voicemail. Anger rose inside her. She knew he was furious, but this was not the deal they'd agreed to. He'd promised to stay in touch if she let him go to Sydney.

She found Gabe's number in her address book and rang it. He picked up after only a couple of rings.

'Abi, is everything alright?'

She took a deep breath. 'I've been trying to reach Hayden for two weeks now, and he's not returning my calls.'

'Really?' False concern laced Gabe's response. 'I'll speak to him as soon as he gets home, okay?'

'Home? Where is he?'

'He's joined the debating team and they have a Saturday session to train for the Premier's Debating Challenge. He's made friends with Malcolm Jones's boy, Freddie. They'll be dropping him home later.'

'Malcolm Jones?' Gabe said it like she should know who that was.

'You know, the member for McMahon. He's making waves in politics and I see him as a future prime minister. Hayden is making key friends; you can rest assured.'

Abi could just imagine Eric's response to hearing that. He'd drag Hayden away from them as quickly as possible and steer him towards kids that were enjoying themselves. *You only have one chance to be a teenager*, Eric would often say. *You make the most of it and begin to grow up in your twenties, not before.*

'Okay,' Abi said. 'Could you have him ring me the moment he comes home? Tell him its urgent.'

'Will do.' Gabe ended the call.

Thirty minutes later, Abi's phone rang, and she saw from the caller ID it was her son. She grabbed the phone from the coffee table.

'Hayden! How are you?'

'What do you want, Mum? Gabe said I *had* to ring you.'

Abi was shocked by the resentful tone that greeted her. 'We had a deal. You're supposed to ring me and keep in touch.'

'Yeah, well, I'm busy, and I don't need extra stress from you. Gabe's helping me to come to terms with Dad's death and what you did, and I just need space.'

Abi was silent. What on earth would Gabe be doing to help Hayden, and what was the reference to what she'd done? 'Are you seeing a counsellor?'

'Yep. He's one of Sydney's top psychologists. He's making me see how traumatic my upbringing's been and how I need to make peace with it and move on.'

'What? Your upbringing? Do you mean what happened with Dad or something else?'

'Look, I don't want to talk about it now. Gavin, the psychologist, said we'd invite you to be part of a session soon, but for now I really need space. I need to come to terms with what you guys have done to me and try and move on.'

What they'd *done* to him? 'Look, I realise this past couple of months has been devastating for you, but if you're talking about things that happened before Dad's death, then I'm really worried. We had a wonderful relationship, all three of us. Dad adored you, and so do I. What's this psychologist suggesting?'

'He's not suggesting anything. He's just listening to what I have to say. Living with Gabe and Imogen has opened my eyes to many things, and how badly you and Dad manipulated me is one of them. Anyway, I have to go. Please don't ring me. I'll be in touch, or Gavin will, to organise a session with both of us.'

'Hold on,' Abi said. 'You're supposed to be coming home in a few weeks for the holidays.'

'Yeah, well I'm not. And now I have to go.'

Abi stared at her phone, realising he'd ended the call. She placed it on the coffee table and stared blankly into space. She knew he'd been angry when he left for Sydney, but none of that anger had been there before Eric's death. What on earth was this psychologist saying to him – and more importantly, if he was a colleague or friend of Gabe's, what lies was he feeding him?

Realising she needed to pull herself out of her funk, an hour after the call with Hayden ended, Abi decided to take advantage of the fact that the rain had stopped and take out her frustrations on the garden beds bordering the apartment building.

She looked up from her digging as Max's voice rang out from down the street. He was a very nice little boy, and she liked Hope as well. Abi had learnt from Max when she'd looked after him that they were from Queensland, not Western Australia, and that his daddy was in prison. That meant Hope had lied on her rental application, but Abi decided it was something to overlook. She paid her rent on time, had improved the apartment and was a genuinely lovely person.

Abi wiped the sweat from her forehead and smiled as Max ran up the path and stopped in front of her. 'Hey, Max, where have you been?'

'To Dot and William's for pavlova and roast.'

'Wow, that sounds like a nice way to spend a Saturday.' She smiled at Hope as she joined them, breathing heavily.

'I can't even keep up with a four-year-old,' she complained, a smile on her lips. 'How are you, Abi?'

Abi's eyes filled with tears immediately. Damn, she wanted to kick herself. Those few words could unleash a torrent.

Hope reached over and touched her arm, her face clouding with concern. 'Hey, I'm sorry. Is everything okay?'

'Don't cry, Mrs Abi,' Max said, his face scrunched with worry. 'It'll be okay. Mumma always says it'll be okay in the morning.'

'And Mumma's probably right.' Abi managed a smile for Max. 'I've got a few things on my mind at the moment, that's all. I'll be okay in a minute.'

'Come up and have a cup of tea,' Hope suggested. 'I've even got a bottle of wine if you'd prefer something stronger.'

'Oh no, I couldn't impose. Just ignore me.'

Max slipped his hand into Abi's. 'Come along now. It'll all be okay.' His voice perfectly mimicked Hope's, and Abi assumed he was giving her the treatment he usually got from his mother. She gave in and allowed Max to lead her up the stairs to apartment nine.

Max led Abi by the hand into the apartment. 'Mumma, you and I need to fix Mrs Abi. She's sad.'

'Okay, Max,' Hope said. 'How about you go and wash your hands and play in your room for a little while.'

Max frowned. 'But Mrs Abi's sad and I'd like to fix her.'

Abi smiled and held out her arms. 'A hug would fix everything if you have a spare one?'

Max grinned and threw himself into Abi's arms. He clung to her for much longer than Abi would have expected.

'Is that better, Mrs Abi?' he asked, pulling away.

'It sure is, Max. I'm all fixed.' She gave him the best smile she could muster.

Hope opened a kitchen cupboard and took out a bag of potato chips. She opened them and poured a small amount into a bowl and held it out to Max. His eyes widened. 'Really?'

Hope nodded. 'You can eat them in your room, if you like, and finish reading your stories.'

Max took the bowl and hurried off.

'Sorry about him,' Hope said. 'He takes everything very literally and likes to fix things.' She grinned as she opened the fridge and took a bottle of wine out. 'And apparently, we need to fix you. Cheap wine okay?' She held up the bottle. 'I'd offer you the expensive stuff, but I left it at the shop by mistake.'

Abi couldn't help but smile at Hope's attempt to make her laugh. 'I'd love one, thank you.'

Hope poured two glasses and the women sat down in the small lounge area.

'Did you want to talk about it?' Hope asked. 'Feel free to say no. I completely understand if you'd just like to enjoy your drink and relax.'

Abi sighed. She probably did need to talk about it, but she was enjoying the friendship she was developing with Hope and didn't want anything to jeopardise it.

'I won't judge you,' Hope said. 'No matter what's happened or what you might have done. I'm here to be supportive.'

Abi stared at Hope for a moment. What she *might have done*? That was an interesting way to phrase something. 'It's not anything I've done. It's Hayden. He's angry with me, blaming me for our situation. We used to be extremely close, all three of us were, and now it appears he's being brainwashed into believing he was manipulated or mistreated before Eric's death.'

'Manipulated?' Hope frowned. 'In what way?'

'I'm not sure. The psychologist he's seeing is going to contact me to be part of one of his sessions. I guess I'll find out more then.'

'I'm so sorry. It's bad enough he's in Sydney, but to turn all of that on you must be very hard.'

Abi did her best to hold back the fresh wave of tears that threatened. 'There have been a lot of changes to deal with. Losing Eric, the house, my job and now Hayden. I'm not sure what my purpose is.'

'You do have the job here,' Hope said.

'I had a very well-paid job with the bank before Eric died. That was taken from me as well.'

Hope raised an eyebrow. 'Taken from you?'

Abi sighed. Even to her, the story sounded suspicious. 'I might as well tell you. Eric killed himself after a property development his business invested in collapsed. Not only did he lose client funds, but he misused them, investing in a scheme he didn't have their authority to invest in. If he'd invested the money where they'd authorised him to, no one would have lost anything, and he'd still be alive. I didn't know anything about the property development, but the money he used was predominately from family and friends. A lot of people lost a lot and are extremely angry with him and with me.'

'With you?'

Abi nodded. 'They assume I was part of it. That I worked with Eric to set them up. Four of the fifteen who invested and lost had loans through the bank that I not only processed for them, but pushed through to meet the investment deadline.' Abi wiped away a tear. 'I honestly believed I was helping them access equity to go into a very safe investment.'

Hope's eyes widened as Abi spoke. 'It's awful Eric would do something like that to you.'

'It was awful, absolutely unforgivable. I still go to and fro trying to work out whether he really could have done something so devious. It seems so out of character. Also, when Eric killed himself, he left a note saying to use his life insurance to pay everyone back. A terrible person doesn't do that, do they?'

'I wouldn't think so. Did you use the life insurance to pay people back?'

'The suicide clause in his policies wasn't valid. There was no payout.'

The two women sat in silence while Hope digested this information.

'You must be amazingly strong to be where you are now.'

'What, in a crappy apartment with a dead-end job?' Abi's hand flew to her mouth the moment the bitter words came out. 'Oh God, I'm so sorry. I should never say anything like that. I'm lucky to have this.'

Hope laughed. 'The apartments are crappy; you don't have to apologise. They aren't exactly what we're accustomed to either, but they'll do for now. Your furnishings have certainly helped improve them. Thank you again, by the way.'

Abi had donated two small couches, a coffee table and a side table from the guest house to Hope, which had helped give the apartment a lift. She'd also given her two single beds to replace the lumpy ones that had been there before. 'I wish I could have given you more, but the reality with these apartments is there isn't a lot of space.'

'What are you going to do about your son? From everything you've said I imagine that is the hardest thing for you right now.'

Abi nodded. 'It is. I think I need to let him grieve in his own way and give him the time and space he's asked for, but it's very difficult.'

'You'll get back on your feet soon enough,' Hope said. 'It might be a matter of applying for more banking jobs.'

'People don't trust me after what Eric did. I doubt I'll ever get a job in the bank again.' She gave a wry smile. 'I wouldn't employ me if I heard my story, so I hardly expect anyone else to.'

'You might have more chance if you disappear from the banking world for a few months or a year, and try again then.'

Abi took a sip of her wine. 'Hopefully.' She wasn't convinced, however. The banking industry was well connected, and she imagined her reputation would follow her. 'Let's change the subject. Tell me about you and Max. Why have you really moved to Melbourne?'

Abi felt a lot happier when she returned to her apartment that evening. They'd finished the bottle of wine between them, and she'd discovered that Hope was very entertaining. It hadn't gone unnoticed, however, that she evaded the questions about why they'd moved to Melbourne. Abi didn't question her further, realising she was making Hope uncomfortable, but she was curious. She'd come home and googled *Hope Faulkner*, but nothing had come up that looked like it was related to her neighbour. She'd put in all sorts of combinations but still nothing. She couldn't even find her on Facebook, Twitter or Instagram. She realised as she looked through the social media platforms that she'd avoided them since Eric's death.

She opened her Facebook page to find over four hundred notifications and twenty-seven messages. She opened her inbox and cringed at the first two messages.

> *You deserve to be bankrupted.*

> *What Eric did was unethical and disgusting. You are a disgrace.*

She hesitated before reading the third one.

> *I'm so sorry, Abi, to hear what's happened. Please let me know if you need anything.*

Jules Stumer lived in London and Abi hadn't even thought to let her know of Eric's death. She wondered who she'd heard from. At least it was a nice message. The first two were from friends who'd lost money. She glanced down the names of the other senders, realising the majority were going to be hate mail. A shudder ran through her. She couldn't imagine sending someone something so hateful. Surely her actions of paying back money, moving into something small and cheap, had to register somewhere with these people? If she was the monster they seemed to think she was, wouldn't she have kept her house and not split the proceeds?

She made a snap decision, and went into the settings and deleted her account. Over ten years of messages, posts and photos, all gone. She did the same with Instagram, deciding not to look at any of the photos she'd posted or the comments that had been added since Eric's death.

Once that was done, she opened her email and started checking through her messages. A lot of spam to delete, but she stopped at one from Cathy, the administration officer from their branch of Bank East. She opened the email.

> Hi Abi. I'm upset you have left the bank and think of you most days. I hope you are coping and things are picking up for you. Dan wanted me to send you the attached. Please don't think he's insensitive. He figured in light of what happened with Eric you might want to consider updating your life insurance policy and take out income protection (assuming you don't already have it). Give Dan a call if you're interested and he'll set it up for you. Let me know if there's anything you need. Cathy. x

Abi stared at the email. It was the last thing she expected someone to send her. She had her life insurance policies with income protection already. The income protection, however, was just the standard policy and did not provide cover for redundancy. If she ever got a decent job again, she'd be updating that policy. She closed the email and found the folder on her computer that housed all the insurance policies. She clicked on the one from Full Life and found her documents. She opened them and read through the fine print, before doing the same with the policy from Life Gain. She'd done this twice already since Eric's death. She wasn't sure why, but she wanted to know for sure that, if she died, there would be a big payout.

Her combined policies were worth the same as Eric's. Right now, she was worth four million dollars dead. That was assuming accidental death, of course. For suicide, she'd have to wait until July thirteenth, her fortieth birthday and the day the thirteen-month exclusion period ended.

She leant back in her chair and thought about that. Right now, with what she'd been able to pay back from the house and contents and her investment, the outstanding debt stood at three million, eight hundred thousand. If she claimed on her life insurance policies, there would be two hundred thousand dollars left over. That would give Hayden a small nest egg. There was possibly money due from Eric's superannuation too, which would go to Hayden. Her reputation would be restored, and Hayden would have some money for university or to give his life a kick-start.

Her phone rang as she considered this. It was Mel. She picked up the phone immediately, feeling guilty that she'd even consider something so drastic. But she hadn't really considered cashing in the policy, had she?

'How're things?' she asked her sister, closing the insurance document.

Silence met her. 'Mel? Are you okay?'

She heard the heaving sound Mel made when she was crying. 'What's wrong?' Abi's hand flew to her mouth. *Please don't be the baby.* Mel's previous miscarriages had torn her apart.

'It's Tony. I told him' – she spat the words out between tears – 'about the baby. He told me he's going to fight me for custody. That it's his baby and I don't deserve it.'

'What?' Abi was horrified. 'Oh, Mel, I can't believe he'd say that.'

'I knew I shouldn't have told him. I don't know what to do. He said he couldn't even bear to look at me because I chose you over him.' She let out a sob. 'I honestly thought he'd come around.'

Abi had too. 'How about I come and have a chat with him? I can come tomorrow if you like. I'll try and make him believe that I wasn't involved with Eric's duplicity. If he doesn't believe or forgive me, there must be some solution that doesn't involve you having to choose between us. That he's even asking you to do that isn't right.'

'Would you do that?'

'Of course.'

'But you shouldn't have to. He's acting like such a jerk that I'm not sure I even want to be with him anymore.'

'Let me chat to him and then see what happens. I'm beginning to wonder if there's more to it. He's usually such a reasonable person. It's completely out of character to see him acting like this.'

Mel let out another sob. 'Thanks, Abs. But don't come tomorrow. I'm helping Crystal move, and then I'm working all week. Come next weekend and stay the night. Text me when you know what time you'll be here.'

'Are you sure?' Abi asked. 'You're so upset, and that's a week away.'

'No, I'll be fine. And by then he might have come to his senses. We'll all have calmed down a bit, at least.'

'Okay, but if you change your mind, ring me and I'll come straight down. Love you, sis.' Abi ended the call. She'd wanted a distraction to take her mind off Hayden and the psychologist's phone call, but this wasn't the type of distraction she meant. A heavy weight settled over her. Would there ever be an end to this feeling of helplessness?

Her phone pinged with a text. Reluctantly she picked it up. It was Alex.

Meet me at Fleming's at 1pm on Monday for lunch. We have a few things to discuss.

Dread immediately filled the pit of Abi's stomach. She needed this apartment, and she needed this job. If Alex terminated her contract, she wasn't sure what she would do.

Chapter Twelve

Monday morning came around quickly and Lucinda's heart sank the moment she rang the day care centre to find they didn't have a place for the day, and it looked like they might not for the remainder of the week. She could rely on Abi for one, maybe even two of the days, but not the whole week. She'd need to ring around other centres. When she'd done this initially, the closest with availability was almost an hour away. The logistics of getting Max there on the bus before work and collecting him after were a nightmare, and would mean an incredibly long day for both of them.

She stared at her phone for a moment before giving herself a mental shake. Why was she even hesitating? Dot and William were the most beautiful people she had been lucky enough to meet. She knew they'd look after Max and he'd have a wonderful time, and right now, if she was to have any chance of making her shift on time, she had no choice but to take them up on their kind offer. She rang their number, finding it impossible not to smile when she heard Dot's excited voice on the other end of the line calling out to William. 'Love, Max *is* coming today!'

Twenty minutes later, it was a relief to drop Max off to the older couple. Max made a beeline for the playroom with the play-dough table as soon as Dot opened the apartment door to welcome him.

Dot laughed. 'I don't think you'll need to worry about him today. If anything, we'll have to drag him away from the toys to get outside for some fresh air. At least it's not raining.'

Lucinda hugged Max, thanked Dot and William, and promised to call them as she was leaving work later that day to let them know what time she'd be picking up Max.

She arrived at Fleming's a few minutes early, and got straight to work setting up the dining room ready for the lunch bookings. She was on her own for the first hour, after which she was joined by two other staff, Lana and Ruby.

'Alex has her fundraising lunch today,' Lana reminded her. 'We'll need to set up two long tables, twenty on each. She's expecting at least forty.'

'What's the fundraiser for?' Lucinda asked. She'd been impressed by the number of causes Alex supported.

'It's a personal one.' Lana spread a white tablecloth across one of the tables. 'Friend of hers has leukaemia and can't afford the treatment he needs.'

'How awful.'

Lana nodded. 'It's made worse by the fact he could have afforded it, but lost most of his money in an investment Alex introduced him to. Friend of theirs has an investment company, and stole most of the clients' money and invested in a property development that went bankrupt. Alex and her husband lost a fortune. It's why they had to close the South Yarra restaurant before it even opened.'

Lucinda stared at Lana. She was talking about Abi's husband. Abi hadn't mentioned that Alex had been affected by the investment. Why would Alex be helping Abi if she had?

'Come on,' Lana said. 'We'd better hurry and finish setting up. Knowing Alex's friends, they'll all turn up an hour early and get stuck into the wine.'

Lucinda was deep in thought as she moved around the dining room setting the tables. Poor Abi. Imagine knowing your husband was responsible for something that had such a devastating impact on people's lives. No wonder she looked miserable a good deal of the time.

By twelve thirty the fundraiser was in full swing and most tables in the restaurant were full. The wait staff were run off their feet. Shortly before the appetiser was served, Alex stood and tapped her glass for everyone's attention.

Lucinda smiled as she watched her boss take centre stage; she had a commanding presence. She seemed more suited to a board-room making decisions and influencing people than running a restaurant.

'Unfortunately,' Alex was saying, 'a number of you here, including Jerry and I, were affected by the downfall of Savvy Investments. My thoughts have been with all of you. But for most of us, our investment represented money – money we can hopefully gain back through hard work and other investments. But for one of our group, the financial loss represents a lot more.'

Many of the guests nodded.

'Our good friend, Paul Murch, could very well lose his battle with leukaemia without the treatment he requires. The family have used all of their savings and remortgaged their house, and are financially drained as a result. The life-saving drugs are now out of reach, partly due to the severe financial loss they endured at the hands of Savvy Investments. We've established a GoFundMe page and I have a small flyer to give each of you with the details. Of course, the proceeds from our lunch today will go to the fund, but that won't even touch the sides. We need some big donations. Even though many of you were affected by the Savvy Investments situation, hopefully you'll still have it in your hearts' – she gave a little laugh – 'and in your bank accounts, to help Paul. Jerry and I will be starting the account with twenty thousand dollars.'

A gasp went up around the table, followed by a round of applause. Lucinda smiled as she watched Alex blush. For people who'd lost a fortune recently, twenty thousand was a very generous donation.

'What I'd like to know,' a woman with a loud, commanding voice said, 'is what she thinks she's doing here?'

Lucinda turned to look at where the woman was pointing. Her mouth dropped open. Abi was standing across the dining room, her face bright red, her bottom lip trembling. Why was she here and how much of Alex's speech had she heard? Lucinda glanced back to see Alex hurrying from the table across to Abi. The colour had drained from Alex's face, and she looked as concerned as Lucinda felt.

Silence fell in the restaurant. It appeared that even those patrons at tables not part of Alexandria's group had tuned in with interest when the woman had outed Abi.

'Don't you disappear, Abi Whitmore,' a balding, overweight man called out. 'You've got a lot of explaining to do, and I for one would like to know why you'd show your face here today of all days? This lunch is for Paul, to give him back a chance at life that you and your husband stole from him.'

'Yes,' another said. 'Why don't you enlighten us as to why you're here, Abi? There are so many rumours flying around, so perhaps you can set the record straight for those of us who are interested.'

Alex was doing her best to steer Abi from the room, but Abi stopped her. She broke away from Alex and walked towards the tables.

Lucinda was holding her breath, her heart pounding as she watched. She so wanted to do something, but right at this moment, she couldn't think what.

Abi drew in a breath and addressed the group. 'I'm afraid there may have been a misunderstanding. I was under the impression I was meeting Alexandria at one. I had no idea about this lunch or the fundraiser.' She lowered her eyes momentarily, before raising them again to meet the hard gazes of the people attacking her. 'I can assure you that I wouldn't have come if I had known you would be here. I certainly wouldn't want to spoil today for any of you. I'm deeply saddened to hear about Paul and will do everything in my power to contribute to the fund. Now, I'll leave you to enjoy your lunch, and once again, I apologise for interrupting.'

One of the women gave a loud snort of disapproval. 'You should be in jail. The only credit I'll give you, Abi, is compared to your coward of a husband, you stayed to face the music. Although from what I've heard you got off scot-free anyway. Stealing money from friends and family. It isn't right.'

Abi stopped and turned to stare at the woman. Her voice was quiet but firm. 'I did nothing wrong, Taya. I had no knowledge of Eric's business dealings, and like those who invested, I believed the money was going into a low-risk capital guaranteed fund. I've assisted people with loans for years – you and your now ex-husband too, if I recall correctly. I don't remember you having any complaints about that, or feeling the need to accuse me of anything then.'

'Leave her alone,' another of the guests said. 'I for one will give Abi the benefit of the doubt that she didn't know she was married to a criminal. Any man who not only runs away from his problems but leaves his wife a huge bloody mess to clean up is not a good man. Abi's as much of a victim as those of you who lost money. You didn't lose your husband and everything you knew to be your life too. Give her a break.'

Lucinda wanted to cheer. Someone was finally standing up for Abi.

'Pills would have been a lot easier,' another said, ignoring the previous comment. 'Just get online and order yourself some Ambien. That's what Trisha Black did, remember? Couldn't get it here so got it in the US. Nice, no-fuss way to go.'

'That's enough.' Alex's commanding voice caused the conversation to stop, and all eyes turned her way. 'As Georgia has just said, Abi is a victim of this mess.' She turned to Abi. 'I'm so sorry. I wanted to meet with you tomorrow at one. If I put today in my message, I was rushed and wasn't thinking. Let me walk you out, and we'll leave everyone else to their lunch.'

Abi shook her head. 'You stay and enjoy your fundraiser. I can see myself out. I'll see you tomorrow.' Chatter started up among the two tables as Abi strode out of the dining room, her head held high. Lucinda cleared some empty plates under the guise of going to the kitchen, and followed Abi out into the car park. She found her leaning against her car, gulping deep breaths.

She reached her and pulled her straight into a hug. 'I can't believe that happened, but you were amazing. You should be so proud of yourself.'

Abi pulled away from Lucinda. 'Proud, why? That was humiliating. I thought Alex had asked me to come in to discuss my job. I was already worried, but after that, I might as well go home and start packing.'

'No.' Lucinda shook her head. 'She won't ask you to leave; she stood up for you in there. She looked genuinely horrified when you walked in.'

'She and her husband lost close to a million dollars. Giving me the wrong appointment time could very well have been deliberate. A chance for those people to attack me. Make sure I know just how much they hate me.' She shook her head. 'I used to sit at the table with them. They were mine and Eric's social circle.'

Lucinda didn't want to believe Alex was capable of orchestrating such a set-up, and deep in her gut she didn't think that she had.

Abi sighed. 'Whether it was a set-up or not, I can't imagine I have a job after this. Alex has been kind to me, but seeing the reaction of our friends, she won't want to be associated with me. I doubt Jerry will allow her to anyway. I'm almost certain that if the meeting she scheduled wasn't to fire me, it will be now.'

'You can move in with us if you need to.'

Abi managed a smile. 'And sleep where? On the kitchen table? Thank you, I appreciate the offer, but you have enough on your plate. I can always go to my sister's or my friend Laila's if need be.'

Lucinda hugged her again. 'If it's any consolation, you were impressive in there. Standing up for yourself. I would have run out crying.'

Abi gave a wry smile. 'Thanks, I guess, and thanks for your support. You'd better get inside before Alex uses this as a reason to fire you. One firing in a day is probably enough.'

'It hasn't happened yet,' Lucinda said as Abi climbed into the driver's seat. She waved as Abi drove out of the car park, determined to ensure it didn't.

Lucinda hurried back into the dining room, picking up her duties where she'd left off, hoping Alex hadn't noticed her absence. Alex was holding court at her table, her voice loud and commanding.

It wasn't until two hours later, after the lunch had finished and Alexandria had farewelled her guests, that Lucinda had an opportunity to speak to her.

'Alex, could I get a copy of the GoFundMe flyer, please? I have some friends who might be able to help with raising money. They can load the details to some of their social media pages. One has over a million Instagram followers, so it might help.' The lies rolled off Lucinda's tongue.

Alex's mouth broke into a wide smile. 'That's so generous of you, Hope. Come with me, and I'll get you a copy.'

'I'm very sorry to hear about your friend,' Lucinda continued as they made their way to Alex's office in the back of the restaurant. 'It must be very distressing for all of you.'

Alex nodded. 'It is. I'm heartbroken for them, and furious, to be honest. So many of us could be helping them with large amounts if it wasn't for bloody Eric Whitmore.'

'Abi looked distraught this afternoon,' Lucinda commented. 'It must be a challenging situation for her. You've been very kind to her, Alex.'

Alex stopped and stared at Lucinda. 'What do you mean by that?'

'The apartment and the job. It was extremely kind of you, that's all. It's given her a lifeline, I think, right at a time that she's needed one. So in addition to the incredible donation you made to your friend's fund today, you should know that it's your kindness that has saved someone else who perhaps needed saving.'

'You mean, you think Abi would take her own life?'

Lucinda shook her head. 'I have no idea. I would hope not. But I do know she's been put in an awful position. Anyway, I think you've done a really good thing and wanted you to know that.' Alex seemed lost for words. Lucinda was hoping that by appealing to her ego, she would save Abi from being fired. 'I should let you know that Abi has gone home to pack up her apartment. She mentioned going to live with her sister.'

Alarm crossed Alex's face. 'Why would she do that?'

'She's assuming after today's ambush that you'll be firing her. That seeing how much your friends hate her, you'll have no choice but to disassociate yourself from her. It's a real shame as she's done an amazing job with the apartments. The gardens are nice and all of the residents have been talking about how the maintenance issues are up to date for once. Did you know that she's managed to get a lot of the work done for free? Two of the tenants are unemployed handymen and have been happy to help out in return for a reference.'

'Really? No, I didn't know that. I can say that for the first time in years I haven't been getting a mass of calls each week about those apartments. I wanted to sell them twelve months ago with all of the work they created for me, but Jerry said no. The land they're sitting on is worth a fortune now but will be worth even more in five years.' The lines in Alex's forehead deepened. 'I didn't set her up today, Hope, if that's what you're thinking. I was as shocked to see her as you were. I still feel sick about the entire situation.'

'Well, I hope you can find someone as good as Abi if you do decide to replace her.' Lucinda took the flyer Alexandria held out to her. 'Thanks for this. Now, I'd better get back to work before my shift ends.' She smiled and left the office, crossing the fingers on one hand that she'd manipulated the situation sufficiently.

Chapter Thirteen

Even though the sun was shining brightly, Abi closed her bedroom curtains the moment she entered her apartment. She took off her suit, put on her pyjamas and crawled under the covers. Numbness settled over her. She'd never experienced cruelness first-hand in the way she had today. People she'd once thought of as friends had gone out of their way to humiliate and embarrass her, and for what? Abi did her best to stop the thoughts that churned in her head, and exhausted, unexpectedly drifted off to sleep. She was utterly disorientated when an hour later, her phone rang.

She lifted it from the bedside table, seeing Alex's name on the screen. She ignored the call and buried her head under the pillow. She would have to fire her another day, or via voicemail or text message. Her phone pinged with a notification only seconds later. Alex had left a voicemail.

Abi put the phone back on the bedside table, telling herself not to listen to it, but her curiosity got the better of her. Exactly what was Alex going to say to fire her? She played the message, her body tense as she waited for the inevitable. But what she heard was a complete surprise.

'Abi, it's Alex. I'm ringing to apologise. I'm so sorry. It was a misunderstanding today. I would never have invited you to that fundraiser. Paul's situation is in no way your fault. I'm sure we'll raise plenty of funds to help him. It's not something you need to worry about at all. I also wanted to tell you what an amazing job you're doing. Hope gave me the impression that you might be packing up and leaving. Please don't. I'll see what I can do to offer you a small pay rise, if that helps. Please let me know you got the message and confirm that you're staying on. If I don't hear from you, I'll pop in and see you on my way home. The actual reason I'd asked you to come in and see me was a friend of mine is looking for someone to manage an apartment block she owns. I thought the extra work might supplement your income, but I wanted to talk through the logistics of it with you and how it might impact what you're doing at our apartments. Anyway, we can discuss that over the phone when you're up to it. But most importantly, I'm sorry about today. I feel I let you down.'

Abi stared at her phone when the message ended, the weight on her shoulders lightening a little. What on earth had Hope said to Alex not only to get an apology but a pay rise too?

She sent a quick text to Alex. The last thing she wanted was her popping in.

> I appreciate your message and would be happy to stay on as apartment manager. Thank you. Definitely interested in the other opportunity. Let's speak tomorrow.

She lay staring at the ceiling for a long time, the situation with Paul Murch returning to her thoughts. If the Murches and their friends still had their money, a lot of it would have been available to Paul for treatment. Tears wet her cheeks as she thought of the distress Eric's actions had caused. How could he have caused such heartache for so many people? He used to be the first to establish GoFundMe pages and donate his own money.

An uncontrollable shudder swept through Abi's body, and she pulled herself up to sitting. Was it *his own* money? Had he been donating his funds or the funds of others? How many people had Eric cheated? She closed her eyes. These types of thoughts had been bubbling under the surface for weeks now, and each time she'd squashed them down, refusing to let them fully form. For if she did, she'd have to accept that she was mourning the loss of a man she thought she'd loved. Thought she'd married. When in reality she was mourning a lying, manipulative cheat.

She reached for the photo album she had in the drawer next to her bed, and started to leaf through the pages. It was an album she'd put together for Eric's birthday the previous year. Twenty years of memories. The best photos of the two of them, and then the three of them once Hayden was born. She studied each photo, looking for something. A crack? A sign? Something to suggest it was all a lie. Bile burnt the back of her throat. She needed to grieve. To come to terms with losing her husband. But how could she, when she was beginning to realise her husband, the man she'd loved and adored for twenty years, was a man she didn't know at all?

As she reached the last page in the album – a photo she'd added after Paul's fortieth, of him surrounded by all of the friends and family at the party – her eyes were so full of tears she could no longer make out the people in the photo. She closed the album and turned her face into the pillow. The pain in her chest was unbearable. She couldn't imagine living the rest of her life without *her Eric*, the man she'd believed her husband to be. More importantly, she didn't want to.

Chapter Fourteen

A little after five, the lift door opened on the third floor, and Lucinda grinned as she heard Max's delighted squeals coming from Dot and William's apartment. She rang the doorbell, and all went quiet for a few seconds before the pounding of feet headed towards the door. It flew open, and Max flung himself into Lucinda's arms. Dot appeared, laughing as she saw them.

'Mumma, I've had the best day ever. Don't want to go to day care. Can I come to Dot's every day?'

Lucinda ruffled his hair and smiled appreciatively at Dot. 'Thank you – you must have given him a wonderful day. I hope he hasn't been too exhausting?'

'Not at all. Come in,' Dot insisted. 'I've told William to boil the kettle and Max has a surprise for you, don't you, Max?'

Max pulled away from Lucinda's embrace and nodded. 'A delicious surprise.' He ran back towards the kitchen, leaving Lucinda and Dot laughing in his wake.

'Really,' Lucinda asked, 'how's he been? He can be full of energy.'

Dot ushered Lucinda through to the open-plan kitchen and living area, and indicated for her to sit down. 'He's been a pleasure. Truly. William took him to the park for an hour mid-morning, which gave me a chance to do a few things. It sounds like they had a ball.' She lowered her voice. 'William makes out that it's me that loves children, and don't get me wrong, I do, but I think he loves them even more than me. We'd love to have Max any time you'll let us.'

'I wouldn't want to take advantage.'

Dot patted her hand. 'You wouldn't be, and we can always let you know if it gets too much. Even if a permanent place does come up at the local day care, I'm sure we'd love to have him at least one or two days a week.'

'Thank you.' Lucinda smiled as Max carefully brought a plate over from the kitchen.

'Look, Mumma, I made this with Dot. And it's healthy.'

Lucinda's eyes widened at the sight of a large piece of carrot cake. 'Wow, this looks amazing.'

He went back to the kitchen and returned with a piece for Dot and then one for himself, which he placed carefully on the coffee table. William brought over cups of tea and then joined them with his own plate.

Max disappeared again, returning moments later with a little red chair which he pulled up alongside the coffee table. 'This is my chair,' he told Lucinda proudly.

Lucinda smiled. 'You've settled in here, haven't you?'

Max nodded. 'William and I were spying on birds from the balcony. They sit in the park in the trees, and we look at them through William's telescope and add new ones to William's list.' He gave a sly smile. 'And I watched a boy on his scooter in the playground, and he didn't even know I could see him! I wish I had a scooter.'

Lucinda laughed. 'It sounds like you've had a fantastic day.'

'Can I come again tomorrow?'

'I'm not sure, Max. If there's a spot at day care, then you'll be going there.' Lucinda already knew there was no way she could ask Abi to have Max. Not after what had happened earlier at Fleming's.

'But I like it here better.'

'We'll see in the morning and work it out then.'

'William needs me here, so it makes sense that I come.'

'Oh,' Lucinda asked, 'why's that?'

'Because he can never find anything, so I am his official finder-person.'

William shrugged. 'It's true. I find this apartment a bit confusing. Nothing's where I expect it to be.'

'And you think a lot of things are *too modern and completely stupid,*' Max said, mimicking William. 'Which is weird when they're your things.'

'He is a bit weird, Max,' Dot said. 'You coming and keeping an eye on him will be for the best.'

William held up his hand, crossing his fingers. 'We'll cross our fingers, Max, that day care is full, and you'll have to put up with us instead.'

Max crossed his fingers and made them laugh as he tried to pick up the last of his cake with them.

'Another slice?' Dot asked Lucinda as she spooned the final piece into her mouth. Lucinda shook her head. 'I'd love to, but we'll be too full for dinner at this rate.'

The doorbell rang and William stood and went to answer it. His voice raised in surprise. 'Jonesy! You're early!'

Dot returned her half-eaten cake to her plate. 'Sorry, love, we did ask him to come later. Men seem to have a problem listening at times. Although you could argue it's perfect timing for you to meet him. He's' – she cleared her throat – 'a lovely man.'

Lucinda smiled, hoping Dot wasn't doing any matchmaking. She hadn't asked about Max's father, so it would be rather odd if that was her plan.

William returned to the kitchen with his arm around a man slightly older than Lucinda. A shiver ran down her spine as his presence filled the room. His stubble accentuated the rugged edge of his jawline, his eyes full of mystery. He was lean yet broad; his shirtsleeves were rolled up to his elbows. Max immediately pointed at his arms.

'Sleeves just like Dadda has.'

Lucinda's eyes travelled to Jonesy's arms. Ink covered his arms from his wrists to where his shirtsleeves started. She had to remind herself that it didn't mean he was anything like Ryan. It was art. She had a tattoo herself on her ankle so she definitely couldn't judge. The way he presented himself reminded her of many of Ryan's friends. Slick, polished and tough. She gave herself a mental shake. She had to stop assuming every male that came into her presence was a criminal.

Jonesy smiled at Lucinda, his dimples and sparkling blue eyes softening his tough-guy image. He held out his hand. 'Hi, I'm Alec, but everyone calls me Jonesy.'

'Hope.' Lucinda took his hand and shook it. 'And this is my son, Max.'

Jonesy held up his hand to Max, ready for a high five. 'Nice to meet you, little man.'

Max high-fived Jonesy with all his force.

Jonesy shook his hand, blowing on it as if it had hurt, before holding out his arms to Dot. 'Don't I get a welcome?'

'Of course you do.' Dot moved into his embrace and Jonesy winked at Lucinda over Dot's head. 'Normally throws herself at me, this one does.'

Dot pulled away, managing a small laugh. 'Enough of that. Come and join us for some cake. Max made it this morning. He's quite a chef.'

Max beamed at the praise. 'It's yummy with a glass of milk.'

'Or tea or coffee,' William added. 'What's your poison?'

'I'll go with the cake-maker's recommendation.' Jonesy winked at Max. 'He sounds like quite the connoisseur.'

Max continued to beam as Jonesy accepted his slice of cake and made all of the appropriate noises over it.

'Now tell us,' William said. 'Where have you been and what have you been doing? It's been a few years since we last saw you.'

Jonesy swallowed his mouthful and brushed the crumbs from his fingers. 'Travelling mainly. I've explored parts of the world I didn't even know existed.' He went on to tell them about parts of Asia and India he'd travelled through. 'Fell in love with yoga, of all things.' Jonesy blushed at the admission.

'Is that why you look so fit?' Dot asked.

Jonesy nodded. 'I try and go most days. It took me a while to find a Bikram studio that I like, but there's a little one tucked away near me in Prahran.'

'Is that the hot one?' William asked.

Both Jonesy and Lucinda nodded in unison. Jonesy raised an eyebrow. 'Do you do Bikram too?'

'I've only been once since moving to Elsternwick. I plan to go more often once we're settled into a proper routine.' Thinking about yoga reminded Lucinda that she'd never contacted Mary. She hadn't been back to a class since their discussion so hadn't run into her either. She'd gone from being suspicious of her, to worrying she might come across as too needy if she contacted her straightaway, to just letting the whole idea slide.

'Can I go and play with the train, Mumma?' Max suddenly interrupted.

'Just for a few minutes, okay, and then you'll need to pack up everything you've played with today, so it's neat and tidy for your next visit.'

'Okay.' Max took his little red chair with him as he retreated to the room with the train set.

'Great kid,' Jonesy said before returning the conversation to yoga. 'You should get back to it. It's so good for your mind. This may sound silly, but life feels a lot less complicated when I'm doing yoga.'

Lucinda smiled. He was stating her thoughts exactly; it was what had helped her through the years in Dorford. 'You're right. I will go back to it. There's a studio in walking distance to us, but I got a weird vibe from there. From one of the teachers. She's friendly, but I don't know, she kind of creeped me out.' And that was precisely it, Lucinda now realised. Mary's scrutiny of her had creeped her out. Her explanation that Lucinda reminded her of someone explained the puzzled looks she'd given her, but it still left her feeling unsettled, which was why she hadn't rushed to organise a play date. She hadn't been back since their discussion, but imagined if she did now Mary probably wouldn't be looking at her so intently. She'd already worked out that she didn't know her. 'Thinking back, it was probably me being a bit unsettled, having just moved. I'll give it another go.'

'I'd be interested to hear if you think it's any good. I'm planning to be around this way visiting Dot and William now that I'm back, so might try it out. It's always good to go to classes with different teachers.'

William and Dot exchanged a look that Lucinda found difficult to decipher. Were they happy at the prospect of seeing lots of Jonesy or not? 'Will do. Now, I'm going to take Max home so we can get our evening routine underway.' She stood and turned to Jonesy. 'It was nice to meet you.' She realised as she said the words that it was. He seemed like a decent guy. 'And thank you,' she said to Dot and William. 'Max has had the most wonderful day. I really can't thank you enough.'

'No need.' William got to his feet. 'Bringing him back to us tomorrow is all the thanks we need.' He pretended to dance a little jig. 'He's making me feel young again, and at eighty-four that's something I'd bottle if I could.'

'I'll ring you in the morning and let you know about tomorrow,' Lucinda said. 'I know he'd love to come back, but I'd like to save you up for when I need help, not when day care's available.'

Dot took her hand and squeezed it. 'Of course, love. Whatever suits you. We're here, and we're usually available, so just know the offer's always there.'

Lucinda squeezed the older lady's hand back to say thanks, before walking through to the other room to collect Max. He hugged both Dot and William, who beamed in delight. Very solemnly, he walked up to Jonesy and held out his hand. 'Nice to meet you, Mr Jonesy.'

Jonesy shook his hand. 'You too, Mr Max.' Max giggled. 'I've got a red kite in my garage at home. I'll drop it to Dot and William for you, and you can fly it for me one day.' He looked over at Lucinda. 'If that's okay with your mum?'

'Of course it's okay.' She smiled. 'And very much appreciated.' First Dot and William, and now Jonesy and a kite. Her concerns about Max settling into Melbourne were quickly being put to rest.

Lucinda saw the light on in Abi's apartment as she turned the key in her own lock. She let Max in and turned on the television in the living room.

'I'm just going to talk to Abi. I'll only be standing outside our door, so if you need anything, just call out or come and get me, okay?'

Max nodded, already mesmerised by the activity on the screen.

Lucinda dropped her keys and bag on the counter before retreating from the apartment. She left her door open so she could hear Max and knocked on Abi's door.

'Abi, it's me, Hope.' She heard a rustle, then footsteps and the door opened. Her heart contracted as she saw Abi's tear-stained face and bloodshot eyes. 'I'm so sorry. That was such an awful day for you. I just wanted to check in and see if you're okay.'

'I was going to come and see you, actually.' Abi held the door open. 'Did you want to come in?'

'No, I've just put Max in front of the television so I can't leave him.'

'Okay. Well, I wanted to thank you for whatever you said to Alex. She left me a message apologising for today and offering me a pay rise to stay on here.'

Lucinda smiled. 'That's the best news I've heard all day.'

'I'm very grateful, so thank you again.'

'No need to thank me. Gosh, I'm still in awe of how you handled yourself. I wish I had that kind of confidence.'

Abi laughed, a sound that came out more like a sob. She indicated her face, doing her best to hold back tears. 'I've not handled myself very well since I got home.'

'You wouldn't be normal if you hadn't come home and curled up in a ball.'

Abi smiled through her tear-filled eyes. 'In that case, I'm completely normal.'

Lucinda glanced towards her own door. 'Would you like to come in and have something to eat with Max and me? I think I have another cheap bottle of wine hidden away somewhere. You could probably use a drink.'

Abi shook her head. 'No, not tonight, but thank you. I'm exhausted. I need to have a good night's sleep and drag myself up tomorrow and work out the next steps forward.'

'Next steps? But you said you still had a job.'

'I do. I guess I mean in general. With Hayden and finances, and just everything. I need to set some goals and give myself a reason to get up each day.'

'Good idea. Drop in when you do feel like a glass of wine, won't you?' Lucinda smiled. 'Even if you don't need the company, I could use it.'

Abi returned her smile. 'I will – and, Hope, thank you. I really mean it, and I could use the company too.'

Chapter Fifteen

Abi dragged herself out of bed the next morning. Her head was heavy from the crying and stress of the previous day. She took a deep breath as she made herself a coffee. The realisation the previous night that she didn't want to live in this new reality, where the man she'd loved turned out to be someone she'd never known, had left her feeling conflicted. Following in his footsteps to cash in her life insurance would have pros and cons. Huge financial pros for those affected by the investment, but cons for the few people who did care about her. Hope certainly wouldn't have imagined that this was what Abi would be thinking about when she'd said she wanted to set herself some goals.

Her phone rang, breaking into her thoughts as she poured her coffee. She glanced at the screen and immediately snatched up her phone.

'Hayden? Is everything alright?'

'No, it's not alright. I need you to be part of my next counselling session with Gavin. There's stuff I need to say to you, but he needs to be there to moderate it.'

'Okay. When is it?'

'This afternoon.'

'And you want me in Sydney for it?' Abi had no idea how she was going to manage that.

She could imagine Hayden rolling his eyes as he replied. 'Of course I don't expect you to fly here today. We'll do a video call. It's at four thirty. Can you make sure you're free?'

'Of course. Are you going to give me any indication as to what it's about?'

'It's about how you and Dad have fucked up my life.'

Abi sucked in a breath.

'I've gotta go. We'll ring you at four thirty, so make sure you pick up.' Hayden ended the call before Abi had a chance to respond.

Tears filled her eyes. She didn't even recognise her son. The hurt, the hatred in his voice. How could you respond to that?

As four thirty rolled around, Abi was glad the psychologist session was being done via video conferencing rather than in person. At least this way neither Hayden nor the psychologist would see her trembling legs and shaking hands. She'd never been so nervous to see her son before.

She took a deep breath as the call came through and she accepted it. However she'd pictured Gavin in her mind, the long-haired, tanned guy in his forties was not at all what she'd expected. He looked like he'd be more at home on a surfboard than delving into the psyches of his patients. He introduced himself and explained the format of the discussion. While his manner was certainly more professional than his t-shirted appearance, Abi immediately picked up on a coolness towards her.

'As you know, I've had a number of sessions with Hayden since he arrived in Sydney, which have proven very productive. He wants the opportunity to speak to you today as there are several things he needs you to know but is concerned about how you might react.'

'*Concerned?*'

He nodded. 'Hayden's main concern is you dismissing him. Apparently, this has been a theme that's run through your relationship with him. If you don't agree or think he's behaving unacceptably, you laugh it off and change the subject. Hayden has asked me to be here to ensure this doesn't happen, and that he has his opportunity to speak.'

Gavin's words silenced Abi. Did she do that? She didn't think so. She was sure she allowed Hayden to speak his mind, and on the occasions she disagreed she would usually question him further to make sure she understood his point of view. She had no problem with them disagreeing, as long as he was sure of his position. Gavin's words were alien to her.

'Let's begin, shall we,' Gavin said. 'We'll let Hayden speak, and then you can respond. If you can do your best not to interrupt him and allow him to finish, that will be the best for this format. You'll have your chance to respond to everything once he's finished.'

Abi nodded. This felt like the most unnatural form of communication she could ever imagine.

Hayden cleared his throat. A vein in his cheek throbbed, the way it did when he was nervous.

She smiled at him. 'Hayds, I'm here to listen. You don't need to be nervous. I'm sure we can work through anything that we need to.'

'Let's let Hayden talk, shall we, Abi?'

Abi nodded, suitably chastised by the psychologist, and waited.

'I'm not nervous. I'm angry. Furious, actually, on many levels. There's the big issue of Dad killing himself, but my anger goes back way before that. You and Dad have controlled my life pretty much since I was born. I've told you many times I want to do things differently, and you've ignored me. Until recently, you dragged me along in what was your picture-perfect life and used me as a decoration. Why you even had kids, I can't imagine. You kept me away from Gabe and the rest of Dad's family too. I'm finally getting to know them, which should have happened when I was a toddler, not when I'm sixteen.'

Abi opened her mouth to object, but Gavin raised his hand to stop her.

'To top it off, you're such a liar. You knew what Dad was up to with the investments. I heard the two of you talking one night about how he'd come across a life-changing opportunity and how everyone would be so grateful to him. That after this, he could probably retire, and you and he could travel and do anything you wanted. So for you to stand up now in front of your friends and even your sister and say you knew nothing about his plans is just appalling. I'm embarrassed to call you my parents. At least Dad killed himself thinking his insurance would pay everyone back. What have you done? Do you actually believe selling all of our stuff and managing a crappy old apartment building is going to help? Of course it's not. You should be visiting every one of the friends who invested and telling them the truth. That you and Dad made a mistake and they're paying for it. Letting Dad take the full blame for it all is just awful.'

Abi was stunned, not only by the venom in Hayden's words but by the facts that he had so wrong. He continued.

'And to let Dad kill himself, how could you do that? They should arrest you for murder.'

'Okay, Hayden,' Gavin interjected. 'Perhaps tell your mum why you think she knew about your father's plans to end his life.'

'You knew what he'd done, and you knew of his plans. I saw the two of you hugging the morning of the day he died, clinging to each other. You knew it would be the last time you saw him alive and you just left and went to work. What sort of monster are you?'

Abi covered her mouth and hurried to the kitchen sink, glad she was so close to it. She turned on the tap as the contents of her stomach emptied. Was this really what Hayden had been thinking in the months since Eric's death? She hadn't realised the extent of her son's distress or the complete mess he'd made of the facts. She washed her mouth out and returned to the table and computer screen.

'Sorry.' She waited to see if Hayden had more hatred he was going to spew at her. He appeared to have finished.

'Would you like to respond, Abi?' Gavin asked.

Abi slowly nodded, but she was unsure where to start. 'I'm stunned,' she began. 'For you to think any of that is true shocks me. I didn't know anything about your father's plans, and yes, I know that he hugged me more that morning than he usually would. He told me he loved me and was just beautiful in the way he spoke.' Abi did her best to contain herself. 'I now know exactly why he did that. He knew it was the last time he'd get the chance to speak to me. I didn't. And as for us talking about retirement and amazing opportunities, we had those discussions all of the time. He liked to think big and imagine the most amazing scenario possible. The talk was around different projects at the time, all legit ones, not the property development. I knew nothing about that.'

'You're still claiming ignorance on that score?' Gavin asked, referring to his notes.

'Complete ignorance,' Abi said. 'There's no way on this earth I would have let him invest in any project without client consent, and I certainly wouldn't have allowed him to take his own life.' She looked at Hayden, her eyes pleading. 'Hayden, I have no idea what Dad was doing, or why, but his note said to use his life insurance. That makes me believe he thought the insurance was valid and wanted to fix the situation.'

Hayden snorted in disgust. 'You let his policy lapse. Why?'

'That's not true,' Abi said. 'Dad changed the policies over last year, and suicide had a thirteen-month wait period. It's as simple as that. If Dad had known that was the case, he might have realised there was no financial benefit in taking his life.'

Hayden's eyes were cold as he weighed up Abi's words. She could tell from the look on his face that he didn't believe what she'd said.

'So you're sticking to the story that you knew nothing and are a victim in all of this?'

Abi nodded. 'It's not a story; it's the truth. Why else do you think I'd be paying people back? I'm trying to put what I can right.'

Hayden shook his head. 'Even doing that you're disrespecting Dad.' Abi had no idea what he meant. 'On one hand, you're saying you knew nothing about what Dad was doing, and the next you're openly admitting he did the wrong thing and you're trying to fix it.'

'He did do the wrong thing, and I am trying to fix it.'

'If you loved Dad, you'd be telling all of them that he killed himself to fix things.'

'I can tell them that, but I can't explain why he manipulated their investments and cheated them to start with. I don't think I'll ever have an answer to that. People are angry, and I don't blame them. I am too.'

Hayden raised his eyebrows. 'You are?'

'Of course I am. He's left me questioning everything I've ever believed when it comes to our relationship.' Abi wiped a tear away roughly with the back of her hand. 'I've been left feeling like my marriage was a lie. What I need you to understand is Dad's actions shouldn't change our relationship. We were both misled by him. I love you, and I'm not sure what else I can do to convince you of that.'

'You can let me live my life. That's what you can do. I don't want to feel any obligation to contact you or see you. I don't believe your sob story about Dad misleading both of us. I'm happy here, and I have real clarity that my childhood was just a way for you and Dad to manipulate me and shape me into a product that you could roll out on display when you had company, and pretend to be proud of me.'

'That's not true,' Abi objected. 'We are both proud of you. There was no pretence at all.' *Not so much now*, Abi thought to herself. It was as if he'd been brainwashed into thinking these things about her. What lies had Gabe been feeding him to make him feel like this?

'Hayden is quite specific in his wishes, Abi,' Gavin said. 'He's asking you to give him space and allow him to live in Sydney with Gabe and Imogen without any additional stress.'

'I'm not allowed to contact him?'

Gavin shook his head. 'Not for the moment. He has a lot to work through and doesn't need the emotional upheaval you bring to him.'

Abi fell silent. She thought about Gavin's words before speaking. 'You want me to step away? Not ring, not visit, not have anything to do with my son?'

'It's not what I want, Abi, it's what Hayden is requesting. Can I make a suggestion? We end this session now, unless Hayden has more he'd like to say, and then you and I speak once Hayden leaves my office. I think it would be good for us to discuss how you're feeling, and also for me to ensure you have clarity over what Hayden is trying to convey.'

She had clarity alright. Her son wanted a complete separation from her. She nodded mutely at Gavin's suggestion and waited to see if Hayden had anything else he needed to say. Apparently he didn't, and he stood without glancing at her and walked out of sight. Abi heard a brief exchange between her son and his therapist organising their next appointment, and then a door closed.

She lay her head on her arms, waves of grief flooding over her. Her son was alive, yet she had a similar feeling to the one she felt for Eric at times. It crept up on her. She was fine one minute and a mess the next. She knew better than to fight it; she needed to feel it and hopefully heal from it. Although she doubted that was possible right now.

'So, Abi,' Gavin was saying, 'it's always difficult when anyone rejects us, but particularly our children.'

'He's got it all so wrong.' Abi lifted her head. 'I knew nothing about Eric's plans. I promise. I'll swear on anything if it makes a difference.'

'It's not important what I do or don't believe,' Gavin said. 'It's what your son believes that matters. And right now he believes you're a liar and you've let him down. His uncle seems to agree with him.'

'You've spoken to Gabe?'

'Yes, I've had a long session with him to get an understanding of Hayden's background. I realise how difficult things have been for him.'

'Since Eric died?'

'Since he was born. Keeping a child away from his paternal family can be very detrimental to their development. Hayden's come to live with Gabe and discovered he has a large family who he's missed out on growing up with. Family is what makes us who we are, Abi. Taking that away from someone can be extremely distressing. That's partly what you're dealing with now with Hayden. There's the current situation, but the bigger picture is that he's always felt that something in his life was missing. He's discovered what that is and is very angry that it was kept from him.'

Abi's voice shook as she spoke. 'Eric's family disowned all of us when he married me. They never showed any interest in Hayden and forbade us from attending family get-togethers because Gabe had an issue with it.' She wasn't going to go into the reasons for Gabe being jealous of Eric. 'Gabe is a manipulative prick. He'll be feeding Hayden and you a bunch of lies. I don't understand why he's doing it, but he's decided he wants Hayden and he gets what he wants.'

'Hayden is my concern, Abi, as he is yours. I listen to everyone in his life and how he's feeling and work from there. I wouldn't be too concerned about Gabe. I'd concentrate your efforts on giving Hayden the space he needs to hopefully give you a chance to mend your relationship down the track.'

'But how do I make him believe me that I didn't know what Eric was doing?' Tears started streaming down Abi's cheeks.

'It's difficult,' Gavin said. 'Building trust will go a long way. That will take time, and right now, I suggest you respect his wishes and give him space. He's asked for no phone calls or visits from you. He'll get in touch when he feels that he's ready. He's angry and hurting. I realise this is difficult to hear as a mum, but sometimes kids are better to be removed from a situation rather than continue to fester in it. Hayden's lucky that his uncle has provided this opportunity for him.'

'So I'm to stay away from him?'

Gavin nodded. 'I'll work with him over the coming weeks and months to explore what makes him tick. You're welcome to call me at any time to discuss him. I can't share what he tells me, but I can discuss his general well-being with you and answer any questions you might have.'

'But I shouldn't expect to hear from him?'

'I hate to be brutal, but Hayden's already asked me how he could cut himself off from you permanently and legally. He doesn't want anything from you right now. I'll be working with him to turn this around, but until I manage to do that, I'd say it's for the best.'

Abi was still staring at her computer screen well after Gavin ended the session. He seemed so sure of what Hayden did and didn't want. And the underlying message was *I do not want you. Stay away from me.*

An image of Gabe popped into her head. Right back when she'd rejected him in favour of Eric, and he'd threatened that he'd get her back. *One day, when you least expect it, I'll take something you love away from you. Then you'll see how it feels.* It appeared that day had arrived.

As she shook off the stunned feeling that had enveloped her following the video call with Gavin and Hayden, a sense of absolute clarity settled over Abi. There were too many people hurting as a result of Eric, and she was the only person who could do something about it. In an instant she could repay all of the debts and leave Hayden in a position to get on with his life uninterrupted. Her heart hurt as she thought of her son. She loved him so much and couldn't imagine a life without him, but right now, that was what it seemed she would have. She couldn't live with that.

She turned on her computer and checked her insurance policies one more time. She couldn't risk any loopholes that they wouldn't pay out. As long as the thirteen-month waiting period was served, they would. She needed to have her will redone to make sure the right people received the amounts they were due.

On top of that, she'd need to ensure Mel and Tony were back together before she did anything. She blinked back tears as she realised she'd never get to meet her nephew or niece. But with the way Tony felt about her, it was unlikely she'd be very welcome anyway. She did need to make sure Tony would be there for her sister. Mel would be devastated, but she'd write her a long letter explaining the reasons for what she felt she had to do. She hoped Mel would forgive her.

A weight lifted as Abi started to make a to-do list. Her phone rang as she added another item. *Laila.* Her heart squeezed as she thought of her friend. Laila and Mel would be the two affected the most.

'I'm on my way over,' Laila said before Abi even had a chance to say hello. 'Just checking you have wine glasses?'

Abi laughed. 'Yes, I took four from the old house. I even have wine, so no need to bring anything.' Other than the wine glasses and coffee machine, Abi had only taken absolute essentials for the kitchen and the rest of the apartment. She had, however, taken a dozen expensive bottles of wine from the cellar she and Eric had established many years ago.

'Nope, already bought your favourite. I'll see you in five.' The phone went dead, and Abi pulled herself up off the couch. She tidied away the files she'd been leafing through and ran a brush through her hair. She contemplated changing out of her sweatpants but decided to remain as she was. Laila was hardly going to judge her appearance.

Laila arrived five minutes later, as promised, with a bottle of Abi's favourite Cab Merlot. 'What's the occasion?' Abi asked as they took the bottle through to the small kitchen and she took two glasses out of the cabinet above the kitchen counters.

'Your fortieth.'

Abi laughed. 'You're a bit early for that. It's not until July.'

'I know, and that's why I'm here now. You need something to look forward to, and so I've decided I'm going to throw you a birthday bash you'll never forget.'

Abi shook her head. 'No.'

Laila smiled. 'I knew you'd say that, which is why I'm here in person to tell you exactly why it will be happening.'

Abi took the bottle of wine from Laila, poured herself a large glass and took a gulp. 'Why on earth would you think I'd want to celebrate my birthday – and more importantly, who's going to come? Everyone hates me, remember?'

'Not everyone.' Laila poured herself a glass. 'And even if it's just a small party, it will be filled with people who do care about you. I'll be grilling everyone when I invite them, and if there is any hint of them being resentful towards you, or blaming you for the investment scandal, then they won't be allowed to come.'

Abi raised an eyebrow. 'I appreciate the thought, but I'd hate to see you waste your time. Other than you and Mel, there's no one you could invite who will meet your criteria. Hope from next door maybe, but I can't think of anyone else.'

'Fine, then it will just be the four of us. But keep the night of the thirteenth free, okay? We're celebrating, and it will be fun.'

Abi realised that nothing she said was going to change Laila's mind. Did it matter? If she went through with her plan, she had the option to exit the world before the party. She smiled. 'Okay, sounds good. Thank you.'

Surprise crossed Lila's face. 'I wasn't expecting you to be that much of a pushover.'

Abi shrugged. She was hardly going to tell Laila that she was beginning to formulate plans of her own for the thirteenth of July. That it was the day she intended to end her life and make everything right. She raised her glass. 'Here's to you. You're an amazing friend, and I love you heaps.'

Laila clinked glasses with her and grinned. 'Finally, something to look forward to. I knew we'd get you back into the land of the living, Abs, I just knew it.'

Chapter Sixteen

On Wednesday afternoon, Lucinda pulled her coat tight around her as she stepped from the bus on to the footpath. She turned, stuffing her hands into her deep, warm pockets, and hurried in the direction of William and Dot's. Her shift at Fleming's had gone over slightly, and she was on a later bus than she'd expected. After her initial reservations about having lunch at their house, within just a few days she'd realised what a godsend they were. It worried her that she was beginning to rely on them. However, the day care hadn't been able to give her a place so far this week, and although Abi had offered to have Max, Lucinda didn't feel right loading her up with extra responsibilities.

It didn't take long for her to reach the apartment block, and she smiled as she rode the lift to the third floor. She'd been so busy thinking about Max on her way home she'd not done her usual scrutinising of everyone on the bus or looked over her shoulder the entire way to Dot and William's. Perhaps she was finally beginning to relax and accept that Lucinda Manning had disappeared. She was Hope Faulkner.

She rang William and Dot's doorbell, her smile widening as she heard Max's excited footsteps pounding down the hallway. He flung open the door with William just behind him.

'Mumma!' He threw himself at her legs.

Lucinda bent forward and hugged him, ruffling his hair at the same time. 'How was your day, buddy?'

'Best day ever! We went to the park, fed the ducks, made cookies, played with the trains, went to the park again to fly the kite and then went to the movies and saw *Nemo*. It's an old film, but William had tickets.' He lowered his voice. 'Don't tell Dot, but William and I shared popcorn, and he's not allowed to eat that.'

William winked at her and put his finger to his lips. 'Secret men's business. Women don't need all the information.'

Lucinda smiled. 'Sounds like a fantastic day, thank you so much.'

'No need to thank us. Come on in. Dot's in the kitchen, and I know Max has a surprise for you.'

'Chocolate chip cookies, Mumma. I made a huge one for you.' Max dashed off to the kitchen, leaving Lucinda with William.

'Before Dot goes into a panic,' William said, 'I do want to tell you one thing that you might not like.'

Immediately the hairs on Lucinda's arms prickled.

'It's young Jonesy. He dropped the kite in this afternoon, and Max saw him and insisted we go to the park to fly it. Dot was very anti the idea. She said you weren't keen on Max spending time with people he didn't know. I hope you don't mind, but we did go, all of us. Jonesy only stayed a short while, just long enough to show Max how to fly it. Dot knew you had concerns about Jonesy and is worried you'll not allow Max to us again. I wanted to get in first and tell you it was my fault and, if you are concerned, we'll never do anything like that again.'

Lucinda could see how worried William was, but she also needed him to know that she'd prefer Max didn't spend time with other people. 'It's not Jonesy himself I have a problem with, William. It's just that I'm very protective of Max. We're new to Melbourne, and I guess I just want to take things slowly. Get to know people at my own pace. We had a few things happen back home that does make me a little wary of people and perhaps take longer to trust them than I might have before.'

The lines deepened in William's forehead. 'Nothing too worrying, I hope?'

Lucinda forced a smile. 'Nothing I want to talk about, but enough to have me a little on edge. In saying that, I have met Jonesy and thought he was a decent guy. But I would prefer you didn't take Max out with anyone I haven't met.'

William nodded. 'Of course. I'm sorry if I've upset you.'

'You haven't. I probably need to thank Jonesy and his kite, not be angry or upset. Max has obviously had a wonderful day.'

William pretended to wipe his brow. 'Phew! Thank goodness. If you're happy for Max to spend time around Jonesy, I'm sure he'd love to pop in and play occasionally. Max told us his dad isn't around anymore, so it might be nice for him to have a man younger than me to entertain him from time to time.'

'What did Max say about his dad?' Lucinda's words were sharp; her heart automatically thumping in her chest. She'd told Max that if anyone ever asked, he was to say that his dad wasn't around anymore and nothing else. She didn't imagine they'd interrogate a four-year-old, and would assume he was either dead or had abandoned them.

'Nothing, just that he wasn't around anymore and that was all he could say.' William frowned. 'He made a real point of that. I took it that he didn't want to talk about him and respected that immediately. We respect that with you too if you don't want to talk about your past.'

Lucinda let out a breath. 'Melbourne is a fresh start for Max and me, so yes, I'd prefer not to discuss our past.'

'Max is a great little boy. You should be so proud. If this is your new start, then we would love to be part of it. Now come on, Dot's probably having heart failure over the thought of telling you Jonesy was involved in our day.'

William was right; Dot was clasping her hands together and pacing the kitchen when they came through.

'It's fine, Dot,' Lucinda said before the older woman even opened her mouth. 'I liked Jonesy when I met him, and I trust your judgement. If you say he's a good guy, then I'm happy for him to be around Max.'

Years seemed to drop off Dot as Lucinda's words sank in. 'Oh, thank goodness. I've been so worried. We know he's a good man, but we also understand your hesitance. He'll be relieved too. He had a wonderful time with Max and the kite. He said that if you were angry or concerned, to call him and speak to his partner, Janice. Janice has seven nephews and raves about Jonesy and how amazing he is with them. I think he hoped that would convince you.'

Heat rose in Lucinda's cheeks. These people were so kind to her. Looking after her son for free and then worrying that she'd be upset with how they'd managed the day. 'No need to convince me of anything,' she said. 'I've mentioned to William that I'd prefer Max doesn't spend time with anyone I haven't met, though.'

'Of course,' Dot said.

'And you will tell me if it gets too much, won't you?'

'It won't get too much. We're hoping you won't put Max in day care, and we can have him all to ourselves, but we do understand if you think it's best for him.'

'I think it would be best for everyone if he has a bit of variety. Partly to give you and William a break, and also for him to socialise with kids his age. He'll be at school next year, and if I'd been living in Melbourne earlier I would have enrolled him in kindergarten, but the waitlists are far too long now. Day care is the only option to give him that kinder experience.'

'Does the local one have a place for him yet?'

Lucinda nodded. 'Yes, next week they can give him three days, so I was going to ask you and William if you could have him for one or two? My neighbour, Abi, is also happy to help out.'

Dot's face fell. 'Of course we can have him for two. Three or four would be better.'

Lucinda smiled. 'I appreciate that, I do, but two would be perfect. That's not to say that we can't see you on one of my days off. You and William are my only friends in Melbourne, and I'd love to spend more time with you.'

Dot's eyes lit up in delight. 'Well, why didn't you say? That sounds perfect.'

Max didn't stop talking as they walked back to their apartment. 'I love it there, Mumma, can I go again tomorrow?'

Lucinda squeezed his hand. 'Definitely. You're going tomorrow and Friday, but then next week will be a little bit different. You'll get to go to day care too and have lots of boys and girls to play with.'

'I like the park better.'

'Well, I'm sure William will take you there again tomorrow.'

'And will Mr Jonesy be there?'

'I'm not sure,' Lucinda answered honestly. 'Do you like him?'

Max beamed. 'He's the best. He's funny, and he asks me interesting questions. I'm very careful with my answers.'

'What sort of questions?' asked Lucinda.

'About my favourite colour, my favourite animal, my favourite place where we used to live, my favourite type of train and bus. All interesting questions.'

'What did you tell him about your favourite place where you used to live?'

'I didn't. I locked my lips and sealed them. I told him my life started when I arrived in Melbourne so he could ask me anything he wanted about that, but nothing about my other life, and nothing about my dad, my grandma or my house.'

Lucinda groaned inwardly. Jonesy was unlikely to have asked Max about any of these things, yet now probably had all sorts of questions. She guessed she'd need to get used to it. It was likely there would be questions once he started day care and school next year too.

'Jonesy told me some things about him,' Max volunteered. 'He's scared of penguins. Isn't that weird?'

Lucinda laughed and ruffled his hair. 'That is very weird, Max, very weird indeed.'

When Lucinda arrived to pick Max up on Friday afternoon, she found a much more subdued version of her son. Rather than racing to the front door and flinging himself on her, he was lying on the couch, his beloved soft toy, Mr Fizz, under one arm, looking at pictures in a book. He looked up and smiled when Lucinda followed Dot into the living area.

'I think we've worn him out,' Dot chuckled. 'It's the quietest I've seen him since we met you. William too, he's gone to have a lie-down.'

Lucinda walked over and sat on the edge of the couch next to Max. 'You okay, hon?'

Max nodded. 'We spent ages at the park, and Jonesy helped me fly the kite.'

Lucinda looked over to Dot. 'Jonesy was here again?'

'You did say you felt comfortable with him, love.' Her smile turned to a frown. 'That was what you said, wasn't it?'

Lucinda ruffled Max's hair, then stood and went back over to where Dot was folding washing at the kitchen table. 'Yes, of course. I'm just surprised he has the time to keep coming over, and I'd hate any of you to feel I was taking advantage and expecting him to be entertaining Max.'

'He loved every minute of it, didn't he, Max?'

Max nodded, turning the pages of his book.

'Doesn't he work?'

'He does, but he has flexible hours with the shipping business.' She gave a little laugh. 'Flexibility is one of the reasons he started it. Never was one for regular business days.'

'This Jonesy you're talking about?' William entered the room, pushing his hand through his hair.

'Yes, just trying to explain to Hope why he's got such flexible hours.'

'Guess it's just the type of business he's in.' William stifled a yawn.

'I take it Max has worn you out,' Lucinda said. 'Dot mentioned you were having a lie-down.'

'Not at all. I wanted to recharge for the next round. Although I assume you're taking him home now?'

Lucinda nodded. 'Yes, we need to walk down to the shops and get some groceries.'

'Will we see you over the weekend?' Dot asked. 'You're most welcome to come to lunch again.'

'Thank you, that's very kind, but I'm concerned we're going to outstay our welcome. So not this weekend, and at this stage I have Max booked into day care Monday, Wednesday and Friday.'

William's face crumpled with disappointment.

'Now now, love, you knew that was going to happen from next week. We'll still get to see Max on Tuesday and Thursday.'

'I know, it's just I feel like there's so much making up to do.'

Lucinda stared at William. 'Making up? What do you mean?'

William shrugged and gave a little laugh. 'Sorry, I'm just a silly old man. I guess because we never got to spend time with our grandson, I like to think of Max as my way of having the grandparent experience.'

'But Max isn't our grandchild.' Dot gave William a sharp look. 'If you go on speaking like that, Hope will assume we're crazy and not have anything to do with us.'

William looked away.

'Sorry, love,' Dot said. 'He can be a bit cuckoo at times.'

'There's no need to be sorry.' Lucinda's heart contracted at the look on William's face. He loved Max; it was written all over him.

'Will we see Dot and William tomorrow?' Max asked, shuffling over from the couch.

'No, not for a few days, buddy,' Lucinda said. 'You'll be back to see them on Tuesday if that still suits.'

'Of course it does,' Dot said. 'And the offer's still there for the weekend if you feel like a meal.'

'Thank you. We have plans with a friend tomorrow, and I'm going to take Max exploring on Sunday, but if anything changes I'll let you know.' Lucinda felt terrible putting them off, but she was sure the novelty of Max would wear off quickly if they didn't start spacing out their time.

'What friend?' Max's face scrunched in wonder. 'We don't have any friends.'

'We do now,' Lucinda said. 'I made a friend at yoga and she has a little boy who is the same age as you. We're going to have a picnic with them in the park tomorrow.' Lucinda had finally rung Mary, feeling bad that it had taken so long. Mary had been delighted to hear from her and Lucinda decided her concerns had probably been paranoia and nothing more. It would be good for Max to meet someone his age outside of day care.

'How lovely,' Dot said. 'Well, I hope you all have a great time. Max, let's get your backpack packed up so you're ready to go home. You wouldn't want to leave your special teddy here. You'll need him tonight.'

Lucinda followed Dot and Max back to the playroom, and they packed up his belongings. He flung his arms around Dot. 'I'll miss you, Granny.'

Granny?

Dot laughed, her cheeks flushing. 'I hope you don't mind, but he asked me if it was okay to call me Granny. As far as I'm concerned, he can call me anything he wants.'

'You said you loved it,' Max objected.

Dot squeezed him. 'I sure did, but I did say I wasn't sure if your mum would love it so much. That might be a name she keeps for her mum.'

Max shook his head. 'No, she's Grandma, and she won't mind. She lives a long way away and won't get to see us anymore. And she's my only grandma, so you can be Granny for sure. And William can be Pa, can't he, Mumma?' He looked to Lucinda for confirmation.

She wasn't sure what to say. They'd known Dot and William for such a short time, but having a Granny and Pa might be what Max needed to help him feel more at home. Three sets of eyes were on her, waiting for her response. It was William's, full of excited hope, that made her decision. 'Of course he can, if you're both sure it's what you like?'

William's face broke into a smile. 'Like? You've just made my day. My year, in fact, and Dot's too. We'll be the best grandparents you ever imagined.'

'Well, adopted ones,' Dot said, giving William a knowing look. She unpeeled Max from her. 'Come on, let's get you and your mum out of here so you can get to the shops before dinner.'

She walked with them to the front door, dropping her voice so William wouldn't hear her. 'That means a lot to him, Hope. He's had a rough time since Billy left our lives. For years it's like he's been stuck at that point, unable to move forward. Young Max has given him a new lease on life. Don't worry, I'll do my best to make sure he doesn't smother you both too much.'

Lucinda smiled. 'Honestly, I can't thank the two of you enough. You're giving Max something I thought he might have said goodbye to forever.'

Dot frowned. 'If you ever need to chat, love, I'm always here. If you're talking about your mum, it's never easy to be apart from the ones we love. If you need an ear at any time, you just let me know.'

'Thanks.' Lucinda realised she'd already said too much. She needed to be careful, as it would be very easy to start talking with Dot and tell her much more than she ever intended.

They said their goodbyes and headed off to the shops, with Max asking a million questions about his new friend Zeb. None of which Lucinda could answer.

Max was hopping from foot to foot the next morning, constantly asking Lucinda what time they could leave for the park. He was desperate to meet his new *best friend*, as he was now referring to Zeb. In the end, Lucinda grabbed the blanket she'd decided could be a picnic rug, and the backpack with the food she'd prepared, and they set off. It wasn't going to hurt to be early. Max could run his energy off there while they waited rather than continually bugging her.

It was a beautiful blue-sky day. The air was crisp, but it was warm in the sun. While much cooler than Dorford at this time of the year, Lucinda was finding she was adapting quite well to Melbourne's unpredictable weather.

They arrived at the park to find the playground already busy with children – from toddlers to preteens – running, screaming and playing. Lucinda set the blanket up in a spot between the play equipment and the lake, so that she could see Max easily and he'd know where to find her. She stretched her legs out, her thoughts travelling to Abi. She wondered how she was. She would drop in on her that afternoon and check.

Her thoughts were cut off as Mary waved from the other side of the park. She'd parked her orange Jeep and was walking hand in hand with her little boy. He had dark shaggy hair and was carrying a large yellow Tonka truck in one hand. If he was a good sharer, Max was going to love him.

Lucinda stood and walked over to them, waving to Max, who was on the slide. 'Max, come and meet Mary and Zeb.'

Max whooshed down the slide and came running over, a massive smile on his face. He ran straight up to Zeb and Mary, who was laughing by the time Lucinda reached them. 'Looks like they're friends already,' she said as the two little boys ran off with the truck towards the sandpit.

'Sorry, I didn't even get to introduce Max.'

'He did it himself. Did you hear what he said to Zeb?'

Lucinda shook her head.

'It was along the lines of *Hi, new best friend Zeb, I'm best friend Max. Let's play.*'

Lucinda rolled her eyes. 'Yes, he's been calling Zeb his best friend ever since I mentioned him. I hope Zeb doesn't mind.'

'Mind? He'll be ecstatic. He doesn't have many friends his age. I've been a bit guilty of being slack with him. With my older kids, I always had play dates and friends over, so I made lots of mum friends, and we all caught up regularly. It's been a bit different with Zeb.'

Lucinda led Mary over to the picnic rug. 'I didn't realise you had other children.'

Mary nodded. 'Three; they're a bit older though. Zeb was a surprise. The older three are on holiday with their grandparents at the moment – my late husband's parents. They have them for a few weeks every year and this year wanted to take them to Fiji.'

'But not you and Zeb?'

Mary shook her head. 'They do see Zeb but decided it was too much to take four of them away when they'd have to spend so much time supervising Zeb. And they weren't going to take me too. They love the kids but had some serious problems with my husband and with me. I think he'd be pretty upset to know they spent any time with our kids after the way they acted towards us, but they went through the courts and made it happen.'

'That must have been difficult.' Lucinda thought back to her own experience of sitting in court, praying that Ryan would be convicted. She imagined Mary's situation had been very different to hers, but no doubt the other woman had also sat there vehemently hoping for an outcome in her favour. 'And I'm sorry to hear about your husband.'

'Thanks.' Mary didn't offer any more, so Lucinda didn't ask.

'It's lovely here, isn't it,' Lucinda said. 'I feel so lucky to have moved into this area. We weren't in a position to afford much, so I was surprised we could find somewhere with such lovely surroundings.'

'Melbourne has lots of leafy gardens and beautiful parks,' Mary said. 'It's a great city.'

'Have you always lived here?'

Mary shook her head. 'No, the kids and I moved here a few years ago. Ironically partly to get away from the grandparents. That backfired, but at least by living in different states, we don't have to see them regularly.' She looked at Lucinda. 'So, what's your story? So far, I know you moved from Perth, you like yoga and have a four-year-old. What made you move?'

'I had a few issues with Max's father and decided we needed a fresh start.'

'You left his father in Perth?'

Lucinda nodded.

'Wow! How are you going to manage that with Max? Won't your ex want to see him?'

'I'm not stopping him. But knowing his circumstances, I doubt he'll be rushing over to see Max. It's all a bit raw, to be honest, and I'd rather not talk about it. Tell me how you got into teaching yoga.'

Mary started talking about her love for yoga and how it kept her sane through her husband's death and being a single parent to four kids. 'I'm lucky that my oldest is fifteen. I had her when I was very young, so she can babysit Zeb for me. It means I can get out and do things. Yoga's my sanity check. You'd get that I imagine.'

Lucinda nodded. She did, and realised how much she was missing it. She'd only worked part-time in Dorford, allowing her to go to classes during Max's kinder hours or when Tess could look after him. She had neither of those luxuries here. She looked across to the sandpit where Max and Zeb were playing. 'Looks like they've hit it off.'

'That's great,' Mary said. 'We should do it again. It's Zeb's birthday next weekend, and with the other kids away, I'm sure he'd love it if you and Max could celebrate with him. I wasn't planning on making a big fuss, just a cake and some of his favourite foods. If the weather's nice, we could come back down here, or otherwise I'm sure he'd love to have Max over to our house to play with his toys. His most beloved toy is a train set, if Max is into trains?'

Lucinda thought of William's train set that Max had fallen in love with. 'He is, and we'd love to come.'

'Great.' Mary smiled. 'I'll text you later in the week. We'll see what the weather's doing and what Zeb would prefer to do.' Her smile slipped as she glanced over to where the boys were playing. She leapt to her feet, her body tensing. 'Who are they speaking to?'

Lucinda looked across, seeing William and Dot standing talking to the boys. 'It's okay, they're friends of mine. They've kind of adopted us. Let's go across and I'll introduce you.' She noticed Mary's hands curl into fists. 'Really, it's okay. They're harmless.'

'Sorry, but after the stunts my ex's parents have pulled to get their hands on my kids, I'm a bit overprotective.'

'No need to apologise or explain, I'm the same.' If only Mary knew just how protective Lucinda needed to be.

The two women walked the short distance to the sandpit, where William was inspecting the Tonka truck and discussing with the boys the different things it could do.

'Hello, Hope dear,' Dot said, taking Lucinda's hand and squeezing it. 'We're just out for our morning walk and saw Max with his little friend.' She smiled at Mary. 'You must be Hope's new friend.'

Mary smiled. 'I'd like to think so. I'm Mary, and this is Zeb.'

'Lovely to meet you.'

'This is my granny and my pa,' Max said, turning to Mary. 'They're my new grandparents.' He lowered his voice. 'I had to leave my old ones. Well, my grandma anyway. 'Cause' – he looked at Lucinda, who gave a quick shake of her head – ''cause, 'cause it's a secret why, isn't it, Mumma.'

Cold chills ran up Lucinda's spine. Max was going to give them away. The lure of Matchbox cars might not have been enough. She ruffled his hair. 'Sure is, bud. Now, why don't you and Zeb play a bit more and then come over to the picnic rug for something to eat and drink.'

'We'll leave you to your catch-up,' Dot said. 'Come on, William, let's leave the boys alone.' Dot shook her head when her husband made no attempt to move away from the sandpit. 'William,' Dot hissed.

William turned and smiled at Lucinda and Mary. 'What I wouldn't give to be four again and allowed to play in the sand.' He sighed. 'Oh well, guess I'll just have to put up with being old and decrepit.' He nodded towards a bench. 'Perhaps we could sit for a bit, Dot. My legs have seen better days.'

Dot rolled her eyes and led William across to the bench.

'Let's go and sit back down,' Lucinda said, and walked back towards the picnic rug.

'How do you know them?' Mary asked.

'I met them the first weekend we arrived in Melbourne.' Lucinda went on to tell Mary about the chance meeting she'd had with the older couple. 'I feel incredibly lucky, to be honest. They've taken us in like we're family. Max adores them, and they're saving me a fortune in childcare fees.'

Mary nodded. 'Just be careful of how attached Max gets. They're not related to you, and if they suddenly decide it's all too much to be around a four-year-old, he might find that rather difficult.'

'It's one of the reasons I have him starting day care next week permanently. A place has finally become available, and while I love both of them already, I also want to give Max some variety and dilute how much time he spends with them. He needs to be around kids his age too.'

The two women lapsed into silence as they watched the boys playing. It wasn't long before the two four-year-olds came racing over, looking for food and drinks.

Lucinda unpacked her backpack, which had a large container of fruit, one of popcorn and some small sandwiches. Mary laughed as she pulled out an almost identical selection of food, and they laid it out for the boys.

'Would you mind watching Zeb for a minute? I'm just going to use the ladies.'

'Of course.' Lucinda took a bottle of water from her bag and poured it into two small cups, which she handed to the boys.

'Back in a minute, Zeb,' Mary said. 'You do whatever Hope tells you, okay?'

Zeb nodded, his mouth full of watermelon.

'Zeb's got secrets just like us,' Max said when Mary was out of earshot.

Lucinda's heart immediately raced. 'That's nice to hear, and of course he can keep them to himself, just like you keep yours to yourself.'

Zeb moved closer to Lucinda and lowered his voice. 'My dad was a bad man too.' He sat back on his heels and grinned. 'Me and Maxy are best friends, and we both have bad dads. Mine would be in prison if he wasn't dead, that's what my brother Eli says.'

Lucinda stared at Max. 'Max, what did you tell Zeb?'

'Nothing at all,' Max said. 'I promise. I never said Dadda was a bad man.'

'He's telling the truth,' Zeb said. 'I worked out he was in prison, which I think makes him a bad man. I asked Max questions, and he nodded or shook his head. He said he wasn't allowed to say anything, so he didn't. But I worked out lots, didn't I, Maxy?'

'Zeb has superpowers,' Max explained to Lucinda, seeming very proud of his new friend.

Lucinda took a deep breath and smiled at Zeb. 'Superpowers are amazing. I hope one of yours is keeping the secrets you find out to yourself. Otherwise your powers might get weak.'

'My superpowers are huge,' Zeb said, flexing his non-existent arm muscles. ''Cause I never tell my secrets. I love secrets, and I'm so good at them. Just ask my mum. She says I'm the best. I have at least' – he held up six fingers – 'this many huge secrets.'

'Me too.' A deep voice spoke from behind Lucinda. She turned, shielding her eyes from the sun to see Jonesy standing behind her.

'Jonesy,' Max yelled and jumped to his feet, high-fiving the big man. 'This is my new friend, Zeb.'

Zeb stood and high-fived Jonesy just as Max had.

'Nice to meet you, Zeb. I've got that red kite in my car, would you like me to go and get it and we can fly it?'

Max nodded. 'Yes, please.'

Jonesy grinned. 'Okay, you guys stay here, and I'll be back in a few minutes if that's okay with your mum?'

Lucinda nodded, pleased for Max and Zeb but slightly confused. What was he doing here? The feeling of unease she'd been doing her best to shake in the last few weeks settled over her again.

'Have a bit more to eat before you fly the kite,' she said to the two boys, who were both standing on their tiptoes trying to see where Jonesy had gone. Lucinda glanced across and saw that William and Dot were no longer on the bench so hadn't seen Jonesy.

Jonesy arrived back with the kite moments later and suggested to the boys that they fly it in the space between where Lucinda was sitting and the lake. 'That way, your mum can watch and pluck you out of the lake if you fall in,' he joked, handing Max the kite.

'Hold on a minute,' Lucinda said to Jonesy as Max ran off with the kite and gave Zeb the handle. 'It's very kind of you to bring the kite by, and I don't want to sound rude or ungrateful, but why exactly are you here?'

'Hey, sorry.' Jonesy frowned. 'I didn't mean to crash your catch-up. I'm on my way to visit William and Dot. William needs a hand changing over some taps. I saw you guys as I drove past and remembered the kite was still in the boot of the car. Thought Max might like it, that's all. He had a ball with it yesterday. I wasn't planning to stay.'

Lucinda nodded. His explanation was reasonable enough.

'In fact, I'll get going right now.' He smiled. 'Knowing William, he's already undoing the tap and hasn't turned the water off yet. Dot will kill him if he floods the place.'

'It's good of you to help them out so much.'

'Their son, Billy, was very good to me. I'm just paying that forward. And I like them, so it's not exactly a hardship. Anyway, I'll leave you and the boys to it. Perhaps get Max to bring the kite back to William's next time he comes over. I know William enjoyed flying it with him yesterday.'

'Sure.'

Jonesy grinned and turned, his eyes searching the park momentarily, coming to rest on Max. 'See you, Max,' he called out. 'Have fun with the kite.'

Max waved before running as fast as he could with the kite, which flew for a few seconds before crashing to the ground.

Jonesy laughed. 'Might take a bit of practice.' He turned back to her. 'Enjoy your weekend, and once again, sorry if you felt I intruded.'

Lucinda smiled, watching him as he walked back towards the road, and she assumed his car. Her eyes settled on the toilet block. She hoped Mary was okay.

As she had the thought, her phone pinged with a text.

> Please pack up my things and bring Zeb to my car. I'm not well. Sorry.

Lucinda stood and looked over to the orange Jeep. She could see a figure inside, and as she looked, the window rolled down and

Mary waved to her. She collected Mary and Zeb's belongings and called the boys over. 'Your mum's not feeling well, sweetie, and has asked me to take you over to the car to meet her. We need to get your truck from the sandpit on the way.'

Zeb's face crumpled in disappointment.

'We'll see you soon, though,' Lucinda promised. 'Your mum's invited us to celebrate your birthday with you next weekend.'

'Yay!' Max shouted.

'Come on, Max, let's walk Zeb over to the car.'

Max and Zeb ignored her suggestion of walking and instead raced each other.

'I'm so sorry.' Mary's eyes darted around nervously. 'I must have eaten something bad. We'll do this again soon, okay?'

'You poor thing, you're very pale.' And she was. The colour had drained from her face, and her lip was trembling. 'You're sure you're sick, and it's not something else? You look like you've had a shock.'

Mary forced her eyes to meet Lucinda's before they flicked back to the park. 'Who was that guy? The one you were talking to?'

'That's just a friend of William and Dot's,' Lucinda said. 'He's spent time with Max before.'

Mary met her gaze. 'How does he know them?'

'He worked with their son, who was also his godfather. Why, do you know him?'

Mary hesitated. 'No, but be careful. I get strange feelings about people from time to time, and more often than not they're right. Be a bit wary of him, that's all.'

Lucinda nodded. It was a strange thing to say about someone you didn't know. 'Okay, thanks. Let me know if you need anything. I can always look after Zeb for you if you need to rest. Otherwise, we'll wait to hear from you about Zeb's party.'

Mary nodded, starting her car. 'I'll be in touch.' She forced a smile and pulled out into the street, leaving Lucinda staring after her.

Lucinda replayed the outing to the park over in her head as she stretched out on the couch a couple of hours later, sipping her tea. Mary disappearing to the toilets and then not coming back was odd. She'd seemed nervous and more on edge than Lucinda herself was.

What was more worrying right now was Max's inability to keep secrets. If Zeb had managed to work out his dad was in prison within ten minutes of them meeting, then what hope did she have of him keeping that secret once he was at day care? She was beginning to think she might need to do something quite drastic with regards to Ryan and the story Max was telling. Did she have it in her to tell him Ryan was sick and over time tell him he hadn't recovered – that he'd died? It was an awful thing to do but, in this case, might be necessary.

She checked her watch. She'd promised to ring Tess at four. It was ten to. She waited until exactly four and then called the number. Tess picked up immediately.

'How are you, Lu? How's Max?'

They spoke for a few minutes exchanging news, before Lucinda asked the question she didn't want to know the answer to. 'Is there any news about Ryan?'

Tess let out a long breath. 'I've got terrible news on that front. He's got an appeal.'

'What? They said it was a non-parole period with no chance of appeal.'

'I know, but the guy in the coma waking up and telling the police he had nothing to do with it seems to have worked.'

Lucinda was silent for a moment.

'Lu?'

'It's the alibi he usually uses. Gets to the victim before the police and lawyers do and pays them enough to get them to change their story. It didn't work before the trial because the victim was in a coma and they couldn't get him to change his story. When's the appeal?'

'He's waiting for a date, but it appears it could be in the next couple of weeks.'

Lucinda sucked in a breath. 'He could be out in a couple of weeks?'

'Possibly.'

'Oh God. Has he contacted you again?'

'Only a brief phone call to check if I'd heard from you and to let me know he thought he'd be out soon.'

Dread settled in the pit of Lucinda's stomach. 'I guess we just keep on as we are, and pray something happens between now and the appeal that stops it from happening.'

'I'm not sure there's much else you can do. Now tell me honestly, how's Max? Is he coping? Can I talk to him?'

Lucinda hung up ten minutes later, after Max had finished chatting to Tess. They'd hardly even had a chance to settle in and already she felt like Ryan was closing in on her. Was she being ridiculous? She'd left Dorford without any kind of trail. She had a new identity. So why did she assume that if he got out of prison he'd be able to find her? The reality was, he could have his colleagues searching for her now, and probably did. But there was no reason to believe they had any idea where she was.

Chapter Seventeen

The rest of the week passed in a daze for Abi. She was still reeling from the conversation with Hayden and the psychologist, but also knew it had been the catalyst for her decision to cash in her life insurance. It was a bizarre thing to consider doing and left her with a mixture of emotions. She found herself laughing at the absurdity of it one minute, and in tears realising she was going to hurt Mel, Laila and possibly Hayden in the process. She wished she could confide in someone about her plan, but she knew exactly how that would end – with her checked into a psych ward. As she made the seventy-minute trip from Elsternwick to Geelong, her mind whirled with what she needed to do. She had to fix the situation with Mel and Tony, but she also needed to spend quality time with her sister. Make sure Mel knew that she loved her. She'd started thinking about the notes she would leave, but each time she sat down to write them, it became too hard. She would need a bottle of wine to get the job done, and still had a few weeks before it would be necessary.

Her biggest problem was working out how she was going to do it. She wasn't going to do what Eric did, not that she had access to a gun now that Eric's collection was in police possession. Also, she had no intention of leaving anyone with that kind of mess to clean up. Her stomach roiled at the memory of what she'd walked in on.

No, it had to be something simple and peaceful. Pills probably. But so far her Google searches had shown her that most over-the-counter pills were not strong enough to kill you. She'd have to take thousands to even make that work. She'd need to do more research and hope that no one was monitoring her searches. She also wondered whether she'd be able to go through with it when the time came.

A little before five, Abi pulled into the driveway of Mel and Tony's modern two-storey townhouse.

Mel appeared at the front door the moment Abi stepped out of the car, a nervous smile playing on her lips. 'I'm not sure this is a good idea,' she said as Abi walked towards her, arms outstretched.

'Why?' Abi hugged her tight.

'I just don't think he's going to want to talk to you. He's been pretty awful in his statements about you and Eric.'

Abi swallowed. This was one fight she refused to walk away from. Eric had destroyed her family and her relationship with Hayden, but she would not let it spill out to her sister and husband. 'He's going to talk to me whether he likes it or not. Can I leave my bag here?' Mel nodded and led Abi into the house. She placed her bag on the kitchen counter and clenched her fists. 'Right, time to do this. I'll be back when I'm back, and whatever you do, stay here, okay?'

'Why, what do you mean?'

'I mean give me a chance to talk to him. Don't come and check on us in case it causes even more problems. I'll make it very clear that you didn't want me to talk to him, that I'm here off my own bat and any problems he has with that he takes up with me, not you.'

Mel nodded, her eyes large with fear.

'It'll be okay, Mel,' Abi said. 'You're pregnant with his child. You've both wanted this forever. It should trump anything else that's going on.'

'I know. But he's so unreasonable.'

Abi placed a hand on each of Mel's shoulders. 'Go and relax. Watch Netflix or have a bath or something, and try not to think about me or him. Hopefully, I'll come back with good news.' Abi smiled at her sister, projecting a confidence she didn't feel. As much as she wanted to fix this, she wasn't sure how receptive Tony would be to a discussion.

Abi knew the conversation with Tony was going to be challenging; what she hadn't anticipated was him refusing to talk to her.

'Go home, Abi. There's nothing you can say that will make this any better.' He stood at the front door of his parents' house, his arms crossed. 'This is between Mel and me, and you're making it ten times worse by being here.'

'It's not between you and Mel,' Abi insisted. 'It's between you and me. Mel's the one stuck in the middle, and it's completely unfair. Making her choose between the two of us; what are you, five?' As soon as the words left her mouth, Abi knew they were a mistake. She needed to stroke Tony's ego, not insult him. She lowered her eyes. 'Sorry, I'm just upset and not sure how to handle this.'

Tony sighed. 'Go home. That's the best way to handle it. Let me and Mel work it out our way.'

Abi shook her head. 'Tony, your wife's pregnant. As much as she puts on the tough guy act, she's scared. The thought of going through this alone is terrifying. Can I ask you something?'

'If you have to.'

'If Eric's investment had been a success and you were sitting here hundreds of thousands of dollars richer, would you still be angry with me? Angry with Eric? Would you want Mel to cut off ties with us, or would you be hoping for another investment opportunity?'

Tony stared at her. 'Abi, Eric didn't just make a bad investment; he made one that went against all of our contracts. One that was illegal. It's not a case that he was working in our best interests and the market downturned. He knowingly invested our funds in a high-risk development that he didn't have our sign-off for. If it had made a lot of money and he'd shared that with us I'm sure I'd be grateful for the financial gain, but I wouldn't be able to trust him ever again. It was unethical and illegal. You can't do that.'

Tony's words were spoken gently and thoughtfully, not at all the yelling match Abi had envisaged, yet they had the same effect that yelling at her would have. The air whooshed from her lungs. He was right. Her legs wobbled, and she reached for the door to steady herself.

Tony grabbed her arm. 'Are you okay?'

Abi nodded. 'Sorry, I think I need to sit down.'

Tony guided her inside the house, down the hallway to the living room. Photos of Tony and his sister Judy as they were growing up covered the walls. Abi sank on to a pale-blue couch and put her head between her hands. She took deep breaths, trying to calm her mind. Eventually, she lifted her head. Tony was sitting opposite her, concern in his eyes.

'You're right,' Abi said. 'If Eric's investment was successful and he'd returned the money and profits to everyone, they wouldn't have necessarily been celebrating. It's more than just the money; it's a matter of trust.'

'You're only just realising this?'

Abi grimaced. 'No, I've known it for a long time. Part of me's hoped new information would come to light to suggest Eric was trying to do something to surprise everyone. To make their lives better. But it hasn't and it won't. I still can't wrap my head around why he did it. He'd provided amazing investment opportunities in the past but was never secretive about them. So why this one? Why didn't he tell us and let us decide if we wanted to go ahead?'

'It's my understanding that five million was the minimum investment the developer was accepting. Eric isn't the only investor to have lost that sum of money.'

Abi's eyes widened. 'Where did you hear that?'

'It was in the papers and on the news.'

Abi winced. She'd done her best to avoid all news channels. She didn't want to read about Eric or anything that had happened. It was bad enough living with the reality of it, let alone being subjected to a journalist's interpretation of the events or suffering through more guilt at the reality of what it had done to others.

She took a deep breath. 'The reason I wanted to visit today was to try and make you realise I didn't know about the property development when I helped you with your equity loan. Like you, I thought you were investing in the guaranteed capital investment. That it was a nice safe way for you and Mel to make some money at little risk, and to be honest, with interest rates so low at the moment, it makes more sense to have any additional funds or equity invested somewhere other than a home loan. I wouldn't have knowingly invested in the property development myself, let alone suggested you or any of our friends did.'

Tony sat up straighter, his eyes widening with surprise. 'Really? Why not?'

'They can be incredibly lucrative, but that comes at too high a risk. You know what I'm like. I've never liked risking money. I'd prefer to earn a guaranteed two percent interest than take a risk to earn ten or twenty percent. It drove Eric mad that I was so conservative.'

Tony's shoulders relaxed and a small smile played on his lips. 'Do you remember the Melbourne Cup a few years back? When

Eric insisted you put five hundred dollars on a horse? He'd won it earlier in the day, so it wasn't really your money, but you almost had a heart attack at the thought and refused to place the bet.'

Abi smiled. 'That was one occasion I wish I had done what Eric asked. If I had, I would have won thousands.'

'I know. That *donkey*, as Eric called it, that you would have bet on had forty-to-one odds. I remember watching him as it rounded the final corner and headed down the home straight miles ahead. I thought he was going to have a fit he was so enraged.'

'I know, but gambling's never been my thing, and he knew it. There was no way I'd risk five hundred on a horse. I'd already spent it, in my mind, on a weekend getaway down the Great Ocean Road. If I'd lost it, I would have felt like I'd lost that weekend with Eric.'

'Did you get your getaway?'

'I did. Mind you, it was with a very sulky Eric. He wouldn't shut up about the horse and how conservative I was. How that bet could have changed our lives.' Abi fell silent as she remembered the conversations that had taken place that weekend. The one thing she'd known for sure was she would never bet on anything again. Eric's reaction was too extreme. It had surprised her at the time, that he thought a get-rich-quick scheme like betting on a horse would work. Now, as she had the thought, she realised that his behaviour in investing in something that promised a quick return wasn't as unfathomable as she'd previously imagined. There were several times in their relationship when he'd laid a bet or invested impulsively, but from what she knew, it hadn't been at the expense of – or risk to – a client.

'Did you ever bet again after that?'

Abi shook her head. 'God, no. It put me off forever.'

Tony sat in silence, deep in thought. Eventually, he met Abi's eyes. 'You really didn't know about the development, did you?'

She shook her head. 'The first I learnt about it was when Eric died.'

'Okay, I believe you.' He sighed. 'It's still hard to believe, Abi. I honestly thought Eric was a good guy.'

Abi blinked back tears. She was relieved that Tony believed her, but hearing his words that he'd *thought* Eric was a good guy still hurt. She'd thought her husband had been a good guy too, one of the best. How wrong they'd both been.

'I owe you an apology,' Tony continued. 'I should have been more compassionate when Eric died, and I should have believed you. I haven't even asked how you're coping. How are you, Abi?'

The tears Abi had been trying to keep at bay spilled on to her cheeks. 'I've had better times.'

'I'm sorry. I should have been more supportive. Even at the funeral, I was pretty horrible.'

'It's okay,' Abi assured him. 'You weren't the only one not wanting to be there. At least you came, which was more than a lot of people, including most of Eric's family, did.'

'How's Hayden coping?'

'Haven't you heard? Gabe came and whisked him off to Sydney. He's seeing a psychologist and seems to believe his problems started well before Eric killed himself. That we were terrible parents, completely manipulative and controlling and he wants nothing to do with us – well, with me.'

'What? That's ridiculous.'

'Not according to Hayden. He's specifically asked that I leave him alone and have no contact with him while he tries to get his head together. He plans to live with Gabe and Imogen to finish his schooling and possibly go on to university in Sydney, with the goal of working with Gabe down the track.'

'But he knows how much Eric hated Gabe. It was hardly a secret and with excellent reason. The guy's a manipulative prick. He's only out for himself; we've all known that for years.'

Abi nodded. 'Unfortunately, he's got into Hayden's head at a time when he needed an out. I just hope Hayden can see through him at some stage. He's angry about Eric, and I imagine sad too, and he's blaming me for all sorts of things. It's still very raw, so I'm hoping time will help him with all of that.' Even as she said the words, Abi was sure that time was going to make no difference. It might if Hayden wasn't under Gabe's roof, but he was, and his uncle could be very persuasive and believable.

'Oh God, Abs, what a mess. What can I do to help?'

Abi smiled. 'Get your stuff and follow me back to your house. I need a drink, so you might have to make up the spare room for me.'

Tony frowned. 'Do you think Mel will take me back? I've acted like a real shit. Giving her ultimatums and threatening her. I'm not sure that I would if the situation was reversed.'

'Tell her you're sorry. It's been a huge shock for all of us, what's happened, and we've all had to deal with things the best we can. Mel loves you and is devastated to think you might not be together when the baby's born. She'll want you back, but she'll want a decent apology first.'

Mel's face, when Abi and Tony walked up the driveway with bags of his clothes in their hands, was something Abi would never forget. Her mouth dropped open, and after a moment's hesitation, she ran down the driveway and threw her arms around her husband. 'Are you coming home?'

He nodded.

She then threw her arms around Abi. 'I have no idea what you did or what you said, but I love you so much.' She stopped at that point, her face clouding over. 'You didn't promise to stay away or anything, did you, so that I didn't have to choose between the two of you?'

Abi shook her head as Mel pulled away from her, and Tony took her hand.

'I should never have made you choose between us. I love you, Mel.' His hand lowered to her stomach, and he caressed it gently. 'And mini-Mel. You guys are my family. I'm so sorry for how I reacted, it's just been such a shock, and I guess I didn't cope with the situation in a very mature way.'

'It's been a shock for all of us.' Mel's eyes connected with Abi's. 'Not something we would ever have expected to have to deal with.' She looked at her husband. 'Abi's been impacted more than anyone. It's so much more than financial.'

'I know.' He looked to Abi. 'And like I said, I'm sorry. From now on I am here to help in any way I can. Just tell me what I can do, okay?'

Abi smiled. 'To be honest, right now the only thing I need from you is exactly what you're doing. Being with Mel and being there for your family and promising you always will be.'

Tony's cheeks coloured as he pulled Mel closer to him. 'That's an easy promise to make.'

The next morning, Abi didn't linger. She hated goodbyes, and while Mel had no idea of the significance of her visit, or what the extra squeeze in her hug meant, Abi did and couldn't trust herself not to break down if she gave it too much thought. Instead, as she drove the seventy minutes to Melbourne, she did her best to think of the positive that had come out of her visit: Mel and Tony were back together. For the first time in months, something had gone right. Thank God.

After freshening up when she arrived home, Abi took one of the bottles of red wine she'd brought from her old house and walked the short distance to the next-door apartment. She knocked on Hope's door and waited. After her visit with Mel and Tony, she needed company. She didn't want to be alone with her thoughts, and on top of that, she owed Hope a proper thank you for convincing Alex to keep her employed.

The door opened and Max stood grinning at her, Hope just behind him. 'Hello, Mrs Abi,' he said in a very formal tone, and held out his hand.

Abi smiled and shook it. 'Hello, Mr Max. And how are you today?'

Max giggled and shook Abi's hand with so much force she thought her arm might drop off.

'Okay, Max, that's enough,' Hope said. 'Let Abi in.'

Abi stepped into the apartment and held out the bottle of wine. 'I brought this as a thank you. Hoped we might be able to open it and have a drink together. I appreciate what you did for me earlier in the week and feel that I haven't thanked you properly.'

'Don't be silly. I didn't do anything that you wouldn't have done for me. I'm just glad you still get to be our neighbour.' She grinned. 'See, it was for selfish reasons that I stood up for you.'

'Well, whatever the reason, how about we have a drink?'

Max ran back into the living area, shouting, 'To the park, to the park.'

'I was planning to take Max back to the park. We seem to live there at the moment. Would you like to come with us? We can take the wine and some glasses.'

Abi nodded. 'The park sounds lovely.'

'Let me get a bag and throw a few things in it.' Abi waited while Hope took some wine glasses from the kitchen and wrapped them in a tea towel before placing them into her backpack. 'Sorry,

I don't have a picnic basket or anything fancy. We can take a rug though, or just sit on one of the benches.'

Abi laughed. 'No need to apologise. I don't have a picnic basket either. I'm not sure I even have a rug.'

'It must be quite an adjustment. Looking at the quality of the furniture you brought with you, I assume your house was pretty swish.'

Abi nodded. 'It was, but it was just a house. Just things. When something like this happens, you realise what's important, and it's not things.'

Hope nodded with a look on her face that told Abi she understood. Once again, it made Abi wonder what Hope's story was.

'Are you ready, Max?'

Max came bounding back into the room. 'Do you think Jonesy will be there with his kite?'

'I doubt it, bud, but you can play on the slide and the swings. Sound good?'

Max nodded. 'Hopefully he will be though. Or Zeb – I'd like to see him again.'

'Sounds like Max has made some friends,' Abi said as they made their way down the stairs to the ground level and turned in the direction of the park.

'Kind of. Jonesy is a friend of the older couple who are looking after Max from time to time, but Zeb is his age. Now tell me, how are things with you? Did you see your sister?'

Abi filled Hope in on all that had happened since they'd last seen each other.

They reached the park and Hope spread out the rug, took the glasses from her bag and poured them both a drink. She clinked glasses with Abi. 'I'm so glad your visit was a success. It's stressful enough having a baby, let alone worrying over finances and your marriage falling apart.'

Abi sipped the red wine. Hope was right; having a baby was stressful. If she went through with her plans, she'd be adding a lot of stress to Mel's pregnancy. It wasn't an ideal situation. She gave herself a mental shake. The whole point of catching up with Hope was to not be alone with her thoughts. She needed some distraction. 'What about you?' she asked. 'How was your weekend?'

Before Hope had a chance to answer, Max came running over. 'Jonesy's here, Mum. Can I go and play with him? He's got a scooter just my size.'

Hope looked across to where Max was pointing. A large tattooed man waved to her, and she tentatively waved back.

'This is getting weird,' she said to Abi. 'He's a friend of Dot and William, and he lives in Prahran. Turning up at the park with a scooter is hardly coincidental.'

'Can I go?' Max asked again.

'Sure, hon, but stay on the path just here where I can keep an eye on you, okay? Can you tell Jonesy I'd like to talk to him?'

Max nodded and ran off. Jonesy high-fived him and then pulled a small helmet out of a bag he had with him. He helped Max put it on and then spoke to him for a minute or two before handing over the scooter.

'I think Max's been given a lesson,' Abi said. 'I take it you didn't know this guy was going to be here?'

Hope shook her head. 'He turned up yesterday with a kite when we were here. It's getting a bit creepy.'

'You'd better have a chat to him. Let him know you're feeling funny about it.'

Hope watched as Jonesy called encouragement to Max and then stood. 'I'll go and have a chat. Come with me; I'd love to get your take on him.'

Wine glasses in hand, they strode over to where Jonesy stood watching Max.

'Hey, Hope, how are you?'

'Good, thanks.' She introduced Abi before getting to what she wanted to say. 'This is a bit much, isn't it? Here with a kite yesterday and then a scooter today? You said you saw us in the park yesterday so stopped. What's the deal today?'

'I'm stalking you.' Jonesy's face was deadpan for a moment before he laughed. 'Sorry, you should see your face. I'm here because I promised William I'd drop the scooter off today or tomorrow. I now have to work tomorrow so thought I'd do it today. I saw Max when I was driving past the park, so thought I'd drop it to him instead of William.'

'He had you buy it?'

Jonesy nodded. 'Said he wanted Max to have his own transport. He had a scooter when he was about Max's age and loved the freedom it gave him, and he wanted Max to have the same. Also, Max has been spying on other scooter riders with the telescope from the balcony, saying he wished he had one.'

Hope nodded. 'That's very generous of William.'

'He is generous. It's one of his kindest features. He's so smitten with Max he'd probably buy him anything he wants.' He grinned. 'Hope you've got room for a pony!'

'That worries me,' Hope said. 'We hardly know him, and he's acting like Max is his grandson or great-grandson. We can't accept all of these gifts.'

Jonesy pursed his lips. 'He's making up for what he feels he lost, that's all. He'll overcompensate with Max, for sure. If you want to stop him, go ahead, but he's just an old man trying to enjoy his last few years. You can't understand what he went through when he lost Billy. His world changed completely. He's never recovered.'

Abi could relate to that; her world had changed completely, too. Different circumstances but same result.

'I get that William's lonely, but I would prefer if you didn't just stop off if you see us. It feels a bit strange, to be honest. Also, if this was supposed to be a gift from William, he might be upset that you've given it to Max.'

Jonesy frowned. 'You're right about William. That was thoughtless of me.' He looked across to where Max was scooting to and fro on the path. 'I can't take it back now. Let me just give William a quick call and see if he's happy with me leaving the scooter with Max, or whether he wants it taken to his place so he can be the one to give it to him on Tuesday.'

Jonesy pulled out his phone and stepped away from the women. They could still hear his side of the conversation. 'Bill, ol' man,' he joked. 'We've had a slight hiccup with Mission Scooter. I'm afraid young Max has already seen it and insisted he ride it. I hope you don't mind, but he's down at the park now on it.' Jonesy's smiled faded as he listened to William. He glanced at Hope and then returned to speaking. 'No, mate, I don't think that would be a good plan for today. Hope's down here with a friend and feels that we're taking over a bit. I just wanted to check whether you want me to leave the scooter with Max or drop it off to you as originally planned?' He nodded. 'Okay, no worries.'

He ended the call. 'William said Max is welcome to keep the scooter, and if he could bring it on Tuesday, he'd love to see him riding it.'

'What did you say wasn't a good plan for today?'

'William coming down to the park to watch Max on it. I feel a bit awful.' Jonesy ran his hand through his hair. 'You were right, he is upset about not being the one to give it to Max. I wasn't thinking.'

Abi watched the exchange with interest. She wondered if Hope noticed the wistful way Jonesy was looking at her? It was lovely for Hope to have found such a caring older couple who wanted to include Max in their lives, but as friendly as he seemed, Jonesy looked like the type of guy who just didn't think. She doubted there was any more to it than that with regards to dropping off kites or scooters. She did feel a little sorry for the older man though, missing out on seeing Max's delight at receiving his present.

'It was very generous of him,' Hope said. 'I'll make sure the scooter and helmet go to their place on Tuesday. Max will want to ride it over.'

'Okay, then I'll be off,' Jonesy said. He smiled at Abi. 'Lovely to meet you, and enjoy your afternoon.'

Abi smiled back and watched as he waved to Max before crossing the playing field towards his car. 'Nice guy.'

Hope nodded. 'He seems to be. A bit clueless though. Who would do that? Be asked to buy a present for someone and then give it to them instead of the person who asked them to buy it?'

Abi laughed. 'It's exactly what I was thinking. Do you think he's interested in you? The way he looked at you was, in my opinion, more than just as a friend.'

Hope blushed. 'No, he's in a relationship. He's just being nice.'

'A friendly guy in a nice package who's possibly missing a few brain cells.'

Hope raised an eyebrow. 'Nice package, hey?'

This time Abi felt her cheeks flush.

Hope squeezed her arm. 'I'm just teasing. I had noticed myself, if I'm completely honest. Let's go and sit back down and enjoy this delicious wine; it's such a beautiful afternoon.'

They returned to the picnic rug and had only been sitting down a few minutes when Max rode over to them on the scooter. 'Can I play on the slide now, Mumma?'

'Of course. Let's take your helmet off, and you can leave it here with Abi and me.' As Hope stood and helped him take off his helmet, her phone pinged with a message. It pinged a second time as she lay the scooter down on the ground.

'Someone wants you, Mumma.' Max pushed his foot in front of Hope, his shoelace undone.

Abi laughed as the phone pinged for the third time. 'Do you want me to read it to you?' It pinged again. 'Sounds like someone's keen to get hold of you.'

Hope frowned as she fixed Max's shoe. 'Weird. Can you read it? It's just at the top of my bag.'

Abi reached across and picked up the phone. '*Leave now*,' she read out. She glanced at Hope. 'That's strange. Hold on, let me see what the earlier ones said.' She clicked on the messages. 'The first three all say the same. *Leave now*.'

'Do we have to leave, Mumma?' Max asked. 'You promised I could play on the slide.'

'Of course you can, Maxy.' She patted him on the bottom. 'Go on and play. Abi and I have lots of wine to drink before we'll be ready to go home.'

'Yay!' Max ran off as Abi handed the phone across to Hope. 'You'd better check who sent you the message.'

Hope looked at the phone, her lips pursing in concentration. 'It's not from any of my contacts. I'll just ring it back and make sure the message is for me.' She held the phone to her ear, removing it after only a few seconds. 'It's from a disconnected number.'

'Probably a mistake in that case,' Abi said.

Hope nodded, slipping the phone back into her bag. 'Weird,' was all she said, but Abi couldn't help but notice her hand was shaking.

Chapter Eighteen

Lucinda found herself pacing up and down the apartment once she had Max settled for the night. The text messages she'd received at the park had unnerved her. She'd found it hard to concentrate on her conversation with Abi. Abi had asked her a couple of times if she was alright, but Lucinda hadn't wanted to explain the situation, so eventually had called Max over and said they should be getting home. As soon as they'd returned home and said their goodbyes to Abi she'd tried calling her mother. There was no answer. She hoped it was just a wrong number, but the lack of information, along with Tess not answering, put her on edge.

It was the second time something strange had happened at the park this weekend. First, there was Mary, and now the message. Was it possible the message had something to do with Mary? She picked up her phone and found Mary's number. She hesitated for a split second, wondering what she was going to say, but then pressed the call button. It went straight to voicemail. 'Hi Mary, it's Hope. Just ringing to see if you're feeling better. Call me to make arrangements for Zeb's birthday.'

She ended the call. Mary's phone was still connected, so it was unlikely that it was her who'd sent the message.

Her phone rang as she had this thought and she swiped it up from the couch, seeing Tess's number.

'Mum?'

'Hi love, I got your message. I'd planned to ring you tonight anyway.'

'Is everything okay?'

'Yes, other than this blasted appeal of Ryan's. It's scheduled for this week.'

Lucinda drew in a breath before asking the question she needed an immediate answer to. 'You didn't send me a message earlier telling me to *leave now*?'

'No, of course not. Why would I do that?'

'I got a message from what soon became a disconnected number. If it wasn't you, I'm assuming it was a wrong number. Other than work and the day care Max is at, no one else has my phone number or knows where we are.'

'That's a bit strange, love. But it wasn't from me. I am worried about you, though. Especially with this appeal looming.'

'What day is it scheduled for?'

'Wednesday.'

'Okay, well, let's do our best not to worry about it until then. There's nothing we can do except keep our fingers crossed.'

'And pray,' Tess added. 'How's Max going, and how are you? Do you need anything?'

They chatted for a few more minutes before Lucinda rang off, promising to call Tess on Wednesday. She sank on to the couch, deep in thought. The most likely scenario was a wrong number. Before this weekend she'd felt like she was finally beginning to relax for the first time since they'd arrived in Melbourne. Now she was completely on edge again.

Lucinda realised she should have had a second coffee as she and Max made their way the short distance to William and Dot's apartment building on Tuesday morning. She'd hardly slept the past two nights, and needed the extra pick-me-up. She'd have to wait until she got to work.

Max scooted happily alongside Lucinda, completely oblivious that she was lost in thought: about Mary's strange behaviour, the text message, and Ryan. What would she do if he got out? If he found her? She shuddered as Max turned into the driveway of the apartment building. She needed to do her best to block out all thoughts of Ryan, get Max settled with William and Dot and make her way to work. She'd need to pay more attention at work today too. The previous day she'd been so distracted she'd messed up three orders and dropped a loaded tray she was carrying.

William opened the door only moments after Max rang the bell.

'Thank you, Pa,' Max said, his face breaking into a wide smile. 'I love my new scooter.'

Lucinda found her lips twitching into a smile as William beamed at Max.

'With manners like yours, I'm sure there'll be more presents to come. Now come on in, and take that helmet off. We'll take your new wheels down to the park later, and you can show me all the tricks you can do on it.'

Lucinda followed them into the apartment, the sounds of dishes clinking together coming from the kitchen. 'I'll just say a quick hello to Dot,' Lucinda said, as William helped Max unbuckle his helmet. She smiled at William, hesitating as he ignored her and continued helping Max. She made her way through to the kitchen where Dot was unpacking the dishwasher.

'Hello, love. How are you?'

'I'm okay, thanks, Dot. Is William okay? He seemed a bit distracted. Perhaps a little annoyed or something?'

Dot pursed her lips. 'Really? That's not on. I'll have a word to him.'

'Oh no, there's no need. I was just worried that I might have done something to upset him.'

'Like stopping me from watching Max receive his gift.' William kept his voice low as he entered the kitchen.

Lucinda turned to face him.

'You're happy for him to have the scooter but stopped me from watching him enjoy it.'

'William.' The warning in Dot's voice did nothing to stop William from continuing.

'I wasn't planning to interrupt your outing, just enjoy seeing my gr—' He stopped as Dot threw him a murderous look. He cleared his throat. 'Enjoy seeing Max receive his gift.'

Had he been going to refer to Max as his grandson? Lucinda looked from William to Dot. William's face was red, anger boiling, whereas Dot looked as if she was going to kill her husband. Something wasn't right.

'William, Jonesy interrupted a catch-up I was having with a friend in the park. As much as I appreciate your generosity, we didn't have plans with any of you on Sunday, and I wasn't going to change that. If the gift is going to cause problems, then I'd rather you take it back. I'm certainly not expecting you to spend money on Max.'

'Of course you're not,' Dot said. 'Jonesy should have brought it to us like we'd planned, and William could have given it to Max today. William, it's not Hope's fault how it worked out, and she's probably sick of Jonesy turning up at the park when she and Max are there.' She turned to Lucinda. 'I'll have a word with him. I'd hate for you to think any of us were intruding.'

Lucinda looked at William; his face was set in a glare. 'I didn't think you or William were intruding, but Jonesy turning up with gifts when he doesn't live around here does seem rather strange. I think it might be best if I look after Max today. I appreciate all your help, but I can't leave him here when William's upset.'

William's face changed immediately and he wrung his hands together. 'Oh gosh, I'm sorry, Hope. I was just so disappointed. Of course we want to look after Max. We have to. It's our job; we have our instructions. Please don't change the arrangement.' He forced a smile. 'You're right. It's Jonesy I should be upset with, nobody else. I'll be less demanding. Dot will make sure of it, won't you, love?'

Dot nodded. 'Why don't you go and show Max those puzzles you were so keen to do, so I can chat with Hope.'

William opened his mouth as if to object, then smiled at Lucinda before going back through to the playroom.

'I'm sorry, love. Max has given him a new lease on life, one that he's missed so much since our Billy died. I'll chat to him about pulling back.'

'Max isn't Billy,' Lucinda said. 'Billy was an adult when he died; he wasn't four. I'm worried William's becoming too reliant on him. What if we had to go away suddenly? How would he cope?'

Dot frowned. 'Is that what you're planning?'

Lucinda shook her head. 'No, of course not. I'm just worried that William's becoming too attached to Max. It's not normal, him saying he has to look after Max and that it's his job. I appreciate the favour you've done me, but it certainly isn't a case of him *having* to look after Max.'

'You're right. It's not William's job. He's getting a little muddled these days. Nothing that would put Max in danger, but enough that I'll need to take him back for another check-up. We saw the doctor a couple of weeks ago, but I think they might need to run some tests.'

'What did he mean by he has *instructions*?' It was a very odd comment.

Dot shifted uncomfortably from side to side. 'He takes his responsibility to Max very seriously, and the doctor did suggest he consider some of his daily activities a job. He's been using that line about a lot of things. That he has *his instructions* to walk ten thousand steps, *his instructions* to eat leafy greens and fish.' She rolled her eyes. 'He uses it whenever he wants something. Last night he had *his instructions* to drink a very large whisky. Having things well ordered in his day gives him a routine and structure, and he copes much better. As soon as something happens away from the plan, it throws him. The scooter was a good example, and I could kill Jonesy. I still don't understand why he did that. It was William's idea and William's present to give.'

Lucinda nodded, thinking back to Abi's words about Jonesy: *nice guy in a nice package who's possibly missing a few brain cells.* She felt sorry for William, but she still wasn't sure she should leave Max.

'I won't leave William alone with Max, if it makes you feel more comfortable,' Dot said. 'I'll join in their games and go to the park with them. Please, Hope, it means so much to William. I do understand your concerns, but I promise you he'd protect Max like a lion would its cub. He adores him.'

Which is part of the problem. Though Lucinda kept her thought to herself.

'Leave him today, and I'll make sure you're happy with William and how he behaves. I think Max has loved all of the attention, so while it might be a bit too much, he does seem very happy.'

Lucinda couldn't argue with that. She sighed. 'Okay. Let's just see how it goes. I do appreciate everything you're doing. Don't get me wrong.'

Dot took a step towards her and pulled her into a hug. 'You look tired. Head off to work and don't give us another thought. Max will have a great day, I promise.'

Lucinda pulled out of the hug and smiled at Dot. 'Okay, thank you. I'll just go and say goodbye to Max, and then I'd better dash.'

Lucinda rang Dot four times from work, something she'd never done before. She was already on edge, and William's weird behaviour had rattled her even more. Dot put Max on the phone each time she rang, and she could hear the pure delight in his voice. He was definitely having a good time. The fourth time she rang, he asked her why she was ringing and could she please stop. 'I want to go to the park but if you keep ringing it will never happen.' Lucinda had laughed, told him she loved him and hung up, promising not to ring back.

In all honesty, her concerns about William were the least of her worries, but it was the one thing she could do something about. The situation with Ryan was a waiting game, and the text message was a mystery she'd probably never have an answer to. Even so, when Alex gave her the option to leave work half an hour early, she took it. She hurried to the bus stop and caught an earlier bus than she'd planned. She was knocking on William and Dot's door just after four thirty.

The door opened, and Lucinda couldn't help but laugh. The largest bouquet she'd ever seen greeted her. A tiny pair of legs poked out the bottom of the flowers. Max stuck his head out so she could see him and grinned. 'These are from William to say sorry.' He pushed them at her. 'And they're heavy.'

Lucinda took the flowers from Max, breathing in their delicious perfume.

'Max is right,' William said, approaching Lucinda. 'They're my apology, which I hope you'll accept.'

Lucinda nodded. 'I just hope we're not overstaying our welcome.'

'Of course you're not. I was being silly about the scooter. I should have been angry with Jonesy, not you. He knew it was a gift I was looking forward to surprising Max with, so I was rather taken aback when I discovered he was the one to give it to him.'

Lucinda nodded. She could understand that. 'Let's forget about this morning and move on, shall we?'

William rewarded her with one of his beaming smiles.

'Hello, love.' Dot joined them. 'I see you got the *little* bunch of flowers William organised.' She winked. 'He doesn't do anything by halves, my William.'

'I don't know if they'll fit in my apartment,' Lucinda said. 'It's not very big. Maybe we could divide them up into two bunches, and you could keep one here? If that's okay with you, William?'

'Of course it is,' William said. 'You do whatever you like with them. Just know that they come from my heart, and the apology is genuine.'

Lucinda followed Dot into the kitchen, and the two women set about dividing the flowers into two. 'You know, I don't think we've even got a vase,' Lucinda said. 'Maybe you should keep all of them.'

'Don't be silly. You can borrow one of ours,' Dot said. She stood staring around the kitchen for a moment. 'If I can remember where any of them are, that is.'

Lucinda laughed. 'Be careful; you're beginning to sound like William.'

Dot gave her a wry smile and then began opening cupboards. Eventually, she pulled out two large vases from the very back of one. She examined them as if she'd never seen them, before holding them up. 'Which one would you prefer?'

'Whichever is your least favourite.'

Dot debated for a moment, then held one out to Lucinda. 'To be honest, I use them so infrequently I'd completely forgotten what I even have. Today's flower purchase would be the first time William's bought flowers in years.'

They arranged the flowers in the vases and Max appeared. 'I've tidied up the playroom. It's all ready for tomorrow.'

'You're at day care again tomorrow, buddy,' Lucinda said. 'You'll be back here on Thursday though.'

Max frowned. 'But William said I would be coming here tomorrow. He promised.'

'He must have got his days wrong, Max. Tomorrow's Wednesday, which is a day care day.'

'Sorry, Maxy old boy,' William said, entering the kitchen. 'Completely forgot about the new arrangement. We'll see you on Thursday, though.'

'Okay.' Max's bottom lip dropped in disappointment.

'Time to go home,' Lucinda said. 'Thank you again for the flowers, William, they're divine.'

William mock-bowed. 'You're welcome, my lady, and once again, please accept my humble apologies.'

Lucinda smiled. 'Nothing to be sorry for. We'll see you on Thursday.'

Max said his goodbyes to the older couple, and they made their way down from the third floor to the apartment building's entrance.

'Oh no,' Max cried. 'I left Mr Fizz in the playroom. I won't be able to sleep tonight.' He immediately burst into tears.

'Don't cry, hon, we'll pop straight back up and get him, okay?'

Max nodded, tears still streaming down his face.

'Let's leave the flowers here for a minute. They're getting a bit heavy.' Lucinda put the vase on a small bench near the lifts and Max pressed the up button. They rode up to level three and stepped out. Max froze as they heard raised voices coming from inside William and Dot's apartment.

Lucinda put her finger to her lips, indicating for Max to be quiet as she strained to listen to what they were saying.

'You can't get angry like that,' Dot was saying. 'We'll regret it if we mess any of this up.'

'It isn't fair,' William replied. 'Us not knowing what the outcome's going to be. It's making me crazy. Maybe we need to talk to her about it.'

There was silence for a few moments before Dot answered. 'We need to be careful, William. Just go along with things for a bit longer.'

Shivers ran down Lucinda's spine as she eavesdropped. What were they talking about?

Dot continued. 'We need to wait and see what happens. Things could be very different by the end of the week. We need more information before we do anything at all. Okay?'

The lift opened, causing Lucinda to jump, and it drowned out William's answer.

'Jonesy,' Max cried in delight.

Jonesy grinned at Max and then Lucinda. 'Just leaving, are you?'

'We came back to get Mr Fizz,' Max said. 'But William and Dot are yelling at each other, so we're waiting for a good time to knock.'

Jonesy's eyebrows drew together. 'Really? That's unusual. What are they arguing about?'

'Dot said they'll regret it if they mess any of this up, and they need to wait and see what happens,' Max said. 'That something might be different later in the week.' He turned to Lucinda. 'That's what she said, wasn't it?'

Lucinda nodded. 'I'm worried he was talking about us.'

Jonesy's face paled and he shook his head. 'No, it won't be.' He lowered his voice. 'Don't say anything to them, but William had some tests done a couple of weeks ago which show a few issues. It looks like he might need some medication to control some outbursts he's been having. They're nothing major and can be treated, but Dot wouldn't want you to know. She's worried you won't let Max visit. William thought maybe he should tell you, so if he does anything weird, it would explain the behaviour. It's a bit of a catch twenty-two for them.'

Lucinda frowned. Dot's story about the doctor visit didn't quite match up to Jonesy's, but then again, she wouldn't want Lucinda to know about any outbursts, even though she had seen one herself. 'He got angry with me this morning over the scooter, which is probably what Dot was referring to. But he's apologised and we're all good. Thanks for the heads-up, though. I might keep Max in day care until we know what's going on with William.'

Jonesy's face clouded over. 'Oh, don't do that. He would never get angry with Max or hurt him. He'll be gutted if you do that.'

'It's only Thursday,' Lucinda said. 'I can say Max is sick or something so he doesn't have to know.'

'You can't lie, Mumma,' Max said.

'No, you can't,' Jonesy agreed. 'I'm not working on Thursday. How about I come over and hang out with them for the day? That way, I can keep an eye on William, and Max still gets his day with his adopted grandparents.'

'I'm not sure,' Lucinda said. It was all beginning to feel too hard. 'I'm thinking day care might be the better option moving forward.'

'Give it a little bit longer. They're good people, Hope.' He rubbed his chin. 'I feel terrible about the scooter. It's me you should be upset with, not them. I do things without thinking sometimes.'

He pulled a business card from his pocket and handed it to her. 'Let me help out on Thursday to make up for it. That way you're not paying for care, Max gets his good day, and William doesn't kill me for upsetting you. My number's on here so you can call me if you want to check up on Max during the day.'

Lucinda nodded. 'Okay. Thank you.'

Max cheered, bringing a smile to Lucinda's lips. Jonesy grinned and high-fived him just as the front door opened.

William's mouth dropped open in surprise as he saw them all standing there. He had Mr Fizz in his arms. He held him out to Max. 'Mr Fizz called out to me that you'd forgotten him, young man. I was just about to bring him over to your house. You've saved me a trip.'

Max scooped the soft toy into his arms and hugged him tightly. 'Thank you, Pa; I'll never forget him again.'

William laughed. 'That's no trouble. We could always have returned him.' His smile slipped as he turned to Jonesy. 'We weren't expecting you tonight. Anything wrong?'

Jonesy shook his head. 'You're getting a bit forgetful, old man. I promised to help Dot put up the new shelves in the laundry, remember?'

William looked blankly at him for a moment and then nodded. 'Of course, silly me. Come on in and you can get started.' He smiled at Lucinda and Max. 'And we'll see you two on Thursday.'

They caught the lift back down to the ground floor, collected the flowers and started to make their way home.

'Do you think Pa's okay?' Max asked as they walked towards the apartment block. 'He seems to forget things, but he never gets angry with me.'

'I'm sure he's fine,' Lucinda said. 'Things can change in our brains as we get older. He might just need some medicine to help him.'

'And I can still play with him?'

'Of course you can.'

Max cheered.

Lucinda was glad Jonesy had been there to explain the argument they'd overheard. The glimpses of forgetfulness and anger they'd seen in William made her wonder if he was developing signs of dementia. She hoped for his and Dot's sake that he wasn't. He was a lovely man and it would be heart-breaking to see him deteriorate. She hoped for Max's sake too that it wouldn't be the case.

As they walked through the front door of their apartment, Lucinda's phone pinged with a text message. She put the flowers down on the kitchen bench and pulled out her phone. The message was from her mother. She settled Max in front of the television before picking up her phone to call her.

'Lu?'

'Of course it's me, Mum. How many other people have this number?'

Tess gave a nervous laugh. 'Sorry, I'm a bit on edge with this whole thing about Ryan getting out. If he does get out, we're going to have to be even smarter with our phone calls. I thought perhaps I should leave the phone switched off and only turn it on when I know I'm here alone.'

'You should do that anyway, Mum. Let's be extra careful now.'

'He called me this morning. Said that he'd be out one way or another by the end of the week.'

A shudder ran through her. 'What did he mean by *one way or another*?'

'I don't know, but the way he said it concerned me. He sounded so cocky. So sure of himself. I guess we'll find out over the next few days what he meant. Now, let's change the subject. Tell me about Melbourne.'

'I wish you could come and visit. We've made a few friends and are beginning to fit in around here.'

'I'm glad, Lu, really I am. Now all we have to do is hope for all of our sakes that this time tomorrow Ryan is still behind bars.'

Lucinda nodded, crossing her fingers as she did.

Chapter Nineteen

Abi put a cross through a box on the calendar she'd attached to the kitchen wall. There were twenty-four days until her birthday. Twenty-four days to put her affairs in order. She was receiving multiple texts a day from Laila, who seemed to be going overboard with party planning. She'd done the same herself for Eric's fortieth, but over two hundred people came to that. She'd be lucky if five attended her party. Laila's latest text said she'd invited Hope. With Mel, Tony and Laila, that would bring the numbers to four guests, at least.

Abi still had the problem of how she was going to end her life. She sighed, sitting down at the kitchen table and opening her laptop. It wasn't something she could put off any longer. She was going to have to work this out.

Over the next hour, Abi wouldn't have been surprised if at any moment the police had turned up to see if she'd committed suicide. The amount of Google searches she'd initiated in trying to find out the best approach to the situation was sure to ring alarm bells somewhere. She was impressed that each time she typed in things like *how to kill yourself* or *can sleeping pills kill you*, the first results to pop up were always suicide helplines. She wondered if this helped many people change their minds about what they were planning to do, or at least made them seek help first.

Her research led her to encounter a problem she hadn't anticipated: it was almost impossible to kill yourself painlessly. She'd assumed she could buy something over the counter which, if she took enough of it, would put her to sleep and she'd never wake up. But it appeared too many people had done that in the past. The drugs today were made with much milder chemicals, so overdose was less likely to lead to death. It was, however, likely to lead to brain damage and all sorts of other horrible results. That was the last thing she wanted to put Mel, Laila or Hayden through. She either needed to be in their lives as a healthy person or not at all.

She continued her search. The state of Victoria had recently passed the Voluntary Assisted Dying Bill, but unfortunately – or possibly fortunately – she didn't meet any of the eligibility criteria. To cash in one's life insurance didn't feature as a valid reason, which mainly revolved around suffering incurable, advanced and progressive diseases.

She was going to have to find pills that would do it. She'd been amazed to discover that Eric's approach, to shoot himself in the head, only had an eighty percent chance of being successful. She shuddered just thinking of what must have been going through his mind in the minutes and seconds leading up to pulling the trigger. Did he feel remorse? Despair? Relief?

As she continued to search, she discovered methadone could do the trick. But where would she get that from? Could she really not find a solution to this? Surely it shouldn't be that hard to kill yourself? Her thoughts went back to the comment made at the lunch at Fleming's. That Trisha Black had ordered Ambien online and used it to take her life. Perhaps that was the answer?

Half an hour later, Abi hummed along to Kylie Minogue's version of 'Celebration' that was blaring from one of the ground-floor apartments. She'd have to go and ask them to turn it down, but right now it suited her mood perfectly. She should be celebrating; celebrating that she'd just ordered enough pills to put an elephant out for the count. Coupled with a bottle of her favourite Merlot and she had her permanent sleeping cocktail. As long as they made it through customs in a couple of weeks, she'd have her means of exiting the world.

Hearing shouting coming from downstairs, Abi decided it was time to go down and sort out the loud-music issue. As she slipped on her shoes, her phone rang. Her stomach clenched as she saw Gabe's name. She'd been tempted to ring him after the discussion with Hayden and Gavin the previous week, but had decided against it. He was a master manipulator, and that was exactly what he was doing in this situation. Eric had always said it wasn't worth talking to him; he thought he was right about everything and would talk and talk until eventually he wore you down and had you agreeing with him.

She considered not answering but then worried that something might have happened to Hayden. She put the phone to her ear. 'Gabe, is everything alright?'

'If you mean is Hayden okay, then yes, physically he is.'

'But?'

'But he's having a hard time dealing with everything. Gavin spoke to you last week, didn't he?'

'He did.'

'So you understand that Hayden wants a separation from you?'

'I understand that he needs time and space to come to terms with his feelings, yes.'

'He wants more than that, Abi. He wants to separate from you, and he wants me to adopt him legally.'

Abi gasped. 'What? You can't do that.'

'We can, actually, but it would be a lot easier with your permission.'

'You'll never get that.'

'Really? You'd prefer to see your son continuing to suffer because of your stubbornness?'

Abi was lost for words. This was not something she'd ever contemplated. She didn't even know it was a possibility. 'Gabe, if Hayden's serious, he needs to talk to me directly. And I don't mean on the phone. He needs to come to Melbourne and spend time with me. If he does that and still wants to ask me to consider this absurd idea, I will at least give it some thought.' She ended the call, not waiting for his response.

With a trembling hand, she put the phone down and closed her eyes. For her son to reject her and then side with the enemy was incredibly hurtful. He was sixteen. Why would he want to be adopted by Gabe? They already shared the same surname. What would it mean?

Her phone pinged with a text message.

> Hayden will come down on Saturday to see you. I'll send you his flight details so you can pick him up. Don't be selfish. This is about Hayden, not you.

Abi stared at the message, anger welling inside her. Was this about Hayden, or was it about Gabe? All these years later, was this his attempt at payback? His words played in a loop in her head. *One day, when you least expect it, I'll take something you love away from you.*

She did her best to silence the words. Regardless of Gabe's motivations, it would be her last opportunity to convince Hayden that she loved him and hadn't done anything wrong. To get him to understand that Gabe was manipulating him. She glanced at her calendar as she had this thought. If she was successful in convincing Hayden of this, could she go through with her plan? She needed to for financial reasons, but if she was able to repair her relationship with him, then it was entirely out of the question. This visit was her last hope of winning her son back, and her last hope for having a reason to live. She did her best to push these thoughts out of her mind as she hurried down the stairs in the direction of the loud music.

'Whoa!' Hope laughed as Abi nearly collided with her and Max at the bottom of the stairs. 'Where's the fire?'

Abi stopped and smiled. 'Sorry, thought I'd better go and sort out this loud music before someone complains. I'm a bit distracted.' She turned to Max, who was riding to and fro on his small red scooter. 'Hey Max, how's the scooter going?' He grinned and pushed even harder down on one leg, speeding away from her in response. Abi laughed. 'Looks like it's going well.'

'He loves it,' Hope said. 'I guess I should be grateful to my fairy grandparents.'

'*Guess?*'

Hope shrugged. 'They're great, but they're a bit suffocating, and William's been acting a bit weird. Anyway, enough about them, what's going on with you? You said you were distracted. Anything I can do to help?'

Abi hesitated only for a second before deciding to confide in Hope. 'My son's returning from Sydney on Saturday to discuss his reasons for wanting his uncle to legally adopt him.'

Hope's mouth dropped open. 'What? How old is he?'

'Sixteen.'

'Can you even do that? And if yes, why would he want to? Is your relationship that bad?'

'Yes, with my permission, he could do it, and I guess *yes* is also the answer to your other question. He pretty much decided overnight that our relationship was horrific and he's been mistreated, and he's not going to forgive me for anything that's happened.'

'Even though none of it's your fault?'

Abi raised an eyebrow. 'I should probably get you to talk to him. You did such a good job with Alex, maybe Hayden would believe you.'

'I'm happy to. Just tell me what time to turn up and I'll be there.'

'I was only kidding, but thank you. I know you would. Now, I was given two bottles of wine by the tenants in apartment four the other day as a thank you for getting their hot water service repaired. Why don't you come over for a drink tonight?'

Hope bit her lip, her gaze moving to Max who was trying to do wheelies on his scooter.

'Or,' Abi said, 'I'm happy to bring the wine to you if that's easier with Max and his bedtime?' Hope didn't respond, making Abi assume she'd put her on the spot. 'I'd better go and sort out this music. No pressure over the wine.' She gave a nervous laugh. 'I'm probably drinking too much anyway. I just thought it would be nice to have a chat and a laugh.'

Hope's face flushed red with embarrassment. 'I'd love to, but I'm expecting a call later, and it might interrupt the evening.'

'Another night then. You just let me know.' Abi waved at Max as she passed him and his scooter, and followed the pathway to apartment two where the music had cranked up a notch louder than before.

Hope's reaction was strange. She could have easily said it didn't suit her, but she appeared fidgety and on edge. Abi would love to know what was going on with her. That message in the park the other day had definitely unnerved her. *Leave now.* Hope had assured her it was a wrong number, but was it?

Abi sighed. She didn't need to get caught up in Hope's problems. She had enough of her own. She stopped outside apartment two and rapped loudly on the door.

Chapter Twenty

Lucinda had been a jittery bundle of nerves all day. Ryan's appeal was scheduled for three o'clock, and now, a little after four, she expected to hear from Tess any minute. Immediately after saying no to Abi, the guilt had set in. She'd said no because, regardless of the outcome, she knew she'd need to absorb whatever information Tess relayed, and having a guest was not going to allow that. But Abi was going through such a horrendous period she should have made the time for her. The disappointment had shown on her neighbour's face.

'Come on, buddy,' she said to Max. 'Let's take your scooter upstairs and have a snack while we wait for Grandma to call.'

Max scooted to the bottom of the stairs and handed his scooter over to Lucinda. She helped him take off his helmet before carrying them both up ahead of him. She glanced at her watch. Surely the appeal would be finished by now?

She unlocked the door. 'Go and wash your hands and I'll cut up some fruit, okay?'

As Max headed to the bathroom to wash up and she moved the scooter and helmet into the small cupboard in the hallway, Lucinda's phone rang. She slammed the cupboard door shut and pulled the phone from her pocket as she moved into the living room.

'Mum? What happened?'

Her mother's reply was so soft, Lucinda could hardly hear her.

'Wait a minute, the line's bad. I'll put you on speaker.' She switched the call to speaker and placed the phone on the coffee table in front of her. 'Can you hear me?'

'I can, and it's good news, love. The appeal was rejected.'

Lucinda sank on to the couch. 'Oh, thank God.' She shut her eyes, willing the tears of relief to stay away. She'd probably be back on edge when he did eventually get released, but at least having some time between now and then gave her the chance to adjust to her new identity and her new life.

'You okay, Lu?'

'Relieved, Mum. Really relieved.'

'Me too.'

'Did you speak to him at the appeal?'

'No, but I've already had a message asking me to go and see him. I'll do that tomorrow afternoon.'

'I'm so sorry I've put you in this position. Part of my leaving was so I didn't have to visit him and go through the charade of pretending I care. Now you're having to do that for me.'

'I'd do anything to keep you safe. You know that. Don't worry about it. The main thing is he's not getting out again for at least a couple of years. Hopefully this appeal stunt will end up hurting his chances of early release as well. Video evidence was brought forward by the prosecution that clearly shows Ryan bashing the victim.'

Lucinda sucked in a breath. 'Really? Why didn't they use that the first time around?'

'Apparently it disappeared from evidence, but the police had backup copies they suddenly found. It all sounded fishy. The prosecution suggested their silence was bought the first time around, but something's happened since if they've come forward. Regardless of why, it was pretty damning evidence. So you can relax for a couple of years at least.'

Lucinda could hear the smile in Tess's voice. 'I wish we were with you, Mum. I miss you so much.' The tears ran down her face.

'Me too, love. Don't get upset though. I might be able to come down for a visit in the next few weeks. I was thinking that I could book a flight through the travel agency in town to Sydney and tell them I'm staying with friends, but I'll also book a flight online to Melbourne from Sydney so I can walk from one gate to the other.'

Lucinda was silent for a moment. She would love to see her mum.

'Lu, what do you think? I thought if I did it that way, if Ryan wants to check up on me he'll find out I'm in Sydney.'

'What if he has you followed and they see you on the plane to Melbourne?'

'Do you think he'd go that far? I truly believe he thinks I'm on his side. I doubt he'll have me followed at all, but at least making the Sydney detour will make it less likely he'd find me.'

'I'd love you to, Mum, I really would. But let me think about it first. I'm just a bit worried it's too early. Ring me tomorrow night after you visit the prison, and we'll talk about it then, okay?'

'Will do. Now, is that gorgeous grandson of mine around?'

Lucinda turned to call out to Max to find him standing only metres away. She flinched. What had he heard and what had he understood? 'It's Grandma, bud. You ready to say hello?'

Max nodded and sat on the couch beside Lucinda. After a few minutes of talk, Lucinda ended the call and turned to Max. 'It was lovely speaking to Grandma, wasn't it?'

He nodded.

'Did you hear what I was talking to her about before you spoke to her?'

Max averted his gaze.

Lucinda took his hands in hers and crouched down to his eye level. 'You're not in trouble if you did. I just need to know what you heard so I can explain anything you didn't understand.'

'I heard you say you miss her and then you cried.' Max hung his head, his face full of sadness. 'Don't like it when Mumma cries.'

Lucinda stroked his hair. 'I do miss her, Maxy, but that's okay because I get to talk to her lots. Did you hear me say anything else?'

He shook his head, his eyes not meeting hers. 'I closed my ears after that, so I heard nothing.'

'Good boy. Now, I think we should start preparing some food for dinner. There's some pasta in the cupboard. Shall we use up the leftover chicken and vegetables and make cheesy chicken pasta?'

Max's eyes lit up. It was one of his favourites. 'Can we invite Mrs Abi for cheesy chicken pasta?'

Lucinda's eyes widened in surprise. 'Abi? Why do you want to invite her?'

'She looks sad sometimes. I don't think she has any friends so we should be her friends.'

Lucinda smiled. 'Well, in that case, how about you go and invite her. I'll stand by our door so that you can see me but she can't, and you can knock and ask. Does that sound good?'

Max nodded and rushed to the front door. He flung it open and was hammering on Abi's door before Lucinda had a chance to follow him.

'Mrs Abi, Mrs Abi,' he called.

'What's all the commotion?' Abi asked, opening her door. 'Is everything alright, Max? Where's Mum?'

'You can't see her.' He giggled, looking over to Lucinda, who now stood in the doorway just out of sight. 'But I can. I'm inviting you to come for dinner. I'm cooking my famous cheesy chicken pasta.'

'I'd love to come, Max. What time would you like me?'

'At dinner time, Mrs Abi.'

Abi laughed. 'Okay, I'll be there at dinner time, and tell your mum I'll bring the wine I mentioned and a special hug for the chef.'

'That's me.' Max clapped his hands together. 'I am the chef, and dinner will be yummy.'

'Excellent. I'll see you at about six, okay? If I get there too early, you can always send me home until you're ready for me.'

'See you at six.' Max rushed back inside the apartment and shut the door. 'Time to cook!'

Allowing Max to help cook meant cleaning up a mess. Max scooped up spilt cheese and stuffed it in his mouth, eliciting a raised eyebrow from Lucinda. 'You have to wash your hands each time you do that. You know that, don't you?'

Max smiled and washed his hands for the fifth time. 'What present should we buy Zeb?' he asked as he ran his hands under the tap. 'I'm going to his party soon, aren't I?'

Lucinda stopped what she was doing, realising Mary hadn't called her back. 'You're right. Mary was going to get in touch with the plans. I'll ring her later to check. As for a present, I'm not sure. What do you think?'

'Maybe some cars like my little ones?'

Lucinda smiled. 'Sounds good. I'll ring Mary as soon as we've cleaned up here and see if it's still going ahead.'

They finished their dinner preparations and cleaned up the kitchen. 'Why don't you go and put some cutlery on the table,' Lucinda suggested as Max danced from foot to foot asking if it was six o'clock yet. 'We've still got an hour until Abi comes over.' Max pulled open the drawer with the cutlery, ready to get on with the job.

Lucinda picked up her phone and scrolled through her contacts until she found Mary's number. She put the phone to her ear and waited. It clicked straight to voicemail. 'Hey, Mary, it's Hope. Just checking to see if you're feeling better and also to ask if you were still planning to have a get-together for Zeb's birthday? Max is excited to see him. Look forward to hearing from you.' She ended the call and put the phone down.

At six o'clock on the dot, there was a rap on the front door. 'I'll get it.' Max ran to the door.

Lucinda switched off the television and stood ready to greet Abi. She felt like she owed her an apology.

The door slammed, and Max reappeared pulling Abi by the hand into the living area. 'I'll serve dinner,' he said.

'No,' Lucinda reminded him. 'Remember we said we'd eat a little bit later tonight so we can have a glass of wine first and chat. And you were going to do something special while we did that.'

Max grinned. 'I'm going to watch *Shaun the Sheep* on the iPad,' he told Abi. 'I'm not usually allowed my iPad after six o'clock, so it's a big deal!'

'It certainly is.' Abi smiled and held a bottle of Shiraz out to Lucinda as Max rushed off to the bedroom. 'Thanks for the invitation. I wasn't sure after our earlier conversation that tonight suited you?'

Lucinda's cheeks burnt. 'Sorry. I was a bit distracted waiting for a phone call.'

'No need to explain. It's lovely to be here. I need to get away from my thoughts tonight.'

'Go and sit down,' Lucinda said. 'I'll get some glasses for the wine, and then we can relax.'

Abi sat down in the small lounge area.

'Have you had any ideas on how to deal with the situation with Hayden?' Lucinda asked. She poured them both a glass of wine and sank back on to the couch.

'I'm not sure what to think about it right now,' Abi said. 'He'll be here on Saturday so we can discuss what's going on, but until I speak with him, I have no idea why he's even contemplating doing this. One thing I know is it wouldn't have been his idea. I doubt he'd even know it was an option, whereas my brother-in-law would.'

'What would being adopted even mean at sixteen? I can't wrap my head around it. I'd understand if he was younger or in foster care or something like that, but he's already living with his uncle, and you're his mother. You've said previously you were close with him before your husband's death. Is that right?'

Abi nodded. 'We were a very tight-knit family. Anyway, let's not talk about it. I can't do anything until Saturday when I speak to Hayden. Tell me about you instead. How's the job going? Is Alex treating you okay?'

The discussion moved to their day-to-day lives, and it was only when Max appeared at close to seven that Lucinda realised time was getting away.

'Sorry, hon,' she said as she glanced at her watch. 'You already made the cheesy chicken sauce so all we need to do is boil the pasta, and we'll be ready to serve.'

'*I'll* be ready to serve,' Max said. 'I am the chef, so I serve the food.'

Fifteen minutes later, Lucinda wiped the edges of the last bowl with a paper towel, ready for Max to deliver it to the kitchen table. His serving technique had caused a few splatters. Lucinda was sure Abi wouldn't be complaining about the presentation once she tasted Max's sauce. It was a delicious recipe.

The three of them squeezed around the small kitchen table.

'Do you like my pasta?' Max asked before Abi had even had a chance to taste it.

Abi scooped up a forkful, rolling her eyes in appreciation when she tasted the food. 'Oh, Max, this is to die for. It's delicious. Thank you.'

Max beamed in delight. 'I should make this for William and Dot one day.' He turned to Lucinda. 'Or maybe for Grandma when she comes. I can't wait to see her.' He shovelled a large forkful of pasta into his mouth, his eyes shining.

Lucinda's gut twisted. He had overheard their conversation.

'I think she'd love it, Max.' Abi turned to Lucinda. 'I assume that's your mum, Hope?'

Lucinda nodded. 'She's not coming to visit, though. I think Max might be a little muddled.'

Max shook his head, swallowing his mouthful. 'No, I'm not. You spoke to her earlier, and that's what she said. She said she would fly to Sydney first and then here and that Daddy wouldn't know anything about it.'

'Okay, Max. Let's finish our dinner, and we'll talk about this later, alright?'

'But I wanna see Grandma.'

'I know you do, hon, and we'll sort something out. But we'll talk about it later.'

Max's eyes widened, and he looked from Lucinda to Abi. He dropped his fork and clasped his hand over his mouth.

'It's okay, Max. You haven't said anything wrong.'

He shook his head, tears filling his eyes. 'I did. It's our secret, and I talked about it. I'm sorry, Mumma.'

'I've got lots of secrets, Max,' Abi said. 'And they are much bigger than being about someone coming to stay. And do you know what? I'm amazing at keeping secrets. I won't tell anyone anything about what you said before. In fact, I don't even remember what it was so I can't tell them anyway.'

Max looked from Lucinda to Abi, a small smile spreading across his face. 'Phew. See, Mumma, it's all fine. Abi is good at secrets, and I'll try to get better at them. I didn't even tell her about Dadda in prison or us escaping, so she doesn't know much anyway.'

Lucinda drew in a breath, unable to look at Abi as Max went back to happily eating his pasta.

Abi spoke, forcing Lucinda to look in her direction. She didn't seem shocked or even surprised. In fact she was behaving as if this was a completely normal thing to learn about your neighbour. 'Let's change the subject for now. I totally understand if you have things you'd like to keep to yourself. As I said to Max earlier, I don't even remember the conversation so certainly won't be repeating anything I've heard.'

Lucinda nodded gratefully.

They continued to eat, Abi doing her best to ask Max questions to break the otherwise awkward silence that had fallen on the room.

After they'd declared Max's meal a success, Abi offered to read Max a story before his bedtime. He rushed off to brush his teeth and a few minutes later called out to Abi that it was Hairy Maclary time.

Lucinda waited until she heard Max's bedroom door close before sinking on to the couch, her head in her hands. It wasn't just that Max had told Abi, it was that he was four and was likely to tell Dot and William, people at day care and anyone else they met. Most people would think nothing of it, but if someone was interested, they might start poking around and trace her identity back to Dorford. If that happened, the likelihood of Ryan finding her suddenly increased.

Lucinda pulled herself up off the couch and went into the kitchen to finish clearing the table. How was this going to work moving forward? Max was little and likely to talk. Maybe her earlier thought that she tell him Ryan was dead would be the way to go. Her heart contracted at the thought of devastating him with news that wasn't even true.

She turned, startled by Abi's voice as she walked back into the kitchen, a smile on her lips. 'Hairy Maclary was a hit, and Max fell asleep reciting the last sentence. I wish Hayden had been that easy at his age. As for Max's secrets and your business, it's none of mine. Really, I don't need to know anything. But I need you to know that I'm here if you need anything at all. No questions, no judgement. You're a decent person and a great mum. I don't need to know anything more than that.'

Lucinda stared at her; Abi was her only real friend in Melbourne, and right now, a friend was what she needed. Someone she could trust and someone she could confide in. She picked up the bottle of wine from the counter and poured them both a fresh glass. 'I think perhaps you do. I'm too close to this situation to see if I'm doing the right thing or not. I could probably use your advice. If you're happy to listen, that is?'

'Of course I am.'

Lucinda took a deep breath and offered Abi a small smile before leading her through to the living room.

A lump caught in Lucinda's throat as she explained the situation she'd escaped from in Dorford.

'You poor thing.' Abi immediately reached for her hand when Lucinda described some of the awful crimes Ryan had committed and the threats he'd held against her over the years. 'Couldn't the police do anything to help you?'

'Ryan's a professional criminal and everyone he associates with is too,' Lucinda said. 'He's not the sort of guy you mess with. Leaving him was a huge risk, but if I'd become an informant or done anything like that he would have got to me. He has too many connections, both criminal and within the legal system, to take any risks. I'm hoping that the way we've gone about things, cutting off all ties and not leaving behind any trail, means they'll find it very difficult to track us down. I've even changed my name and have official documents with my new details.'

'Wow.' Abi's eyes were wide listening to Lucinda.

'My real name is Lucinda. But continue to call me Hope. It'll get too confusing otherwise, and risky.'

'Of course.'

'I'm worried that Max is going to get us into trouble. He thinks he's doing a great job keeping secrets, but like you saw tonight, he slips up from time to time. While my preference is to have him in day care more days a week, it might be less risky to have William and Dot looking after him.'

'You're not worried he'll tell them too?'

'I am, but I'm not sure they'd have anyone to tell if he did. I'm thinking of telling Max that Ryan's dead so that becomes his story. He's unlikely to focus on Ryan being in prison or us escaping if he has that to contend with.'

Abi's mouth dropped open, causing Lucinda to flinch.

'I know it's extreme, but this is an extreme situation. Even if I can contain Max, for now, he'll have to go to school next year, so then the risk starts all over again. There are quite a few months between now and then to put a story in his head that he can tell people and make him think we no longer have any secrets.'

Abi nodded. 'It's extreme, but it makes sense. If you do decide to tell him that, pre-warn me so I can make sure I am extra kind to him. Also, I'd be happy to look after Max for you any day that you don't have somewhere else for him. He can help me do some gardening around the apartment block, or we can just play. I'm home most days, so it isn't a problem.'

'Thank you,' Lucinda said. 'As much as Max loves William and Dot, I'm not sure if it's going to be a long-term solution.'

'It only has to be until the end of the year. You won't need them at all once he's at school. There's after-school care in the afternoons when you need it, or he can come to me for a couple of hours.'

Lucinda smiled. Abi was being so kind. 'Thank you. I won't want to take advantage of you, though. It probably will be easier once school starts, and I guess we can put up with William and Dot for the next seven or eight months.'

'What is it about them that makes you feel uncomfortable?'

Lucinda thought about her answer. 'It's funny because they're lovely, lovely people, but there are a few things that have happened that have just felt strange. I think part of it is they're just too full on. William in particular. My mum adores Max, but she's never wanted to see him every day – or, to be honest, even look after him for consecutive days. She's always been great, and when I've needed her she's looked after him, but she's the first to say that being a grandparent is ideal because you can enjoy a few hours and then hand them back. William and Dot are having Max all day, and then William's getting upset if he's not going to see him the next day. To be fair, it's William that worries me, and Dot has been upfront that he has some medical issues going on. Possibly dementia, I think. I hope it's not, for both of their sakes. He's wonderful with Max, but having seen him blow up at me, I'm a little cautious of leaving Max with him. Jonesy said he'd drop in tomorrow and hang out with them for the day. Just check that William is okay with Max and give me some peace of mind.'

Abi raised an eyebrow. 'Is that all he's doing it for? I still think the way he looked at you when I met him was more than just being friendly.'

Lucinda blushed. 'He's in a relationship, and he hasn't given me that vibe. He's just really close with Dot and William and doesn't want to see them disappointed. And anyway, I'm still married, and after that experience I'm never going near another man again.'

Abi's eyes filled with sympathy. 'That I can understand. Do William and Dot pop up unexpectedly at the park, like Jonesy does?'

'Occasionally.'

'They live near the park, don't they?'

'Overlooking it,' Lucinda said, her face changing as she realised what she'd said. 'William birdwatches from the balcony of the apartment, which is why they chose the park side of the complex to live on. He sits out there with his telescope and bird book and makes lists of the different birds.'

'And spies on you and Max at the same time?'

'I'm not sure that he's spying, but I'm beginning to wonder whether if he sees us that's his cue to go for a walk.' Lucinda sighed. 'I'm probably not being fair. The first time we met them at the park, they told me they walk every morning and afternoon, so they probably haven't changed their routine at all. It's always been early morning or afternoon that we've seen them there.'

'I imagine you're warier than most people would feel the need to be. What you've been through would put you on edge and make you suspicious of people, even those trying to be kind.'

Lucinda gave a small smile. 'That's an understatement. I spent the first couple of months looking over my shoulder every time I went out. I half expected Ryan or one of his colleagues to turn up at the door most nights too.'

'Do you think he's looking for you?'

'He'll have someone searching. We've been gone for quite a long time now though, so I'm hoping that's a sign that he has no idea where we are. Only Mum and a friend in Dorford know we came to Melbourne, so I can't see there's any way he'll find out. Even if he did, it's a big city, so finding us would be difficult.'

Abi nodded and sipped her wine. 'To think I thought I was going through a difficult situation. It's nothing compared to what you're going through.'

Lucinda spluttered on her drink. 'To lose your husband the way you did, causing you to lose your job, your home and your friends, and then have your son leave to live with the enemy? I think it's more than comparable. It's a lot worse.'

Abi smiled. 'Listen to us. Arguing about whose life is the biggest mess.'

Lucinda laughed. 'To be honest, having you to compare notes with has given me a real lift. It's not the same talking to Mum on the phone.'

'I'm here if you need anything at all, Hope. I mean it. Whether it's to look after Max or just to have a chat when you need to. We've both been through a difficult time, and I know I could use the support, and hope you can too.'

Lucinda raised her glass, the weight she'd felt settle on her earlier lifting. Abi was exactly the type of friend she needed in her life right now. Kind, non-judging and sympathetic. She just hoped she could be as much of a support to Abi as she could already see her neighbour being to her and Max.

The way he looked at you was, in my opinion, more than just as a friend. Abi's words repeated in Lucinda's mind the next afternoon when she arrived at William and Dot's apartment building to collect Max.

That morning, good as his word, Jonesy had arrived at William and Dot's the same time she and Max had. Lucinda felt guilty that Jonesy was giving up his day for Max, but he assured her it was fine. 'There are a few jobs I want to do around the place for William, and I'll get Max to help me with those. My eyes need a rest from the computer screen too. I've spent too many hours the last few days tracking lost shipments.'

Now, as she caught the lift up to the third floor, she wondered if there was any truth in what Abi had suggested. No, she was being silly. Abi had seen him for only a few minutes, and there was no way she could deduce that from their brief conversation. Perhaps she'd said it just to flatter Lucinda? Regardless, it wasn't appropriate to even be thinking about.

Lucinda rang William and Dot's doorbell, expecting to hear Max rush to answer the door in his usual fashion. But instead, it was Dot who opened it, a broad smile on her face. 'Hello dear, come on in. The boys should be back any minute. Max insisted Jonesy take him back to the park, for the third time today, to practise another trick on his scooter.'

Lucinda smiled. 'Trick?'

Dot rolled her eyes. 'Wheelies. He can lift the front wheel off the ground now and is trying to get the back one up too so he can leap over cars.'

Lucinda laughed. 'We'll assume he's talking about his Matchbox cars.'

'Hopefully. Would you like a cup of tea while we wait for them? William's having a rest. I think having Jonesy as well today has worn him out. Too much talking and planning, as well as entertaining Max.' She raised a finger. 'Correction. Too much entertainment from Max.'

'How is he, Dot? Jonesy mentioned he was having some tests done, and he was a little worried.'

Dot frowned. 'Jonesy shouldn't have said anything. I didn't want to worry you before we know what's wrong, if anything. We're going back tomorrow for the results. He's getting a little forgetful, which makes him agitated at times.' Her face coloured. 'Which you've seen of course. When we spoke to the doctor earlier in the week, they thought some medication would be enough to curb the agitation, assuming nothing else presents itself.'

Lucinda nodded. It was what Jonesy had told her the other day.

Dot squeezed her arm. 'You're doing a wonderful thing for us, you know. If you'd met William twelve months ago, you'd have seen an old man giving up. Max has given him a new lease on life, and I couldn't be more grateful to you.'

Guilt flooded through Lucinda as she thought of the previous night's discussion. Of the plan to get through the year, and once Max was at school no longer have to rely on William and Dot.

'I'm glad for William and for you. I won't stay for tea, thank you. I'll gather up Max's things if that's okay, and go and meet him and Jonesy at the park. It's getting a bit late, and I'd like to get Max home for dinner.'

'Of course. Let me give you a hand. We can't have him forgetting Mr Fizz again.'

Lucinda slung Max's backpack over her shoulder and walked the short distance from Dot and William's apartment to the park. She could see Max riding the scooter down a small incline, a blue cape with a large *M* on the back of it flying out behind him. She smiled, wondering if the cape was another gift from Dot and William or whether Jonesy had brought it with him. She'd decided to stop questioning the generosity of these people who'd adopted them with open arms, and just be grateful. They were giving Max the normality of grandparents and family that she'd thought they'd left behind in Queensland.

'Hey!' Jonesy waved as she made her way towards him. He was perched on a park bench watching Max go up and down the incline. His smile broadened as she reached him.

'Hi, Max.' She waved to her son as he came flying down the incline again. He lifted his front wheel, performing a little jump, whooping in delight as he achieved his purpose. He came to a stop next to her, and accepted the hug she gave him before taking off again.

Lucinda laughed and sat down next to Jonesy. 'Thanks so much, he looks like he's had a great day.'

'I should thank you. I've had a great day. It's amazing experiencing life through the eyes of a child. No cares, no worries, just living in the moment.' He sighed. 'Wish I could do that every day.'

'It'd be nice, wouldn't it?'

He nodded, looking faraway.

'Is everything okay?'

Jonesy snapped his attention back to Lucinda and smiled. 'Definitely. Just thinking, that's all. How are you going? Getting to yoga lots?'

Lucinda shook her head. 'Juggling work and Max makes it tricky.' Jonesy's question made her realise she still hadn't heard back from Mary. She hoped everything was okay with her. It was strange to suggest a catch-up for Zeb's birthday but then not organise anything. 'I will try to get there soon.'

Jonesy nodded, the faraway look in his eyes returning. 'Have you ever wished you'd done things differently, so that you weren't in the position you currently are?'

Shivers ran down Lucinda's spine at his words. Had Max said something to him about their situation? She cleared her throat. 'Has Max been saying something about us? He's got a rather vivid imagination, I'm afraid.' She laughed, hoping her next words would sound convincing. 'We had a friend over last night, and he was busy telling her that he was adopted and that his real parents worked for the circus. His dad is a lion tamer and his mum swallows fire.'

Jonesy laughed.

'And,' Lucinda continued, 'I've heard many other stories from Max. Let's see: there's the one that his dad is a pirate with multiple treasure chests; there's the one that I'm going to the moon on a space mission; we've then got the one that his dad's in prison; the one that we won the lottery, but we're pretending we're poor so no one asks for money; then, of course, the story that Max is an alien and is only visiting earth for a short time.'

Jonesy was laughing even harder now and Lucinda relaxed. She'd deliberately inserted the dad's-in-prison story hoping it would sound as far-fetched as the other stories she'd made up.

'He's got a great imagination,' Jonesy said. 'But no, it wasn't anything Max said. I was thinking about my own life, my choices that now make things a little difficult to move forward how I'd like to.'

That wasn't what Lucinda expected to hear. She watched as Max tried unsuccessfully to lift his wheel off the ground, reached the bottom of the incline and turned around and scooted back up to the top.

'I'm a good listener if you want to share anything.'

Jonesy shook his head. 'No, not really. All I can say is I wish my circumstances were different. Max is a great kid, and he's reminded me of what's important. I just wish I could change a few things in my life, but I'm kind of locked in.'

Lucinda wondered if he was referring to his work, his relationship or something else altogether? Before meeting Ryan, she probably would have said that we all make our own choices and if he wanted to change things then he could and he should. But she knew from personal experience that you didn't always have the freedom to do what you wanted. Other people and circumstances could prevent it.

'If there's anything I can do, just let me know. I owe you for everything you've done for Max. Where did the cape come from, by the way?'

'Dot made it. She's a great sewer, so it gave her a project. Super Max, apparently. And you don't owe me anything.' His eyes locked with hers as he said this. 'Just know that I wish my circumstances were different. You're a great mum and Max is a great kid, and I wish . . .' He let his words peter out.

What was he going to say? That he wished he was available? Was Abi right with her analysis of the situation? Was Jonesy interested in her?

He gave a little laugh. 'Not sure what I wish really. Just that everything turns out well for everyone, I guess.'

Lucinda didn't respond. The conversation was taking a weird turn and she didn't know what to think of it. Was he concerned about William's diagnosis? It seemed strange that he didn't just come out and say it if that was the case.

'I'd better get Max home. I want him in bed early tonight as he's got day care tomorrow.' Even though she was concerned about Max saying too much at day care, she wasn't going to change anything this week. She'd half contemplated asking Abi to look after him, but was aware that Abi would be preparing for her son's visit so probably didn't need the extra responsibility of looking after Max.

Jonesy stood when she did and followed her over to where Max was inspecting the wheels on his scooter. 'Time to go, buddy,'

Lucinda said. 'We need to get home and start on dinner. I love your cape, by the way.'

'I'm Scooter Max,' he said proudly, making Jonesy laugh.

'I thought it was Super Max?'

Max shook his head. 'Nope, that would be a silly name when I have a scooter. Are you coming home for dinner with us too, Jonesy?'

Jonesy shook his head before Lucinda had a chance to respond. 'I've been spoilt having you to myself the last couple of hours, and I'm sure your mum wants to hang out with you. I'm going to go back to see William and Dot, twist their arms and see if they'll let me take them out for dinner. I'll see you some time next week, though. I'll check with Dot as to when you're next coming and make sure my visit is on the same day.'

'Yay!' Max yelled. 'Yay, Jonesy.'

Lucinda gave him a grateful smile. 'I can't expect you to be there every day he goes to their house.'

'I won't be,' Jonesy said. 'But for the next few visits, I can.' He turned to face Lucinda. 'I want the best for both you and Max, and I'll do my best to make sure that happens. Just know . . .' He hesitated, searching for the words. 'Just know that this is important to me. And as I said earlier, if circumstances were different . . .' He trailed off again, leaving Lucinda staring at him.

A feeling of unease settled over her. There was something he wasn't saying. Was it as simple as admitting he liked her, but he was conflicted because he was already in a relationship?

Lucinda's gut told her it was something else, something she needed to be careful of. She gave herself a shake. Her paranoia was rearing its ugly head once again. She needed to accept she had three people looking out for her and Max, and appreciate it, rather than continually questioning it.

Chapter Twenty-One

Abi found thinking about Hope's situation a distraction as she prepared the spare room for Hayden's visit. She really should be working out exactly what she was going to say to him, but her thoughts kept wandering back to the situation next door. You heard stories about people fleeing from their marriages and changing their identities to start a new life. She just never expected to meet anyone who'd had to do that. She could understand Hope's decision, though. Her husband was dangerous. She wondered how Hope had ended up with him in the first place. She was an intelligent and attractive woman and could have had her pick of guys, Abi would have thought. But from what Hope had said, her husband was a Jekyll-and-Hyde type of character. Charming one minute; manipulative, abusive and threatening the next. How sad that Max was caught up in all of this. At least they'd been able to escape and start a new life. She couldn't imagine living like that. It would always be at the back of your mind that you might be found or caught out using the new, fake identity. Perhaps over time you got used to it and it eventually became your normal.

She finished making Hayden's bed and glanced around the room. She'd made it as homely as possible but could already imagine what his reaction would be. The whole apartment was only slightly bigger than the large bedroom he'd had to himself. His flight was arriving at eleven the next morning. While she'd been watching every cent she spent, she was willing to splash out to cook something he'd enjoy. She wasn't sure that a rack of lamb would win back her son, but it certainly wasn't going to hurt.

The next morning Abi was up at five. She'd hardly slept and had spent a good part of the night scrolling through old photos and videos of Hayden's childhood. She'd put together a memories presentation that she wanted to show him. Eric's business dealings were a completely separate issue to the accusations Hayden was making about his childhood. She wanted to remind him of not only how close they'd all been, but that his childhood wasn't manipulative and abusive as he now seemed to think. She shook her head. Where he'd even got that from she couldn't imagine. He wasn't five; he was sixteen. He should know better.

By nine thirty she was on the road heading towards the airport. There was no way she was going to be late. The plane probably hadn't even left Sydney yet, but that wasn't the point. She wanted to be parked and at the gate ready for its arrival. Nerves fluttered in the pit of her stomach as she turned on to the West Gate Freeway on-ramp. She didn't even recognise her life and was beginning to doubt she had any hope of appealing to Hayden's sense of family or loyalty. While she'd never thought of her son as materialistic, when he'd left Melbourne, nothing much had changed. She'd still had her Audi, the house and their belongings. That had all changed now, and she wasn't sure how he was going to feel about it. Living in Gabe's multi-million-dollar Sydney mansion was not exactly a downgrade.

Abi turned on the radio, allowing the music to distract her for the remainder of the drive. She pulled into the airport car park with forty minutes to spare. She'd go and get a cup of coffee and hope it helped calm her nerves. A stiff drink would be a better option, but so early in the morning, with a drive and a conversation to be had, it was not a good idea.

Hayden's plane landed on time, and Abi was waiting as the passengers began to disembark. Expecting the usual lengthy wait, Abi was surprised when her son emerged third from the plane.

Tears filled her eyes as soon as she saw him. His face radiated a healthy glow and he sported a new haircut and clothes. He was exceptionally handsome, and her heart swelled with pride. His eyes connected with hers, and she drew in a breath. Eyes that had once danced with fun and excitement were filled with hardness. This wasn't going to be easy.

She was surprised that he allowed her to hug him. 'How are you, Hayds?'

He pulled away from her. 'Let's go and get my bag, and we can talk later. And I don't like Hayds anymore, okay? It's too childish.'

Abi nodded, chastised. He'd said he always knew who his really good friends were as they called him Hayds. She wondered what he'd do if he saw any of his Melbourne friends. Ask them to call him Hayden, she guessed.

They collected his bag and made their way out to the car park and the old Toyota Abi now drove.

Hayden raised an eyebrow. 'What happened to the Audi?'

'Sold, along with the house and most other things. You'll see a few changes now that you're home. Changes I can't say I love, but I'm getting used to.'

'I'm not home, and I'm glad you've made changes. You can hardly drive around in an expensive car and live in a fancy house after what's happened. People would hate you.'

'I think quite a few hate me regardless of the changes I've made.'

'Yeah well, that's to be expected.'

Abi chose not to respond to this comment as they climbed into the car and drove towards the exit. Instead, she moved the conversation to what she considered to be safer ground. 'How's school?'

'Amazing. The facilities are incredible, as are the teachers. I can't believe Dad didn't offer to send me there years ago. He went there; he knew how good it was.'

'Not very practical when we lived in Melbourne.'

'We could have moved.'

Abi raised an eyebrow. 'Dad's business and my job were in Melbourne. Moving to Sydney for schooling wouldn't have made any sense, especially when you had excellent schooling here.'

'That's debatable.'

'What about friends? Are you planning to catch up with anyone while you're home?'

Hayden turned to face Abi. 'Are you serious? For a start, I'm going back to Sydney tomorrow. I have school on Monday, so no, I haven't made plans, and secondly, I haven't kept in touch with anyone. I deleted all of my social media accounts. The last thing I need is someone posting something on my Instagram account or anywhere else that links me back to what Dad did. Thanks to Gabe and Imogen I'm able to have a completely fresh start in Sydney. There's no way I'd jeopardise that.'

The hatred and anger that spilled with every word Hayden spoke cut like a knife. Abi knew he'd wanted to get away from her and the situation with Eric, but cutting everyone off?

'What about Pete? You guys have been friends since you were three. You've even cut him off?'

Hayden nodded. 'I contacted him before I left and told him I'd look him up one day, but for now, I need a new start.'

Abi remained silent, unsure what to say to that. She thought of Hope's situation of needing to start again and not wanting anyone to know where she was. Completely different reasons, of course, but a fresh start required cutting yourself off from your past. Her gut churned at this realisation.

'What time is your flight back tomorrow?'

'One o'clock.'

Abi gripped the steering wheel tighter. She had just over twenty-four hours to convince her son not to cut her off. If she didn't, when she dropped him back at the airport the next day, she'd be saying goodbye forever. While she had her plan to end her life, part of her had assumed that her relationship with Hayden would be the thing that prevented her from doing this. With him in her life, she had a purpose. Without him, forced to live with the mess Eric had left her, she didn't.

Hayden's reaction to the apartment was not what Abi expected. He'd nodded his head in what looked like admiration or satisfaction. She wasn't sure which.

'As I said, it's not what we're used to, but it's home for now and has provided me with a job.'

Hayden put his bag on the spare bed and joined Abi in the living area. 'I'm surprised Alex gave you a job. She must hate you right now.'

'She has more compassion than most people,' Abi said. 'Their business is doing well, and they have this as an asset. Losing money in the investment put a halt to their expansion plans, but it hardly ruined them. Alex doesn't blame me for what happened.' She did her best to push the memory of the disastrous lunch at Fleming's away.

Hayden nodded. 'Well, good for her. I'm less forgiving, and as Gabe's already told you, I want you to sign off on Gabe and Imogen being allowed to adopt me.'

Abi's legs wobbled and she sank back on to her chaise lounge, holding on to the arm for support. She'd planned to show Hayden the photos and video compilation she'd put together, remind him of how much he was loved and then have this conversation. She wasn't prepared for him to launch into it in such a cold manner.

She closed her eyes momentarily, aware he'd sat down on the chair opposite her and was impatiently tapping his fingers on the armrest. She opened her eyes. 'Why?'

Hayden shook his head. 'Really? You need to ask?'

'I don't understand why you need, or would even want, to do that. You share the same name as Gabe already and are living under his roof. I can't imagine you're planning to tell people he's your dad, are you?'

Hayden shrugged. 'I hadn't thought about that. Probably not. I want them to be my legal guardians. I don't want you to have any say in anything I do, and I want people to assume they are my family.'

'But they already are your family. Being adopted by them just isn't necessary. I'd understand if both Dad and I were gone and you were younger, but at sixteen you're practically independent.' As the words left her mouth, Abi realised that, if she agreed to this, in three weeks Hayden would be orphaned and the adoption idea wouldn't be as crazy as it sounded now. It seemed ridiculous to her, as she was still alive and up until Eric's death they'd had a wonderful relationship. Not that you'd know that now. Anyone meeting her and Hayden for the first time would see the intense hatred in his face and wonder what on earth she'd done to make this happen.

'You don't get it, do you, Mum? This isn't a case of it will all blow over and I'll come back to you. I will never forgive you and Dad for what you did. Both the investment scheme leading to his death and also the way you treated me for years before.'

'Okay, that's what I want to get to the bottom of,' Abi said. 'What do you mean by what we did the years before? We only ever did the best for you.'

'That's not what I now know. Gabe's filled me in on how devastated Nanna and Granddad were that you kept me away from them. You brainwashed me into thinking they didn't care about me. That's an awful thing to have done when they were asking you to visit or let them come and visit.'

Abi's mouth dropped open. Eric's parents had washed their hands of Eric the day he'd left Sydney to be with Abi. When Hayden was born, they'd shown no interest in him at all. Eric had used Hayden's birth as an opportunity to try to reconnect with his parents, assuming they'd want to get to know their first grandson. They'd declined Eric's invitation to come and visit. He'd pretended it hadn't hurt, but Abi knew it had. 'Gabe's been filling your head with lies. Your nanna and granddad turned their back on your dad when he and I got together. They disowned him and weren't interested in anything he did after. That included your birth, his death and everything in between.'

'Gabe told me you'd say that. Just like you'd probably say that you had nothing to do with the rift between him and Dad.'

'I didn't. They didn't get along, and that was that.'

'Because you told Dad if he had anything to do with Gabe, you'd leave him.'

'What? I never said anything like that. Why would I?'

'Because Gabe broke your heart when he ended your relationship, and it was your way of paying him back. And of paying Nanna and Granddad and the rest of the family back. You told him that one day you'd make him pay for what he'd done, and you used Dad and me to do that. Did you even love Dad, or were you just with him to get back at Gabe?'

Abi stared at Hayden, finding it hard to believe what she was hearing. Gabe was feeding him blatant lies.

'You don't have to answer that if you don't want,' Hayden said. 'Nanna already told me it's what happened. They're so happy, by the way. She said she's sad about Dad, but if he was alive, they would have died without ever getting to know me. Now they have the rest of their lives to spend time with me and enjoy me. So much for what you and Dad always told me – that they'd disowned us.' He shook his head in disgust. 'I can't believe I fell for all of your lies. Makes me feel so stupid. As if my own family would have turned their back on me.'

'They did.' Abi was doing her best to control the anger that was building in her. 'Your uncle is telling you so many lies I don't even know where to start unravelling them.'

Hayden rolled his eyes. 'And Imogen's lying, and Nanna and Granddad. Let me guess, you're the only one telling the truth?'

Abi didn't respond. The sarcastic tone in his voice sent shivers down her spine. How was she going to get through to him?

Hayden got to his feet. 'I'm going to go and lie down and read. I've got heaps of study to do in preparation for Monday. We can talk more over dinner.'

He left the room, Abi staring after him. She needed to come up with a new plan, and quickly.

A few hours later, when she called him for dinner, she had a plan.

'Okay,' she said as they sat facing each other at the small dining table. 'You've asked me for something, which I am considering. But before I give you my blessing to be adopted by Gabe and Imogen, I need you to do something for me.'

'What?'

'I need you to listen, that's all. After we eat, I want to show you something I put together for you, and I want to explain a few things. Can you agree to at least be open to listening?'

Hayden nodded as he cut into his lamb. 'Let's not ruin our meal. I'll listen after dinner. There's no point cooking my favourite foods and then wrecking them with whatever lies you're planning to tell me.'

Abi let the comment go and did her best to stomach the meal she'd put together. She wasn't hungry and just wanted to get on with the rest of the night. When they'd finished, she opened up her laptop and asked Hayden to sit down in one of the armchairs. She placed the computer on the coffee table and let the slideshow she'd created play. It started at Hayden's birth and went right through until the week before Eric's death. Photos and videos made up over an hour of memories.

She paused a few times, wanting to discuss the video they'd just seen with Hayden. But other than a few grunts he wasn't going to get into any discussion. She persisted, stopping at the video of Hayden catching his first barramundi.

'Remember that,' she said. 'Do you remember what your dad said to you after you pulled it in?'

Hayden shrugged.

'He said he couldn't be prouder watching you defeat something that fought so hard, but then having the compassion to remove the hook and release the fish. He said if you approached life with the same determination and compassion you'd shown with the fish, you'd always come out on top.'

Hayden turned and stared at Abi. 'Look, I get that you're trying to show me all the great times we had, but they mean nothing. Yeah, Dad said that but so what? Do you think I care about the words of someone so cowardly? He hardly approached his life with determination and compassion, did he? He approached it as a cheat and a coward.'

Abi stared at her son. She wasn't sure why she wanted to defend Eric, but she did. For Hayden to question the unconditional love both she and Eric had showered on him was heart-breaking. 'I agree that what Dad's done is awful, Hayden. But it doesn't change how he parented you or how much he loved you.'

'We'll have to agree to disagree on that one. Now, do I have to watch the rest of this slideshow or can we just turn it off?'

Abi hesitated for just a second before continuing to play the video. Maybe something would jolt a feeling of belonging in Hayden.

It didn't. Twenty minutes later, he yawned. 'Okay, so what else are you planning to say? You said you wanted me to be open to listening.'

Abi nodded. 'I need you to believe I didn't have anything to do with the financial mess we're in.'

'What difference does it make whether I believe you or not?'

'It makes a huge difference to me.'

'Well, I'm sorry, but I don't believe you. And even if I did, it would make no difference to what I want now.'

'Hold on. So even if you knew I had nothing to do with it you'd still act like you despise me and want to legally separate from me?'

Hayden nodded. 'It's not an act. I want a better life, and Gabe can give me that. Gabe's forgiven you for the way you've treated him, but I don't think I can. This goes way beyond the money. This is about family. You cut me off from my family and for sixteen years had me believe that all I had was you and Dad. I have a whole extended family who've mourned me for that time. That was all you, not Dad. Granddad told me that he'd asked Dad many times to join them for Christmas and each time you'd said no way. Dad went along with you.'

Abi did her best to keep her voice steady as her anger mounted. 'That's not true. Not true at all. We were never asked to Christmas. The rift between Dad and Gabe has been going on for years, and your grandparents chose to side with Gabe.'

'The rift's being going since you met Dad.'

Abi fell silent. That was true, but the information Hayden had was wrong.

'What does it mean for us if I agree to this adoption?'

'It means I have no obligations towards you. I become a permanent member of Gabe's family, and we break all ties.'

'We have no contact at all?'

Hayden nodded. 'It will make my life a lot easier to be moving forwards and never looking back.'

He might as well have slapped her.

'I'd miss you if that happened. A lot.'

Hayden didn't respond.

God, where had this harsh, uncaring teenager come from? 'And if I don't agree to the adoption?'

'Then nothing changes. I go back to Sydney and live as part of Gabe's family. When I'm eighteen, I can make the decision myself, and you'll have no say in it.'

'So, there's no difference whether I say yes or no then. It's going to be the same result anyway?'

'Same result for you, but not for me. Saying yes gives me a sense of closure and freedom. A chance to embrace a new life and the family I should always have had in my life, and would have had if it wasn't for you.'

'But you'll have that regardless, you've just said so.'

'The family part yes, but not the closure. I'm never going to forgive you for keeping me from my family, so our relationship is over. It's whether or not you love me enough to do it on my terms. That's what we're talking about now.'

Tears slid down Abi's cheeks. Her son hated her. He absolutely, passionately hated her, and it seemed there was nothing she was going to be able to do to change this. She wiped her cheeks and stood. 'I'm going to bed. I'll give you my answer in the morning.'

Hayden nodded, picked up the remote and flicked on the television. The coldness in his face and eyes reminded her exactly of Gabe. Fury bubbled under the surface as she thought of Gabe and then Eric. The husband she'd adored. The husband whose actions had led her to this moment when she was unable to defend herself against his lying family. There were many things she would never forgive Eric for, but losing the most precious thing in the world to her, her son, was the one that hurt the most.

Abi made her decision long before she fell into a fitful sleep in the early hours of the morning. What choice did she have? Saying yes to Hayden might at least mean that when she said goodbye to him he listened to her and believed what she was going to say. It was going to be the last time she saw her son face-to-face, and she was going to do her best to say the things she felt he needed to hear, that hopefully he'd look back on after her death and realise were sincere.

She showered and dressed before coming into the living area. Hayden's door was open, but he wasn't in his room. She pushed open the doors that led out on to the tiny balcony and breathed in the crisp winter air. She heard a small boy's laughter from the path below and looked down to see Max running after a soccer ball, screaming with delight as he reached it. He turned and kicked it back in the opposite direction.

She continued to watch as Max ran back and forth, his screams getting louder as his kicks got higher. Eventually, he picked the ball up, walked over to a large rock and sat down. 'Come and chat to me,' he called out.

Moments later Hayden strode into view. He sat down next to the little boy, and while Abi couldn't make out what he was saying, the two had an animated discussion. After a few minutes, Hayden got up, fist-bumped Max and walked back around the side of the building out of sight.

'Mumma, I've got a new friend,' she heard Max calling to Hope, who appeared at that moment. She took his hand, and the two of them disappeared from view.

The front door of Abi's apartment opened, and Hayden walked in carrying a large paper bag and two cups of coffee.

'Figured you probably didn't have the coffee machine anymore.' His eyes travelled to the kitchen bench as he handed her a cup. 'Although it looks like I was wrong.' He shook his head in disgust.

'You begrudge me keeping the coffee machine? The one from the guest house, mind you, not our expensive one. The auction people said I'd get about eighty dollars for it, which is why I kept it. I don't see you going without any luxuries, by the way. Looking at your clothes, you're living a more extravagant lifestyle than you ever were here.'

Hayden didn't respond. Instead, he took two plates from the cupboard and placed the pastries on them. 'Your favourites.'

Abi blinked back tears. Now he was doing something nice, or was he just buttering her up so she'd agree to his request? She decided it was better not to ask. 'I saw you talking with Max,' she said instead. 'He lives next door.'

Hayden nodded, sitting down at the table with his coffee and pastries. 'He's a cool little kid. Said he's on the run and his mum was now going undercover with a different name.'

Abi did her best to contain her surprise. 'Did he say anything else?'

'I asked him what he was running from, and he said he wasn't sure. That his dad was in prison and there were lots of secrets that he didn't understand. If it's true, it all sounded pretty messed up. His mum seemed nice. Not someone running from anything. I think he's been watching too much TV.'

Hope was right that she needed to shut Max down quickly. While Abi thought the idea of telling him his father was dead was extreme, it looked like Hope might need to. 'Hope's lovely,' Abi said, 'and I agree, she doesn't seem like someone on the run.' That much was true; Abi doubted anyone would pick that up about her.

'So, have you made a decision yet?'

Abi didn't have to ask about what. She nodded. 'Yes. I'll agree to go along with what you want. I would like you to listen to one more thing from me, though, before you cut off all contact, assuming you still plan to do that?'

Hayden smiled. 'Really? I didn't think you'd agree. Thank you.'

Tears threatened Abi's eyes once again. 'I'll agree because I love you. I need you to know that and never question it. I'd do anything for you, Hayden, including allowing you to cut me out of your life if that's what you want. I do want you to be careful, though. Gabe's very controlling and manipulative, and I can see he's already having a great influence over you.' She held up her hand to stop Hayden from interrupting. 'Just listen. I'm telling you this because one day I hope you'll look back and realise that your memories are the ones you need to be listening to. Gabe's fabricating information to make me look bad, and his reason for doing this is revenge. He never dumped me, we hardly dated. We went out a couple of times. I knew he wasn't right for me, and before I got to tell him that, your dad turned up. It was love at first sight, and I had to be careful how I told Gabe as he was always so competitive. He didn't take it well, and neither did your grandparents. In his anger, he swore that one day he'd take something I loved away from me. He's doing that now with you. I don't need you to defend him or give me your opinion, I'm telling you exactly how it was, and one day I hope you can see this for yourself. In the meantime, I can only wish you the very best.' Tears began rolling down Abi's cheeks. 'I want every success for you. I want you to be happy. I want you to find love one day, and I want you to be loved. I want you to know how much I love you, and will every day for the rest of my life, and beyond.' Hayden stood and came over to Abi, allowing her to embrace him. She held him tight, savouring this moment. 'That's what I want you to remember – that I love you, okay?'

Hayden nodded. 'Thanks, Mum. I'll never forget that you're doing this for me.'

Abi buried her face in his broad chest, a numbness settling over her. No *I love you.* No *I've changed my mind and want you in my life.* Just *thanks.*

The numbness she felt stayed with her as she drove Hayden to the airport, as she said her final goodbye, and as he walked through to the airbridge and disappeared, not once turning around.

Chapter Twenty-Two

Lucinda and Max were returning from the park with Max's scooter when they saw Abi's blue Toyota pull into the driveway of the apartment block. The outing to the park had been to try to distract Lucinda. Tess had promised to ring her after her visit to the prison on Thursday, and she'd heard nothing. She'd rung and texted her mother's prepaid phone but had had no reply. She'd already decided that if she heard nothing today, she would find a payphone and ring her at work on Monday. She'd hardly slept the last few nights, and found herself snappy with Max and unusually moody.

Seeing Abi, she wondered how the visit with her son had gone. She'd met Hayden earlier that morning when he'd spent a few minutes kicking a ball with Max. He was polite and seemed like a nice boy. She couldn't imagine him cutting all ties with his mother and hoped they'd managed to sort things out.

One look at Abi's face when she emerged from her car immediately told Lucinda that things hadn't gone well.

'Why don't you ride your scooter up and down the path for a few minutes,' Lucinda suggested. 'I just want to have a quick word with Abi.'

Max didn't need convincing and sped off to the far end of the path before turning back in the direction he'd come.

Lucinda walked over to Abi. 'You okay?'

Abi shook her head. 'I need to curl up in the foetal position for a few hours. I couldn't talk him around. He's gone back to Sydney with my permission to separate from me.' Her voice cracked as she forced the words out.

'Oh, Abi, I'm so sorry. I can't even begin to imagine what that must feel like. I met him this morning, and he seemed like such a lovely boy. I was sure you'd work it out.'

'He's been brainwashed by his uncle and grandparents. Some of the lies he's been fed are just awful. It's hard to believe Eric's family could hate him so much that they'd turn our son against us, but it appears they do.'

'Do you want to come up for coffee and take your mind off things?'

'No, but thanks. I need some time to be alone. I'll be okay in a day or two; it's just getting my head around what's happened and the next steps for me.' A flash of pain crossed her face.

Lucinda squeezed her arm. 'I'll pop in tomorrow morning to check on you, okay?'

Abi forced a smile. 'There's no need, but thank you, I appreciate the offer.' She turned and began to walk away, then stopped and faced Lucinda. 'Actually, I should probably tell you something Max said to Hayden.' She went on to relay the conversation they'd had. 'I was thinking about him and assume he's confused about what's going on, which is why he's suddenly talking. You might want to consider your idea of telling him his father's gone or give him a much better story than the one he's currently telling.'

Lucinda sighed. 'Thanks, I'll work something out. I'm not going to send him back to day care this week, so at least the number of people he can tell is limited, but still, I don't want William and

Dot knowing, or Jonesy. He's supposed to go to them tomorrow, so I'll need to think up something quickly.'

'I'll look after Max tomorrow for you,' Abi said. 'It'll be my pleasure and will help me snap out of this mood. I promise I'll be upbeat and make it a fun day.'

'I'd love you to,' Lucinda said. 'But are you sure? You've been through a lot this weekend.'

'The distraction of a four-year-old is exactly what I need. And I might even take him out, if you're happy for me to do that? I'm sure I can borrow a car seat from the couple in apartment one, and we can take his scooter off to a different park. It will get him away from William's birdwatching too.' She gave a wry smile as she made the suggestion.

Lucinda stepped forward and hugged her. 'Thank you. You're a lifesaver. I'll ring William and Dot and let them know of the change of plans. Can I drop him over at eight?'

'Of course.' Abi pulled out of the hug. 'I'll see you in the morning.'

Lucinda watched as Abi walked towards the stairs that led to the second floor. She was such a strong woman. She wasn't sure how she would have coped in Abi's position – losing her husband and her son so close together.

'Mumma?' Max's call broke into her thoughts as he came hurtling at her on his scooter. 'Where's Mrs Abi gone?'

'Home, Maxy, which we need to do too. I need to make a phone call to William and Dot about tomorrow. You're going to have a day with Abi instead as she wants to take you in the car to a different park where you can ride your scooter.'

Max's eyes widened. 'Really? A proper outing with Mrs Abi?'

Lucinda nodded. 'You can just call her Abi, hon. She doesn't need to be called Mrs Abi.'

'Can I take Mr Fizz with me?'

'Of course. Now, take off your helmet and let's go upstairs and have a drink. You must be so thirsty after all of that scooting.'

With Max sipping his water in front of the television, Lucinda picked up her phone and called Dot and William's number. William answered.

'I was just thinking about you and Max,' William said. 'There's a small tribe of boys at the park on their scooters, and it made me wonder what Max was up to today.'

'He's already had a good session on the scooter,' Lucinda said, glad that it appeared William didn't already know this. Perhaps his telescope really was for birdwatching and he wasn't spying on them. 'I wanted to let you know that Max won't be coming to you tomorrow. He's going out with another friend for the day.'

'Oh, that's a shame. I was planning to do some bug investigations with him with the magnifying kit. Never mind, we can do that another day.'

William didn't sound disappointed or angry; he seemed completely normal, as most people would with the change of plans. Lucinda was relieved.

'Will he still be coming to us on Tuesday?' William asked.

'I'll give you a ring tomorrow, if that's okay? My shifts might be changing this week, and I won't find out until I'm at work tomorrow exactly what days I'll be working. Sorry to mess you around.' It wasn't true, but Lucinda wanted to buy some time while she worked out how she was going to manage the Ryan situation with Max.

William gave a little chuckle. 'It's no problem, Hope. We're not exactly rushed off our feet with other obligations. You just let us know what you need us to do. We're here for you and Max anytime. I'd better go. Dot wants me to help her bottle some jam this afternoon, and I'm in charge of sterilising the jars. Tell Max we'll miss him tomorrow, but we'll have lots of fun things to do when we do see him.'

Lucinda said her goodbyes and ended the call, relieved it had gone so well and William hadn't created any fuss.

The next morning Max woke early, excited at the prospect of spending the day with Abi and going to a new park. At eight o'clock they knocked on Abi's door, which opened immediately. Abi gave Max a huge smile. 'I've been looking forward to this morning ever since your mum said it was okay for me to look after you today. We're going to have so much fun.'

'Thank you,' Lucinda said, taking in Abi's pale face. 'Are you sure you're up for this?'

'Definitely. As I said, the distraction will be good for me. Lying around feeling sad isn't going to help me at all.'

'If you need to talk about it, I'm always here. I'm not sure I can fix anything, but just getting it off your chest sometimes helps.'

Abi nodded. 'Thanks. Now, you'd better get to work, and Max and I should get our day started.' She turned to him. 'How about we make up a picnic and then take it to a new park? I've already put a car seat in my car, so we're all set to go. There's a track there for bikes and scooters, with traffic lights and road signs, as well as a massive fort.'

Max's eyes widened.

'Bye, Maxy,' Lucinda said, pulling him to her for a hug. 'You be on your best behaviour for Abi, won't you.'

'Yes, Mumma. I love you.'

'Love you too, bud.' She planted a kiss on his forehead.

'I should be back by about five thirty,' she told Abi as Max ran into the apartment and disappeared. 'Just ring me if there are any problems.'

Abi smiled. 'We'll see you at five thirty, and I'm sure we won't need to ring you. Have a great day.'

Relief settled over Lucinda as she hurried down the stairs and crossed the street to the bus stop. She knew she didn't need to worry about Max when he was with Abi. For a start, she knew everything about them, so there were no secrets to be kept. She had a son of her own, so looking after a boy was nothing new; and most importantly, Lucinda trusted her.

As she climbed on to the bus, Lucinda checked her watch. It was nearly eight fifteen. Her mother should be at the salon opening up by now. She should have enough time between getting off the bus and her shift starting to ring her. Her body tensed as she thought of her beautiful mother. If something had happened to her, she'd never forgive herself.

Lucinda got off the bus and crossed the road to a park opposite Fleming's. She had twenty minutes before her shift started, which was perfect for making the call to Tess.

She reached the payphone near the toilet block, grateful that the park appeared to be empty. Picking up the handset, she slipped her money into the slot, her body tense as she willed Tess to answer. On the fourth ring, she did.

'Trims and Tones, this is Tess.'

'Mum—'

Lucinda stared at the phone. Her mother had hung up. She lifted her finger to call her back, then stopped. It might have been deliberate. She couldn't ring again if her mother was in danger. What should she do now?

She crossed over to a bench and sat trying to formulate a plan. A couple of minutes passed, and her mobile phone rang with a number Lucinda didn't recognise.

'Hello.'

'Oh, Lu, thank goodness. I'm calling from the phone box down the road. It's too risky to call on the work phone. The police might have it tapped.'

'The police? Why would they do that?'

'Because Ryan escaped and they want to know where you are.'

Lucinda froze. 'What?'

'I went and saw him on Thursday as he asked me to, and he didn't tell me what he was up to but alluded to the fact that the appeal was irrelevant and that he would be out very soon. He thanked me for all the support I've given him and said he'd be in touch once he had Max, so I could visit.'

Lucinda was silent, trying to process what her mother was saying. 'So you could visit? If he's escaped from prison, surely he'd be hiding, not organising visitors?' She pressed her fingers to her forehead as it began to throb. 'Explain to me how a prisoner escapes.'

'I have no idea, but he had it planned for a while. He told me on Thursday that he was scheduled to be transferred to the higher-security prison in Almain. He escaped somewhere between the two facilities. I'm assuming he must have had help from the guards. He implied on other visits that he was well-looked-after as he had so many connections. That's all I know. The police wouldn't tell me any more.'

'When did you talk to the police?'

'They came and questioned me for three hours on Friday, as I was the last person to visit him. I had to tell them that you and Max left Dorford because you were scared of him and that he threatened you. They want to know where you are so they can question you too. I told them that you'd cut all contact with me and I didn't even know if you were still in the country.'

Lucinda's stomach churned as she listened to her mother. 'I guess stick to that story.'

'There's something else, Lu. Yesterday I had a phone call from a woman. She said I needed to tell you that you were in danger, that the people around you are connected to Ryan. That you need to leave now. She said there was a safe house in New South Wales. I have the details for it here.'

Bile rose in Lucinda's throat. *Leave now.* 'Who was she?'

'She wouldn't say, but she sounded nervous. I tried to get more information from her, but she wouldn't tell me anything, which made me suspicious of her. She cut me off in the end. I'm worried that Ryan had her ring me and he's waiting for you at the safe house. The timing of the phone call seemed too coincidental. He escaped, and two days later I get that call. You need to decide, but I think it's a set-up.'

'Oh God.' Lucinda bent over double, willing her breakfast to stay down. 'I have no idea what to do.'

'You could go to the police and ask for protection. They told me if you contacted me that I was to tell you to do that. Ryan's escape could be a good thing in the long run. Once they catch him, he's going to go to jail for a very long time. You won't have to worry about him anymore.'

'But he controls so much from inside,' Lucinda said. 'While he's alive I think I'll always have to worry about him.'

'I'd better go,' Tess said. 'I've ordered a phone online that should arrive today or tomorrow. The other prepaid stopped working, which is why you haven't been able to contact me. I'll ring you as soon as I get the new one working.'

Lucinda's hands trembled as the phone call ended. What should she do now? She could get Max and run, but to where? If Ryan did know where she was, which she doubted, she'd be being watched, and he'd have her followed. What worried her the most was Ryan's message to Tess, that he expected to have Max soon and she could visit. But if he knew where they were, wouldn't he have had someone visit her weeks ago? Why go through all the pretence of not knowing with her mum if he really did?

Lucinda took a deep breath. The one thing she agreed with Tess on was that the safe house phone call sounded like a set-up. That whoever rang had wanted Tess to pass on the message and encourage Lucinda to take Max and go there. The one thing that did unsettle her, though, was the wording Tess had used. *Leave now* was the same message she'd received by text in the park the day after the strange catch-up with Mary.

She needed to speak to Mary, just to rule out that she had anything to do with any of this. She quickly searched for Yoga Life's number and rang it. Her foot tapped as she waited for someone to answer.

'Good morning, Yoga Life, this is Shelley.'

'Hi, Shelley. I was wondering if Mary's at the studio now or is teaching any classes today?'

'No, sorry. Mary's no longer with us.'

Lucinda sucked in a breath. 'Really? Do you have any idea where I could contact her? Her mobile's going to voicemail each time I ring it.'

Shelley hesitated. 'Are you a friend?'

'Yes. I've been trying to reach her for a few days now, so I'm getting worried.'

'So are we,' Shelley said. 'She came in about a week ago, agitated. Said she was leaving Melbourne and needed her final pay. She wouldn't say what had happened, but it was weird and went against all of the plans she'd previously told us for her and her kids in Melbourne. No one's heard from her since.'

Lucinda's heart began to race. 'Do you know what day she came in?'

'It was Saturday afternoon. I only remember because Luke dealt with her, and he filled me in on Sunday morning when I was teaching. I can take your number if you like, and if anyone hears from her, I'll ask them to contact you.'

'That would be great, thanks.' Lucinda gave Shelley her number before ending the call. A cold shiver ran down her spine. Mary had left Melbourne the afternoon they'd caught up in the park, when she'd acted weird about Jonesy. If Mary had sent the *leave now* text and made the call to Tess, what would be her motivation to do that? If she thought Lucinda was in danger, she could have just told her when they were in the park. It didn't make sense, but it certainly made her feel uneasy.

Lucinda glanced at her watch. She had five minutes before her shift. It was tempting to ring in sick and go home to spend the day with Max.

'Hope?' Alex waved to her. She was walking through the park with a coffee in hand on her way to the restaurant. 'Thought that was you. Is everything okay?'

Lucinda stared at her. She wondered how she'd react if she told her the whole story. She'd be fired, for a start, for misrepresenting herself.

'Hope?'

Lucinda gave herself a mental shake. 'Sorry, I was miles away. A few problems with my mum. Nothing that won't sort itself out, I hope.'

'Do you need the day off? We're a bit short on staff, but family comes first.'

Lucinda smiled, appreciating her boss's concern. She probably should take the day off but what was it going to achieve? She wasn't going to run. The evidence that Ryan knew where she was wasn't reliable enough. While she didn't want to take any risks, she also didn't want to have a knee-jerk reaction that unnecessarily upset her and Max's lives. If anything, the workday would distract her. 'No, I'll be fine for today. Although I might need to change a few shifts around for the rest of the week. Can I work that out and talk to you this afternoon?'

'Of course.' Alex glanced at her watch. 'We'd better get moving. I have a meeting at nine, and it never looks good when the boss is late.'

Lucinda fell into stride next to Alex, the weight and worry she'd thought she'd finally shed settling firmly between her shoulder blades.

Chapter Twenty-Three

Abi smiled as she watched Max speeding around the well-designed bike track on his scooter. She was impressed to see him stop at the set of traffic lights before racing off through a small tunnel once the light turned green. After half an hour of non-stop scooting, she called him over to the bench where she sat and held out a drink bottle to him.

'Scooter Max never wears out.' He drank from the bottle, suddenly removing it from his mouth and letting out a squeal. 'Look, Mrs Abi, look!' He pointed across the park, where an elderly couple sat on a bench. He waved to them, and they waved back.

Abi knew before she asked. 'Who are they, Max?'

'That's my granny and pa. They're called Dot and William, but they said they'd be my grandparents. Can I go and say hello?'

Abi hesitated. The whole point of today was to keep Max away from the older couple. Why on earth would they be at this park? Had they followed her? 'How about you take me over and introduce them to me. I've heard so much about them, and I'd love to meet them.'

Max's eyes danced with delight.

'But Max,' Abi said, 'remember what Mumma's said about your secrets. She's shared some of them with me, but she doesn't want you saying anything to William and Dot, okay?'

Max pressed his lips together and pretended to throw away the key. 'I won't say anything. I just want to show them how good I am with traffic lights.'

Abi followed him across to where the older couple sat.

'Hello, Maxy boy,' William said. 'Fancy bumping into you here.'

'Hi, I'm Abi,' Abi said, introducing herself. 'Max is spending the day with me today.'

'I'm William, and this is my wife, Dot,' he said.

'What a coincidence,' Dot said. 'We decided to do a bit of park reconnaissance today, so we'd have somewhere new to take Max later in the week. A friend of ours, Jonesy, mentioned this one to us.'

Abi nodded. 'It's a lovely park.'

'It is,' Dot agreed. 'We found another lovely one not far from here too. It has a nice big pond with ducks on it. We thought that would be another good one to visit and feed the ducks one day. We're so lucky to have so many options around us.'

'Where are you off to after this one?'

'To Thomas Street in Hampton,' William said. 'According to my research, it has a fort that's bigger and better than this one. I thought we'd check that one out too.'

Dot shrugged apologetically. 'It gets us out of the house and gives our very under-utilised car a run. It's a beautiful day, so having a picnic in the park is very appealing.'

Abi forced a smile. Everything they were saying sounded completely reasonable but this was far too big a coincidence. What was their motive for being here? Were they really that lonely that they would follow a four-year-old around? It didn't make any sense. She wasn't sure what to say to them. She knew one thing for sure: Hope needed to know, and she needed to confront them.

'Can I go and play, Mrs Abi?' Max asked, interrupting. 'I'll come back for a drink soon.'

Abi hesitated. Part of her thought she should take Max home. But was that over-reacting? The older couple weren't in any way threatening; it was just that with the concerns Hope had already voiced, the situation made Abi very uneasy.

'Mrs Abi?'

Abi realised all three of them were staring at her, waiting for an answer. Staying a bit longer wouldn't hurt. It would give her a chance to speak to the couple and see if they revealed anything unusual about themselves. 'Of course, Max, you show us your skills on the bike track.'

Their eyes all turned to Max once his helmet was re-buckled, and he took off.

'We're lucky to have Max,' Dot said. 'As I've said to Hope, he's given us a whole new lease on life. Hasn't he, love?'

William nodded, his eyes fixed on Max. 'He sure has.' He turned to Abi. 'Do you have children?'

She nodded. Although once Hayden was officially adopted, did she? 'A sixteen-year-old.'

'How lovely,' Dot said as Max scooted back to the group.

'Can we go and look at the fort, Mrs Abi? I want Pa to see it so he can decide if it's better than the other one he's going to look at.'

'If Dot and William are happy to walk up there then I think that would be fine.'

William looked to Dot. 'Did you want to stay here? I can go with the lad and Abi and then come back.'

Dot shook her head. 'No, I think I'll be okay. I've had a few aches and pains this morning, that's all,' she said by way of explanation to Abi. 'Nothing that won't sort itself out.'

William frowned. 'I think you should stay here. We won't be long.'

‘Only if Abi stays and keeps me company,’ Dot said.

‘Oh no, sorry, I can’t do that. I know that you’re very good friends with Hope, but Max is in my charge today. I can’t hand him over to William without Hope’s permission.’

Dot smiled and got to her feet. ‘Good, then that settles it, we’ll all go. It’s comforting to know Hope has someone so responsible looking after Max. Some people would be sitting staring at their phones, not paying any attention at all.’

The three adults walked slowly in the direction of the fort, Max scooting to and fro to make sure he stayed in their sight.

Dot was puffing and clutching her side by the time they reached the fort.

‘Are you okay?’ Abi asked.

Dot nodded and sat down on a bench at the entrance of the play area. ‘Just need to catch my breath.’

William helped Max unbuckle his helmet and propped his scooter up next to the bench. He turned to Abi. ‘Are you okay for me to go and explore the fort with Max? You should be able to see us from here.’

Abi nodded. ‘I’m a bit worried about Dot, though, William. She looks very pale.’

William focused his attention on his wife. ‘Her blood sugar might be a little low. Have you got any jelly beans, love?’

Dot shook her head. ‘I didn’t bring my bag.’

‘I’ve got some lollies in the car,’ Abi said. ‘Why don’t I go and get them.’ She turned to Max. ‘You can play on the fort if you like. William will need to stay with Dot while I get the lollies, but he can come and explore with you as soon as I get back.’

Max nodded and ran off.

‘I’ll only be a couple of minutes,’ Abi said. ‘Can you keep an eye on Max? The car’s only a short distance so I can watch him while I’m gone, but an extra pair of eyes would be good. Like I said, he's in my charge, so I don't want anything to happen that could worry Hope.'

'Of course,' William said. 'Max has three of us looking out for him, so I don't think Hope will be complaining.'

Abi hesitated before hurrying to the car, looking back to the fort every few seconds as she went, pleased that she could see Max's blue cape billowing out behind him as he ran from one area to the next. Once at the car, she took the lollies from the glovebox, then hurried back towards them. Halfway back, William got up and walked over to the fort. She was surprised he'd left Dot on her own, but perhaps it was a sign she was feeling better.

Abi smiled and waved to Max. He was standing on top of a small pillar calling to her to watch him. He jumped off and ran laughing to William.

'How are you?' she asked as she reached the bench. Dot's colour was looking better.

'I'll be fine, dear. Max called for William to join him, so they've gone to explore. He's such a joy, that little boy.'

Abi handed her the bag of lollies. 'Have a couple, just in case it is your blood sugar.'

'It's not,' Dot said. 'I couldn't say anything in front of William, but it's something else. I'm getting a lot of pain in my abdomen.' She winced and bent over as she said this. 'I saw the doctor last week, and they're running some tests. Hopefully, it's nothing serious.' She remained bent over, her face twisted with pain.

Concern flooded through Abi. 'Dot, I think you need to have someone look at you. This isn't right.'

Dot groaned in response.

'I'm going to call William back and have him take you to the hospital. You need medical attention.'

Dot shook her head. 'No, don't call him. He can't see me like this. I don't want him to know.'

'You can't hide this from him, Dot. He's your husband, and he's going to notice.'

'I just don't want him to worry until I know what it is.'

'Can I call someone else to come and get you? I'd offer to take you there myself, but I have Max, and I can't see how I'd explain to William what I was doing.'

Dot rummaged in her bag. 'I'll call Jonesy, get him to make up a story that he needs my help. William can take himself home. He won't suspect anything.'

Abi frowned. 'I think you should tell William. He needs to know.'

Dot squeezed her eyes shut and took several deep breaths before reopening them. 'Not yet. I'll get checked out first and then decide.' She scrolled through her contacts on her phone and called Jonesy's number. Abi listened to the one-sided conversation.

'Hi, love, my stomach's playing up rather badly. I think I might need your help.' Dot listened to whatever Jonesy had to say before replying. 'At the park, the one you recommended with the fort. We bumped into Max and Hope's friend Abi who's looking after him. Love, I need you to make up a story, so William thinks you need my help. I don't want him knowing I'm going to the hospital.'

She listened for a few more moments before ending the call.

'He'll be here in about ten minutes. He's a good man, our Jonesy.'

Abi wasn't sure what to say to any of this. She still thought Dot should tell William, but it wasn't her place.

'Could you go and tell William that Jonesy rang and he's picking me up? Tell him he needs me to help with the curtains for the new house and they have to be up today for the houseguests that are arriving tonight. Just tell him I forgot I'd agreed to help this morning.'

Abi hesitated as Dot curled over in pain again. 'Are you sure it's okay to leave you?'

Dot nodded. 'Jonesy won't be long.'

Abi slowly rose and walked over to the fort, glancing back at Dot every few metres. The older woman was watching her in between grimaces.

'Everything okay?' William asked as Abi approached him and Max. They were looking down the barrels of pretend guns, discussing a battle that seemed to be taking place in their imaginations.

'Jonesy just called,' Abi said. 'Dot was supposed to help him with some curtains this afternoon. He's stopping by in about ten minutes to collect her. She said to let you know that she'd completely forgotten.'

William rolled his eyes. 'And she says I'm developing dementia. I guess that puts our park exploring off for the afternoon. I'll head home, I think.'

'Not yet,' Max said. 'Stay and play forts.'

William grinned. 'Okay, Max, if Abi agrees, I'll stay a little longer.'

Abi nodded. 'I'll sit with Dot until Jonesy arrives.' It was on the tip of her tongue to say more about Dot and being worried about her, but she didn't. She didn't know this couple, and she needed to respect the older woman's wishes.

William and Max went back to the fort to continue their game, and Abi returned to the bench where Dot was sitting.

'I'm so sorry, Abi,' she said. 'Here you are having a nice day out with Max, and you end up having to babysit us.' She met Abi's gaze. 'Please don't tell Hope you saw us. She might not let Max come to us if she thinks there's something wrong with me.'

Abi shook her head. 'Sorry, I'm not keeping anything from Hope. As I said earlier, I'm responsible for Max today, and anything that happens should be reported back to her. She needs to be able to make decisions about her son with all of the facts present.'

Dot's face fell, but she nodded. 'Okay, I understand. Please tell her that I'm keeping this from William until I know what I'm dealing with.'

Abi nodded and the two women lapsed into silence. A few minutes later a shadow fell over them.

Abi looked up to find Jonesy smiling at her. He immediately turned his attention to Dot.

'How are you, Dot?'

She gave him a weak smile. 'I'm okay, but dreading the walk to your car. Something's not quite right inside.'

'I'll prop you up and help you,' Jonesy said. 'Let me just say a quick hi to William and let him know that I'll drop you home later. I assume he's in the fort with Max?'

'Yes, they're playing a game,' Abi said.

Jonesy nodded. 'Nice to see you again, Abi. Give me a minute and I'll be back for Dot.' He hurried over to the fort just as Max and his blue cape appeared, William right behind him. Max said hello then hurried off to the other side of the fort while Jonesy spoke to William. Once they'd finished speaking, Jonesy clapped William on the back and returned to Dot and Abi.

'William didn't look concerned, so he's believed Jonesy's story,' Abi said.

'Good.' Dot kept her response short and Abi couldn't help but notice her face screw up in pain once again. They needed to get her to the hospital.

Jonesy was back quickly and helped Dot to her feet. He put an arm around her. 'Lean into me and I'll help you back to the car.'

Dot did as he said and they started a slow shuffle towards the car park. Jonesy looked over his shoulder at Abi. 'If you could get on Dot's other side, it would be a lot quicker.'

Abi glanced round at Max and William, who were busy with their game.

'He'll be fine with William, Abi. Hope has him look after Max all the time. You know that.'

Dot groaned.

'I really think we need to get Dot some help,' Jonesy said.

'Of course.' Abi cast aside any reservations and hurried to Dot's side. With the two of them propping her up, they reached Jonesy's car in a matter of minutes.

'Thanks,' Jonesy said. 'Tell Hope I'll call her later tonight and tell her how Dot is. She can let you know.'

'Okay, that'd be great.' She looked in through Dot's window. 'Look after yourself, won't you. I won't say anything to William.'

Dot patted her hand that was resting on the car windowsill. 'Thanks, love, that's very good of you.' She squeezed her eyes shut again.

'Okay, we'd better go,' Jonesy said. 'See you later, Abi.'

She gave them a quick wave and hurried back up the path to the fort. Max's scooter and helmet were at the bench with his backpack where she'd left them. She looked up to the fort but couldn't see William or Max. No doubt they were playing in one of the sections on the far side of the fort. She walked up to the entrance, her eyes scouring the equipment. Three little boys were playing tag in one section, and a girl was sitting near the drawbridge pretending to stir a pot. But there was no sign of Max or William. Her heart rate quickened as she hurried into the fort and started searching each area. They couldn't have gone far in the few minutes she'd left them. She searched every section. Nothing. Had William taken Max to the toilet? There was an amenity block only a hundred metres from the fort – between it and the car park. She hurried to it, calling out their names. There was no response.

She pushed open all the doors, even those to the men's room. Nothing.

Abi's legs felt weak. She did her best to ignore her racing heart rate and pulled herself together. They had to be close by.

As she exited the toilet block a white car in the car park caught her attention. It was reversing out of its spot quickly, too quickly. It bumped the car opposite. A lump caught in Abi's throat as she saw blue material hanging out of the door. Max's cape. She sprinted in the direction of the car as it straightened, ready to exit the car park. She was still twenty metres away when she saw the driver of the car was William. He didn't look her way, but she caught a glimpse of Max's little face in the rear passenger window. He raised his hand and waved, a huge grin spreading across his face.

Abi stared after the car as it pulled out of the car park and drove off. She'd left the backpack on the bench with her keys in it. She raced back, grabbed the backpack and Max's scooter and helmet. By the time she'd returned to her car, it was too late. William's car was out of sight.

Her entire body started to shake. Had William kidnapped Max? Max wasn't distressed, he'd waved to her happily from the back of the car. But why had William done that? He'd said his original plan for the day was to go and look at more parks. Was that what he was doing now? Jesus, what should she do? She needed to contact Hope. She couldn't call the police because of Hope's situation.

She pulled out her phone and found Hope's number. It went straight to voicemail. It was probably in her locker at Fleming's. She did a quick search for the restaurant's number and rang that. Alex answered.

'Alex, it's Abi Whitmore. Is Hope available, please? Something rather urgent's come up.'

'She's setting up tables, Abi. Can she ring you on her break?'

Abi swallowed down the lump in her throat. 'No, it's urgent. I'm looking after her son, and someone's taken him.'

'Oh Jesus, I'll get her.'

'Alex, don't say anything to her, let me explain. It might not be as bad as it sounds.'

'Okay, hold on.'

A few moments later, Hope was on the line. 'Abi, is everything alright?'

Abi took a deep breath and then explained what had happened.

'What? William drove off with him?'

'Yes. It all happened so quickly. Dot took a turn, and Jonesy came and got her to take her to the hospital. I had to help her to the car, and when I returned, William had packed Max into his car and was driving off. Max looked fine. He waved happily to me out of the window with a big grin on his face.'

The line was silent for a moment.

'Hope?'

'I'm just trying to piece this all together. What were they doing there to start with?'

Abi explained that the older couple said they were filling in their day doing park reconnaissance. 'They said they were going to a park in Hampton with a fort next. I'm wondering if William got it in his head to take Max there too.'

'Possibly.'

'I wasn't sure whether to ring the police?'

'Not yet,' Hope said. 'Can you come and pick me up from work? We'll go to the park in Hampton and then to their apartment and see if they're there. William's been acting strangely for some time. I'm hoping this might just be another episode with him acting out of character.'

'He seemed completely fine at the park,' Abi said. 'He and Max were having a great time.'

'He'd never hurt Max, so I know we don't need to worry about that. I'll tell you more when you pick me up.'

Abi ended the call, threw Max's scooter and helmet on to the backseat and, heart thumping, drove towards Fleming's.

Chapter Twenty-Four

As soon as she ended the phone call with Abi, Lucinda turned to tell her boss she needed to leave, but Alex waved her on. 'Just go, I know something's happened. Ring me later when you find Max, okay?'

Lucinda nodded, unable to find any words, and rushed out of the building, willing Abi to drive quickly. She'd kill William when they found him. She just hoped that he'd decided on the spur of the moment to take Max to explore a new park and there was nothing more sinister to it. He was so besotted with Max, and her cancelling their day could have sparked all kinds of emotions in him. He'd done an excellent job hiding it if he had been upset. God, this was not what she needed today of all days. She'd just found out her husband was out of prison and now this. A shiver ran down her spine. The two things couldn't be related, could they? Of course they couldn't.

Jonesy. She needed to speak to him. She pulled out her phone and found his number. He answered on the second ring.

'Hope? Everything okay?'

'No, it's not. Do you know where William is?'

'I left him with Abi and Max at the park in Caulfield about twenty minutes ago. Don't tell William but Dot's had a bit of a turn. I'm taking her to the hospital now.'

'William took Max. He drove away from the park with him. Abi's just rung me distraught.'

There was a momentary silence at the end of the line before Jonesy spoke. 'Okay, look, he's old and he's harmless. He's probably taken him off to a different park or to have some fun. I don't think you need to worry that Max will be hurt.'

'I'm not. I just want to know where he is, and I want him back. Abi's coming to get me now. She said William mentioned another park with a fort he was going to check out this afternoon. They might have gone there.'

'The one in Hampton?'

'I think so.'

'Okay, go and check that one out and if he's not there ring me. I'll get Dot settled with the doctors and head back to their apartment in case he took him home.'

'Okay, thanks. Abi's here. I'd better go.'

Hope ended the call and ripped open the passenger door of Abi's car as it screeched to a stop. Abi's face was pale, her lip trembling.

'I'm so sorry, Hope, please believe me.'

'Don't worry, it's not your fault. William's not well, and I doubt he realises the fuss he's caused. Let's go to the park in Hampton, and if they aren't there, we'll go back to their apartment. Jonesy said to call him and he'll meet us there.'

'We might have to call the police if they're not there.'

Hope nodded. 'Hopefully it won't come to that.'

They travelled to the park in Hampton in silence. Hope jumped out before Abi had even killed the ignition. The park had a few children playing in it, but there was no sign of Max.

'Let's go to their apartment,' Hope said. 'It's just around the corner from us. I'll give you directions when we get closer.'

They climbed back into the car, and as Abi started it up and began driving out of the car park, Hope caught a glimpse of an older man sitting on a bench that had been blocked from view by a small bush. It was William. 'Stop!'

She pushed the car door open and sprinted across to the bench.

'William, where's Max?'

William looked up at her, tears rolling down his cheeks. 'He lied to me.'

'What? Who did? Max? William, where's Max?'

William shook his head, the tears getting heavier. 'No, Max would never lie. My grandson lied, that's who lied. He said if I did what he told me, then Max would be part of my life forever. That Dot and I would have partial custody.'

Coldness enveloped Lucinda. 'Your grandson said this?'

William nodded. 'We uprooted our lives for him. Lied to you and went through all of this for nothing. We'll never see Max again.' He was sobbing now.

Abi caught up to Lucinda, her eyes filled with concern.

Lucinda's heart was in her throat. She had one question she needed answered. 'William, who is your grandson?'

He looked at her through his tears. 'Ryan. Ryan Manning.'

Lucinda's legs crumpled beneath her, and she would have hit the ground if it weren't for Abi catching her and helping her on to the edge of the bench.

'Ryan, your husband?'

Lucinda nodded. 'He escaped from prison. I only found out this morning.'

'William,' Abi asked. 'Where's Max now? Did Ryan take him?'

William shook his head. 'A friend of Ryan's. They're delivering him to Ryan. Ryan's somewhere in New South Wales.'

'We have to call the police,' Abi said.

'He lied to us,' William said. 'To all of us.'

Lucinda ignored William. Right now, her focus was on getting Max back. She didn't even want to think about the fact that William and Dot had befriended them right from their first weekend in Melbourne. Ryan had known all along where they were.

'I need to ring Jonesy,' Lucinda said. 'See if he knows anything.' She called his number. There was no answer.

'He took Dot to the hospital, so might not be able to answer,' Abi said.

William snorted. 'Dot's fine. It was all part of the plan. They'll be at the apartment packing. Jonesy works for Ryan.'

'What?' The word roared from Lucinda's mouth. 'Are you serious? Do you realise the danger you've put Max in? Ryan's a dangerous man. He's not someone you mess with.'

The colour drained from William's face. 'We just wanted a relationship with Max. He's our great-grandson.'

'Why didn't you tell me?' Lucinda practically screamed at him. 'You were taking instructions from someone who's in prison. Didn't it cross your mind that that wasn't okay? That it might end badly? God, did you even find out why he was in prison?'

Abi took hold of Lucinda's arm. 'Come on. We need to find Max.'

Lucinda shook her arm free. Abi was right. William was not the priority right now, Max was.

The ten minutes it took to travel from Hampton to Elsternwick were the longest ten minutes of Lucinda's life. It was one thing when she'd thought Max was with William, who he trusted and loved, but quite another to think of him with a total stranger. She blinked back tears thinking of how frightened he must be.

Abi pulled to a stop outside William and Dot's apartment building, and they hurried out of the car to the lifts and up to the third floor.

Lucinda banged loudly on the door. 'Dot, Jonesy, I need to speak to you.'

The door opened immediately, and Jonesy stood on the other side. 'I'm just leaving. If you want Dot, she's inside.'

'I don't want Dot; I want my son, that's what I want. Where is he?'

'He's being transported back to his father.'

'His criminal father who just broke out of prison?'

Jonesy nodded. 'I'm sorry, I really am. I hate that I was part of this, but I had no choice. Your husband's holding a lot over me. And to be fair, neither did Dot or William. While he promised them access to Max, he also threatened them if they didn't follow his instructions.'

Lucinda stared at Jonesy. Everything that had happened with William, Dot and Jonesy had been orchestrated by Ryan? Her phone pinged as she tried to wrap her head around what was happening. She checked her message.

QF444 to Sydney, connecting through to Dubbo. Send police to the airport NOW. Namaste.

Jonesy stepped from the apartment and pulled the door shut. 'Look, Hope. I'm sorry about what's happened, but I also know that I need to leave. I assume you've already called the police?'

She shook her head. 'About to.'

Jonesy met her eyes for just a split second. 'I am sorry.' He turned and hurried from the apartment as Lucinda, with a shaking hand, drew her phone from her bag and called triple zero. She quickly explained what had happened and that she believed her son would be put on a flight to Sydney. The police told her to wait outside the apartment block. They would send a car to get her and would alert the airport authorities immediately.

Lucinda turned to Abi, doing her best to hold it together. 'I should never have run. This is all my fault.'

'It's not your fault,' Abi said. 'The main thing right now is staying strong and getting Max back. We can evaluate it all later. For now, just be strong and focus.'

Lucinda took deep breaths as they travelled back down to the ground level, trying her best to go with Abi's words. Being strong and focused was what she needed to do. A police car pulled up outside the building a few minutes later.

'Come with me.' She grabbed Abi's hand and pulled her into the back of the police car.

Lucinda answered all of the questions the police asked, admitting she was operating under a false identity and had fled Dorford in fear of her husband. She provided the police with a photo of Max from her phone, which they immediately sent to airport security and their officers at the airport.

The siren was blaring as they raced along the Tullamarine Freeway in the direction of Melbourne Airport. 'We're confident we'll have your son waiting for you when you arrive,' one of the officers told her. 'So far it appears they haven't checked in or been sighted. That will change very quickly.'

Lucinda couldn't respond. The fear that had settled over her was like nothing she'd experienced before. Even if they got Max back, what did it mean? Ryan had the capability to orchestrate this, a complete set-up ever since she'd arrived in Melbourne. He had the connections and the ability to destroy her, and quite possibly would. She tried to push the thoughts from her mind. Right now, her only concern should be Max's safety.

The police car pulled up outside the departures terminal and the two women were hurried inside. One of the officers took a call on the way in. 'Okay, great news. We'll be there in a minute.' He turned to Lucinda. 'They've been stopped at the gate. A woman's in custody and Max is being looked after. We'll go straight to him now.'

Lucinda hardly felt the squeeze of her hand Abi gave her. Her focus was on following the police officer and getting to Max. They were rushed through the security screening and into an administration section of the airport. Police officers stood outside two doors. They pointed to one. 'The child's in there.'

Lucinda raced to the open door and stopped. She didn't know whether to laugh or cry. Max was wearing one of the police officer's hats, his Scooter Max cape flapping out behind him as he saluted the officer then continued to march around the room. He looked like he was having a ball. He stopped when he saw Lucinda. 'Mumma!'

Lucinda rushed in and took him in her arms, her tears flowing freely down her cheeks.

Max squirmed out of her grip.

'Are you okay, Max? Has everyone been nice to you?'

He grinned. 'I've had the best day. First, there was Abi, then William took me on an adventure to a strange place where Mary was waiting. Then she told me Zeb was having his birthday at the airport, so she was going to bring me to the party. But when we got here, we couldn't find him, and then the police came to chat with us. I think they took Mary away to find Zeb and they've let me play in here ever since.'

Mary? Lucinda had no idea what the connection between Mary and Ryan was, but if she'd warned her, why was she now at the airport in police custody?

Lucinda turned to one of the police officers. 'I don't understand what's going on.'

'We're trying to work that out ourselves,' the officer said. 'The woman Max is referring to as Mary seems to have a connection with your husband. Her real name is Theresa Barrett.' He glanced at his notepad. 'Wife of Hunter Barrett, who, according to Theresa, worked with your husband prior to his death five and a half years ago.'

An uncontrollable shudder swept through Lucinda's body. *Hunter Barrett.* He'd got on the wrong side of a client by trying to sell him low-quality drugs. He'd borne the brunt of his client's fury when he'd been attacked with a baseball bat. Hunter had died three days later, leaving behind a pregnant wife and three kids. Her hand flew to her mouth. Was Theresa the pregnant wife? But she'd left Dorford immediately after Hunter's death, and Ryan had never mentioned her again. Why would she be working for him now?

The officer cleared his throat. 'Theresa is adamant that her involvement in your son's abduction was forced, that she had no choice. She was allegedly under threat from your husband. She says she also tried to warn you to leave Melbourne via several text messages. Is this true?'

Lucinda nodded. 'Yes. I still have them on my phone. They didn't give enough detail for me to know if they were real or not.'

The police officer nodded. 'Okay, we need to get you to the station for questioning. Is there someone who can look after Max for you?'

'I really would prefer he come with me,' Lucinda said. 'After everything that's happened, I don't want to let him out of my sight.'

‘That’s understandable, but it might take a few hours. We’ll need to talk to him first, but then he will be free to go. He’ll get pretty bored waiting at the station.’

‘I can wait with him or take him home,’ Abi said. ‘I won’t leave the apartment this time, and I’ll call the police if anything at all happens that seems suspicious.’

Lucinda hesitated before nodding slowly. As much as she didn’t want to let Max out of her sight, hanging around the police station for hours was not ideal either.

‘Okay,’ the officer said. ‘Now, let’s get Max organised. He can travel into the city with you to the station, and stay with you while we get a statement from Mrs Whitmore as to exactly what happened at the park, and then we’ll need to speak to Max. Once that’s done, they’ll be free to go. We’ll escort them home with protection. We’ll then need you for a few hours.’

Lucinda nodded, realising that she was no longer in control of what was happening. For now, she was going to have to go along with what the police said, and hope that they really could protect her and Max.

Lucinda was exhausted, her nerves completely frayed by the time the police told her they’d finished questioning her for now and they would drive her home. In the five hours she’d been at the police station, they’d confirmed Ryan had been found in the safe house in New South Wales.

‘Unfortunately, the situation isn’t under control as yet,’ the officer told her. ‘Ryan and those he’s holed up with have weapons and are threatening to use them. We believe the house is about to be stormed.’

‘What will happen to him?’ Lucinda asked.

'At this stage, all I can say is he won't get away. Over forty officers are surrounding the house. There's no getting out of this one.'

Lucinda had gone through hours of questioning so that the police could establish her every move since leaving Dorford. The relationship she'd formed with William and Dot, and Jonesy's involvement in it all. Lucinda still found it hard to wrap her head around everything. To think she'd thought herself lucky to have met such a lovely couple in William and Dot. To now find out that Ryan had set up the first meeting and everything following it was just awful. He'd been alerted by one of his colleagues the moment she'd boarded the bus from Dorford to Brisbane, and he'd had her watched from that point forward. So much for her exiting Dorford discreetly. She should have known better. Ryan's contacts spread far and wide.

From what the police had learnt from William and Dot, it appeared Ryan had manipulated his grandparents. Previously estranged from them, he'd used the lure of Max to develop a relationship. They hadn't known of Max's existence until Ryan had contacted them from the prison after he'd been sentenced. He'd promised them partial custody and involvement in Max's life if they went along with his plan. He'd told them all he was doing was establishing for the courts that Lucinda needed help. That sharing custody with them would be a perfect arrangement moving forward and would mean once he was out of prison he would be able to spend time with Max under their supervision. It had all sounded quite reasonable until he'd had one of his criminal associates visit them. They'd been told there would be detrimental consequences if they didn't go along with his instructions, or if they told Lucinda anything.

Meeting Max and Lucinda had made it easy for them. Ryan's associate had brought them to the hotel in Melbourne the first night Lucinda had checked in, with strict instructions that they were to have a casual conversation over breakfast. To plant the seed of moving to Elsternwick. They'd fallen in love with both of them immediately and couldn't imagine a life without them. They'd then been told to await further instructions. It had been weeks before Ryan had allowed them to 'bump into' Lucinda and Max in the park. Dot had told the police that waiting those weeks had been torture for them, and they'd gone along with everything Ryan had said, scared he would change the plans or stop them from seeing Max if they did anything wrong.

Before being allowed to leave the airport, Lucinda had asked to speak to Mary. She needed to work out exactly why she'd become involved.

The police agreed to a supervised five-minute meeting between the two women. Nerves flitted in Lucinda's stomach as she entered the room. Mary was staring at her hands, her face pale. She looked up the moment Lucinda entered.

'I'm so sorry.'

Lucinda shook her head. 'I'm here to thank you. You don't need to be sorry.'

'I should have warned you properly that first day in the park. It was when I saw Jonesy that I realised who you were and how I knew you. When I first saw you at yoga, you were vaguely familiar, but I couldn't place you. We never officially met in Dorford but I did see you at a barbecue once. You smiled at me, but then one of the kids dragged me away, so we never got to speak. What I noticed then, and again when you first came to yoga, are your eyes. They're stunning, but as your hair is so different and you said you were from Perth I couldn't work out where I knew you from. When Jonesy appeared, I made the connection to Ryan immediately, and that's when I worked out who you were. The fact you'd also changed your name made me realise you'd probably run. But it was too late by then. Jonesy saw me and reported back to Ryan that I was here, and he assumed I was helping you.'

'You know Jonesy?'

Mary nodded. 'He was close with my late husband, Hunter. Hunter was killed when a drug deal went wrong, and I left Dorford.'

'I remember. The police told me your real name is Theresa Barrett. Do I call you Theresa or Mary?'

'Mary. Like you, I changed my name when I left Dorford. I needed to start again. I hated what Hunter had done for a living and didn't want any association with it.'

'I remember when your husband died, how upset Ryan was.'

Mary bit her lip. 'And I honestly thought he was genuine in helping me with my fresh start. He organised a GoFundMe account and added his own money to it. It set me up and gave me enough money to move. I didn't realise at the time it came with strings attached. It meant I owed Ryan and he called in his favour today.' Her face paled further and she swallowed a sob. 'Jonesy saw me in the park that Saturday, and later that night when I was packing up getting ready to leave Melbourne, I had a visit from him. He told me that, after all he'd done for me, Ryan was very unhappy that I'd been helping you. I tried to explain that I hadn't helped you, that our meeting was a pure coincidence and I'd only just made the connection, but they didn't believe me. I was told that I needed to stay away from you, and I would be required to help move Max back to his father.'

'And you went along with it?'

'I had no choice. He threatened my kids, and I know it wasn't an empty threat. I was promised that as soon as Max was returned to Ryan, nothing else would be expected of me and I could live wherever I wanted and wouldn't be contacted again.'

Lucinda stared at the woman standing in front of her. 'It was a huge risk sending those text messages and ringing my mum.'

'I know, but I couldn't stand by and let it happen to you or Max. I'm so sorry, though. I had no idea how to do it properly. I couldn't go to the police, and I couldn't risk revealing who I was. I feel like I've made such a mess of things.'

'God, no. I have Max back, and once they get Ryan, he'll be going away for a very long time. I'm incredibly grateful to you.' A tear slid down Mary's cheek. 'What's going to happen to you now?'

'I don't know. I'll be taken down to the station soon for a formal statement, and I guess I'll need to speak to a lawyer.'

'Surely they'll believe you weren't given a choice? I'm happy to speak to them if you need me to, to explain what sort of person Ryan is. That if he threatened you, you'd have to listen.'

'Thanks. I'll give the lawyer your details.'

The two women stood in silence for a few moments. Eventually, Lucinda spoke. 'I'm sorry that you got caught up in all of this.'

'Me too. And I'm sorry Ryan's put you through what he has. Hopefully, once this is all resolved, we'll both be able to live normal lives and not look over our shoulders the whole time.'

Lucinda nodded. She'd give just about anything for that.

As she sat in the back of the police car on the way home, Lucinda's thoughts turned to William, Dot and Jonesy. The police had confirmed that they had been taken into custody. As much as Lucinda wanted to hate them for what they'd done, she couldn't. She knew what it was like to be controlled by Ryan, and it appeared all three of them had been under his control. Although she wasn't so sure about Jonesy. If he'd been involved with Mary's husband and Ryan, he'd probably done things over his lifetime that had come back to haunt him. All his talk about wishing he'd done things differently in the past now made sense.

She thanked the police officers for the lift, nodding as they reminded her of her need to remain in the area, as more questioning would be required over the coming days, and hurried towards the apartment block. She was puffing by the time she hammered on Abi's door.

'Who is it?' Abi's voice came from the other side.

'It's me, Lucinda. I mean, Hope. I mean, God, I don't know what I mean.'

The door swung open, and Abi gave her a nervous smile. 'Max is watching *Peppa Pig*. I hope that's okay.'

Lucinda nodded, then burst into tears. It was all too much. Abi embraced her immediately. 'I'm so sorry about today. I can't believe I fell for their tricks. I honestly thought Dot was having some kind of turn.'

Lucinda pulled back and wiped her eyes. 'You don't need to apologise. I've had them looking after Max for weeks. There was something a bit off, but I thought it was William's ill health, nothing like this.'

'Come in,' Abi said. 'I opened a bottle of wine to breathe as soon as I got home. I thought we'd need it tonight.'

Lucinda followed Abi into the apartment. The one thing she knew for sure was that she needed a glass of wine.

The bottle of wine disappeared far too quickly; its usual relaxing qualities absent as Lucinda realised her nerves were still a mess. Abi had made some sandwiches for Max's dinner, and he'd fallen asleep in the middle of the chaise lounge.

Lucinda blinked back tears as she watched him sleeping, his arms around Mr Fizz, his face peaceful and full of innocence. How differently the day could have turned out. She'd just got off the phone with her mother. Tess had cried tears of joy when Lucinda explained that she'd gone to the police and they knew everything.

She also warned her mother that she should expect a visit from them.

'I don't understand why Ryan didn't tell me he knew where you were,' Tess said. 'He acted as though he believed that I had no idea and we were searching for you together.'

'He's a professional manipulator, Mum. He would have known that everything he told you was relayed to me. Making sure I knew of his plans to get out of prison and to take custody of Max. It was all deliberate. He wanted to scare me and make sure I knew that he was still in control. That ultimately things would play out exactly as he said. By acting like he didn't know where Max was, there was no reason for me to be suspicious of William and Dot having any connection to Ryan. Thank God he decided to use you like that and didn't hurt you, or worse. At least you won't have to visit him again. None of us will.'

'No, but I can visit you,' Tess said. 'I'll speak to the police tomorrow, and assuming they don't need me to stay here I'll get a flight down tomorrow afternoon. We don't have to hide anymore.'

'We don't, but still be careful, Mum.'

Tess promised she would and said she was going to hang up and start packing.

'You can both stay here tonight if you want to,' Abi said. 'If you'd feel safer?'

'No – thanks, though. We'll only be next door, and the police are driving by regularly. I can ring them if I'm worried. The landline works in the apartment, and I'll organise a new mobile tomorrow.' She gave a wry laugh. 'I guess I can pull out all of my real identification this time. I'm no longer in hiding.'

Abi smiled. 'Do I call you Lucinda now?'

Lucinda nodded. 'Yes, please. I thought Hope was a great name. That moving here gave me hope for a new start in life. But it hasn't exactly turned out that way.'

'It has in some ways,' Abi said. 'You're no longer running from your husband, the police know what's going on, and after the attempted abduction they will be able to provide you with protection. I'm sure Ryan won't be entitled to any visits or custody if he's ever released.'

Lucinda smiled at Abi. 'Sorry to get you caught up in all of this. I'm sure after the weekend you had, this was the last thing you needed.'

Abi gave a small laugh. 'I said I wanted a distraction from my weekend and you certainly gave me that. I haven't given Hayden or what's happened a thought all day.' Her face clouded over.

'But you are now.'

Abi nodded. 'But that's okay. It's going to take time to come to terms with the new arrangement. I'll be okay. Let me help you out with Max. From memory, sleeping four-year-olds can get quite heavy. I'll bring his scooter around tomorrow. It's still in the car.'

Lucinda's phone rang as she stood ready to help Abi with Max. She slipped it from her pocket and answered it. It was the police. She sank back down on to one of Abi's kitchen chairs as she listened. Ryan had been caught.

'Unfortunately, the siege didn't end peacefully,' the officer said. 'Shots were fired, and Ryan Manning was killed.'

Lucinda squeezed her eyes shut. The officer was still talking, but she wasn't registering what he was saying. The call ended, and she opened her eyes to find Abi standing next to her, her face full of concern.

'It's over,' Lucinda said. 'He's not going to be released. He's dead.'

Abi sucked in a breath. 'Are you okay?'

Lucinda nodded. 'He's gone, Abi. He's finally gone. Max and I are free.' She stood and Abi pulled her into her arms. An overwhelming sense of relief settled over Lucinda. Her jailer was gone.

No more looking over her shoulder. No more worrying they'd be caught. After years of being controlled, she could live her life again. She pulled out of Abi's embrace, grateful for her friend's support but knowing she needed to be on her own.

With Abi's help, she lifted Max from the chair. She blinked back tears as she stared at his innocent face. With all that had gone on, the one thing she could be grateful for was that the people who'd tried to take him had cared for him. He'd felt loved and safe the entire time. He wasn't going to be traumatised by the events, which was a relief. She, on the other hand . . .

Chapter Twenty-Five

Abi was relieved that life seemed to have calmed down again after the events two weeks ago, with Max and the failed abduction. Lucinda hadn't decided whether she would stay in Melbourne or go back to Queensland, but for the moment she was required to remain where she was until William, Dot, Jonesy and Mary had faced the courts and sentencing. Abi had looked after Max on a few occasions for Lucinda but had chosen to stay in the apartment and cook with him and make play dough or do paintings. She wasn't willing to risk going out. Tess, Lucinda's mother, had arrived the day after the abduction, so she'd been able to help Lucinda out with babysitting and had kept her company. She was planning to stay another week, which worked perfectly as far as Abi was concerned. It meant she would be here for her fortieth birthday party and would be a comfort to Lucinda after Abi was gone.

The box of Ambien had arrived over a week ago, and Abi shivered each time she looked at it. Her own death sentence staring back at her. She'd splurged on her favourite bottle of red wine, which she intended to take the tablets with. She knew she needed to be careful that she didn't take too long ingesting them, or they might put her to sleep before she'd taken enough to do the job.

Laila was contacting her daily to organise details for the party. She felt guilty that it was never going to go ahead, but she'd told

Laila numerous times that she didn't want a party. That she wanted to celebrate with Mel, Laila and Lucinda, and that was all. Laila still wasn't listening though. She'd done her best to try to convince Abi that she still had friends who supported her. Abi sighed at the thought. These *friends* had been noticeably absent during the last few months, and the idea of facing anyone at her birthday made her squirm uncomfortably. She felt awful with what she was going to put her friend through, and Mel and Lucinda for that matter, but her mind had been made up for some time. The timing gave her the added bonus of not sitting through an excruciating party.

She had an appointment with Ross at Law One at four, just over an hour away, to go over the final details of her new will. She'd contemplated changing lawyers, but as he knew her and Eric's history, if he was questioned by the police after her death he'd be able to confirm she had checked all of the life insurance policies numerous times to ensure they would pay out. Her will should be finalised and ready for signing, with all of the beneficiaries clearly listed. Once that was done, it was just a final countdown and finding an opportunity to say goodbye. She planned to make a trip out to visit Mel and Tony, drop in on Laila under the guise of party planning, and do the same with Lucinda and Tess. She'd take a nice bottle of bubbles to celebrate Lucinda's freedom from her husband and to say her goodbyes. Not that anyone would know she was doing this.

She checked her watch as she put the finishing touches on her make-up. If she left now, she'd have time to grab a coffee at the cafe below Ross's building. She'd not allowed herself to buy any food or drinks out since Eric's death, but this week she decided she would make some exceptions. It was her last week to enjoy the simple things, and she was going to make an effort to.

Shortly after arriving for her four o'clock meeting, Ross passed the documents across to Abi for signing. 'The will has been updated as per your instructions.' He watched her as she took the pages from his hands and started to read through it.

'Is everything alright, Abi?'

She looked up. 'What do you mean?'

'It's just that you've really pushed for this will to be drawn up, and are very specific that it needs to be divided between the clients affected by Eric's business. I'm just concerned that it all seems rather rushed, that's all.'

Abi put the papers down. 'Ross, I could walk out of here and get hit by a bus. Imagine if that happened. Of course, we're assuming I'm going to die of old age so these payouts won't happen for many years, but what if I don't? What if there's an accident or a natural disaster? People die every day. I thought you'd be encouraging people to keep their wills up to date.'

'As long as that's all it is and you're not planning on speeding things up.'

Heat crept up the back of Abi's neck. 'As if I'd do that to my family.' She shook her head and averted her eyes back to the document.

'It's just that originally you wanted specific amounts left to those affected by Eric's business dealings, but with the investigation still going on, you've left it more general. That it is to be divided equally amongst any clients who have been affected. If you waited until the investigation was complete, you could name clients and allocate amounts to them.'

Abi nodded. 'I can always update it once the investigation is finalised.'

'That should be this week,' Ross said. 'A meeting has been organised tomorrow for me to discuss the findings with the investigations team. I decided I would represent Eric.'

'Really? Why?'

Ross shrugged. 'I'm hoping this investigation will find plenty of profitable investments. If it does, after the clients have their monies returned, there may be money to distribute out of the company to help pay back some of the debt. I want to make sure that this is all done in the best interests of everyone.'

'Thank you. That's really generous, but I'm not sure I can pay you.'

'I'm not expecting you to, Abi. That's not why I'm doing it. Now, you realise that the current will doesn't leave Hayden with much, don't you?'

Abi shook her head. 'Two hundred thousand is a decent amount to give him a boost in the event of my death, and I'm sure my brother-in-law will look after him if something did happen to me.'

'Okay, well, if you want to sign it, I'll have Rosemary come in and witness your signature.'

Ten minutes later, Abi returned to her car with mixed feelings. On the one hand, she felt like a weight had been lifted from her. She had a plan and it was coming together. But then the reality of what she was going to do once again settled on her shoulders. Could she really do this to the people who cared about her? Would they ever forgive her? She pushed the thoughts from her mind and turned the key in the ignition. She'd made her plan and she needed to stop analysing it and just get on with it.

Abi pulled out on to St Kilda Road, debating whether to make the drive out to Geelong to see Mel or stop in and see Laila. She started early, so was often home by four. It was a little after five now, so unless she'd gone to the gym or had a hot date, she was probably at home.

Abi stopped at one of her favourite florists in Clarendon Street before continuing to Laila's cottage in Port Melbourne. She knocked on the door, the large bouquet of lilies spilling from her arms.

'Wow.' Laila's eyes widened as she took in the flowers. 'They're beautiful. What's the occasion?'

'Just wanted to say thank you.' Abi passed the flowers to her friend. 'You've been wonderful since Eric . . . well, since he died. And you were wonderful before that too. I just wanted you to know that I appreciate everything you've done and love that you're such a good friend.'

Tears instantly filled Laila's eyes. 'That's so lovely, Abi. I love you, you're very special to me, so of course I'm there for you, just like you always are for me.'

Abi blinked back tears of her own. This was going to be harder than she realised. She had to try to stop the thoughts of what Laila was going to go through next week when she was gone.

'Come in,' Laila said. 'I've got some bubbles in the fridge, and what better way to start getting into birthday celebrations than to drink champagne midweek.'

Abi followed her down the narrow hallway that opened out into a large kitchen and open-plan living area. Laila's cat, Foxy, stretched in his position in front of the open fire, one eye opening to check who had arrived before curling up and going back to sleep.

'Wish I was Foxy sometimes,' Laila said. 'How nice to have no stress, no worries, yummy food and plenty of cuddles. The perfect life.'

Abi nodded. It certainly was.

Laila put the flowers in a vase then opened the fridge and took out a bottle of Taittinger.

'Are you sure you want to drink that?' Abi asked. 'It's a special one.'

'For a special friend.' Laila eased the cork from the bottle. 'I've got a case of this for Saturday, so you'd better be ready to have a big night. I've lots planned.' Guilt settled in the pit of Abi's stomach. 'Do you want me to tell you who's coming?'

Abi shook her head. 'Let's leave it as a surprise. Like I said when you first started to plan it, I can't believe anyone will show up other than you and Mel, so I'm happy to find out on the night.'

Laila grinned. 'Good. Now tell me what's been happening. The last time we caught up, you'd just had all the drama with Hope or Lucinda or whatever we call her now. Anything else to report?'

They spent the next hour chatting and reminiscing about funny things that had happened leading up to previous birthdays. Eventually, Abi decided it was time to say her final goodbye and leave.

'I really meant it when I said you mean a lot to me,' she said as they reached the front door. 'I want you to always know that, okay? Sometimes I don't say how I feel, but I'd never want you to wonder. Our friendship is more important than any other friendship in my life.'

Laila hugged her. 'Ditto, and thank you. It's not the stuff we normally talk about, but it is nice on occasion to let each other know how we feel. I had planned a speech on Saturday night about you, but you're getting in a bit early.'

Abi smiled, conscious of the tears welling up in her eyes. 'That speech would be about me, and I wanted to say something to you. Something I want you to always remember. You're the best, Laila, you really are.' She leant forward and hugged her friend again, before turning and hurrying towards her car. She didn't want Laila to see the tears that were cascading down her cheeks.

The next afternoon, Abi's stomach churned as she made the drive out to Geelong. She'd rung Mel the night before and said she was taking her and Tony out for dinner and to be ready by six, so they could have a drink or two beforehand.

She pulled up in front of their townhouse right on six, the boot of her car full of presents. She hesitated as she went to get them. Mel would think something was up if she suddenly brought them all in. Maybe she'd be best to leave them with a note for Mel to find . . . after.

Part of her wanted to see the delight on Mel's face as she opened presents containing baby clothes, toddler clothes and all sorts of baby paraphernalia, but it was something she realised she was just going to have to miss out on. Losing the opportunity to attend the birth of her nephew or niece and seeing them grow was one of the hardest aspects of her decision – that and the possibility of reuniting with Hayden at some stage, of course.

She shook her head, trying to clear her mind, and made her way to the front door. It swung open and Tony greeted her with a beaming smile and pulled her into a hug. 'Hey sis-in-law, great to see you.'

Abi laughed and hugged him back. She pulled away eventually, drawing in a deep breath. 'Something smells delicious in here. I am taking you out for dinner, you know.'

'No, you're not,' Mel said, appearing in the hallway. 'You can't afford that right now, and I'm making your favourite Peking duck pancakes.'

Abi's mouth watered at the thought. 'But you can't afford it either at the moment, remember? Tonight was supposed to be on me. I didn't even bring any wine as I thought we were eating out.'

'We've got it covered,' Tony said. 'Mel's not drinking but you and I can. I've made the spare room up already.'

Abi laughed. 'Good plan. Please let me go to the bottle shop at least, and contribute something.'

Tony took her by the shoulders and marched her down the hallway to one of the stools at the island counter in the kitchen. 'Nope. We've got bubbles and your favourite Merlot and news.'

Abi looked across at Mel. 'Baby news?'

'That's extra news,' Mel said. 'We have some money news first.' She crossed the room and put an arm around Tony. 'You tell her, as you made it happen.'

Tony blushed. 'I didn't actually, Eric did.'

'Eric?'

Tony nodded. 'Do you remember when Mel and I got engaged?'

'Of course.'

'Well, remember at the engagement party Eric said he wanted to talk to me, that he was going to take me out the back and kick some sense into me to make sure I always looked after Mel? He made a big joke out of it in front of everyone.'

'I remember.' Abi did. She'd been surprised by how protective Eric had been towards Mel. Surprised and delighted that he considered her family and loved her like she was his sister.

'Well, he didn't kick any sense into me. He told me that he was thrilled for us, that he thought of Mel as his own sister and couldn't imagine a better brother-in-law. We had a few drinks and toasted each other and what great blokes we were.' He laughed at the memory. 'And then he gave me something.' He walked over to the bench and picked up a piece of paper and handed it to Abi. It contained numerous lines of computer code. She looked up at Tony. 'What is it?'

'On that night nine years ago, Eric gave me fifty bitcoins. We laughed about it as they were worth two dollars each. He said a hundred dollars was a good amount for an engagement present, but I had to keep them for at least ten years, if not longer, as they were going to be worth a fortune. I'd completely forgotten about them until the other day, when a guy at work was complaining that he'd never bought any.'

'Abi,' Mel said, her eyes shining with excitement. 'They're worth nearly thirteen thousand dollars now.'

Abi smiled. 'That's great. You'll be able to buy something for yourselves or the baby.'

Mel frowned. 'That's it? I thought you'd be more excited for us.'

'Well, I am, but thirteen thousand isn't going to pay back your debts.'

'Thirteen thousand each, not in total. It's over six hundred and fifty grand and going up every day.'

Abi's mouth dropped open. 'You're kidding?'

Tony shook his head. 'Nope! The bitcoins are worth more than double what we lost. We can't believe it.'

'Have you cashed it in?'

'Not yet,' Mel said. 'We think we might cash in half of them and keep the rest.'

Abi nodded. In the next few weeks they were going to get an additional three hundred thousand dollars, once her will was settled. She wished she could tell them so they could keep their bitcoins if they thought they would continue to increase in price.

'Did Eric buy any for you guys?' Tony asked.

Abi nodded. 'He did, but he sold them all a few years back. He'd be kicking himself now.'

'We're happy to give you some of them,' Mel said. 'Help you out a bit.'

Abi shook her head. 'Nope. I'm just so happy it helps you.' And she was. In fact, she couldn't ask for a better outcome for them. 'Now, where are those bubbles, it's definitely a night to celebrate.'

It was after one when Abi's head hit the pillow. Mel and Tony were in a much better place than they had been only a few weeks ago. Financially secure once again, a baby on the way, and by the looks of things, madly in love. She was so happy for them. Her eyes welled when she thought of what Eric had done. He'd always talked about bitcoin being the next big thing, but she'd been sceptical. She'd happily gone along with him spending a few hundred dollars on them but hadn't felt comfortable investing thousands like he suggested. What a pity she'd not only questioned him but then encouraged him to sell them a few years back.

Even after a late night and too much champagne, Abi was up at seven and ready to leave by eight. Both Mel and Tony needed to leave for work, so she said her goodbyes, giving them both an extra-long hug.

'I'm so glad things have worked out how they have,' she said to Mel. 'Remember how much I love you, okay? You're so important to me, and I want the very best for you and the baby, no matter what.'

Mel swatted her away. 'Too much champagne makes you emotional. But I love you too, and we'll see you on Saturday night, don't forget. The big four-oh. We can actually afford a present for you now.'

Abi shook her head. 'Last night was my present. Really, don't get anything. There's nothing that I want other than you knowing you're the best sister anyone could ever have.' Abi didn't wait for a response. Tears had been threatening since she woke up and she didn't want Mel to see them. She pushed her sunglasses on to her face and slid into the driver's seat.

'See you Saturday,' Mel called as Abi backed out of the driveway and pulled into the street.

Abi only made it a few kilometres down the road before she had to pull over. She could hardly see through her tears. She'd known this would be hard, but it was beyond that. The pain in her chest was excruciating. She imagined having a heart attack must feel something like this. She knew it was heartache, not a heart attack, but the enormity of her feelings of grief was overwhelming.

She did her best to take deep breaths and calm herself, eventually finding her breathing steady again and her eyes dry. A dull headache started and she closed her eyes, wishing she could squash every emotion she was currently experiencing. The reality was, the pain she was feeling now would be gone for her on Saturday, but it wouldn't for Mel or anyone else that cared about her. She was going to put them through this agony. She turned the key in the ignition, questioning whether she really could go through with it. For all of the good she was trying to achieve, would the pain and suffering she inflicted be more damaging than the current situation where people were suffering financially?

She drove slowly towards the main highway between Geelong and Melbourne. The fact she was questioning her decision meant perhaps she wasn't ready to make it after all.

Her thoughts were interrupted by her phone ringing. She hesitated, not recognising the number on the car's old touchscreen. She chose to answer it. She needed something to distract her from her current line of thinking.

'Abi, it's Ross.'

'Ross? Is there an issue with the will?'

He cleared his throat. 'No, I wanted to speak to you before you hear this yourself. The investigation team will, of course, be in contact, but I'm pretty sure the media's got wind of it, so I didn't want you hearing elsewhere. As you know, I met with them yesterday to go through their findings.'

Abi's heart began to race. She wasn't sure if she was ready to hear this. 'What is it?'

'The investigation's uncovered that the property development isn't his only failed investment. A few months ago he lost a substantial amount of money in a copper mine that closed in Western Australia. Share prices fell from over a dollar to twelve cents in a matter of days. Unfortunately, Eric had a lot invested, and like the property development, it appears it was invested without client consent. It wiped three million dollars from the business.'

'What? You're kidding?' Abi knew the mine had closed. At the time, Eric had been frustrated that it had happened so quickly without enough warning to sell shares. He had assured her it was a very small investment, which profits in the company would cover. It obviously wasn't.

'Unfortunately, I'm not kidding, and several other unauthorised investments have been uncovered.'

'How can they be unauthorised? Eric's clients sign a contract when they first invest. They're generally leaving it up to Eric's discretion as to where he invests the money.'

'True, but unfortunately many of these investments haven't been recorded on any client statements, yet their money has been used. Eric's done an excellent job of falsifying statements and hiding his business from clients. Both the losses but also a lot of wins. He's reported *safe* investments and small returns to many clients when he's actually used their funds in much higher-risk investments. Investments that he's taken the profits from and reinvested in new opportunities. From what has been uncovered, he's taken some of the money out of the company but not huge amounts that would make you suspicious. Whether he was waiting for a really big payout to take the money, or whether he would have continued to reinvest we'll never know. But when the copper mine failed, he had a problem. A three-million-dollar problem. How does he explain to his clients that their *safe* investments have been lost when the companies he's said he's invested in have actually turned a profit?

Suddenly he's in a world of trouble, which we assume he tried to fix with the property development. Unfortunately, what it's shown is that the unethical and illegal dealings have been going on for many months and none of the money can be recouped.'

Abi pulled the car over to the side of the road, opened the door and vomited on to the curb.

'Abi? Are you okay?'

She leant back in her seat, wiped her mouth with the back of her hand and ended the call. She couldn't talk to Ross or anyone right now. She could only imagine what discussions were taking place among Eric's clients and their families. They would be devastated.

She squeezed her eyes shut. Had she known her husband at all? You heard stories of people being clueless of what their partners were up to, but surely she should have seen some signs that he was . . . that he was a lying, cheating, unscrupulous bastard. Her eyes flicked open, and she started the car and manoeuvred back into the street. Feelings of anger, grief and bewilderment churned within her. The one thing that Ross's phone call had done was make her decision a lot easier. She could make a difference, and she could escape this nightmare. Both of which she intended to do.

Abi woke the morning of her fortieth birthday after a restless night. As hard as she'd tried, pushing thoughts of Eric and his betrayal from her mind wasn't possible. She dressed in her favourite pair of worn, comfy jeans and a black knit jumper. Comfort clothing. She'd spent most of the previous day writing letters to Hayden, Mel, Laila and Lucinda. She had no idea what Lucinda would tell Max, and felt terrible that she was putting any of them through this, but unfortunately it was a reality of the situation.

It was only eight o'clock. In theory, she was being picked up at four by Laila ready to be taken to the surprise birthday location. Guilt gnawed at her that Laila had gone to a lot of trouble to put something together for her birthday, but it didn't change what she'd planned. She had to do this now.

She did a final check around the apartment. She'd tidied everything the previous day to ensure there wouldn't be too much for anyone to do. She'd left a box with Hayden's name on it full of USB sticks with family photos on them. She'd made a copy for Mel too. She put them on the kitchen table along with the letters, which were all sealed in envelopes. A form with practical information was also printed out. Her lawyer's details, a copy of her will, even though Ross would have that, and Alexandria's contact details as well as Gabe's. They would both need to be told once she was gone: Alexandria for the practical side of needing an apartment manager, and Gabe so that he could tell Hayden. She couldn't imagine what it would be like for any of them reading the letters or hearing the news – particularly Laila, who would find her this afternoon.

She checked that the front door was unlocked. Even though every fibre in her body wanted to lock it and ensure one hundred percent privacy, she needed Laila to be able to get in later and find her. She did one last walk around the apartment. Everything was in order.

She took the wine from the cupboard and the container of pills. She'd decanted all of the pills from their packaging into a plastic container. She already knew that once she was ready to go, she would need to work fast – swallow them all in a few minutes to ensure that she didn't fall asleep or pass out before she'd ingested enough. The bottle of Merlot to increase the effects of the pills had seemed like a good idea . . . until now. Drinking at eight o'clock in the morning held no appeal at all. She couldn't leave it too long, though. She needed to make sure she was not revivable when Laila came to collect her at four. The last thing she wanted was to go through all of this to wake up in hospital having her stomach pumped, and find it was all for nothing.

She grabbed a wine glass from the cupboard and took it over to the couch. It might be too early, but a couple of sips and she'd probably get the taste for it. It would be her last chance to enjoy a beautiful Merlot, so she needed to ignore the clock and pretend it was afternoon drinks. She poured a glass and then tipped the pills on to the coffee table. She shook her head, not quite believing she was going to put these into her body. She took a sip of her wine, and another, still staring at the pills. Normally after a sip or two her body would relax, but not today; she was more wound up than ever.

With her heart racing, Abi took a large gulp of wine, refilled her glass and picked up three of the pills. She figured she could wash down three at a time no problem, and just keep doing that until they were gone. It would be close to seventy mouthfuls. That was a lot. She'd deliberately not eaten anything since she'd woken, realising she needed the capacity in her stomach for two hundred pills. They weren't going to fit on top of a bowl of muesli.

She closed her eyes momentarily, saying goodbye to her life. Even at this point, it was hard to imagine that she'd be gone in a matter of hours, probably less with this quantity of pills. She reopened her eyes, picked up three pills and popped them in her mouth. She was about to wash them down with a mouthful of wine when a piercing scream erupted from outside her door. It was followed by another, and her door flung open. 'Mrs Abi, help me, Mrs Abi.'

Abi spat the pills into her hand and rushed to help Max. 'What's happened?'

He pointed at his hand as he gulped for air. 'I got stung by a bee. Don't tell Mumma.'

'Quickly, come and sit down. Where is Mumma, and why aren't we telling her?'

Tears ran down his chubby cheeks. 'I snuck out to ride my scooter after Mumma told me I wasn't allowed to. She was in the shower. I'll be in big trouble.' His chest heaved as he began to sob.

'Let me have a look at your hand, Max. We need to remove the stinger and then we'll put some ice on it. Will you trust me to help you?'

Max nodded, held his hand out to Abi and closed his eyes. She could see the sting site. She used the edge of her fingernail to remove the stinger, then hurried to the fridge and took an icepack from the freezer. She brought it back over to Max. 'Put this on it, and it will help with the pain. I've got some aloe vera gel we can put on it too, which will help, and Mumma might give you some Panadol if the pain gets really bad.'

'If what's *really* bad?' Lucinda appeared in the hallway of Abi's apartment. 'Sorry to barge in but I came out of the shower and Max was gone. I heard him in here, thank God.'

'He's been stung by a bee,' Abi said. 'I've taken the sting out and put some ice on it. I was just saying you might want to give him a painkiller.'

Lucinda stepped further into the living area. 'Thank you so much. You're a lifesaver. Max, I've got painkillers back in the apartment, let's go and get you one.'

'Mrs Abi has lots,' Max said, pointing to the coffee table. 'Lots and lots.'

Lucinda's eyes flitted from Max to the coffee table and then to Abi. Her mouth dropped open. 'Oh my God. You weren't . . . ? Have you taken any?'

Abi hung her head in shame. She couldn't even get this right.

'Abi!' Lucinda's voice was verging on hysteria. 'Have you taken any of the pills?'

Abi shook her head.

'Thank God.' Lucinda let out a long breath before walking over to the kitchen table, picking up the paperwork and envelopes. 'Why didn't you speak to me? This is not the answer.'

Oh, but it is.

Abi said nothing. Today had taken a lot of organising; she really didn't want to have to delay it.

'It's not what you think,' she finally said. 'Can you and Max just go home and leave me in peace? I'm working out a few things, and I need some time to myself.'

'If you let me take those pills, I'd consider leaving you alone for a few minutes,' Lucinda said, 'but not much more than that.' She picked up the plastic container from the coffee table and swept all of the pills into it, clicking on the lid and moving it to the side. She then picked up the letter addressed to herself on the table and opened it.

'Don't—' Abi began, but Lucinda held up her hand.

'Nothing you say right now is going to stop me reading this, Abi. I need to know what I'm dealing with.'

Abi sank into an armchair and buried her head in her hands. Why had she got involved with her neighbour? It had been nothing but trouble from day one, with Lucinda's background and the lies she'd told, to Max's abduction and the trouble with the police. She should have kept to herself.

'Abi?' Lucinda's voice was gentle. 'Your letter is beautiful. I know I'm not supposed to have read it now, with you here, but I'm glad I have. You can't do this.'

Abi didn't lift her head.

'Look, I have to get Max fixed up. I want you to come next door with me. We'll give him some Panadol and put him in his room so we can talk. I'm going to ring the police if you don't come, so that's your choice.'

Abi looked up. 'You wouldn't.'

'Of course I would. I don't want this' – she gestured around the room – 'on my conscience for the rest of my life. You're not going through with this; not on my watch. Now, come on. Get anything you need, which doesn't include the pills and booze, and come with me.'

Reluctantly, Abi pulled herself up to standing and followed Lucinda and Max out of her apartment.

Chapter Twenty-Six

Lucinda's hand was shaking as she pushed open her door and let Max and Abi in. She couldn't believe what she'd just walked in on. What if Max hadn't disobeyed her that morning and had stayed inside watching television? They had no reason to visit Abi until the party that evening, and by then it would have been too late. They had a bee to thank for intervening before Abi took her own life.

She indicated for Abi to sit on the couch, got the children's Panadol from the cupboard and told Max to go and lie on his bed. 'I'll bring you some medicine and the iPad in a minute. You can rest and watch some *Peppa*, okay?'

Max nodded, still holding the icepack on the sting. Lucinda poured out the medicine and took it in to him with the iPad. He drank it, and she found a compilation of *Peppa Pig* episodes on YouTube and switched them on. 'Call me if you want anything. I need to talk to Abi, but I can come in straightaway if your hand hurts or you need me.'

Max nodded. His tears had stopped and he was looking brighter.

Lucinda closed his door and returned to the living area. She sat down on the couch opposite Abi, not really sure what to say.

Abi spoke first. 'Sorry. I didn't mean for you to walk in on that. Max came flying through the door without knocking. He's never done that before either. I had planned it so it would have been Laila who found me, not you, and certainly not Max.'

'Why?' Lucinda asked. 'You've been through so much and made so many changes in your life. You're an inspiration, Abi. I'm in awe of how you've coped.'

'But I haven't coped,' Abi said. 'I've got through each day partly knowing that it would all end today. It gave me a reason to live, to put my affairs in order. To say my goodbyes, not that anyone knew I was saying goodbye. I can't live knowing how many people's lives have been affected by what Eric did. This helps fix it.'

Lucinda raised an eyebrow. 'What do you mean?'

'My life insurance will provide everyone who's lost money with a payment. It's what Eric thought would happen when he took his life, but he hadn't realised the suicide clauses in his policies weren't valid. As of today, suicide is covered in both of my policies. At least some of the money will be returned as soon as my will can be acted upon.'

'But people won't want that, Abi. They won't be able to live with themselves knowing you've done this for them. I know I wouldn't be able to.'

'You saw the hatred yourself at the lunch at Fleming's. There's a guy who can't get his cancer treatment because of Eric. Some people lost their savings. Alex was affected in a big way. Money is everything to some people, and I discovered this week that it wasn't just the property investment that Eric lost money in. The investigation into his business shows there are many more people affected. I can guarantee that the majority who get their money back wouldn't ask that the situation be changed. They'll be happy.'

'I won't be. Laila won't be. Your sister and son won't be. Alex won't be, and other friends of yours won't be. People will be devastated by your decision.'

Abi snorted. 'There are no other friends. I can guarantee if Laila has managed to get anyone to agree to come tonight, they will have cancelled by now. I know the story about Eric hit the news yesterday. No one will want to be associated with me or have anything to do with the Eric scandal.'

'Your real friends will. It's not about quantity, it's about quality. That's what tonight's about, Abi. It's about making you realise that there are people who really care about you and love you. It's going to be a great night, I promise.'

Abi sighed. 'My day was planned. I really have no intention of changing it.'

'I'm going to call the police, or the ambos, or whoever deals with attempted suicide if you don't agree to my terms.'

'Your terms?'

Lucinda nodded. 'I can't stop you from taking your life. I can make it harder for you, but ultimately I can't monitor you twenty-four-seven. I can, of course, ring the authorities, but I'm not sure I'd do that. Here's my offer. You stay with Max and me all day today, so I can watch you. You come to the party tonight, and if you don't walk away at the end of the night feeling truly loved by the friends who attend, then I'll give you back your pills and won't come near you for a few days. You can do whatever you like.'

'Really? You won't tell Laila or Mel, and you'll let me . . . well, you know, do it?'

Lucinda nodded. There was absolutely no way she'd allow Abi to do this, but she wasn't going to tell her that now.

'And all I have to do is come to the party?'

Lucinda nodded again.

'I don't have anything to wear,' Abi said. 'I wasn't planning to go.'

Lucinda laughed, the tension draining from her body. 'We'll give Max an hour to rest and then we'll go shopping. We'll even book you in for a blow wave. You'll look amazing.'

Abi nodded, then closed her eyes. Lucinda's heart went out to her. She'd obviously spent ages planning this day, and at no point would she have thought to prepare for the unlikely event of a bee sting. While Abi was no doubt cursing the bee, Lucinda could only thank God for Max's encounter with it.

Chapter Twenty-Seven

Abi stared at herself in the mirror. Having confiscated her pills, Lucinda had allowed her to go back into her own apartment to put the finishing touches on her make-up and find the wrap-around shawl she would need as the cool evening air approached. Lucinda, she discovered, had a love for charity shops and was terrific at plucking out vintage clothing. At the second shop they visited she'd found an Audrey Hepburn–style dress with a modern twist. The embroidered lace and layers of tulle gave it a sophisticated look, and it fit Abi's slim body like a glove. She would never have thought of looking in a charity shop but was glad they had. The dress would have been worth hundreds, but the thirty-dollar price tag was a steal.

A heaviness nestled firmly between her shoulder blades as she picked up her bag and went next door to join Lucinda. For her, this was hardly going to be a celebration. She sent Laila a text saying she would be at Lucinda's having a drink. She'd taken the open bottle of Merlot back with her. It wasn't quite how she'd imagined drinking it, but it was her fortieth, and a few drinks might help to push away her sense of failure.

Lucinda was wearing a black dress, a heart-shaped pendant around her neck. She looked gorgeous and was fussing around Max when Abi returned.

'Mum should be back any minute to look after him,' she said, as Abi put the wine on the kitchen counter and sat down at the table.

'Are you sure she doesn't want to come? Max could come for a few hours.'

Lucinda shook her head. 'No, she's happy to stay with Max. She leaves on Monday, so she wants to make the most of it.'

'I certainly do,' Tess said, coming down the hallway. 'I've done my Melbourne shopping today, and tonight and tomorrow Maxy is all mine.' She stopped when she reached them and gave a low wolf whistle. 'Look at you two stunners. Do we have time for a drink, or do you have to go?'

'Laila's collecting us, so we can pour one and see how we go.' Lucinda picked up Abi's bottle and poured three glasses. She raised hers. 'To Abi. A very happy fortieth birthday.'

'And may there be many more,' Tess added, having no idea what had unfolded earlier.

They sipped the wine, a smile forming on Lucinda's lips. 'That's the nicest red I've ever had. You certainly have class, Abi Whitmore.'

Abi's cheeks flushed. 'Not sure about that. Good taste in wine perhaps, although I doubt what I was going to do with it would be classified as classy.'

Tess raised an eyebrow, but Lucinda shook her head. 'I'll just say goodnight to Max and then we should get ready to go. Laila's probably parking as we speak.'

She was right. A couple of minutes later Laila arrived, in a luxurious burgundy ankle-length dress. She hugged Abi. 'Happy birthday, precious friend. It's so good to see you.' She gave a nervous laugh. 'You know I had this weird feeling that something was going to go wrong today. That you were going to ring me and say you couldn't come to the party. Thank God you didn't do that. I'd have a lot of explaining to do.'

Abi didn't answer. She could hardly say she wouldn't have dreamt of cancelling.

Lucinda came to her rescue. 'Abi's been with me all day. Insisting we get hair and make-up done and wanting a second opinion on her dress. You had nothing to worry about.'

Laila smiled. 'Good. Now we'd better go. Pre-dinner drinks are calling.'

Abi laughed as Laila insisted she put a blindfold on before getting into her car. 'You're kidding, aren't you?'

'Nope. I definitely don't want you guessing where we're going.'

'Why? Will I refuse to go in?'

Laila laughed, not answering. 'Just put it on. I've gone to a lot of effort for tonight, so you have to do what I say.'

Lucinda nudged her. 'Yes, you do.'

Abi pulled the blindfold over her eyes and allowed Lucinda to guide her into the car. 'It would have been easier doing this once we were in the car, you know.'

'Complaints, complaints,' Laila said.

Abi allowed Lucinda to put on her seat belt as Laila made all sorts of weird noises in the front seat. 'What are you doing?' Abi asked, after the distinctive chink of glasses filled the car. The pop of a cork was the next familiar noise and then the filling of a glass.

'Put out your hand,' Laila said, and Abi obeyed, the stem of a champagne flute immediately pushed into it. 'A Taittinger traveller for the road,' Laila said. 'And one for Lucinda. I'll join you once we arrive at our destination.'

Abi sipped her wine, the delicious bubbles dancing on her tongue. 'Thank you,' she suddenly said. She realised her behaviour hadn't been particularly grateful up to this point. 'I can't wait to see where we're going.'

She didn't have long to wait. Ten minutes later they pulled to a stop and Lucinda took her champagne flute from her. They helped Abi out and, with one on each side, escorted her into a building. It had a familiar floral smell to it, but Abi couldn't put her finger on where she'd smelt it before.

Still side by side, they guided Abi into an area where music was playing.

'Okay,' Laila said. 'Feel in front of you for the table, and then you can sit down.'

Abi did as she was told.

'When I tell you, you can take off your blindfold, okay?'

Abi nodded. She strained to listen to any noises around her, but other than the music it was quiet. She did register Laila's – and she assumed Lucinda's – footsteps moving away from her.

'You can take it off now,' Laila called from somewhere further away.

Abi slipped the blindfold off, blinking as the room came into focus. She was seated at a large round table, suitable for ten guests, in the dining room of Fleming's. The lights were dimmed, and silver and blue balloons filled the ceiling. She was alone, yet the table was set beautifully, and a small table off to the side was filled with presents.

She jumped as a hand touched her back.

'Happy birthday, Mum.'

Abi swung around to find Hayden sitting behind her. He rose and moved into the chair next to her. 'Hayden?'

He smiled. 'Don't you recognise me? Is the suit too flash?'

She gave a nervous smile. 'I wasn't expecting you to be here, that's all.' Her eyes darted around the rest of the room. 'Where's everyone else?'

'I asked Laila to give us some time before the party begins. There are some things I need to say to you. That I want to say to you.'

It was on the tip of her tongue to say that he'd probably said enough when he'd last visited, but she didn't. Instead, she remained silent.

'I need to tell you that I'm sorry.' Hayden's cheeks coloured as he spoke. 'I'm not really sure where to begin, but I do want you to know that I'm ashamed of how I've acted towards you since Dad died.'

Tears welled in Abi's eyes as she reached across and squeezed Hayden's hand.

'I was angry, I know that. I couldn't believe that not only could Dad do something so dishonest but that he'd take the coward's way out. Blaming you was the easiest way to release some of my anger.' He shook his head. 'I still can't believe it, to be honest. He was my hero. I idolised him and wanted to be just like him. It completely threw me that I could have been so wrong about someone so important to me.'

Abi wiped her eyes as she listened to the hurt in Hayden's voice. 'I get it, Hayd, it was a complete blindside and betrayal for both of us.'

Hayden nodded. 'Then I had Gabe feeding me a whole lot of stories about Dad and you trying to keep me away from the family. It made me see red. That I'd missed out on so much and now was in this awful situation. He was also adamant that you knew about the investments and had worked with Dad to get money out of friends and family.'

'That's not true.'

Hayden put his hands up to stop her. 'I know. It's just at the start the news articles implied you were responsible and then once Gabe got involved, he did his best to convince me that was the case. It was when he tried to suggest you'd always cheated friends and family that things didn't sound or feel right. I know I didn't see Dad's behaviour coming, but I do know you. You're the first to help people and give them extra when they need it. You'd be the last person to ever cheat anyone out of anything.'

Relief washed over Abi at his words. 'You know, Gabe never forgave me for choosing your father over him. He threatened to pay me back one day, and I believe that's exactly what he's been doing since Dad died.'

Hayden nodded. 'A couple of weeks ago, I went to visit Nanna, and her sister was there. My great-aunt.'

'Rhea?'

'Yes. She was refreshingly blunt when it came to matters about the family.'

Abi nodded. She'd met Rhea a few times when she and Eric started going out and, like Hayden, had admired her straight-talking. She was very good at putting Eric's mother in her place, which had been amusing to watch.

'Nanna left the room to get the tea tray, and she started speaking about how lovely it was that I'd decided to forgive the family for the treatment of you and Dad and embrace them again. I asked her what she meant, and she filled me in. She knew that it was you that had ended the relationship with Gabe to be with Dad and that he'd threatened you. That she'd tried to make Nanna and Granddad realise this, but they'd refused to listen. And from that day forward, Gabe fed the family stories about Dad not wanting to be associated with them anymore and you refusing invitations. Rhea said it was never you and Dad who abandoned the family, it was the family who did it to you. Apparently, they didn't show any interest when I was born or even come and visit?'

'Rhea did.' Abi remembered how strange it had seemed that the only member of Eric's family who'd made the trip to Melbourne to meet Hayden when he was born was an ageing aunt who they hardly knew. She'd flown down and come to the hospital for an hour with presents. Admired Hayden and then flown back to Sydney that afternoon. 'But none of the rest of the family did. We took you up to Sydney when you were a few months old, but we might as well not have bothered. They'd disowned us by that stage. Gabe had done a real number on us.'

'I spoke to Gabe about Rhea when I got home, and he admitted he hadn't been honest. He didn't fully go along with Rhea's interpretation of who rejected who, but he did admit some of his behaviour was done in retaliation for where he felt he'd been wronged.'

'His ego was wronged, and that's about it,' Abi said.

Hayden laughed. 'Yes, I realise that's the biggest part of his anatomy. Look, he's given me an amazing opportunity with my schooling, but I've recognised that he's been grooming me to be someone he wants me to be. I don't want to forget where I came from, any more than I want to forget what you taught me.' Hayden squeezed Abi's hand. 'I love you, Mum. I hope you can forgive me.'

Abi drew him to her without hesitation, tears rolling down her cheeks. 'Of course I do. Does this mean you're back in my life again?'

'Of course. I'll still finish school in Sydney; I'd be silly not to. But I'll be home for the holidays, and we'll chat during the week. I'll be applying for uni in Melbourne too. There's no reason to do that in Sydney. Ultimately, I'll want to be where my family is, and that's you.'

Abi squeezed him to her harder. She'd just been given the best birthday present possible.

Hayden pulled back and laughed. 'Now, the rest of your guests are probably dying to say happy birthday. I'll go and tell Laila they can come in.'

Abi did her best to wipe her cheeks, hoping her make-up wasn't spoiled, as Hayden went to get Laila. The door opened, and the small group of guests moved into the dining room.

'Happy birthday, Abi,' Jerry Goldberg called out. He had a drink in one hand and his other arm around Alex, whose face lit up with a genuine smile. Mel and Tony followed behind, with Lucinda and Laila both carrying bottles of champagne. Jude and her husband followed them in, each holding strings with balloons attached. With Lucinda and Hayden, it made a group of ten.

She stood as they approached the table, not really sure what to say. She was completely overwhelmed with what Laila had done for her. She hadn't organised a group of people who Abi knew despised her; she'd organised people who were her friends and had supported her.

She thought back to Lucinda's words. *It's not about quantity, it's about quality. That's what tonight's about. It's about making you realise that there are people who really care about you and love you.*

She blinked back tears as she saw the genuine warmth and love in each of their eyes. Even Jerry, which was a little bit of a surprise. Alex had said how upset her husband was, but he certainly wasn't showing any of that now.

'Thank you,' she said first to Laila and then Alex. 'Having my party here is so generous of you.'

'Don't be silly,' Alex said. 'You're our friend, Abi. We both admire how you've carried yourself the last few months, and want you to know we're here to support you.'

'No matter what others say,' Jerry added. 'I'm guilty of not being as supportive as I could have been, but tonight's a new beginning. A new decade for you and a new attitude for me.' He raised his glass. 'Happy birthday, Abi.'

They all raised their glasses.

'Abs, you are an incredibly strong woman who I feel privileged to call my friend,' Laila said. 'You've handled yourself with dignity and integrity, and we can all learn a lot from you. I love you to the moon and back and would do anything for you, as I know you would for me. I was thrilled to be able to put this party on for you and, to be honest, surprised that you actually turned up.'

A ripple of laughter went around the table as Abi caught Lucinda's eye. How different tonight could have turned out if it weren't for Max and his bee sting. Lucinda gave her a small smile. Abi knew it was a secret that Lucinda would never share, and for that she was incredibly grateful. She looked around at Hayden and Mel and her friends and could hardly believe she'd nearly walked away from all of this. It was definitely the best birthday she'd ever had, and the one that she would always be the most grateful for.

Nine Months Later

Abi took the photo frame from the drawer she'd stuffed it in nine months earlier, and stared at the image of her husband. Of a man, it turned out, she hadn't really known. He stared back at her, his eyes crinkled at the corners as they did when he laughed. She missed that laugh, and she missed the Eric she'd known and loved. But any time she had those thoughts, the other side of Eric filled her mind. The liar, the cheat, the man who'd left her to pick up the pieces. She hoped one day she could move on from the feelings of hurt that resurfaced when she thought of him, but for now, she would just take each day at a time and be grateful for what she had, and try to enjoy life to its fullest.

The party for her fortieth had proved a turning point. Having Hayden back in her life and a small group of friends show her how much she was loved gave her the will to live again. She was so grateful that no one other than Lucinda knew what she'd planned.

She'd taken on managing a small apartment complex for a friend of Alex's in addition to her job as apartment manager at the Elsternwick apartments. Weirdly, with all that had gone on, it felt like home. She might move out at some stage, but she loved having Lucinda and Max as her neighbours, and while they remained in Melbourne, she saw no reason for any of them to move.

She returned the photo to its drawer. She wasn't quite ready to throw it out. Perhaps when she was, it would be a sign that she was moving on. She glanced at her watch. She'd promised Max she'd meet him and Lucinda at the park at three to watch the scooter races. Apparently, he'd organised ten other boys, and they were all meeting to battle it out on the perimeter track that surrounded the park. She smiled, thinking about him. He'd turned five and was loving his first year of school.

It was amazing to think that Mel and Tony would be going through the school system in a few years too. She couldn't wait to see them the next day. Hayden had flown down from Sydney, and they were going to drive out to Geelong for Lilian Abigail Dwyer's christening. Abi had been touched when she'd learnt of her niece's name, and even more touched when Mel asked her to be Lily's godmother.

Abi moved into the kitchen and picked up the picnic hamper she'd prepared for the outing. Lucinda wouldn't be expecting her to bring anything, but she felt like celebrating. She had so much to be grateful for and particularly to Lucinda, who had saved her life. She shuddered to think what devastation she would have left behind if she had gone through with her plan, particularly for Hayden. It would have been unforgivable, and she knew she was so lucky to have had a second chance. She'd always be grateful to Max, Lucinda and the bee.

She left Hayden a note, letting him know that she'd be at the park and would be making them a special dinner later. It was nice to see when he did return to Melbourne that he was catching up with some of his old friends again. It appeared they too had moved on from *what Hayden's dad did*, and were treating him like they always had.

With a spring in her step, Abi walked from the apartments towards the park. A huge smile crossed her face as Max waved to her. 'Mrs Abi, I'm going to win the race. Are you going to watch?'

'Of course I am, Mr Max. I'll just go and find your mumma so I can sit with her and cheer you on. Does that sound okay?'

'Awesome,' Max called as he scooted off for his practice lap.

Abi laughed as she walked in Lucinda's direction. She'd found a spot in the shade of a flowering gum tree and was waving Abi over.

'He's still mad about his scooter.' Abi placed the picnic basket on Lucinda's rug and sat down next to her.

'I know,' Lucinda said. 'I suggested we get a second-hand bike, but he said no, he loves the scooter so much. He's almost outgrown it, I think, but he insists it's still fine.' She frowned. 'He says it reminds him of William and he misses him.'

Abi sighed. 'Poor Max. I don't think he'll ever really understand what happened to William and Dot.'

'I know. He loved them like they were his grandparents; not all that surprising considering they were actually blood relatives. And they loved him. William absolutely adored him. I feel very sorry for them.'

Abi nodded. 'But not sorry enough to change anything?'

Lucinda shook her head. 'No. I'm glad they didn't go to prison, as they were in many ways victims of what happened too, although they should have known better than to go along with any of it. But I could never trust them. I still can't get it out of my mind how I believed they were old and doddery and the things I was seeing were a result of old age. When William couldn't find things in the apartment, for instance, I assumed he was developing some form of dementia. Mind you, Dot helped with that one, suggesting he was having tests. It never occurred to me that the apartment was rented through Airbnb, so no wonder he couldn't find anything – none of the belongings were his in the first place. The telescope on the balcony was to watch us at the park, not the birds or stars like they told us. Ryan forbade them from contacting us when we first moved to Elsternwick. He wanted to make it look like we really did bump into each other again. Apparently, it drove William mad being that close to Max but not being able to talk to him, so at least watching him at the park gave him some connection.' She shuddered at the thought of them being spied on. 'William's angry outbursts are easier to understand too. He wanted to tell me who they were, but Dot was too scared of the repercussions, particularly as Ryan, through Jonesy, told them they'd lose all access to Max if they did. They were also threatened physically. His anger was pure frustration, dementia had nothing to do with it.'

'Have they sent you any more letters?'

'No, just that first one. I didn't respond so I guess they got the hint.' Lucinda had had to fight back tears reading the letter William and Dot sent her. It was first and foremost an apology. They should have been honest with her from the start rather than allowing Ryan to bully, scare and manipulate them into betraying her. Dot said the stories they told Lucinda had been fabricated by Ryan to make her feel sorry for them and let them into her life. Their son Billy, Ryan's dad, had died ten years earlier but of a drug overdose, not an accident as they'd led her to believe. Ryan had estranged himself from his family before his father's death, and they hadn't heard from him until he'd contacted them from prison. The fact he was married with a child, their great-grandchild, had been an enormous surprise.

Ryan had organised for Jonesy to visit William and Dot to make it very clear that if they valued their lives, they would go along with his instructions. What really blew Lucinda away was how convincing Jonesy had been. She'd truly believed he had a long-standing relationship with William and Dot, and that the things they'd said about him being *like a grandson* were true. He'd never even met their son Billy, let alone worked with him. His connection was through Ryan. The story had been cleverly crafted, and they'd all played along.

The upside for Dot and William in following Ryan's instructions, other than staying alive, was they would get to have a relationship with their great-grandson. For William, the chance to have a relationship with Max was too good an opportunity to pass up. He felt like a complete failure when it came to his own son and grandson. He'd not been able to influence either of them to make good decisions in their lives. Both had ended up involved with drugs and in and out of prison. He convinced himself this time it would be different. With Max, he could make amends for not being a better father and grandfather. *It's why he went a bit over the top ensuring Max was happy*, Dot had written in the letter.

They'd also wanted Lucinda to know that they'd loved every minute they'd spent together, and if she could ever find it in her heart to forgive them, they would love to see both her and Max again. Lucinda hadn't responded. She'd felt torn at first. She knew they were decent people who'd been put in an awful situation, but that didn't help her. She'd almost lost her son because of them, and even with Ryan gone, she could never trust them again.

'Do you think it was fair that they didn't go to prison whereas Jonesy did? I know he was involved in all of it, but I actually thought he was a nice guy,' Abi said.

'The difference was he knew exactly what he was doing. Ryan lied to Dot and William. He had Jonesy withhold the information about the plans to abduct Max until the day it happened. From what I understand, Jonesy told them what to say and how to act and continued to turn up to make sure they were following instructions. I actually feel awful that I was worried when I overhead Dot and William arguing and asked Jonesy to be with them on the days they had Max. Thinking back now, I realise they were arguing about whether they should tell me what was going on.'

'You weren't to know that, and you have to hand it to Jonesy – he was persuasive.'

Lucinda nodded. 'He was convincing all around. Not just in convincing me he was a good guy, but to Dot and William too. On the one hand, he threatened them that they had to go along with his plans, but he also made them believe that part of what he was doing was because he believed I couldn't cope with Max on my own. That I would need help, and they were the perfect people to fill that role. I believe he regrets his involvement; he as good as told me he wished he could change his past before the abduction even happened, but he owed Ryan from years before, and criminals collect. His biggest mistake was ever getting involved with Ryan in the first place. Which was mine too, I guess.'

'Yes, except you got Max out of Dorford and away from being controlled by Ryan, whereas Jonesy got a prison sentence. Max isn't really missing out not having William and Dot,' Abi added. 'He has your mum back in his life, plus all his new school friends, and you and me, and Hayden when he's home.'

'He does miss seeing Mum regularly like he did when we lived in Dorford.'

'But you'll see her in a couple of weeks when you fly back to visit. Do you think you'll decide to stay in Queensland?'

Lucinda could hear the question in Abi's voice and knew her friend was hoping she wouldn't be making a permanent move. 'No chance. We're used to Melbourne and its unpredictable weather and busy streets. As crazy as it's been, I feel like we fit in here. I love living next to you, and even though the apartments are small, it strangely feels like home.'

Abi nodded. 'I feel the same.' She laughed and pointed as Max went tearing past. 'Go, Max! He's getting really fast on that thing.' She opened the picnic basket once he was well past them and pulled out the champagne flutes. 'I thought we should celebrate. So much has happened in the last year and we're both still here, both doing well, and our lives are improving each day. And I need to thank you again.'

'You're not talking about the bee incident, are you?'

Abi laughed. 'Code for *kill myself day*.'

'I prefer to call it the bee incident, and you can stop thanking me. I'm just so glad we're sitting here now, and I'm not here on my own reminiscing about what a great person you were.'

Abi poured the champagne and handed Lucinda a glass. 'Here's to you. To your bravery for leaving an abusive situation and for not looking back.'

Lucinda raised her glass and clinked it against Abi's. 'And here's to you. I've never met anyone as brave as you, Abi. Any time I think I can't handle anything, I just look at what you've been through and where you are now. You're an inspiration.'

Abi blushed. She fell silent for a moment before speaking. 'You know, I think of you as two different people. The before version and the after.'

Lucinda laughed. 'I guess I am. The Hope and the Lucinda.'

'You might be Lucinda now, but for me, you were my Hope. My last hope, I guess. Without you I wouldn't have a relationship with Hayden, I wouldn't be watching my niece grow and I wouldn't be enjoying – or even living – life. I would have left behind heartache and pain for people who have done so much to show me how loved I am. Regardless of your name, you'll always be a symbol to me. My symbol of hope.'

Lucinda smiled and squeezed Abi's arm. 'I think we were destined to meet. To be there for each other. To help and support each other. Instead of being weighed down and looking over my shoulder the whole time, that weight has lifted.'

'It's more than a weight that's lifted,' Abi said. 'Life's changed for both of us. We're no longer suffocating. The worries have disappeared, and most importantly, we can breathe.'

ACKNOWLEDGMENTS

It's so lovely to see my books come to life and be enjoyed by so many readers around the world. Thank you to everyone who has purchased *Her Last Hope*, and special thanks to those who've taken the time to message me and/or leave a review on Amazon. I'm very appreciative of you sharing your thoughts and comments and hope you'll enjoy more of my available titles.

To Sammia Hamer and the team at Lake Union Publishing; thank you for the amazing opportunity you've provided and for the quality and professionalism you bring to each process.

To the brilliant Celine Kelly, thank you! Your editorial suggestions and insights are invaluable. Once again, it has been a pleasure to work with you.

To Gillian Holmes, thank you for bringing the final editing touches to the story, which have undoubtedly tightened and strengthened it.

To Sarah Whittaker, your inspirational cover designs have created an amazing brand for my books, and I particularly love this one – thank you!

A big thank you to Judy, Maggie and Ray for providing feedback on early versions of the story.

To Robyn, the dedication isn't enough. Thank you for your wisdom and friendship. It means the world to me.

And lastly, thank you to my wonderful network of writers and friends who love to chat about all things books. It is lovely to have the support and friendship of such a passionate group.

ABOUT THE AUTHOR

Louise has enjoyed working in marketing, recruitment and film production, all of which have helped steer her towards her current, and most loved, role – writer.

Originally from Melbourne, a trip around Australia led Louise and her husband to Queensland's stunning Sunshine Coast, where they now live with their two sons, gorgeous fluffball of a cat, and an abundance of visiting wildlife – the kangaroos and wallabies the most welcome, the snakes the least!

Awed by her beautiful surroundings, Louise loves to take advantage of the opportunities the coast provides for swimming, hiking, mountain biking, and kayaking. When she's not writing or out adventuring, Louise loves any available opportunity to curl up with a glass of red wine, switch on her Kindle and indulge in a new release from a favourite author.

To get in touch with Louise, or to join her mailing list, visit: www.LouiseGuy.com.